Don't miss the first Kyle Swanson novel

KILL ZONE
A Sniper Novel

"Tight, suspenseful…Here's hoping this is the first of many Swanson novels." —*Booklist*

"The action reaches a furious pitch."
—*Publishers Weekly*

"A renowned sniper, Coughlin recounts battlefield action with considerable energy." —*The Washington Post*

And look for the authors' non-fiction
***New York Times* bestseller**

SHOOTER
The Autobiography of the Top-Ranked Marine Sniper

"One of the best snipers in the Marine Corps, perhaps the very best. When I asked one of his commanders about his skills, the commander smiled and said, 'I'm just glad he's on our side.'"

—Peter Maass, war correspondent
and bestselling author of *Love Thy Neighbor*

ALSO BY JACK COUGHLIN

*Shooter: The Autobiography of the
Top-Ranked Marine Sniper*
(with Capt. Casey Kuhlman and Donald A. Davis)

ALSO BY DONALD A. DAVIS

Lightning Strike

The Last Man on the Moon (with Gene Cernan)

Dark Waters (with Lee Vyborny)

DEAD SHOT

A SNIPER NOVEL

GUNNERY SGT.
JACK COUGHLIN,
USMC (RET.)

WITH
DONALD A. DAVIS

St. Martin's Paperbacks

This is a work of fiction. All of the characters, organizations, and events portrayed in this novel are either products of the author's imagination or are used fictitiously.

DEAD SHOT

Copyright © 2009 by Jack Coughlin with Donald A. Davis.
Excerpt from *Clean Kill* copyright © 2009 by Jack Coughlin with Donald A. Davis.

Cover photographs:
Photograph of soldier © AP Photo / Jim Macmillan
Background photograph © Remi Benali / Corbis

For information address St. Martin's Press, 175 Fifth Avenue, New York, NY 10010.

Library of Congress Catalog Card Number: 2008036237

ISBN: 978-0-312-35948-5

Printed in the United States of America

St. Martin's Press hardcover edition / March 2009
St. Martin's Paperbacks edition / December 2009

St. Martin's Paperbacks are published by St. Martin's Press, 175 Fifth Avenue, New York, NY 10010.

10 9 8 7 6 5 4 3 2 1

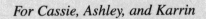

For Cassie, Ashley, and Karrin

1

THE GREEN ZONE
BAGHDAD, IRAQ

It was just a matter of waiting. Juba was good at waiting. Patience was an important tool for him, as it is for all snipers. The Iraqi desert sun baked and parched him, but his soul remained calm, soothed by the instructions of his two fathers and the sure knowledge that the hunt was on. Once again, he was the sword of the Prophet. *God is great!* he whispered, feeling guilty for breaking his oath and speaking the words of praise.

He had been in the hole for three days, shaded only by a few bushes during the hottest part of the blistering afternoons. He let his face and neck become sunburned and measured his rations carefully, eating and drinking only enough to survive. The last chocolates from his field rations had been eaten, and he had intentionally drained the last water from his canteens the previous day. He was hungry, and thirst clawed at his throat. Good.

Throughout the time in the hide, he had heard sporadic traffic passing unseen only fifty meters away and the occasional boom of an explosion somewhere down the track. Each morning an American patrol rolled past, clouds of dust following the big vehicles. He could have gotten help anytime he wanted it. Didn't want it.

On the fourth morning, the sun was up and the temperature was climbing when he saw the faraway dust clouds kicked up by the oncoming patrol. No wonder they were so easy to ambush. He crawled from the hide, brushed away the signs of his stay by brooming the area with a bush, and staggered to the road. The vehicles now could be seen with the naked eye, which meant they could see him, too, a wobbling soldier alone in the desert.

He held up his hands as if in surrender to the first Bradley Fighting Vehicle that approached, with its .50 caliber machine gun trained on him. Then he collapsed. A lieutenant of the U.S. 1st Cavalry Division instantly recognized the disruptive pattern camouflage uniform and weathered beret worn by the British soldier and jumped down to help. They pulled him into the shade of the big vehicle.

Sweat caked the dusty face and dirt clung to the filthy uniform, and when they started pouring some water into his mouth, he greedily grabbed for the canteen. The American pulled it back. "Easy, pal. Just a little bit at a time. You're gonna be okay." He offered another sip. A medic smoothed a wet salve on the sunburned face, neck, and hands.

Juba slowly responded in a British accent, haltingly explaining that his sniper team had been discovered a week ago and his spotter killed in the ensuing fight. The Englishman had evaded the searching insurgents, found this road before dawn today, and walked next to it since then, hoping that a friendly force would spot him before the insurgents did. The Americans were unaware that his uniform and the rifle hanging from his shoulder had been stripped from a British soldier he had killed outside of Basra.

Juba was able to stand unaided by the time a helicopter arrived, and he thanked the American soldiers and climbed into the bird. Within thirty minutes, it delivered him to the landing pad of a military hospital inside the Green Zone of Baghdad. A stretcher team met him, but he waved them off, and they led him into a cool corridor, then into a big room where other soldiers lay on cots. A nurse helped him remove his tunic and stuck a needle into his arm to start a slow drip of hydrating fluids. He had been outside in the heat for so long that the fresh liquid going directly into his veins, plus the air-conditioning, caused a deep and instant chill, and he began to shake as if he were freezing. The nurse recognized the reaction as normal and wrapped a blanket around his shoulders as a doctor came over to check him. Exhaustion, sunburn, and dehydration, but no wounds. Juba lay back on the cot, enjoying the brief rest and the air-conditioning.

As the IV drip was finishing, a courteous U.S. intelligence captain came to his cot, having already notified British commanders that their man had been rescued. "They thought you were dead," said the captain, settling into a chair. He thought the guy looked like hell. "So what happened out there, Sergeant?"

The officer took a few notes as Juba repeated his tale of a mission gone wrong. "Sorry about your buddy," the American said and put away the notebook. "Bad shit."

"Part of the job, mate." Juba sighed and leaned back on the green sheet of the metal-framed cot.

"Your instructions are to rest up and then return to your unit as soon as medically fit," said the captain.

The busy doctor in uniform came by just long enough to look him over for a final time and remove the needle. "I've signed your discharge slip, Sergeant. You're going to be fine except for a few aches and pains and that sunburn. Drink a lot of water and have some chow. Here's some ointment for the burn, and if you need more, just come by the pharmacy. You want something to help you sleep tonight?"

"No, sir. I've dealt with worse than this."

"Okay, then. You're free to leave. Good luck."

The intel officer was still there. "Come on with me, soldier, and I'll take you over to the mess hall, then give you a chit for a bed tonight in the guest quarters. Your orders from British HQ are to rest up and then report back to your unit. Meanwhile, you're a guest of Uncle Sam."

Juba pushed himself from the cot, acting wobbly, then drew himself erect and stretched, turning side to side. The body was lean and muscular. He put on his tunic. "Thank you, sir, but I plan something a little more upscale. I'm going to get a hotel room, raid the minibar, take a long shower, get some decent food, and then sleep for two days."

"I hear ya," said the officer. "I've got everything I need. Stay safe." He waved Juba through the door. The sniper ducked into a bathroom, locked himself into a stall, dropped his trousers to retrieve some documents from a plastic bag that had been tucked just above his right boot, and put them in his shirt pocket. He came out, signed for his rifle at the makeshift armory, and left the hospital. Back on the hunt. Closer than before.

He took his time crossing the military areas of the Green Zone as he made his way over to the new Nineveh Hotel, a five-star, four-hundred-room edifice that offered safety, opulence, an indoor Olympic-sized swimming pool, a gourmet restaurant, and other luxury conveniences to foreign visitors, diplomats, and business executives. The gleaming signature spire and a communication array on the roof made it the tallest building in Baghdad.

Despite the outward appearances of commerce, Baghdad remained a military town, and it was not thought strange at all when Juba unfolded the papers that he had carried in the plastic bag and handed them to the concierge of the Nineveh. The documents allowed him to commandeer the corner suite on the twelfth floor for an unspecified "military necessity," the code that unlocked any door in the city. The civilian led him to the suite and joked during the elevator ride about how things were improving. Soft music played in the background.

Juba thanked him, locked the door, and dumped his gear and clothes. He showered, shaved, cleaned his uniform, and put it back on. He snatched three pillows from the bed, piled them on the small dining table in the center of the suite, and stacked his pack atop them to provide a solid support for the long rifle. Crawling on his knees, then his stomach, he moved to the sliding glass door that led onto the balcony and pushed it open by a narrow six inches. Then he wiggled back about seven feet and stood in the shadows of the room, overlooking the neat front garden with lawns of grass that was irrigated to a deep lush green.

Juba lifted his L115A1 long-range rifle, made by Accuracy International UK, the standard weapon of a British sniper. It fired a .338 Lapua Magnum round that was accurate up to 1,100 meters, and it had a Killflash silencer on the muzzle and a bipod. He had zeroed the weapon two days ago and was confident it would hold enough for the task today. From his position, he could see the outside world, but no one on the ground could see him.

Juba had exchanged the standard Schmidt & Bender PM II telescopic sight for the better Zeiss version used by the Germans, and he peered through it to examine the foot traffic along the pathways. A wolf eyeing a flock of sheep. The people below seemed startlingly close through the clear optics. The first potential target to stroll through his kill zone was a civilian wearing a loud Hawaiian shirt and tan trousers. Too easy: a foreign contractor who meant nothing, and killing Americans was not his mission today. It had to be the man with the secret. Sooner or later, he would come along, if the intelligence was correct. Juba would wait. He knew how to wait.

He put down the rifle, sat in a soft chair, and flipped through the English-language newspaper that had been delivered free to the hotel room and checked the football scores to see if Manchester United had won.

He sipped chilled water from a plastic bottle. Scorching outside air oozed through the slightly opened door and did battle with the room's buzzing air conditioner. The flat-screen color television set mounted in the wall was on, and he adjusted the volume slightly to the loud side. News readers rattled on about next week's royal wedding in London, elevating the event steadily so that by Tuesday, the marriage of the prince and his girlfriend would be considered the most important thing in the world. Millions of people would watch. As a British subject, he vividly remembered the legends of the glory days of the monarchy, lessons that had been pounded into him as a student and later as a soldier defending the Crown. He planned to be there for the wedding.

Juba was slightly under six feet in height and slender at 170 pounds, with the fair hair of his British mother and the dark eyes of his Arab father. His skin was several shades darker than the normal Briton, more of a nice California tan that had been darkened even more by his work in the desert. It helped him move with ease in the twilight gulf between Christians and Muslims. Juba could be anybody he wanted to be, and for the past few days, he had again chosen the familiar role of a British Army sniper. It was his best disguise, because he once had been awarded the coveted sniper's patch of two crossed rifles with an *S* between the barrels.

After reading the sports in the newspaper, he put his

eye back to the scope and considered the next possible target, an approaching soldier who, despite the midday heat, wore a helmet and a flak jacket. This had once been the safest place in Iraq, the International Zone, home of the giant U.S. Embassy. It once had been known as the Green Zone, and although bureaucrats changed the name to better claim that the war was the effort of many nations, the Green Zone name stuck. Juba was tempted by the soldier, for he always enjoyed the challenge of placing a bullet in the small gaps of the armored vests or between the ceramic plates. Not the mission: Let him pass.

An hour before sundown, four soldiers in full armor appeared, moving in a box formation as they escorted a smaller man toward the Coalition Headquarters building where the first formal interrogation was to take place. The soldier on the left front corner was talking and making sharp, descriptive motions with one hand, probably an officer directing the prisoner transfer. Except that the man was not a prisoner, more a valuable guest of the Coalition. He had arrived yesterday in Baghdad, with the secret locked in his head. The Iraqi physicist planned to hand the information to the Americans and the British officials, but he had made too many mistakes in escaping from the laboratory in Iran. The biggest error was in trusting his co-workers, who were able to provide almost a minute-by-minute schedule for the defector. Then Juba had been summoned.

The traitor could not be allowed to reach the interrogation room alive. Juba pressed his cheek into the cool stock, his fingers roving with familiarity over the rifle to make sure it was ready. They were three hundred yards away, and he checked the flags on the government building. He estimated the wind at seven to ten miles per hour full value, right to left, which would move the fired round two inches to the left at two hundred yards. He adjusted the scope to compensate. Humidity was zero.

He settled the scope on the officer and looked for a weakness. The waving arm! The officer was describing something, and his right arm windmilled to make his point. Juba exhaled and let his heartbeat slow almost to nothing. Under the arm, that's the place.

At two hundred yards, almost point-blank range, he squeezed the trigger back, slow and steady and straight, just as the American raised his arm above shoulder level. The big rifle fired, and the Killflash ate up the noise as the bullet entered beneath the right armpit of the officer, smashed down through the rib cage and exited out of his lower left side, crushing bones and shredding every organ in its path. The officer died before anyone could reach out to help him.

Juba accepted the light recoil and cycled another round into the chamber as the startled group stopped in its tracks. He brought his scope to the small man in the middle. They had heard nothing, but the colonel had just been shot! The soldiers spun around, looking for the threat but leaving the target uncovered. The Iraqi automatically bent down, turning to aid the fallen American. That exposed the left rear side of his neck, and Juba centered the crosshairs right there and pulled the trigger again. He was able to see the vapor trail of the bullet, which impacted right below the base of the skull and ripped out the throat when it came out the other side. Two catastrophic kills.

Juba put aside the rifle, ducked down to the floor, crawled forward, and reached up to slowly close the door to the outside patio. He went back, retrieved his kit and the rifle, tossed the pillows back onto the bed, and left the room.

He increased his pace through the lobby and hurried

outside with other armed soldiers and civilian private security company guards who were moving into the attack
area. A Quick Reaction Force would arrive within minutes, and uniformed men would be all over the place,
with all sorts of weapons pointing everywhere, and Juba
would be just another soldier with a gun. He made his
way through the crowd and walked out of the Green Zone
unmolested.

That evening, a small Royal Jordanian Airlines Fokker
plane took off on schedule from the Baghdad International Airport. On its manifest was a quiet Canadian civilian engineer with fair hair and dark eyes. Juba was
going to London.

The secret that Saddam Hussein had taken to his grave
remained safe. The Palace of Death was secure.

2

Captain Sybelle Summers of the U.S. Marine Corps walked purposefully into a secure briefing room at Incirlik Air Force Base in southeastern Turkey. Many of the combat-ready Marines who were to conduct the mission recognized her immediately, and the others knew her reputation as operations officer of a special operations unit known as Task Force Trident.

"Oh, oh. It's the Queen of the Night," muttered a lance corporal. "We've stepped in it. They don't use the Bride of Dracula on small jobs."

"Count Dracula divorced her for spousal abuse," whispered the man next to him.

"Shhh. Summers will kick your ass if she hears you."

The experienced warriors of the Marine Special Operations Command (MARSOC) normally shied away from taking orders from women, but Summers was different. She wore a black jumpsuit with the silver railroad tracks insignia of her rank glinting on the collar of a turtleneck sweater and projected a maximum "don't give me any shit" attitude as she walked to the podium and flipped open a file folder. Her short black hair, dark blue eyes, and lithe figure disguised the fact that she was the only woman ever to make it through Force Recon training.

"Settle down," she snapped, and the MARSOC team quieted. "We are going after a High Value Target tonight in Iraq, and I don't want any of you jarheads to screw this up. Mustapha Ahmed al-Masri has surfaced again, stirring up the Kurds in northern Iraq, and the intelligence pukes have pinpointed his location. They list him as the number two for al Qaeda in the region, which is why he has been designated an HVT and we have been assigned to stop him."

She walked around the podium to the front and nodded to her left. A door opened and a man stepped in, also wearing a black jumpsuit and with his face covered by a pull-down mask. A long rifle of a sort they did not recognize was slung over his shoulder. Sniper.

"Batman?" whispered the lance corporal.

"Maybe a holdup," joked his partner.

"CIA spook. Definitely."

Summers spoke. "You guys will assault the house at 0500, and I'll leave it to the other briefers to give you the details. By the time you arrive, this gentleman and I will already be on the ground, closing the back door. He is masked simply because you do not need to know who he is. The two of us have been attached as special operators for this mission. Far as you are concerned, we aren't here, and we will go in and extract on our own."

As she finished, other briefing officers came forward with their maps and timetables. The lights started to dim. "If you see al-Masri, kill him. The best bet is that he will haul ass once the attack starts, and we will be waiting. You absolutely must remember that this is friendly territory and be sure not to have civilian casualties. If you screw up and shoot at us, even by mistake, he will shoot back, and I guarantee that you don't want that to happen.

Be very careful when you pull the trigger. Know your targets. That's it. Good luck and good hunting. Captain Barnes will continue your brief." She spun on her heel and disappeared out the door with the masked man.

Once they were in the Humvee and driving to the helicopter pad beside the ten-thousand-foot runway, Kyle Swanson rolled up the mask, changing it into a watch cap. His face itched. "Damn, Sybelle, you are a woman of few words." He changed his voice to imitate her grim briefing cadence. "'Shoot at us and he will shoot back!' Way to inspire confidence in the troops."

They both laughed. "I had to get their attention. We don't want any mistakes out there."

"I knew about half the guys in that room," Swanson said. "Worked with some of them. It's always strange not letting friends know who you really are." In special ops, he had a million aliases but no real name at all because he was officially dead.

The Turkish night was crisp and starlit, with a slice of a coasting moon. A giant Air Force cargo plane roared overhead on its landing approach, hauling more material from the States into Incirlik, a major supply dump that fed the war in Iraq. Adana, a modern city of a million people, was less than ten miles away, and the Mediterranean washed onto beaches within easy access. For special operations types, it was a good location. You could get a decent hamburger and a cold beer, jump on a bird and fly off on a quick combat mission, and be back in time for a hot shower and a movie.

Swanson brought the Humvee to a halt beside a hangar, and they both got out and suited up with their web gear. Summers removed her shiny captain's bars because they were entering the world of hiding, blending, and deceiving, a dark place where nothing must reflect light. She had assigned herself to this mission for several reasons, one being that she still spoke the language of her childhood, although her Kurdish last name had disappeared when her father had died and her mother remarried an American. It was a welcome asset.

A U.S. Air Force lieutenant approached, saluted, and introduced himself as their command pilot. He would not be going with them, however, and behind him sat a tiny HTX-I helicopter, the rotors already turning lazily on battery power. Commonly called a TAXI, it would be controlled by pilots far away from the action, with this lieutenant in charge of getting them launched and then handing the flight over to another controller cruising far overhead in an electronics warfare plane.

The TAXI had been perfected by the U.S. Special Operations Command as a revolutionary tactical delivery system for particular missions and could deliver up to four operators to an exact point, then speed away to some nearby isolated site and shut down, roosting there patiently for days if need be, while solar panels recharged the batteries. When summoned, it would zip back in to pick them up. Except for the reconfigured overhead rotor, it hardly even looked like a helicopter. With no pilot, copilot, or loadmaster and with the giant internal combustion engines gone, weaponless and without armor, the unique helicopter was a blend of ultralight, stealth, and modern fuel cell and electronic technologies. It possessed extraordinary range and was virtually invisible to searching radar while its passengers sat in pairs, side by side, encased in a sleek aerodynamic bubble. The HTX-I wore the X designation to indicate it was still in the experimental stage, nothing more than an idea on the drawing boards. The media had never even picked up a scent that it was already operational.

Swanson and Summers climbed in, checked their gear, buckled up, and put on their headsets as the flight engineer closed the hatches and backed away, speaking into a radio to the controller. The reaction was immediate, and they heard no roar of engines as the TAXI rose from the landing strip like a quiet elevator, with only a slight whipping sound from the rotors, then flitted away on its run to the border. Swanson watched the lights of Adana disappear behind them. It was like sailing on a quiet lake.

At an exact GPS location, the TAXI slowed to a crawl and went close to the ground and then into a motionless hover. They jumped out, boots crunching desert sand, and ran to some nearby clusters of trees. The contact who had alerted the Americans about the presence of Mustapha Ahmed al-Masri was waiting, and Sybelle spoke to him in Kurdish, apologetically explaining to him that she was just a mere translator for the man with her.

Satisfied that as a woman, she was still an underling, the man guided them into the village and pointed them to a flat place in a ditch. The road beside them ran straight for a while, then bent right, and at the curve was the house that was to be attacked.

Sybelle and Kyle slid into the dry gully, and Swanson unlimbered some of his gear, setting up shop. Sybelle thanked the guide profusely and told him he was now free to go and wait for the main force that would be coming in on the other end of town. The guide disappeared into the night.

"Let's move," she said.

Kyle was already packing. They had no intention of staying in a place known to a local. Trust went only so far. "That house on the left. We go over the wall and get some protection, and I can brace the rifle on top of it."

They moved out quietly, and Sybelle spider-dropped over the wall and landed without a sound on the far side. Swanson turned the knob on the gate, opened it, and walked through. Sybelle raised her middle finger in response.

During the next hour, they created a hide by using material found around the yard, and Kyle placed his personal space-age sniper rifle, the Excalibur, on a solid rest. Sybelle set up a spotter's scope. Both had a clear view of the target building. They created a range card by measuring distances to points in the target area as they waited in the early morning chill.

At five o'clock, dawn was only an hour away, and parts of the village stirred as men and women prepared for the coming day. Kyle and Sybelle received a radio alert that the assault team was on its final approach, and almost immediately, the attack began with the buzzing approach of two big troop-carrying helicopters. Lights began snapping on throughout town by the time the birds landed on a soccer field a block east of the target. As the other Marines charged for the house, one of their snipers found a high position and took out the al Qaeda guard in front. Swanson and Summers, in the rear of the house, never took their eyes off of the target area.

"I have movement at the door," whispered Sybelle. "Tall man. Must be al-Masri's huge bodyguard."

"I see him," responded Kyle. In the scope of the Excalibur, strings of numbers scrolled in constant movement as the computer measured the distance and figured the trajectory. So close, wind would not be a factor. Swanson held his fire.

"Second target. I identify him as al-Masri."

Kyle studied the figure. "I confirm. Target in sight."

As gunfire snapped in the house, the two men ducked into a small automobile, with the bodyguard driving, and the vehicle charged into the street with its lights off. Once again, the foot soldiers of al Qaeda were left behind to become martyrs while the leader escaped.

"Not this time," whispered Kyle. He pulled the trigger. The .50 caliber weapon fired with a jarring *BOOM,* and the recoil kicked his shoulder as the big bullet slammed into the engine block hard enough to make the vehicle jump. A second round then went through the windshield and shattered the head of the bodyguard as the out-of-control car swerved sharply and slammed into a parked truck with the crunch of metal and glass.

"Target down. Other one getting out." Sybelle's voice was perfectly calm, a monotone devoid of emotion.

"Confirm the other one is getting out." Kyle took his time racking in a third round, giving the man a moment to open the door. Al-Masri was alone in the empty street. His men were all dead or captured, and he knew that an American sniper had him in plain view. It was time to quit. He dropped to his knees and held his hands high over his head.

Kyle shot him through the chest, and the al Qaeda officer flopped over on his side. A final shot went into his head.

"Both targets down," said Sybelle.

Kyle grabbed his rifle and pack, and Sybelle picked up her scope and gear and called out the signal for the controller to send in the TAXI for pickup. They hustled out through the gate and back to the landing zone, where the little bird arrived two minutes later. They jumped in and were gone.

The fighting was over in the house. The nest of terrorists had been wiped out to the last man, and the Marines would secure the area.

"Was he trying to surrender?" Sybelle asked, wiping some camouflage greasepaint from her face. "Might have given up some intelligence."

"I saw a weapon," Kyle said.

"Yeah," she said. "Me, too."

3

They arrived back at Incirlik with plenty of time to shower, change clothes, and have breakfast before their next flights. With the special op done, they could mix anonymously with the crowd. Lines of soldiers and airmen and Marines talked in a garble of background noise, and silverware and china clinked a tinny chorus. The aroma of cooking eggs, sausage, and bacon rose like a cloud from the grills as cooks in stained whites kept the food moving to the steam tables. Air Force chow halls were the best, so although the flyboys wore bus driver uniforms, Kyle was always happy to share their food. He stacked a tray full of the good stuff, while Sybelle settled for bran flakes and fruit. Plenty of black coffee. They found a small table off to one side and put down their trays.

"What are you going to do on your R-and-R, Kyle? Two weeks is a long time."

"Rack time. Sleep. Wake up and then go back to sleep. I'm tired." He drank some coffee and thought back over the last few months, during which he had been constantly on the go. The two weeks spent stalking a terrorist in Chechnya had been exhausting, and before that he was looking for a drug operation buried deep in Brazil's giant rain forests. Leading a Filipino marine unit against an island hideout of Islamic terrorists ended in a screwed-up firefight. Last night's raid into Kurd country seemed like just another routine day at the office for Swanson, but even professional hunters get tired.

Sybelle studied him as they ate. Kyle Swanson: the legend himself, the ghost arisen. He was not a big man, 5'9" and 175 pounds, with muscles that were sinewy rather than bulging. The kind of guy with remarkable endurance who could fight all day, long after the bigger guys gave out. Gray-green eyes and sandy brown hair that was longer than normal, even by civilian standards, around an angular face. He was neither handsome nor unattractive, just unremarkable, which was exactly what he needed to be.

On paper and in all government computer banks, Swanson was dead, and he had a tombstone in Arlington National Cemetery to prove it. Two years ago, Kyle was the best scout-sniper in the Marines, a veteran shooter who was often tabbed for special ops work by other agencies. Then General Bradley Middleton had been kidnapped as part of a plot to topple the United States government and put the Pentagon beneath the thumb of a private military contractor. Kyle was on the rescue team sent into Syria, and although the rest of the force had been wiped out, Swanson pulled Middleton to safety while most of the Syrian army hunted them. He was badly wounded in a final firefight, and his fiancée, Shari Towne, was murdered by the plotters in the United States.

Important people realized the value of a single operator in the modern-day climate of terrorism, and it was decided that Kyle Swanson, with no living relatives, should cease to exist. He accepted the deal, with one condition. After recovering from his wounds, the billionaire maniac responsible for killing Shari Towne was soon thereafter found dead on a Colorado mountain, shot through the head in what was ruled to be a hunting accident.

With the fake burial at Arlington, and Kyle's entire identity and fingerprints wiped away, Task Force Trident was created around him, with General Middleton in charge and Sybelle Summers as the operations officer. Swanson was virtually the invisible man, free to take on any assignment. He could kill anybody, anywhere, and walk away untouched by law.

But he had never fully recovered from the death of Shari, his bride-to-be, and one of the reasons that Sybelle had come out from Washington for this otherwise routine operation in Iraq was to evaluate his physical and mental condition. She found that he still had his normal cold edge and the hard shell that made sure nothing got inside. Swanson simply did not care about much. Kyle's problem was not about being dead but about continuing to live with himself.

"Middleton wants me to report back on how you're doing, Kyle." She held the warm mug of coffee in both hands. "I know you can still shoot straight, but how's your head?"

"You mean, am I crazy?"

"Are you?"

"Of course. I have to be crazy to do this job!" He grinned. "No. At times, I get tired of being dead. It can be a pain in the ass. I mean, having to wear a black mask in that room with other Marines? I knew half of those guys but couldn't even say hello. I have to check my latest fake passport every morning to remember my name for the day. They even gave me a set of Dutch identification papers a while back. Do I look Dutch to you?"

"Got to be tough," she agreed. The ultimate loner. "Tell you what. You're obviously exhausted and running on battery power alone. So take your R-and-R and rest up, get drunk, get laid, and sweat out a hard physical conditioning program. Then come back to Washington and let's figure out how to slow down the workload. They can't expect you to cover the whole world by yourself."

"Is the general complaining about me again?" Swanson and Middleton had not gotten along for years, dating back to their first encounter during the First Gulf War. Middleton had come across Swanson after a particularly vicious firefight and saw the sniper trembling as he reflected on the carnage he had caused during the battle. Swanson always had found a few moments alone after a fight to bring himself back to normal, but Middleton had mistaken the reaction as evidence of incompetence. Not only had he tried to get Swanson kicked out of the Marines, but he also used the term "shaky" in the official report. The attempt failed, but the ironic nickname of "Shake" stuck, for his friends knew that Kyle Swanson was anything but unreliable in battle. It had taken the rescue in Syria to start Middleton and Swanson on a path of mutual respect and friendship.

"No. He's just concerned. We all are. Without you, there is no Task Force Trident."

Kyle finished a final slice of toast and pushed away his plate. "Well, Captain Summers, tell the folks back home that I am just skippy. I still believe in our mission. I still hate terrorists, and I'm still willing to kill whoever the president decides needs a good killing."

Within a few hours, Summers left for Washington aboard a military transport, and Kyle climbed into a Sikorsky S-76 helicopter. It was shining white except for two narrow bands of dark blue stripes and a gold corporate symbol on each side marking it as part of Excalibur Enterprises Ltd., the holding company for the many businesses of British tycoon Sir Geoffrey Cornwell. The sleek bird was a combination executive passenger vehicle and all-around workhorse, and Kyle was the only passenger in its spacious and soundproof cabin. The aircraft had no ties to anything military, and its flight log for the day recorded just a routine trip for a company executive, but in the world of clandestine operations, Sir Jeff was known to occasionally lend a hand for off-the-book operations. Kyle strapped into a comfortable leather seat as the powerful Turbomeca Arriel 2S2 engines revved up, and in minutes the Sikorsky was up and heading toward the Mediterranean Sea. The steady low throb of the engines helped him fall asleep almost instantly.

"We're landing, sir." The pilot's voice on the intercom aroused him after what seemed only a few minutes, but when he checked his watch, Swanson saw they had been in the air for more than an hour. The blades were slapping hard, and from the cabin window, he could see the square landing deck of a luxurious yacht with the same color scheme as the helicopter. The sparkling *Vagabond* seemed to rise from the waters to meet the wheels of the descending bird, which touched down lightly on the landing deck.

"Home, sweet home," said Kyle Swanson as a crewman pulled open the door from the outside. "Thanks for the lift, guys."

He stepped to the deck while the chopper was still shutting down its engines and ducked away from the powerful downdraft of the rotor blades. A woman moved toward him from the cabin area. She was Lady Patricia Cornwell, in a blouse of blue silk and dark slacks, with a silver necklace and earrings. "Welcome back, stranger," she said, giving him a tight hug and handing over a cold beer. Her eyes took in everything: the weary movement, the sun-reddened skin, a slight limp. He had been gone for almost two weeks. No questions. "Jeff is on his way back from a NATO meeting and should be aboard before the storm arrives."

"Good to be here, Pat. Lord, I'm tired." Clouds were gathering on the horizon, and crewmen in crisp uniforms hurried about, coiling rope and lashing canvas to get the big yacht ready for the approaching heavy weather.

Pat gently touched a small bandage taped on his chin. "Did you forget to duck?"

"Cut myself shaving," Swanson answered with a laugh.

"You seem to do that a lot these days." She punched him lightly on the shoulder. "Why don't you go take a nap before you fall asleep on your feet, Kyle? We will call you for dinner at seven."

"Yes, m'lady." He walked away across the teak deck and disappeared into an open hatch, heading for his own cabin as the yacht shifted beneath his feet on the rolling waves.

Pat stared out to where the black waters met the graying sky. An unhappy soul, she thought as the breeze pulled at her hair and clothing. She knew that he would fall asleep fully clothed and that they would not see him at dinner.

Swanson heard a soft bump against the hull and immediately smelled rot and decay. He knew who it was before he shrugged out of bed and went on deck to peer over the rail. Below, bobbing in a long, low craft that rode easily on the churning water, was the Boatman, grinning up at him. Dead people sat erect on the benches, three to a side.

"You've been busy," Kyle observed.

"Wars. Revolution." The Boatman shrugged with a low cackle. "I always have many waiting to go over." He pointed a finger of ivory bone toward a narrow ridge of fire in the north, a glowing rim between the black of the

night and the black of the sea. When the Boatman pulled on a long oar to steady the craft, the wind pushed the soiled black robe around his thin figure, and his skeletal face flashed an evil smile of broken teeth.

"So what do you want? You already have a full boat, and I ain't planning to go with you."

"Not yet. But very soon."

"Fuck you."

"I have retrieved the two souls you just killed."

"Good. They thought they were going to paradise and each would collect his six dozen virgins."

The Boatman cackled. "They were wrong." There was a long pause. "You are a good and reliable supplier."

Kyle spat overboard. "And you are nothing but a bad dream. I'm going to wake up soon and you will be gone."

The Boatman placed his hand against the white hull of the Vagabond *and gave a push, then leaned onto his oar, and the little boat swung away. A few more sweeps put some distance between them before the specter turned and spoke again. "Yes? That is true, but I am never too far from you, awake or asleep. I will be back when you finally decide to put a pistol in your mouth and finish self-destructing. It will be a special trip, and you can have the whole boat to yourself."*

The shuttle craft paddled away with its cargo of corpses, the Boatman disappearing into the storm, trailing a croak of laughter.

When Kyle awoke, he was standing outside on the rolling deck of the *Vagabond* in his bare feet with wind-driven rain sluicing over him, drenching the clothes in which he had fallen asleep. Lightning sizzled off the water and thunder rumbled through the night sky as he held the rail in a death grip. Just a dream. Just the damned dream again.

Swanson had been trained for years to keep his emotions in check while on a mission, when precision and control frequently marked the difference between success and failure. It was after the shooting, when he was alone, that he allowed his thoughts to deal with what had happened, and the process was not always pretty. Now, the Boatman had become an unwanted part of that procedure.

All of the storms in the world could not wash away what really troubled him, so he staggered into the main cabin, pulled a bottle of tequila from the bar, and went back outside. Rain didn't bother him. Cold didn't bother him. Killing people didn't bother him.

What gnawed at his brain was the simple equation that Shari was dead and he was still alive. He upended the bottle and took a large swallow, feeling the tequila bite in his throat, then he sought shelter from the thundering gale in the corner of the superstructure and drank himself back to sleep. About four o'clock in the morning, a pair of *Vagabond* crew members found him curled up there, wedged between a locker and a lifeboat, and they hauled him back to his cabin, stripped off the wet clothes, roughly toweled him down, and left him on the bunk beneath blankets.

"We've got a new mission." Major General Bradley Middleton made himself comfortable in his Pentagon office by opening the lower right-hand drawer of his desk and propping a spit-shined shoe on it, loosening his tie, and unbuttoning his collar.

Master Gunnery Sergeant O. O. Dawkins, one of only forty-five men in the Marine Corps to hold that highest enlisted rank, occupied most of the sofa. Double-Oh had helped write the book on special operations. Next to him sat Sybelle Summers, who had just flown in from Turkey.

In a chair of burgundy leather sat U.S. Navy Lieutenant Commander Benton Freedman, whose hair was always tousled, as if he had just gotten out of bed. He was a brilliant computer geek, engineer, and master of all things technical. At the Naval Academy, he was given the nickname of "Wizard" because he seemed to perform witchcraft with electronics and possessed an astonishing memory. Middleton yanked the Navy guy into what was essentially a Marine operation when Trident began, where his nickname became "the Lizard."

The other member of the team, Swanson, the Dead Guy, was missing, starting an R-and-R.

Middleton pointed at Freedman, whose busy brain had been sucking information from the folder in front of him. "Lizard, summarize it, with anything you have picked up from other sources."

"Yes, sir," Freedman said, not looking up. "An Iraqi physicist who we thought had disappeared in 1992 showed up two weeks ago in Baghdad. He arranged a surrender to an Army intel officer and claimed to have vital information about a new weapon of mass destruction at a place he called the Palace of Death."

Sybelle, studying her red fingernails, interrupted. "A WMD? I thought we killed that old horse and buried it a long time ago. Everybody looked everywhere and nobody found anything."

"Save the questions and comments," said Middleton. "Go ahead, Lizard."

"Other than saying it was a chemical-biological agent, he was reluctant to give much real information until he was formally given immunity from prosecution and protection for himself and his family. He was kept under wraps until yesterday, when a meeting was set up at Coalition Headquarters for the first formal interrogation, and he was being delivered by an armed escort of four soldiers. A sniper picked him off before he got there and also killed the officer in charge of the escort detail."

"Talk to me, Double-Oh," said Middleton.

"A good piece of shooting," said Master Gunny Dawkins as he went through the photographs of the corpses. "The first bullet hit the officer by going through the unarmored point beneath the armpit of his vest and took out the internal organs right to left, including the heart. Then the Iraqi was hit in the jugular vein along the neck, just above the collar of his armored vest, left to right. Exit through his throat." He closed the folder. "One of those might be a lucky shot. Not two. This sniper hit what he was aiming at, and both victims bled out on the spot. My conclusion is that this was another attack by Juba."

The general closed the drawer with his foot and slid the chair forward so he could rest his arms on the desk. "What's your take, Captain Summers?"

"I agree with Double-Oh. It's got to be Juba, sir. Shoots, kills, and disappears. We don't know whether he is just one man or several different snipers, whether he is even real or just some Arabian fairy tale to pump up the spirits of the jihadists. Whatever, he's the best they've got, and pulling off an assassination like this in the Green Zone enhances his reputation."

Freedman did some calculations in his head. "I figure the shooter had a target area of no more than an inch. The unprotected opening between the vest and the sleeve of the first victim was only about an inch wide, and the sniper squeezed a bullet in there. The second shot was exact enough to hit the vein, an even smaller target. I can work up the ballistics, angles, and all that if you want."

"Not necessary," said Middleton. "The people in Baghdad are doing that, and we will have their data when it comes in. What is interesting is that he knew exactly who to shoot and when the target was going to appear in a certain place at a certain time. Total inside information."

"Liz, did the informant say anything else worthwhile before he got popped?" Double-Oh crossed his right leg over his left knee, taking up even more space. Sybelle pushed him.

"An intel report arrived just before we came in here for the meeting," interjected Middleton. "The scientist said he had escaped from a laboratory in Iran, and he gave a general location near the Iraq border."

"He used that particular word, sir? Escaped?"

"Right. So, people, that's our mission. We are going to do a little snoop and poop and find that mysterious lab."

Middleton stood and stretched, throwing his arms wide, then put his hands on his hips. "So we're going in. Sybelle, you will stay here this time and oversee the operation. Spin up an infiltration team and get them over to Doha. Double-Oh, you will lead the team on the ground. On your way over, detour out to Sir Geoffrey's boat and pick up Swanson. Give them a briefing, and then you two hustle down to Kuwait. Order anything you need through Lieutenant Commander Freedman."

The Lizard blew out a short breath of relief. He did not like to travel far from his desk. "Sir, is it wise to use Gunny Swanson on this? According to Captain Summers, he really needs some down time."

Double-Oh answered. "Liz, if there is any fucking chance at all that we might bump into Juba while we run this job, I want our best shooter along to cover my ass. I'll put my money on Kyle, tired or not."

"Then he can sleep on the plane to Kuwait," said General Middleton. "Get to it, people. Go get me some pictures of this Palace of Death."

4

The royal wedding of Prince William and the beautiful Barbara Seldingham, the future king and queen of England, was a plum for the press. A billion people would gather around television sets from Africa to Australia to watch the splendid event. *A billion!* Maybe more.

Television stations wanting to personalize the coverage could send a reporter and crew to London but could not transport their own mobile rigs overseas and had to lease the needed technical equipment. Every such company in the region had been booked for months in advance, and others were created just for that purpose.

Edinburgh All-Media Ltd., in Scotland, was one of the small companies founded to serve the huge demand. It had filed papers for a business permit, found a storefront office, then bought and reconfigured two vans especially for commercial television use, including external generators to power computers and editing gear inside the cargo areas. One was immediately rented by a television station in Little Rock, Arkansas, and the other was leased to a cable company in Italy. The two trucks were given distinctive purple and white paint schemes.

Juba wore a jumpsuit that matched those colors as he

drove the lead van away from the city center and onto the City of Edinburgh Bypass, the A720. He slipped on dark sunglasses as he turned east, directly into the morning sun, and drove on until the A720 merged with the A1 at Old Craighall Junction. The second van followed, and they crossed the border at Lamberton.

They made the journey of a twisting 420 miles to London in a single day, entered the city, and maneuvered to the cordoned-off far end of Kensington Park that had been reserved for the regiment of production trucks that would support the television horde. There was a short line of trucks waiting to get in, and the two vans from Edinburgh All-Media slid into position at the rear. A policeman told them to stay with the vehicles until the security teams cleared them. For thirty minutes, they followed as the line grew shorter until Juba drove onto a special parking pad caked with detection sensors, where a four-man squad and their bomb-sniffing dog thoroughly combed the vehicle and found nothing. Once cleared to be inside the quarantine area, a van could not leave until after the wedding.

Juba was given a map with a specific parking slot highlighted with a yellow marking pen: the very back row, against the Cyclone fence. The other purple and white van had a slightly better spot, one row in front and about fifty yards away, to the left. The Italians had more clout than the station from Arkansas.

The driver of the second van caught a late train back to Scotland, where he would dismantle the little office of Edinburgh All-Media Ltd. Juba did not have far to go: he was spending a few days with his mother and father at their small place in the West Midlands, the home of his boyhood.

In the Med, a streak of sunshine as bright as a spotlight came through the slightly parted curtains over the porthole and hammered the face of Kyle Swanson until he woke up. It was almost noon. Everyone passing in the corridor outside had been content not to awaken him and had tip-toed around his cabin door. After stretching, he took a shower and shaved. By the time he put on fresh jeans and a golf shirt and running shoes, he almost felt human. His head hurt.

Stepping outside, he found that the storm had passed on and had been replaced by a calm green sea and a sunlit sky, and the *Vagabond* was heading east at about twenty knots, churning into the deep water. No land was visible. A squadron of seagulls followed the white wake, and the temperature was warm.

Up one deck, he entered the main cabin of the yacht, a spacious lounge with a full bar in one corner and a com-fortable arrangement of sofas, soft chairs, and heavy an-tique Chinese tables. A giant flat-screen television set and an electronic entertainment center were built into one bulkhead. Sir Geoffrey Cornwell was hunched forward and reading news reports flashing on the screen of a lap-top computer. A retired colonel from the British Special Air Services, Jeff had built a fortune making and selling state-of-the-art weapons systems. He seldom got excited and was very aware that warriors handled stress in differ-ent ways. It was not exactly a secret that they got drunk on occasion to deal with the stress.

Jeff raised his shaggy eyebrows. "Rough night?"

A carafe of chilled orange juice was on the buffet, and Kyle poured a glass and drank it before answering. He filled a thick ceramic mug with coffee and picked up a small bowl of fruit at the buffet. "Was drunk. Now so-ber." No apologies.

Lady Patricia was reading a magazine beside a large window that provided a panoramic view of the passing sea. She looked up, took an elegant pull on a small, thin cigar, and blew away the smoke. "You are our wayward boy, Kyle. You were quite naughty last night, but we've seen you worse. Do it again, however, and I shall spank you."

"Is that an offer, m'lady?" He smiled. Conversation made his head hurt.

"Don't act the little pervert now. Ask Dr. Russell to give you something for your hangover."

"I'm fine," said Kyle.

"Spoken like a true warrior. You are truly a hard man, Kyle Swanson," Sir Jeff said without looking away from the screen.

They sat in silence for a while, comfortable, and Kyle let his eyes close. In two minutes he was asleep again, with his head back against the sofa. Pat looked over at Jeff, who gestured that she should keep quiet. "Let him be," he said. Jeff had just checked one of his e-mail accounts and found an encoded message from Washington. Trouble was on the way, and Kyle was going to need all the sleep he could get.

Captain Rick Newman was in a garage on a military base in North Carolina, up to his armpits in grease as he worked on his latest automotive restoration project, a 1955 Chevy Bel Air two-door hardtop with fender skirts. The outside skin of the old car was in decent shape, not much rust; the original baby blue and cream paint scheme was still visible, the chrome running trim undented. The interior needed major renovation, but it would just take some time and money to make it cherry again. The engine, though, a rare 350 V8, was for shit, and the deeper he dug into its guts, the shittier things got. It would cost a fortune to replace the whole thing, which was against the rules for a serious hobbyist and car trader like Newman. He had bought the car for nine thousand dollars at an Alabama estate sale and planned to restore it personally and sell it on the upside of $50K. It would take years. "Hey, Cap'n! You got a phone call over here," shouted a motor pool Marine.

Rick wiped the grease from his hands and picked up the receiver. "Captain Newman," he said.

"Hey, Rick. This is Sybelle Summers calling from Trident in Washington." The voice was some hybrid of a normal tone, authoritative sandpaper, and a purr.

"Hi, Sybelle. Long time," he said, suddenly alert. "What's up?"

"We've got a job for you, my friend. Get back to your office right away and call me back on a secure line. Top Secret."

"On my way," he said. "Fifteen minutes." He hung up, closed the Chevy's hood, and hurried away to clean up and get to his desk. The Bel Air would have to wait. Newman was part of a Marine Special Operations Company that comprised four platoons. The rotation had one platoon in Iraq, one in Afghanistan, one in training at this secret base in North Carolina, and the fourth on ready alert, sitting on a short leash, ready to go anywhere in four hours.

When he spoke to Sybelle Summers on the secure link, her orders were quite simple and explicit. He was to choose five more designated operators for a black mission, get over to Camp Doha, in Kuwait, and link up there with Master Gunnery Sergeant O. O. Dawkins, who would give them a full briefing. Eight men would be going in, and Newman's group would provide the guns in case something went wrong.

She gave him only a brief overview to help pick the specialists he would take and said he could plus up with scouts, snipers, or anyone else he needed. Trident would chop them from their current assignments and arrange the temporary duty. To Newman, it sounded like he was

going to need shooters to provide firepower for a special
op. He had plenty of good ones from which to choose. He
would rather work with people from his own team, highly
disciplined and well trained, who already knew each
other. His group would click together like a well-oiled
military machine. Hughes, Tipp, and Rawls for certain.
Two more and himself. The addition was easy. His group
was six. Double-Oh made seven. Who was the eighth?

Newman began making calls of his own.

Darren Rawls faked a move to the right, pulled back, and
went up and up and up. Rawls, with a thirty-one-inch verti-
cal leap, seemed to levitate in slow motion as he flicked
his wrist and delivered a jump shot from the top of the
key. His sneakers hit the concrete court as the ball finished its arc to the basket with nothing but net. "Game
over, Rabbit. Pay me the money," he told Joe Tipp, a
lanky white boy who was better at football than hoops.
Both were sweating hard in the North Carolina sun that
baked the hidden, off-limits military installation. They
were the lead instructors in an escape and evasion training mission and had started the young members of the
platoon through the assigned exercise at dawn. The first
and fastest would be approaching the finish well after
dark. At sundown, when the trainees were exhausted but
feeling confident about having made the distance, Rawls
and Tipp would hunt them down, one by one, and capture
them. Then the fun would begin in the interrogation hut.
Until then, they might as well play ball or take a nap.
Their beepers sang out at the same moment.

Travis Hughes was out pillaging and terrorizing the coun-
tryside on his Suzuki Hayabusa GSX1300R. The speed
limit was 65 mph, but Hughes had not pimped out his
bright red rice-burner to go 65. The Marine staff sergeant,

a sniper team leader, wore a blue bandanna around his head, dark sunglasses, creased black leathers with an Outlaws patch, and biker boots. Long red hair flew behind him as he stormed back toward the base. The blonde at the bar had been with Marines before, and when the beeper stuttered on his belt, she knew he was gone. She walked with him outside and gave him a long wet kiss when he powered up his machine. She nibbled his ear and said, "Stay out of trouble this time, Travis." Hughes revved up the bike. "Don't think I can do that, darlin'," he said and launched the motorcycle out onto the road, laughing into the sharp wind that whipped around him. He bent low over the handlebars and cranked it up to a comfortable 110, hauling butt back to the base.

LONDON

Television reporter Kimberly Drake was only two years out of journalism school and still a little fish, even within her Arkansas station. She wanted to be considered a serious journalist, not just a talking head, and sometimes felt that her good looks were no advantage whatsoever. Every station had a beautiful anchor or weathergirl, and she could no longer even imagine an unattractive woman hosting a television newscast. To break out of Little Rock, Kim needed some big stories, and once she had earned her spurs and boosted her reputation, she could jump to a bigger station or at least a cable network.

Then, out of nowhere, the station management decided to send its own correspondent to the royal wedding, just like its big competitors, as part of the continuing battle for advertising dollars. Kimberly would have happily either screwed or killed her news director to get the assignment but did not have to do either. Since the rest of the reporting staff was male and the female anchor was too pregnant to travel, nobody else even wanted the assignment! To the guys, it was just a wedding. Fluff, not like a Super Bowl or a war.

The station gave Kim the job but put very little money behind the trip. Tom Lester, a veteran cameraman, accompanied her, along with a young engineer who would work as a soundman for the stand-ups. The shoestring budget meant they operated out of a small purple and white production van that the station had hired at bargain basement rates.

Kimberly did not care. As she left the Royal Wedding Command Center Press Office in London with her new laminated credentials on a chain around her neck and walked toward the media production area in Kensington Park, she felt like a real reporter for the first time in her life.

It was not until late that night that reality sank in. Because of her low status, Kim's truck had been assigned a space far away from the parade route, on the very back row. From the camera position atop the van, she could overlook the vast media lot that had been cordoned off, and she was jealous that another purple and white van from the same company, rented by an Italian cable operator, had been given a slightly better spot about fifty yards away.

She had never seen so many media types. British journalists were as aggressive as pit bulls, and reporters and television people from dozens of other countries were arriving, also wearing press credentials for the big event. There were hundreds of them around, many of whom she recognized, although they did not know her. The network people were right at the front! Media money was everywhere. Private residents had fled the city and rented out their apartments and homes at exorbitant rates. Restaurant prices doubled around the heart of the press operations because the reporters were on expense accounts.

Kim Drake stood atop her van and sipped a cup of coffee and stared out over the media throng. She had to admit she was a little fish over here, too. A guppy swimming with sharks. *I'll show them. I'll show them all.*

5

THE MEDITERRANEAN SEA

Master Gunnery Sergeant Dawkins set foot on the spotless deck of the *Vagabond* with supreme confidence, for he, too, was a creature of the sea, having spent much of his life on boats and ships, beneath the water in submarines or flying over it in planes and helicopters. It was good to be back in his element and out of Washington on this sunny Monday morning, ready to take his best bud, Kyle Swanson, on another hunting trip. He left his luggage aboard the bird, since they would be leaving again soon.

Swanson, Lady Pat, and Sir Jeff were waiting at the edge of the helo deck, and they took him to the stern, where a table beside the swimming pool had been set with china and silver utensils and white napkins. The chef had started the eggs when the helicopter was five minutes out, and now an enormous selection of delicious food was rolled out by a female crew member dressed in whites.

Double-Oh plunged into the meal, hardly aware that the others were only nibbling at the feast since they had already had breakfast. The conversation was mild chatter, waiting for him to finish eating before getting down to business. The four of them were family in many ways, except by blood. The brotherhood of spec ops warriors was tight, and the men had known each other for years. Lady Pat was their den mother.

Swanson had joined the Marines while still a teenager, and it was Dawkins, then a staff sergeant, who first discovered that the awkward boy had a remarkable ability in the unique craft of long-distance precision firing and was also a natural in combat. Over the years, as they both rose in rank, Dawkins remained Kyle's mentor and eventually spun him off for use in special operations work by nonmilitary government agencies.

One of Kyle's more interesting assignments had not involved combat at all but was serving as a special Pentagon adviser to Sir Jeff Cornwell in the development of a new-generation sniper rifle that they called the Excalibur. It took several years of off-and-on work by Swanson, and although he always kept people at an emotional distance, he was drawn in by the magnetic friendship Jeff and Pat offered. When he had introduced them to Shari Towne as the girl he planned to marry, she also was taken under the protective wings of the Cornwells. Family. Kyle had thought for a while there that he really had one. Then Shari was murdered, and Kyle almost came apart. Pat, Jeff, and Double-Oh had been helping piece him back together slowly over time. Keeping him busy was important.

Dawkins finally finished eating and filled his coffee cup again. Lady Pat motioned for the crew member to clear the table, and the four of them were soon left alone on the deck as a soft Mediterranean breeze blew across the stern of the *Vagabond*. Pat pulled a soft shawl of Scottish wool around her shoulders to stay warm.

"I am leaving for London tonight to attend a reception for the royal wedding and then spend a lot of Jeff's money on new clothes," she declared, looking at Swanson. "But before I leave you boys to talk about whatever the new mission may be, I have something serious to say to you, Kyle."

He smiled. "What's on your mind?"

"You are still grieving for our dear girl Shari. Her death left a hole in your heart, a deep hole that you think can never heal, and you think that withdrawing into all of this black ops work will protect you," she said. "I did not like how you got so stupefied drunk that you didn't have sense enough to come in out of the rain. You're acting like some dumb ostrich sticking its head into the sand and thinking it cannot be seen. It isn't working, is it?"

"Instant psychobabble from Dr. Pat? You know everything?" He was instantly defensive.

She stood, and he saw tears in her eyes just before she slapped him so hard that his ears rang. "Don't you dare speak like that to me, Kyle Swanson! Do you believe that you are the only one who loved Shari? That your heart was the only one broken when she died? I still cry when I think of her. I am thankful that she was in our lives at all."

"So how did you get over her, Pat? What's the secret?" He was growing angry. He did not like to talk about Shari, even with Jeff and Pat and Double-Oh.

She had a hand on each hip and glared at him. "You think that Jeff and I got over her? How wrong you are. You *never* get over that kind of loss. You just . . . eventually . . . come to accept it as something you cannot change. The sun comes up in the morning, the clock ticks, and Shari will still be dead. You cannot climb into the coffin with her." Pat pulled her wrap tight around her shoulders. "Wake up, Kyle. Shari's been gone for more than a year, and you are condemned to live with the rest of us now. I want you back, the real Kyle Swanson, not some war junkie who is on his way to becoming an otherwise useless alcoholic."

She turned, shook her head, and walked away to the main cabin.

Swanson fell back in his chair. *Jesus Christ. She just beat the crap out of me.* Kyle had been disturbed for months when he could no longer mentally recall every detail of Shari's beautiful face, nor smell her fragrance, although he could still imagine her touch and her laugh. He was losing her. She was fading over time. "What's your opinion, Jeff?" he asked.

"What she said." He drank some coffee and unblinkingly returned Kyle's stare.

"And you?"

Master Gunny Dawkins picked up his briefcase and pulled out a folded map. "I'm your friend, not your confessor. Whatever it takes, as long as it takes. But if you get fucked up on booze or dope and get me killed, I shall be very unhappy. Now can we please move past this Oprah moment and talk about the fucking mission?"

Double-Oh laid out the map, pointing at a grid location close to the southwestern tip of Iran. "This is where the defector said the so-called Palace of Death was located, almost within rock-throwing distance of the border. We know from the satellites that there's nothing important down there except the port town of Khorramshahr. Beyond that is just a lot of dirt, which is why the boss wants to put some boots down and take a look."

"Could the walk-in just have been looking for a quick cash payment with his allegedly secret information?" Kyle asked. "Peddling bogus information to Americans is not exactly new in Iraq."

"Not bloody likely if someone went to the trouble to assassinate him in the Green Zone. There was a reason." Jeff sat back and folded his hands over a growing belly, the price of success. He was no longer young and jumping out of airplanes.

"That was a perfect stalk and shoot," Double-Oh looked over at Kyle. "We're sure it was Juba. The description from the hotel people matches what we know about him, and he did everything but leave his autograph. So somehow he's involved, too."

"Lots of loose ends," said Kyle. "But why Iran? It would be a lot more credible if an Iraqi scientist emerged from Syria, since that's where Saddam stashed his big weapons, up around al-Baida, and in the Bekaa Valley in Lebanon. Iran and Iraq hated each other after eight years of war and a million casualties. I cannot see this level of cooperation, even so many years later."

Sir Jeff picked up the map and studied it. "Unless . . ." They could almost see the wheels turning in the man's brain. "At the end of that war, there were months of negotiations before the two sides agreed to the solution brokered by the United Nations. Very little was changed in the long run, but some deals were made concerning captured territory and the shared use of the Shatt al-Arab waterway."

"History lesson number 42," said Kyle. "What is your point?"

"What if this Palace of Death thing was one of the back-channel agreements, something even the UN people did not know about? Hussein and the ayatollahs overlooked their differences long enough to make a deal for the future."

Double-Oh was interested. "Meaning us?"

"I'll get to that. What was the major thing people remember about the Iran-Iraq War? The use of chemical weapons by Iraq to blunt Iranian frontal assaults. Later came the biochem attacks in the Kurdistan region. You certainly remember the Arab saying that 'the enemy of my enemy is my friend.' Both sides consider America to be the Great Satan, and both sides anticipated that sooner or later, one or both of them would be facing us in combat."

Kyle finished his coffee. "So these crazies, the mullahs and Saddam's thugs, start planning something way back in the 1980s? A jointly owned and operated bioweapons factory? Then they never used the product?"

"If they were trying to come up with something really new and effective and deadly, perhaps it just wasn't ready in time for the Gulf War, and things tightened up quickly during the current war. The United States sold weapons to both sides during the Iran-Iraq fighting, and so much matériel and cash has been lost or stolen during the current war that it cannot even be counted. Throw in the massive support the United States supplied to the Afghan rebels that fought the Soviet Union and it is reasonable to believe they had access to plenty of raw materials and plenty of time for development."

"So you think there really may be something to this Palace of Death idea?"

"The name is just a name, like Saddam's 'Mother of All Battles,' but they have to call it something. Whatever is out there needs to be uncovered."

"That's the job. Kyle and I are heading down to Doha to pick up a MARSOC team, then go in early tomorrow morning." Double-Oh stood and put away his map. "Give my apologies to Pat for my not being able to stay longer. I still have some money she hasn't stolen from me at poker."

Kyle shook hands with Jeff. "Tell m'lady I'll be thinking about what she said . . . and for her to have a good time in London. I'll be back in a few days."

Sir Jeff slapped him on the shoulder. "Right. Only wish I was going with you." He walked them to the helipad and waved as the helicopter lifted away.

The Marine assault team arrived at Camp Doha in Kuwait as fast as it could be assembled and flown out of North Carolina. They boarded a plane on a sunny afternoon, flew most of the night, and got off to find themselves in the desert sun of Kuwait. A waiting helicopter ferried them to a secure barracks in the special operations sector of the sprawling American base at Camp Doha, north of Kuwait City.

Every member of the team had been to Doha before, during previous tours in Iraq. It was Little America. Uncle Frosty's Oasis, the Marble Palace, the beach, and great Mexican food downtown at the La Palma. Pizza, camel races, ice cream. Doha was not a hardship post.

They knew, however, that this was not going to be vacation time, for the first thing they saw in their barracks was a stack of hazmat suits on a table by the door. They pawed through the stack and picked out correct sizes, tossed the suits onto the bunks, and followed Captain Newman over to a private room in a mess hall for chow. Afterward, he disappeared for a briefing, and the rest of them ambled back to their small barracks. Special operators do not linger in the daylight when starting a mission, and they were glad the sun was going down.

The lights were off, and Travis Hughes was the first one through the door, feeling for the switch. He was snatched from his feet by a big, meaty arm and thrown to the floor, where someone jammed a knee into his chest and pressed a knife to his neck.

Darren Rawls, the next through the door, thought Hughes had tripped and fallen. Then he felt a pistol barrel being jammed under his chin so hard that his head was forced back.

The lights snapped on. Master Gunny Dawkins removed the pistol he held on Rawls and looked furious. A guy with a black mask had Travis Hughes pinned to the floor.

"You people get in here!" Dawkins bawled in a parade ground voice. "You're supposed to be hot shit MARSOC troops, and you are bumbling around like a bunch of Girl Scouts. Walked right into an ambush! You are on a mission, goddammit, and a lot of you would be dead by now if we were a couple of terrorists. There is no safe place over here, not even in Doha. So pull your heads out of your asses, right now!"

The other Marines sheepishly filed into the room and gathered around Double-Oh. The man in the mask sheathed his knife and held out a hand to Hughes. "Get up, Trav," he said. The voice was familiar. The masked guy sat on a bunk, and Captain Newman entered, locked the door, and joined Double-Oh at the front. The attention of the men was totally in focus now because they had been professionally embarrassed by letting down their guard.

"Here's the drill," Newman said. He explained the snoop-and-poop mission and told them they would be providing fire support, if necessary, for Master Gunny Dawkins and the other man, who would be principal investigators.

Dawkins then took over. "I know that you do not like going into a possible firefight with someone you don't know covering your back, so we have to break a rule here tonight. You all have clearance for Top Secret material, and you will never speak of what we are about to tell you to anyone, ever. Understood?" He looked around and received nods from each of the six men. Then he nodded, and Kyle removed his mask.

"This is Gunnery Sergeant Kyle Swanson. Because of special ops purposes, he was declared dead back after the Syrian mess. We both now work for Task Force Trident, which you don't need to know much about."

"Haaaayyy! Shake!" hooted Travis Hughes, while others shouted "Dude!" and "Muthafucka!" and "Awrite!" They clapped, and a few gave him high fives. Everyone knew Swanson, or knew of him. "Quiet down," barked Double-Oh. "Save the happy horseshit reunion crap for later. Right now, everybody get a couple of hours' sleep. We leave at 0200 hours. Be ready."

LONDON

Juba showed his pass and walked without incident into the media grounds in Kensington Park, carrying his bag of tools. A small army of technicians was laying down rivers of cable, lighting specialists were clamping big, glaring bulbs into position, soundmen were rigging microphones, and makeup artists flung powder puffs and eyeliner on the TV news readers while writers pounded out copy and producers pulled their hair in frustration. Juba was just another tech and made his way effortlessly through the dozens of production trucks and the forest of satellite dishes atop thin poles. He spotted the distinctive Edinburgh vans and went toward them.

A pretty young woman was seated on the steps of the truck, working on a laptop computer that was balanced on her knees. She looked up with a start when she realized someone was standing in front of her. He wore a technician's purple and white jumpsuit with a belt of tools hung around his narrow waist. Even in the dark, he looked as if he had a deep tan. "May I help you?" she asked.

The man referred to a scrap of paper. "Are you Miss Drake?"

"Yes."

"I'm from Edinburgh All-Media. They sent me down to give the vans a last-minute look to be sure you don't have any problems tomorrow. Is your engineer around?"

"Sure. He's inside." She led him into the cargo bay. "Harold? This tech is from the rental service and wants to see if anything is wrong."

Juba followed her in, shook the hand of the engineer, and turned back to Kim. "Nothing is wrong, Miss Drake. Just a precaution, mind you. We want everything to go smoothly for you tomorrow. So, have you encountered any problems?" he asked Harold.

"Nope, but glad you came around to check." The engineer had on a headset and was working a bank of lighted dials. "I'm setting the uplink to go live. Let me know if you need me."

"Right. Won't be a minute." Juba studied the desktop area, dropped to the floor to look at the underneath wiring, and clicked a flashlight to see into small places. He opened the engine and played around in the compartment, climbed to the top and back down, then crawled beneath the truck, where he removed two cans of aerosol spray from his toolbox. Each was labeled as a commercial product that was widely used to blow blasts of clean air onto delicate computer components. Juba twisted the exterior coverings and pulled out the canisters within, then carefully attached them to small clamps above the exhaust pipe from the muffler. Tiny bits of explosive plastique were on the tips of the canisters, and he joined them with a common wire to a small detonator. It would go off when a certain cell phone number was dialed, and the contents of the canisters would be released.

While he worked, Kim Drake continued preparing for her upcoming live shot for the six o'clock evening news back home. She had managed to snare a good report, standing in front of the palace with one of those tall soldiers in the red coat and funny-looking fur hat. When she was done filming, she stepped away from the spot, and a press officer ushered in another reporter to do the same thing. The news director back home loved it and set the report for the evening news.

Juba finished just as Kim was doing her makeup at a

mirror in the van. "Pardon, Miss Drake, if you don't mind. May I snap a few photos of you and Harold and your cameraman? Hate to be such a bother, but the company wants some pictures for its adverts after you lot are gone. Drum up more business for us in the lean times, you know." The request was so polite that they all agreed, and Juba took out a digital camera.

"Just wait until I finish my hair," Kim called. "I look horrible." He shot a series of pictures of Harold at the controls while he waited.

Kim snapped off the light and stepped forward. "Any time you're ready."

"Are you famous, Miss Drake?" He clicked two pictures.

"No, not yet. Working on it." Broad smile, hands on hips, blond hair in helmet hairspray mode. American Idol.

"I find that difficult to believe. Obviously you're talented, or you would not be here." Two more pictures. "Very good. My thanks to all of you. The company will be pleased up to get these. You are okay here, so I'll just be off now to check the other van. Some Italian chaps."

He repeated the drill with the Italian van, where only a technician was on duty. There was one big difference. Inside the truck, Juba tilted the driver's seat forward and unscrewed a panel door, and the aroma of fresh coffee filled the interior. "That smells good. Are you brewing a pot of coffee down there?" asked the man at the console.

Juba explained over his shoulder that they packed coffee around some of the more sensitive avionic components to absorb excess moisture because the damp climates of Scotland and England played havoc with the delicate equipment. In reality, the strong coffee smell masked the scent of the large brick of C-4 explosive attached to a small lead-lined box. Sniffing dogs had moved right over it during the final security inspections. Juba fished out his camera and took a few pictures, then reached inside the lead-shielded compartment and clicked a metal switch attached to the explosive, which lay beside a large aerosol canister. The weapon was armed. He set the timer on a backup detonator, poured in some fresh coffee beans to cover it, screwed the panel back in place, and lowered the seat.

"There. That's it, now. I will be going along. Good luck." The technician paid no attention as he left.

Kimberly Drake was in a pool of bright light, facing a TV camera on a tripod and smoothing her navy blue jacket over the pink button-down shirt. Her hair and the top half of her outfit were perfect, but since she would only be shown from the waist up, she also wore jeans and white sneakers. She held a microphone in one hand.

She seemed to be talking to herself, muttering as she rehearsed her report. As Juba passed, she glanced up. "Thanks for coming by," Kim said. "Keep watching TV and maybe you'll see me someday, rich and famous."

Juba returned the smile. "I have no doubt of that at all, Miss Drake. I am sure that after tomorrow, the entire world will know your name."

"One can always hope," she said. " 'Night."

6

The dull black special ops helicopter sliced high above the border between Iran and Iraq in the cold early morning hours at 175 miles per hour, and wind howled through the open cabin. Three heavily clad men stood attached to safety harnesses behind the 7.62 miniguns mounted at the side door and the port side escape hatch and a .50 caliber machine gun on the lowered rear deck. The U.S. Air Force pilots had engaged the stealth capabilities of the big MH-53J Pave Low III Enhanced helicopter, such as the infrared engine exhaust suppressors, and the sensor package in the craft's bulbous nose sniffed for danger signals.

The Pave Low had gone across the border at a high altitude but then swooped down like a hawk through the night, the pilots trusting the terrain-following radar as they hurtled the machine forward only a hundred feet off the deck. The biggest helicopter the Air Force had, the versatile Pave Low, a direct descendant of the Vietnam-era Super Jolly Green Giant, was the platform of choice for covert insertions and extractions deep in enemy territory. Two large General Electric engines fed the huge single rotor that allowed extra armor plating, and it could fly in any sort of weather. The eight Marines aboard were an extremely light cargo for the helicopter, for thirty more could have fit into the cavernous cargo space. That absence of weight allowed the Pave Low to perform even more niftily than usual.

Kyle Swanson hunched against the icy blast, protected somewhat by the extra insulation and activated charcoal lining in his bulky hazmat suit. The Mission Oriented Protective Posture (MOPP) outfits were to protect them against chemical, biological, and aerosol agents, but the heavy rubber gloves, masks, and booties made Kyle feel as if he were wading through syrup. On top of the suits, they carried full combat loads, including double water, ammo, and chow for three days.

Swanson breathed steadily, easily. The goal was reconnaissance only, so they would not be going into a hot LZ. It was to be hide-and-seek and not a combat engagement. In fact, Kyle would regard it as a failure if the lightly armed Marine team made any contact at all with Iranian armed forces.

The crew chief's voice cut through the communications link into Swanson's black flight helmet, telling them to get ready. Kyle signaled: two minutes out.

The Marines wobbled to their feet and grabbed handholds as the chopper flared into a hover and lowered. Double-Oh was at the head of one stick of Marines, and Captain Newman led the other, and through the open hatch they could begin making out some details of the land below. Kyle was in the rear to make sure everybody got off. At a motion from the crewman, they all scrambled down the rear ramp and had to hop only about a foot to hit the dirt. Swanson watched them all go, gave a signal to the crew chief, and leaped from the lip of the ramp himself as the Pave Low tilted nose down and soared into a two-thousand-feet-per-minute climbing turn for the return to Camp Doha.

* * *

The team sprinted into a perimeter position and hit the
dirt with weapons covering all 360 degrees. It was dark
out there and also very quiet, an almost tangible feeling
of solitude after the racket of the helicopter insertion.
Swanson unpacked the chemical and biological detection
devices and scanned the area. To give themselves plenty
of distance from the suspect site and minimize contamination danger, they had landed four kilometers away.
There was nothing dangerous on the breeze. He peeled
off his hood and the rebreathing mask and motioned for
the others to do the same. They had to do a fast march to
find an observation point, and the Marines quickly shed
the MOPP suits, which prevented anyone from doing
anything quickly.

Newman did a map check with Double-Oh through
the red lens of a flashlight and a GPS locator and determined they were just where they were supposed to be.
Had they come in by parachute, they would have been
scattered all over the terrain, but instead they had landed
and could move as a cohesive unit. "Rawls," whispered
the captain. "Lead out." Newman pointed in a specific
direction, and Darren Rawls stepped away, flipping down
his night vision goggles and going over a rise. One by
one, the others followed him, weapons at the ready and
moving deeper into hostile Iran with every step.

The quietness was eerie and unsettling. Even in the middle
of the night, *something* should be moving about, but there
were no birds, no small predators, no night-foraging animals at all. A few empty shacks. There were some sickly-
looking trees, and the fields over which they walked were
just dirt, with no growing crops, nor evidence of a har-
vested one. Nothing. An agricultural dead zone near a
major waterway.

Kyle kept a close read on the dials of his instruments, but they remained steady and in the neutral zone. "Some wicked shit," he said to Double-Oh. Whatever had killed everything was no longer around, but its evil sign was everywhere. He spoke to Captain Newman. "Palace of Death should be only a half mile now. Let's set up a security position here and then patrol out to find an observation point."

They were exposed on a plain, and daylight was not far away, but they could not hide in a gulley or a low wadi. Chemicals and biologicals were heavier than air and tended to settle into the lowest points around, and the dirt in a hole might still grip some of the deadly material. The team would have to make a home on high ground, but there was little of that available. While everyone else took a break and filled up with water, Joe Tipp and Travis Hughes ventured closer to the designated area and came back within thirty minutes, puzzled.

"There's nothing much out there," Hughes reported. "Didn't see anything but a small bunker complex inside a fenced area. Apparently deserted."

"No palace?" asked Swanson.

"None," Hughes said. "I thought we would find something like Cinderella's castle. This thing looks like a small parking garage on the bad side of Detroit."

"Huh," Kyle grunted.

"And get this: The fence is about ten feet high and topped with razor wire, but the gate is hanging unlocked and open."

Joe Tipp said they had found a decent overwatch site to the south about four hundred meters away, along the single road leading into the site from the nearest population center, Khorramshahr.

"Okay, then, Captain Newman. That's our OP," Kyle said.

"Roger that. You, Double-Oh, and Tipp set up there, and the rest of us will establish a good support position here. Let's go," Newman said. Tipp took point, and Swanson fell in behind him, reading the dials, while Double-Oh walked at the tail end. The rest of the MARSOC team began building hide sites and gathering bushes for camouflage.

The OP was in an area where a washboard of ridges began and expanded higher and higher into the distance, so it did not stand out like a pimple on the flatlands. Once at the crest, the three Marines had a clear view of both the road and the target site, so they made themselves a hide among low, decaying trees and thin weeds. In a few minutes, a powerful spotter scope, a pair of binos, and the scope of the sniper rifle were examining the structure, inch by inch, parsing it in every way possible. The clouds had parted, and illumination was good. Not so much as a dog barked.

"Ain't nobody home down there, Shake," said Double-Oh after watching for a half hour. "Place is run-down and empty." Wind had covered up most vehicle tracks, which indicated nothing had been driving around recently, and they could see no footprints.

"Yeah," said Kyle. "I don't think we're going to need to watch this for three days. It *feels* empty."

"Spooky," said Tipp. "So we stay here all day and go in tonight? Why not go in right now and be done with it?"

Swanson shook his head. "We only have a good hour left before daybreak. We need to take our time in there. Remember, slow is smooth, smooth is fast."

"Too risky right now," added Double-Oh. "I don't think anyone is down there, but there may be some activity in the area. We'll watch it all day, then go in as a four-man team tonight. The other four guys will set up a firing position here while we make a thorough snoop." He found the keypad on his digital communications terminal and typed a message that flashed up on Captain Newman's DCT. *Send Rawls.*

Darren Rawls, carrying a heavy machine gun, appeared at the OP in a few minutes as the other three wiggled around to make room for him. He smoothly set up the weapon, which gave the OP more firepower. Then they began a rotation of two men on watch while the other two slept for a few hours. It was going to be a long day in Iran.

With the sun up, they had a clearer view of the surrounding area. A main highway led out of the city, heading northeast, and the road the Marines were watching seemed to be an isolated track that led only to the site. It was about ten miles long. Two guard posts, one a mile from the site and the other near the wire, were abandoned. Not a vehicle came up the road all day.

Rick Newman crawled to the OP as the sun started to set and found all four of the men there already wearing their heavy MOPP suits, except for the hoods and masks. He agreed to accelerate the mission by a day and went back to bring forward his other Marines and do a communications update. The helicopter was scheduled for 0400.

Swanson, Double-Oh, Joe Tipp, and Rawls hurried through the open gate and stacked beside the gaping entrance to the building, then plunged through as a group. They did a hasty search and clear of the small layout, and Kyle read the dials: nothing dangerous. Their flashlights, however, scanned the walls in four bright circles, and the evidence of a recent fire was clearly visible. Kyle reached out a finger and swiped a path through a deep layer of soot.

A freight elevator was in one corner at the edge of an exterior loading dock, and a broad staircase led down into darkness. The Marines descended in pairs on each side, and Double-Oh kicked the door at the bottom. It burst open to reveal another empty room, which must have been an office before it was destroyed by fire. Through another door at the rear, and down another staircase, they found the tangled debris of what once had been a laboratory.

While the others stood in protective positions, Kyle waved his wands and sensors throughout the room. Whatever the monster that caused so much destruction was, this was where it was born and probably also was where it died. There was no sign of an accident, so the fire was likely deliberate. Apparently the occupants had thrown in some thermite-style grenades after soaking the place in flammable liquids. Fire is the best way to destroy chemical and biological agents, which vanish in the flash of intense heat. The blackness of the soot was even thicker in the ruined laboratory, and the MOPP booties were almost ankle deep in the stuff. The dials remained steady and harmless.

One more door, one more staircase.

They were far underground now, and since fire burns up, not down, the damage was not as great as on the lower level. Kyle found a bilingual sign at the top of the staircase with Arabic script and Korean lettering. Just as in Syria, the underground bunker complex had been built by North Korean engineers.

A central square room was the hub of six separate corridors, and a pair of Marines went down each of them.

"Jesus Christ!" muttered Double-Oh as he and Kyle came to a stop outside a barred cell door. The walls were also scorched back here, but the fire had cooked hotter above, and it would have required some time to reach back along the concrete fingers, where there was a minimum of oxygen. The scorched bones of a human being lay beside the door inside the cell, as if he had been trying to pull the bars apart in his last minutes during the process of suffocation and incineration. Apparently the flammable liquid also had been splashed inside the cages prior to the fire. The poor inmates had been doomed to burn alive.

Every cell held the same gory story. A dead person in each. Swanson scanned them, and there was some light ticking on one of the meters. He backed away.

"Okay, guys. Rawls, you take a position at the top of the stairs by the entranceway while the rest of us break out our cameras and document all of this for the intelligence people to figure out." He wanted to take the contaminated body out with them, but there was no way to secure it to prevent whatever infection it carried from spreading. He would have to settle for cutting a few samples from the corpses, sealing them in double plastic ziplock bags, and wrapping those tightly with duct tape.

The three Marines removed their hoods and masks, then put them back on because it was so hard to breathe deep inside the bunker complex. It was like standing inside a giant fireplace. They worked as fast as possible, wanting to clear out of this building, go home, and take a shower. "Palace of Death is right," said Joe Tipp. "Not much to look at, but the name is sure accurate down here."

Captain Newman's voice sounded suddenly in their earpieces. "Get out now! Somebody's coming fast!"

They were on the bottom floor, documenting the tiny cells and their inhabitants, when the call came in. Racing up three floors on slippery stairs while wearing MOPP booties was pointless. There was no way to make it in time, and when they cleared the final doorway into the upstairs office area, Rawls was motioning for them to take cover. Two vehicles raced through the open gates and braked to hard halts with the headlights shining on the building.

One was an old Range Rover, and in it were a young man who was driving and a woman as a passenger. The second was a military truck with a squad of armed men wearing Iranian Revolutionary Guard uniforms, chasing the people in the Range Rover and not hunting for U.S. Marines.

"Hold fire," Captain Newman said over the intercom. The Marines on the overwatch and inside the building observed what was happening with their fingers on their triggers. Swanson had left the sniper rifle behind for the building search. He brought his small M-4 carbine to bear on the group and focused the scope.

The soldiers had surrounded the front vehicle and were yelling for those inside to get out. The doors opened, and the driver exited and was immediately pummeled to the ground and dragged a short distance away, still in the pool of bright light. The woman got out slowly, but she, too, was smashed to the ground and hauled over beside the prone driver. She struggled to her knees, pleading; "I am just looking for my brother!"

A soldier in a beret, possibly an officer, shouted at her. "You are a traitor and a spy! You were told to stay away from this place. Your infidel brother has run away."

"No," said the woman. "He would not do that. He is only a student and loyal to our country."

"Another traitor." The soldier pulled out his pistol and kicked the driver in the ribs. The man groaned. "And I know who you are, too, only too well. The president of the university student council. A man who speaks loudly against our government. You did not come out here just to find her brother."

The driver said nothing, and the soldier gave a signal for several of his men to move in and begin savagely beating the young man, who curled into a fetal position. The woman screamed and was grabbed when she tried to protect him.

"Call in the helicopter, Captain," Kyle said on his radio. "We're going to stop this."

"Negative, Swanson. Our mission does not include contact. As long as they stay outside, we sit tight. Just in case, I'll put the bird on standby."

There was laughter as the beating and kicking continued until the driver stopped moaning in pain and went silent, unconscious.

"Traitor," said the officer. He walked over to the still figure on the dirt, raised his pistol, and fired two shots into the head. He turned to the woman. "You were warned several times. You disobeyed our instructions. A worthless woman troublemaker." He balled up his fist and hit her in the head, and she fell over.

The soldiers put aside their weapons and moved closer, keeping her in the full light of the vehicles. One reached out and tore away her headcover, revealing the terrified face of a beautiful young woman with long black hair. They began to grab at her clothing, laughing and calling insults.

Kyle said to Double-Oh, "I think we need to take her back for interrogation."

"Good idea," Dawkins replied.

"Are you sure of that?" came the voice of Captain Newman.

Kyle replied, "My mission, my call." They were all under his command, there only to support him.

"Roger that. Pave Low inbound."

Swanson said, "All members listen up. I'll take the first shot, and my target is the officer with the pistol. Double-Oh, take the target to his immediate left. Rawls, you have the target to his right, and Tipp takes the guy next to the vehicle." He paused while he scanned the area again. "Captain Newman, your four men take the two targets behind the vehicle. Ambush commences on my shot."

The officer was only twenty-five meters away. Kyle pulled the crosshairs of his scope on the man's head, steadied his own breathing, and pressed the trigger. There was a single crisp retort of gunfire, and the officer's body stood still for a moment, then fell backward with half of the skull and all of its contents missing.

The other Marines opened on their targets, and the IRGs were caught in a cross-fire from the observation point and from inside the building. It was almost impossible to miss, and the Iranians had stacked their weapons prior to assaulting the woman.

"Cease fire, we're coming out!" yelled Double-Oh, and the four Marines charged from the building into the remaining IRG troops, moving forward in a line and with their weapons tight on their shoulders. In ten seconds, the entire Iranian squad had been wiped out, and the shooting stopped.

"Let's go," Kyle said as he plucked a grenade from his web gear to throw into the army truck. Tipp popped one free for the Range Rover.

Double-Oh slung his weapon, leaned over, and easily scooped up the terrified woman in his huge arms. "Don't worry. You're safe now. We won't let anything happen to you." He began trotting back to the observation post. Then there was a burst of automatic weapons fire. The big master gunnery sergeant grunted in surprise, paused for a moment, and then resumed his run, staggering the last few feet until he collapsed facedown among the Marines.

"Goddamn! Blow that fucking truck away!" Kyle yelled as he lobbed the grenade. Some soldiers had stayed behind with the truck and remained unseen in the firefight. A hurricane of bullets now shredded the vehicle, which lurched hard under the impact until the grenade exploded and the truck detonated in a ball of flame.

Kyle scrambled up the incline and dropped to his knees beside Double-Oh, looking at the bullet hole. "Oh, fuck," he said.

7

Jeremy Mark Osmand—Juba—awoke from a disturbed sleep into an unsettling moment during which he did not know where he was. The former British paratrooper was drenched in sweat. *Why does it still bother me?* Familiar and terrible memories flooded up during long nights and sat on his chest so heavily that he could hardly breathe. Palestinian kids blown apart by Jew rockets and Russians doing the same thing to Muslim children in Chechnya. A baby dead on its dead mother's breasts in Afghanistan, flies on their open eyes. Pakistan, the Balkans, Colombia, Ecuador, and, for too many months, Iraq.

Then he realized that he was not in some war zone but safe at his family's home in England, awakening to the smell of cooking eggs and sausage. His mother had gotten up before dawn because she knew he had to leave again. He showered and dressed in a blue Armani suit and a D&G Bengal stripe shirt with a solid blue tie, with soft black Cole Haan shoes, and a Fortis watch on his wrist. The upscale clothes were just another uniform, one that said "successful business executive." He looked around his old room. Soccer trophies, club flags, ribbons, and photographs of the young striker scoring goals. His old prep school jacket with the golden crest on the pocket still hung in the closet. Yesterday's hero.

He went downstairs. The house was small and immaculate, everything in exactly the same place it always was. A photograph taken ten years earlier would show the same furniture in the same spots, the time difference marked only by the changes in the faces of the people in the pictures. They were all younger then. He lifted his mother from the floor and twirled her in a circle in the tiny kitchen.

"Stop that this minute, Jeremy," she commanded with a giggle. "I am cooking! The toast will burn." As if that were important. He loved her without reservation.

Martha Goodling Osmand thought her son traveled too much, although she had put in more than a few miles herself as a young firebrand human rights attorney when she went out to the hellholes and recorded what the devils were doing. An Israeli bullet shattered her knee during a raid on a Palestinian refugee camp on the West Bank and clipped her traveling wings but not her spirit. Now she worked from home, hosting a Web site to help Muslim refugees.

His father, Dr. Allen Osmand, came into the kitchen and gave his wife an affectionate good-morning peck on the cheek. A thin man with a neat beard, he, too, was impeccably dressed for work. The doctor sat across from his son at the table.

"How long do you intend to keep up this schedule, Jeremy?" his mother scolded as she poured hot tea. "When are you going to get your company to assign you to the home office here in England? I want to be able to play with the toes of my grandchild before I am too old."

"Look who's talking." He laughed. "You two hauled me all over the world as a kid, taught me languages, how to travel and to get along with people. Now you complain because I'm taking advantage of that training to make a living." He sipped the tea and cut his toast into triangles, dipping them into the egg yolk. "I am just a poor salesman, forced to hustle for my next meal at some five-star restaurant in Berlin or Paris, and it's your fault." He looked at the clock. Almost time to go. "Are you going to watch the wedding today, Mum? Not going down there, are you?"

"Oh, wouldn't dream of getting mixed up in that crowd. Barbara is quite lovely, and a fine match for Prince William, but my leg tells me to stay here and watch it on the telly. A volunteer from Amnesty International is dropping by to help me catch up on some work on the site."

His father spoke. "We expect things to be quiet around the hospital today because of the wedding, so Professor Grosvenor and I should have the lab almost to ourselves." Jeremy nodded. Good. Perfect alibis, if ever needed.

Father and son finished their tea, and after hugging his mother, Jeremy went to the car and tossed his travel case into the back seat. As his father drove, the son wrote a note and handed it over: "You *must* stay out of London today." The father read it and gave it back, with a slight nod of understanding. The son tore it into little pieces and fed it out the window, bit by bit, along the morning highway.

Jeremy leaned back and studied his father, who held the steering wheel lightly with the gentle, sure hands of a talented surgeon, a man who had worked hard his whole life only to see his dreams crushed. He deserved better. The young medical student had fallen in love with England the moment he set foot in the country from his battered homeland of Lebanon. The golden history of the British Empire enthralled him, and he trekked all over the country, wanting to become part of it but knowing that he could never really be a true Englishman because of his deep skin color, his dark eyes and hair, and the accent;

a foreigner forever. To close the distance between him and the society of which he so desperately wanted to be a part, he committed the greatest shame of his life, abandoning his country of birth to become a British citizen.

Aziz Osman gained a reputation as a brilliant young doctor who healed patients of high social status. That was until the old and cancer-riddled Lady Wallendar died beneath his knife. It mattered not that the obese woman was in her eighties, and an extraordinarly poor candidate for any sort of surgery. When Osman opened her up, he found the liver, stomach, kidneys, and heart almost destroyed. Then she had a myocardial infarction while on the operating table, and it was all over in twenty minutes. Lord Wallendar had wanted a miracle and, by God, had paid handsomely to get one. He blamed Osman, and from that moment the surgeon was tainted as just another worthless wog sawbones. The big door of class slammed shut, with Osman on the wrong side, and his practice and dreams evaporated. *Wog!* The acronym for "worthy Oriental gentleman" was the ultimate sneer.

The doctor determined that his children should not have to face that same barrier, and after taking the advice of friends, Aziz Osman went to court and formally anglicized his name. Aziz became Allen; Dr. Osman added a single letter and became Dr. Osmand. The next year, his son was born, and Jeremy Osmand grew up about as English as a boy could be.

The car pulled up at the new St. Pancras International train station in King's Cross, and Jeremy removed his bag and went inside. Since he would be traveling to the Continent, he ran the magnetically encoded card through a reading device and passed smoothly through customs and an X-ray tunnel, for he had nothing to hide. Once in the sterilized zone for departures, he would not have to go through customs on the other end of his journey, the Bruxelles-Midi station in Belgium. The high-speed Eurostar departed at 6:10 A.M., with Jeremy resting comfortably in seat 55 on the aisle of the first-class, nonsmoking car number 9, reading an *International Herald Tribune*.

The Eurostar sped into the mouth of the thirty-one-mile Channel Tunnel, dashed through the Chunnel, and popped up in Europe. Two and a half hours after leaving London, he was in Brussels. He took a cab to the Silken Berlaymont Hotel on the Boulevard Charlemagne, asked for and got early check-in, and went directly to his room. With the wink of a tiny green light above the handle, the electronic coded card opened the door.

Jeremy Osmand turned on the television and placed his cell phone on a small, polished table beside the soft chair facing the set, then hung up his jacket and brewed a pot of tea in the little kitchenette. He checked his watch again and transformed himself, the genial personality of the pleasant Englishman sliding away like the discarded skin of a snake. His feelings shut down. He became Juba.

Security agencies were in overdrive, for nothing could be allowed to mar the wedding or threaten the royals. The streets around Buckingham Palace and St. Paul's Cathedral were searched a dozen times, and officers were posted in every building along the route. Security cameras were everywhere, their little eyes probing and curious. Uniformed policemen from the boroughs were brought in for duty, and Scotland Yard's Special Branch detectives threaded through the throng. British soldiers in combat gear were stationed in plain view.

Tuesday was a national holiday in Great Britain, and about seven hundred thousand people were jammed into the parks near the palace—Kensington, Hyde, Green, and St. James's. Each person had been searched before being allowed through the security cordon. The Royal Wedding Command Center in the Palace Gardens had been going nonstop for seventy-two hours before the ceremony and was not to stand down until William and Barbara left for their honeymoon at a private place unknown to the general public.

Every cop in England was looking the wrong way.

The wedding went off without a problem, and the royal couple signed the register after the ceremony and walked back down the red carpet, with Barbara needing help from her bridesmaids to maneuver the twenty-five-foot train of her antique lace and ivory silk gown. The prince and his smiling, radiantly beautiful bride stepped into sunshine amid nonstop cheers and hurrahs and got into a special open landau drawn by a matched team for the trip back to the palace, escorted by the glittering Horse Guards.

Juba, in Belgium, watched the carriage depart and gave it a three-minute start through the adoring crowd. He held his cell phone in both hands. When he finally dialed a number, the call bounced off a satellite and into London. It caused a dart of electricity to pulse across the microscopic gap between two strips of copper, closing the circuit in the small bomb beneath the floorboard in the purple and white press van rented by the Italians. It was a crude device, but all he needed to generate an explosion from the C-4 to rupture the lead container.

The explosion detonated the gas tank and caused a secondary eruption. The Edinburgh van tore apart as the blast peeled away its sides and knocked over the antennas of several nearby trucks. Flying pieces of metal became deadly shrapnel, and all four members of the European technical crew and three passersby were killed. Although the unruffled BBC commentators, far from the scene, continued describing the parade, the explosion was clearly heard by thousands on the ground, and the plume of smoke in the rear of the media headquarters in Kensington Park was seen by millions of television viewers before the camera intentionally swung away.

The horses pulling the landau of the prince and his new princess broke into a fast trot, and the mounted guard closed around them, sheathing their ceremonial swords and pulling free the carbines attached to their saddles.

Kimberly Drake was stunned. The unexpected explosion had smashed her against another truck, and she toppled to the ground, out of breath and dazed. She shook her head to clear the cobwebs just as the strong hands of Tom Lester, her cameraman, scooped her up.

Tom Lester, a photojournalist for more than twenty years, had stepped over a lot of bodies in a couple of wars. Any explosion that did not kill him was someone else's problem, but he had not seen one in London since the IRA had quieted down. He looked at his reporter and saw no blood. Just shock. He poured water into a cupped hand, wiped her face, and gave her a drink. That was enough tender loving care, and he shook her by the shoulder. Hard. "Wake the fuck up, Kim! Pull yourself together! A monster story just fell right on your lucky little head!" He turned to see the young engineer looking out of the doorway of their van. "Get back inside, Harold. Get us up live to Little Rock right now. Move, kid! We're not here as sightseers." He snatched his camera and looked it over, wiped the lens, then hoisted it to his shoulder and adjusted the eyepiece to frame the fire, the debris, and the dead.

Kim was pegged to the spot by indecision over whether to cover the story or help the bleeding victims around her. Lester shouted, "Get with it, Drake! This story is all ours for the time being, but others are going to be coming. It's your moment, girl. Grab it with both hands."

"But these people, Tom . . ."

"Fuck 'em," he snarled. "We all take our chances in this game. They caught it, we didn't. Shit happens. The medics will be here in a few minutes for them anyway, and our job is to cover the goddam story! You make up your mind right now whether you want to be a reporter or Florence Nightingale. You stop to help those poor bastards and you can kiss your career good-bye." He had to keep her focused, keep her mind busy, or she would falter. Fucking newbie.

Harold ran up and rigged them with collar microphones and earpieces. "We've got the station. Go!"

"Kim? What's happening over there?" The familiar voice of the news director back home in Arkansas comforted her.

"There was some kind of explosion in one of the TV vans," she said. "It was not close to the parade route and probably has nothing to do with the wedding. Maybe an overheated generator or something."

Lester broke into the conversation through his own microphone. "Fuck that! The goddam thing blew up almost right next to us! I've got some great fucking shots here, dude. Bodies and fires and all kinds of good shit. Kim and I are alone with it right now, but it won't last long. Get us on air!"

The voice in her ear told her to stand by and be ready to go live. The news director took a few moments to confer with the station management. Fire and destruction always made good television, even better when media people were involved, but this was frontline action and a royal wedding at the same time, and their reporter had it! "Get your thoughts together, Kim. We're going live in about one minute, as soon as we offer you to the network and cables." The additional revenue from such an exclusive report could cover the budget for Kim's entire trip.

Her heart flopped, but Tom flashed a thumbs-up and gave a smile of encouragement. The network was going to carry her report! No other reporters were at the smoldering site yet because they had been out of position, trying to get close to the parade route. Kim pulled out her hairbrush and a small mirror, but Tom Lester slapped them from her hands, saying the unkempt look of the blond hair dangling over her forehead and the dirt on her face and jacket added authenticity. He did not want her to see the trickle of blood working a crimson path down her dirty cheek. A button had torn from her blouse, enough to give a glimpse of a lacy black bra. Sexy as hell. The voice in her earphone started a nineteen-second countdown. Then she heard the godlike tones of the network anchorman saying, ". . . and here is reporter Kimberly Drake at the site of the explosion. Kimberly?"

In his hotel room in Belgium, Juba smiled as he recognized Kim Drake. She had her opportunity, just as he had predicted. He dialed another number, and this time a soft pop no louder than a firecracker went off unheard beneath the van rented by the Arkansas station. The contents of the canisters bled invisibly into the air, crawled out from beneath the van, rose, and spread.

Kim's mike was live. Her dream was coming true. She was on live network TV! Once she started to talk, her nerves calmed and the training kicked in. Nothing fancy. *Let the pictures speak while you give the who, what, when, where, why, and how.* The network news directors were impressed with the kid.

* * *

Crew Manager William Warner of the London Fire Brigade was chewing a chocolate and peanut energy bar when the first explosion detonated less than a hundred meters from his truck. He had kept his team on full alert during the wedding, so they were already in their bulky coats, overtrousers, and fire boots. The truck was rolling in seconds, its lights flashing, the horn honking and the siren shrilling to push a path through the crowd as the crew slapped on helmets and pulled on gloves.

There were some casualties but only a small area of actual damage, and his firefighters were on it immediately with suppressant chemicals, then waded into the charred debris with their tools. Some cleared a circle for emergency medical personnel. Walker found himself bumping against a small American news reporter with a microphone in her hand.

Kim had finished her first report, but the appearance of the fire truck and its flashing lights gave her more material. Tom had them in his eyepiece as they dove into work. *Let the pictures talk!* Her throat was very dry; her eyes started to mist, and her skin itched. Probably the smoke, she thought, and plunged ahead with her work.

She had expected to be shoved aside by the big firefighter because that is what would have happened in the States, but this was England, where people valued courtesy. William Warner let her stand her ground because nothing important was happening anyway and his people had the work in hand. He coughed.

Warner had listened to the reporter and agreed with her quick conclusion that this had the look of an accident, maybe an undetected electrical fire inside the truck that set off a gas tank leak. Only an off-the-cuff hypothesis by an untrained observer, but a pretty good guess. Arson investigators would sort it out soon enough. He had already given basically the same report to the Command Center; the situation was under control. He felt a tug on his sleeve. The disheveled young reporter thrust the microphone at him, and Warner leaned down to answer the question. The telly camera was pointed at him.

Kim cleared her throat, then had to do it again before speaking. Exposed portions of her skin were stinging as if she had been attacked by a swarm of bees, and she felt woozy. She wouldn't let that sideline her. "I am standing with an official of the London Fire Brigade," she said. "Sir, what can you tell us about this explosion?"

Warner was about to answer that all was quite well, that it was an accident, when he actually looked at her. The girl's face was flushing bright red, and she was rubbing her forearm, where a gelatin-like substance was clinging. Then a sharp chirp squealed from a rectangular device attached to the thick collar of his coat. He jerked his head up. More chirps were coming from the crew's uniforms, and his firefighters turned to him with alarm and shock on their faces. They were in the midst of thousands of people, and their hazardous materials detectors were singing like mad canaries.

"Get your rebreathers on and button up!" he yelled. The reporter was collapsing at his feet, clawing at her skin as she sucked in air, having trouble breathing. Her eyes rolled back. The cameraman was falling to his knees.

"Oh, dear God," Warner said, slapping down his own face shield as he grabbed the radio that was on the frequency of the Royal Command Center. "Red Alert! Crew Chief Warner in Sector Kensington Three. Red Alert! Dirty bomb! I repeat: *Dirty bomb!*"

8

Dawkins was a big, strong man who had more muscle tissue than an ordinary person to protect his organs, and the adrenaline coursing through his system gave him the extra burst of strength he needed to reach the Marine position while still carrying the woman. Then his eyes closed and he toppled hard to the ground.

Marines do not have medics, but they have a brotherhood relationship with combat-trained Navy corpsmen. Corpsman Rick Suarez trained alongside the MARSOC Marines, even having the mission specialty of being a demolitions expert. Suarez jumped to the side of the wounded Double-Oh even before Kyle scrambled to them.

They used knives and surgical scissors to slice away the thick gear harness, then tore open the MOPP suit and the T-shirt to get to the wound. A lot of blood was spilling from a small entry hole on the right side of the muscled back.

"Help me turn him over to see if there is an exit wound," Suarez said. There was none, but Kyle could hear oxygen gurgling from the bullet hole, and air flowed out like bubbles in water. They had him propped in a sitting position.

Double-Oh was in the Golden Hour, the vital sixty minutes between the instant a man is hit and the time a field hospital gets him on the table. Keep him alive back to Camp Doha and his chances of recovery improved considerably. Each minute was a treasure.

Captain Newman was on his radio. "Whiskey One-Niner, this is Hotel Seven. I have one emergency evac. Forty-year-old male. Gunshot wound to the back."

"Roger, Hotel Seven," said the smooth voice of the helo pilot. "We are inbound and will meet you at designated pickup zone. Three minutes. We have a PJ aboard." A PJ was an Air Force pararescue specialist trained in emergency medical procedures.

"Roger that," said Newman.

"Alert the PJ that it's probably a collapsed lung with internal bleeding. Vital signs appear shallow," Suarez called over his shoulder. Newman repeated the information.

"Help me here, Shake. We have to dress the wound and help his breathing," Suarez said. He rummaged around in his first aid kit, found morphine, and tossed it aside because he could not administer it to an unconscious man. Then his hand closed around a thin plastic card about the size of a driver's license. He pushed it against the bleeding wound. Above that he secured a pressure bandage with medical tape.

Kyle kept holding the unconscious man in a sitting position, talking to him with a stream of vulgarity and insults, just as they usually spoke to one another. Maybe Double-Oh could hear him and maybe he couldn't, but if Kyle spoke normally, then his friend might recognize the voice and believe the wound was not serious. That would inspire hope. Getting all sappy and sorry would have the opposite effect.

"I ain't got time for your crap tonight. Patch up your

fat ass and haul it to the hospital, then wait around to see if you bleed out. Probably have to dig your grave by myself and then put up with a bunch of Pentagon pukes at your funeral. You stand up out there like a fucking carnival target and get shot by that amateur? Jesus Christ, Dawkins, you are supposed to be some kind of Superman black ops dude, and I swear you would trip over a crack in the sidewalk if somebody wasn't around to lead you around like a blind mutt. You did this on purpose, didn't you? Just to get some attention and another medal and polish your résumé before retiring. Anyway, what did you leave me in your will? You ain't really got nothing I want but maybe that Ford truck, so I'll take that. Dammit, don't you die until you buy some better stuff, you hear me?"

The time for stealth was long past, so Captain Newman had designated their current overwatch position as the pickup zone for the Pave Low extraction. There was no indication of any more vehicles on the road from the city, but that would not last long if the Iranian patrol was supposed to report in at regular intervals. The roar of the approaching helicopter grew louder, and as soon as it touched down, Marines grabbed the legs and arms of Double-Oh and got him into the open door.

Swanson came next, with his hand tight around the wrist of the girl to help her aboard and strap her in. She took a last look around at the carnage of the ambush, knowing she had escaped certain death, and did not resist. Whatever lay ahead was better than being another corpse for the Palace of Death. Then the Pave Low was gone, leaving no trace that it had ever been in Iranian airspace.

The twin engines strained as the helicopter grabbed for altitude. The PJ wrapped a blood pressure cuff on Double-Oh, leaned in close to use his stethoscope, then reported to the pilot. "Breathing is ragged, heartbeat still strong. Vital signs weak but steady, so he's holding his own. We can keep him stable until we land. Notify the docs to prepare for a serious gunshot wound in the back. The lung is punctured." The corpsman cleared an IV needle, found a vein in the arm for a hydrating solution, and then adjusted an oxygen mask over Double-Oh's pale face. He cut away the field bandage, cleaned the wound, administered some medication to the opening, and recovered it with a thick, large sterile bandage.

Kyle could do nothing to help and snapped his mind back to the mission. "Captain Newman, we got everybody?"

"Roger that. I counted them coming on. All plus one."

Plus one. The woman. Swanson, seated beside her, was suddenly aware of how they must look to her eyes, a group of large foreign men with faces greased with camo warpaint, laden with weapons and helmets and packs. The attempted rape, followed by the unexpected ambush, followed again by being snatched aboard a helicopter—her senses were overwhelmed, and she sat staring straight ahead, her arms clutched about her. He removed his cap, laid aside his weapon, and pulled a box of baby wipes from an onboard pouch, using the soft papers to wipe away some of the grime and grease on his face. Then he handed her the box. The small gesture was an icebreaker, forcing her to act, to make a minor decision.

After a moment, she pulled out a few papers and wiped her own face, with a small smile of appreciation and a nod.

"Don't worry," Kyle said in Arabic. "You are safe with us."

"They killed my friend," she whispered.

"I'm sorry we couldn't save him, too."

The woman sniffled and pulled away her scarf to dab

at some tears. Lustrous brown eyes, firm cheekbones, a pretty face. She asked in English, "You are Americans?"

"Yes. U.S. Marines," Kyle said, then changed the subject and handed her an unopened bottle of water. "What were you two doing out at that place so early in the morning?"

"We went out looking for my brother, a student. He was taken prisoner last week because of his political views, and we learned yesterday that he was being held in the forbidden zone. We wanted to help him escape." She spoke with a slight British accent.

"But it was some kind of secret military installation," Kyle said. "You had to know that."

The woman nodded. "The site was being evacuated because the work, some government project, apparently has been completed. People were leaving, trucks hauling away equipment. We felt we could be safe if we moved in a hurry." She began to weep, a nervous shudder shaking her body. "My brother was just a headstrong boy."

Kyle recognized that physical shock was setting in, but he would not touch her, for in her country, no physical contact whatsoever was allowed between unmarried and unrelated men and women.

"Did you see anyone in the building?" she asked softly.

"I'm sorry. There was no one alive in there when we arrived," he said.

As she sobbed, her shoulders heaved, and finally she leaned against Kyle's shoulder for support as the helicopter jarred through the sky. "He was just a child. Only sixteen."

He let her lean against him but remained silent. The girl had just broken a huge religious and cultural taboo, and Swanson knew she had reached some momentous conclusion about her life. He would not tell her that her brother was probably one of the six unfortunate inmates who were found dead and locked in individual cells. Instead, he said, "Try to relax. We'll be in Kuwait soon and sort things out. You'll be okay."

Travis Hughes watched the interplay between Swanson and the woman carefully, again observing the duality of the complex man. The Marines had expected Shake to remain the coldhearted son-of-a-bitch leader who was perfectly capable of standing in the shadows and letting those Iranian assholes rape the girl rather than take the chance of compromising his mission. With him, the mission always came first.

Nevertheless, no plan ever worked perfectly. Sooner or later, you had to face something unexpected, and Swanson had made an instant decision based on factors that Hughes was only now adding up. It wasn't really the rape at all that triggered him.

If they allowed the IRGs to kill her, the fuckheads probably would have thrown the bodies into the building anyway. Then again, if they were any sort of soldiers at all, they probably would have at least taken a quick look inside the building. Chances of exposure in either case were almost certain, so the mission was already compromised.

That meant that the Marines were going to have to smoke the Iranian troops anyway, so Swanson decided to take them down hard and fast to prevent any information from being radioed back to their headquarters. The woman obviously was not with the soldiers, therefore she was against them, which made her a good possible source of intelligence, but only if she was alive. Kyle had decided all that in the space of a few seconds and triggered a rescue.

It was not a heroic act. Swanson had just figured that was the best way to salvage the mission and at the same time gain a bonus of intelligence. Now he sat over there talking quietly to her and letting her cry on his shoulder, as if this whole effort had been mounted just to save her.

Travis was impressed. He leaned close to Joe Tipp and motioned at Swanson. "I think ol' Shake has a girlfriend," he whispered.

Two clusters of people were waiting at the hospital helipad when the Pave Low came to rest at Camp Doha. They were standing apart, grouped by their specialties, as if on different teams. Just because everyone wore the same uniform did not mean they were friends.

The first small group was comprised of medical personnel, and even before the helicopter cut its engines, they hurried forward with a rolling stretcher. The team of medics helped maneuver Double-Oh onto the gurney, and the entire group ran off toward the emergency room of the base hospital, a young triage doctor trotting along behind calling instructions ahead into a handheld radio. Swanson checked his watch. Double-Oh had made it with time to spare in the Golden Hour, and now the professionals could get to work.

The second group was more rigid and moved with serious purpose: four grim soldiers wearing armored vests and carrying weapons. They approached as the MAR-SOC Marines climbed out of the helicopter and gathered their gear.

"Captain Newman?" called a tall man. "I'm Lieutenant Zahn, sir. Military Police. We've been sent to collect your enemy combatant for interrogation."

Rick Newman was surprised. "What?"

"Your prisoner, sir. We'll take her now."

Newman looked over at Kyle Swanson and shrugged his shoulders. His brief situation report during the helicopter ride had somehow been read as the team bring-

ing home a valuable enemy prisoner. Swanson had his
face turned away from the soldiers but shook his head
slightly. *No.*

"Afraid there has been a mistake, Lieutenant. We rescued a civilian who got caught in the middle of a firefight,
that's all. You can stand down. We will turn her over during our debriefing."

The woman understood every word and pushed closer
to Kyle as fear grew inside of her. She had heard how
Americans interrogated prisoners.

"Sorry, Captain. I don't know anything about that, but
our orders are to bring her in immediately because she is
a suspected terrorist." The lieutenant waved his hand, and
three MPs, two male and one female, moved forward.

While the officers had talked, Kyle had helped the Iranian girl from the helicopter and moved her in behind the
MARSOC Marines, who appeared to be lounging about
watching the episode with disinterest. When the MPs
stepped forward, however, they were met by a solid wall
of special ops warriors. Darren Rawls, Joe Tipp, and Travis Hughes stood between the MPs and their target. Kyle
was close behind but did not want them to see his face.

"Okay, fellows, move aside," ordered the lieutenant.
"Your part of the mission is done, and now we have to
deal with the captive."

"Sorry. Can't help you," said Travis Hughes. "Sir."

"Lieutenant, you can lead us to the debriefing room if
you wish, but that is all," snapped Rick Newman.

Lieutenant Zahn was not used to having his orders
disobeyed. He squared up before Newman and sharpened
his voice. "Captain! I am giving you a final warning. You
and your men will stand aside and give us the enemy
combatant or you will be placed under arrest."

Darren Rawls grabbed the lieutenant and leaned into
his face. "You want her? Well, you will have to come and

take her. Sir." The rest of the team formed a knot around the woman and Kyle. Then Rawls pushed the lieutenant so hard that the man sprawled on the helipad.

Newman stepped forward and extended his hand to the fallen officer and pulled him up. "Be careful there, Lieutenant. Easy to trip and fall around here. How about taking us over to the debriefing room now? You can't have her because we won't give her up. The woman is already in the custody of the CIA, and you don't know shit about what is going on, so let's cut the crap and get on with things before somebody gets hurt."

Zahn brushed himself off. He made a mental note about that big black guy who'd shoved him and would settle that score later. "Yes, sir. This way, sir."

The MARSOC team moved as a group toward a convoy of waiting vehicles that would take them over to another part of the base. The MPs posted themselves in a square at the front, back, and sides of that formation, as if taking the whole group to the brig.

"You are CIA?" the woman asked Kyle softly as they walked to the Humvees.

"No," he said quietly. "But those people don't need to know that. And don't worry. You will be treated well here."

"So who are you, then?"

"Me? I'm nobody."

Major Jim Riley, a surgeon, was ready, scrubbed, and gowned as he pushed open a swinging door with his elbow and stepped into a bright, cool operating room of the 856th Combat Support Hospital. Sterilized implements gleamed on a steel tray, and everyone around him was also gloved and masked.

Before them lay a huge soldier with a bullet hole in the back. The patient had been stripped, cleaned, put to sleep, and thoroughly prepped. There was an IV of blood and another of a hydrating solution. The vital signs were being constantly measured and displayed on monitors.

Dr. Riley had been working in the hospital too long to be shocked by the condition of any patient, since there was a never-ending river of them. He studied the X-rays on the light board and moved over to the table. "Very well now. Everybody ready? Let's save this guy's life today."

"My name is Delara Tabrizi, and I teach at a girls' school in Khorramshahr." She sat at a small table in a well-lighted room with a cup of tea. Across the table were two intelligence officers who had been alerted about the unique circumstances and acted with respect and politeness. Adding to her comfort were Darren Rawls and Travis Hughes, still in combat gear and face paint, sitting beside the door to prevent a recurrence of the incident with the MPs at the helicopter. There was always somebody who did not get the word, and Captain Newman had ordered them to stay with her until final arrangements could be made. Delara was already considering them to be "her" Marines; she believed they would protect her against any rough interrogation and was ready to answer the questions of the officers.

She had already made up her mind. "I am now the only remaining member of my family," she said. "Everyone has been murdered by the government and its brutes, because we were part of the educated, moderate class. I will tell you everything I can in exchange for political asylum. I know that if I return to Iran, I may be killed, but we must go back."

"Why?" asked an interrogator.

"I know of another facility, such as the one from last night, and my brother may still be alive there."

"Just tell us where and we will send in another team."

She shook her head negatively. "No. It is near my home village in the north, and I can lead you there. You cannot find it on your own."

The officer gave her a slight smile. "Believe me, Miss Tabrizi, when I say that our technology and satellites can find almost anything, anywhere."

Delara returned the mirthless smile. "So, have you found it yet? No. You didn't even know it existed until I just told you."

The officer studied the young woman. Stubborn. Determined. Knows that if she is caught by the Iranians, she will be killed, and yet she is willing to lead a raid back into the country. "Let me discuss it with my bosses and see if they want to put together a mission. Meanwhile, we will put you up in a safe location and let you rest and clean up while we work this out."

Delara said, "I want the same team that was used before."

"We may not be able to do that. A fully capable and fresh team probably will be chosen."

"No substitutes," she insisted and turned to look at Rawls and Hughes, both of whom were nodding agreement. She remembered not only the rescue in Iran but also the confrontation at the helicopter. "I trust these men to bring me back alive."

In another room in the same building, Kyle Swanson and Rick Newman were being debriefed, going over the mission step by step. Swanson handed in the bag of flesh samples he had cut from the dead body, and it was transferred to a secure biohazard container. The digital cameras with their documentation were sent off to be copied and analyzed.

"The place was burned to a crisp," he told the intel officers. He described the construction of the underground laboratory complex. "Everything was destroyed. Looked as if they flooded it with gasoline or something, then popped some thermite grenades to set it all off. The heat would have been tremendous, certainly enough to burn off any evidence of chemicals or biologicals being produced there."

"You found prisoners in there?"

"What remained of them. Way back in individual cells at the end of the tunnels. The poor bastards were probably guinea pigs for experiments and were disposed of like everything else."

Newman described the sudden arrival of soldiers at the site and the ensuing ambush, and how Master Gunny Dawkins had been wounded. Swanson gave his version of the same subjects. The intelligence officers were running out of questions when one asked, "Why do you think the scientist who was assassinated in Baghdad gave up this site?"

Kyle gathered his gear. "That's for you intel guys to figure out. Maybe the girl that we brought in can shed some light on it. My wild guess is that the scientist figured that everything connected with the place was going to be eliminated, including him. So he ran. He just didn't run fast enough."

9

PARIS

Leafy vines tangled like thick ropes around the bars of a big wrought-iron gate that had stood open day and night for almost ten years on a quiet street in the Nineteenth Arrondissement. The property owner had tired of having to open and close it. Thieves came over the walls, despite embedded shards of sharp glass and alarm systems, so what was the point? Then a new owner had arrived and there still was no need to close the gate, for hard-eyed men stood guard, and word spread among the footpads of Paris that it was better to prey on targets that would not cost them their lives. The house now belonged to al Qaeda.

The neighborhood in the northeast section of Paris was in an inevitable transition toward a gentrified future, but pockets of the past still existed in its multiethnic heritage. The mixed aromas of foreign food and spices wafted from the restaurants, and people of all nationalities moved through the streets. Juba was just another face.

Shadowed by the foliage of the gate, he entered the old courtyard and smelled the combined scent of flowers and rot. The concrete slabs of the parking area were uneven, buckled by a century of shifting earth, and a creamy white Mercedes was parked in the center. Juba brushed his hand across the hood as he walked by. Warm to the touch, so the vehicle was recently used, probably to deliver Saladin to the meeting at the three-story home.

A nervous young man with a ragged haircut over a thin hyena face stepped from the shade of the doorway and motioned Juba to stop. The visitor was expected but would be searched nevertheless. Juba obediently raised both arms, then very slowly lowered his left hand to open his Prada sport coat wide enough to show the guard the holstered pistol that rested on his left hip. The young man's eyes went to the gun, which would have to be removed before the visitor could go inside. Juba helpfully opened the coat a bit more, using the diversion to keep the man's attention away from his right arm, which was slowly extending all the way up. When the elbow locked straight, a mechanism strapped to the inside of his forearm was tripped and a small Ruger pistol and silencer slapped into Juba's palm. He shot the approaching guard twice in the head at a distance of only three feet, the blood and brain matter spraying backward onto the paving stones. Juba grabbed the bleeding corpse by the shirt and hauled it into the cool, dark space beneath the stairwell.

He checked his clothes to make sure no blood had spattered on him and then trotted up the steep, curving stone staircase, making plenty of noise so the second bodyguard knew he was coming. His feet slapped with a steady rhythm against the old stones that a scrubwoman had washed by hand that morning. As he neared the top, the gun was hidden at his side. He huffed a bit, as if panting, and called to the guard. "Long way up," he said in French. This man was larger, standing with his hands crossed in front of him. He had a lot of bulk that was more fat than muscle. A thick unibrow stretched in a line across both eyes, and a few gold teeth glinted on the left side of a frowning mouth. A ragged scar ran down his forehead.

He was not alert because the visitor had been cleared by the entryway guard. Juba came up the final few steps, raised the Ruger, and fired his last three bullets. The scowling man collapsed where he stood.

Juba put the little gun away and gave the fallen man a look of utter contempt. *They still do not train them well.* The bodyguards chosen to protect the head of the entire al Qaeda operation in France should have been the best combat veterans available instead of a couple of waterfront thugs hired because they looked mean and could handle themselves in a barroom brawl. Both died because they were stupid. He stepped inside the house.

The door opened into an area between a neat kitchen that was the color of buttermilk and a living room where tall windows gave a view of other courtyards and buildings on this crowded edge of the city. The fading sunlight was orange and bright. He blinked. As his eyes adjusted, two silhouettes in the living room became a pair of middle-aged men seated in comfortable chairs directly across from each other, separated by a low table.

"My son! Welcome, welcome," said one, rising and coming to greet him with hugs and traditional cheek kisses.

Juba bowed his head. "Father. It is good to see you again." He had not seen his spiritual father, the man known as Saladin, in six weeks and was pleased to find him smiling with a warm greeting, particularly under the circumstances. Al Qaeda was demanding that he hand over the formula, and that Juba deliver it in person. Both of them realized their lives would be worthless the moment that the details of the new and virulent nerve agent were out of their possession, so that could not be allowed to happen.

Saladin appeared undisturbed. He had a handsome face with a well-trimmed beard and sharp black eyes that flashed intelligence, and he was dressed in a dark business suit and a subdued pearl gray tie. Actually taller than Juba, he weighed less and was thin. "You look well, and you have done well," he said as he squeezed Juba affectionately on the shoulder. "I am so proud. Come, please, and meet our host."

The second man stood. In contrast to Saladin, he wore a cheap suit that could not be buttoned over his stomach, and his belly overlapped the creased belt. The collar tips of his brown shirt flared like dirty wings, and a clump of chest hair had wiggled out above the second button.

"Let me introduce our new friend, Youcef Aseer, a very important leader among our al Qaeda comrades," said Saladin with some deference. The fat man's tiny eyes did not leave Juba's face.

"I am honored," said Juba and gave a slight bow. He was not about to embrace this unclean fat man who carried the smell of shallots and sweat.

"No, it is I who enjoy meeting you, the famous Juba. Your work in London has left the infidels in panic. God is great! Well done, young man." The voice was oddly small for such a large man.

They took seats, and Saladin got straight to business. "I know you were surprised by this summons, Juba, but something very important has happened to change our plans. Since the London episode, Youcef Aseer has been designated by al Qaeda to see that we all should henceforth work together. It is a great opportunity for us. Al Qaeda offers a generous sum of money and also manpower— dedicated foot soldiers, street demonstrators, and willing martyrs—that we can use in certain situations. In turn, we supply the formula and our field leadership. They want a strike in France, to subdue this wicked nation like a whipped puppy."

Youcef Aseer chuckled. "We are closer here than in

any other Western nation. One good push is all we need! Imagine an Islamic government in France!"

Saladin clapped his hands. "Exactly, my friend." He turned to Juba. "Our friend Youcef here is now within our small circle of trust. You are to do as he says, Juba. Do you understand that?"

"Yes, Father." Juba understood very clearly: Al Qaeda was taking over.

"Good. See, Youcef! I told you there would be no difficulty. It will be good to work with al Qaeda again," said Saladin. "Let Juba see your list."

The al Qaeda chieftain handed over a small envelope. The small move was peremptory, the sort of wave of a hand that a master gives an underling. This was his home, and his bodyguards were skillful. Unless these two renegades cooperated, he would have them killed.

Juba rose from his chair, and since he could not go between the two because of the table, he circled behind the al Qaeda leader. "Excuse me. The light is better by the window." He looked out at the fading sunlight playing with shadows on the rooftops and ran his thumb beneath the gummed flap of the envelope, pulled out the paper, and read three names, three addresses, all in the southern part of the country. Of course. The port of Marseille had been the initial arrival point for the first waves of immigrants from North Africa.

Aseer grinned. "The first is a judge who has sentenced our brothers to long terms in prison, the second an undercover detective with a particular skill for infiltrating our group, and the third simply a worthless traitor. Juba, I want you to kill them all to show that our enemies cannot escape the Prophet's justice."

"And the attack in France?"

"You leave that to us. We will have our own chemists

and physicists construct the weapon under your supervision."

"It is not yet ready. The London experiment showed the dispersal rate remains too high."

"Another batch just like that will be more than enough for our purposes," said Aseer. "We will finish the refining process as time allows."

Juba nodded and turned to Saladin. "When do you wish me to start, Father?"

"Immediately, my son. The sooner you complete this, the sooner we can move on."

They both knew that they would not be moving at all if they remained in the grip of al Qaeda.

"Very well." Juba slid the note into his jacket's right pocket. The light was dim and purple in the room as he walked back toward his chair. When his hand emerged from the pocket, there was something in it, invisible in the dying, gloomy light. Passing directly behind Aseer, he moved in a blur and looped the strand of piano wire around the neck of the al Qaeda man and yanked hard on the wooden handle in each hand. The wire sliced into the throat like a razor, and the fat man grabbed at the tightening garrote until his eyes bulged and his tongue hung out.

Juba's hatred of al Qaeda pulsed through his strong biceps and forearms and hands and into the killing wire as he slowly lifted his victim all the way over the back of the chair while the struggling man clawed to hold on to the life draining away from him. He could have finished it quickly but did not want death to come easily to this piece of al Qaeda filth. He tightened the wire more, strangling the man as he twisted the body out of the chair and let it fall onto a burgundy rug that was almost the same color as the blood oozing from the deep neck wound. Aseer urinated in his pants as he died.

Saladin remained calm. What a macabre pleasure it was to watch his son at work. The moves were so clean and economical and perfect, like a ballet dancer's, and there was a cold passion to his mastery of so many skills. A maestro of death. "Imagine, Juba, this fool actually believed we were frightened." He spat on the body.

"They will come after us again."

"No, I think they will simply become a customer. This death signals that the formula still belongs to Unit 999 and no one else. It took us twenty years to develop, and we have repeatedly had to defend our ownership. Now that we are so close to success, no one can be allowed to stop us."

Juba washed his hands in the kitchen sink. "I will take care of this one, and our men will remove the two guards."

"Very good, my son." Saladin refilled his cup of strong coffee. "The London task was flawless, but of course I expected nothing less from you. I assume the announcement is ready for distribution?"

"Yes. I downloaded the pictures I took in London onto discs and posted them, along with your message, by FedEx, to North Korea, China, Brunei, and Tehran. The packages will arrive at any time, and someone will have to sign for them, which guarantees delivery."

"Then it is done. The word will spread from those seeds. Now we wait."

"You can wait, my father. I have no time to waste. I will relax when it is all done."

"Would you rather be back in Iraq, taking target practice?" Saladin teased his assassin.

"No. Paris is better. It is too bad that I cannot stay longer. I long for a few days in which I can just be a pure Muslim and sit at your feet again and study the Koran. Physically I am fine, but spiritually I am an empty vessel. My role is difficult."

"Which is why you are the only one who can do it," replied Saladin. "I promise plenty of time in the future for you to walk openly as one of the faithful and even go on a hajj to Mecca and Medina. For now, you must remain who you are. The Prophet bestowed special gifts upon you, Juba. I know your inner struggle and intercede with prayers for you every day. Until the right time comes, you must carry on. You know that."

"Yes. I am but an instrument of the Prophet. Show me the path and I will follow. But tonight I leave for Iran again to observe one final test. The director of our remaining laboratory there thinks the formula will be complete after a final adjustment improves the staying power of the gel. The gas in London still spread too fast."

Saladin laughed to break the serious tone. "Good. We are finally so very close to the end. After you dispose of this trash, we can go out and have time for a nice dinner before you leave."

Juba opened the door and summoned two more men to help with the corpses as the slow sun set and the lights of Paris illuminated the night. Saladin stood at the window, feeling the rhythm of the city alter from a daytime center of commerce to a nightscape dedicated to personal pleasures. He liked this house and decided to stay here for a while.

He heard the men removing the body behind him but did not turn to watch. The al Qaeda fool actually believed an Islamic government could be seated in Paris. It was true that France had more Muslims than any other Western European nation, but that was still less than 10 percent of the overall sixty-four million Frenchmen. Aseer must have thought he commanded some German army. Al Qaeda thought in such small terms.

If Saladin had any real problem that evening, it was the knowledge that he must devote considerably more energy to his protégé. Anyone who did not think twice about setting off a device that condemned unknown hundreds of people to painful deaths obviously required careful handling.

He wondered if Juba ever looked deeply into a mirror or thought about the deadly paradox that he had become. The sniper felt betrayed by his home country, England, and most recently by al Qaeda, which had recruited him so many years ago. He had lost *faith*! Saladin had long listened to Juba's spoken outward devotion to Islam and his dream of cutting himself off from the outside world and living like a penniless peasant in the service of the Prophet. The true dedication, however, was not there, and the dream was so unrealistic that it could never be fulfilled.

For while he was a skilled assassin and soldier, Juba's motives were muddled and corrupt. He lived in the moment and was never more alive than when in combat, where his senses tingled with anticipation. He was a perfect fit for the sniper hides and the combat holes, but those assignments did not last forever. In between, in the down time, he had learned to live the good life. He had been ordered to do so and had been declared exempt from violating the Koran! Years of five-star hotels, luxury cars, exquisite tailoring, top-shelf whiskey, and the company of beautiful women in trendy clubs was the lubrication that kept the deadly machine running and ready to strike. The adopted and addictive Western lifestyle cost a great deal of money, and that was the rub: the final rivulet of water needed to bring down his stone bridge back to Islam. Juba had lost his religion, and probably everything else, and didn't really know it. He had learned to like money more than the stern lifestyle preached by the fanatics.

Saladin played along, keeping him on a leash, just as a snake charmer must carefully play a cobra in a basket.

Cobras do not care who they bite, and Juba no longer truly killed for any cause, not even vengeance; he killed because he enjoyed killing.

LEBANON
2002

Saladin remembered his own coming to terms with the future, sweating on the day he stood before Saddam Hussein. At the time, he was just an anonymous lieutenant colonel in the Iraqi army, second in command of the United States Battalion of Unit 999, Saddam's elite terrorism force. The unit was charged with developing what the Iraqi leader called "special ammunition for special circumstances," meaning terrible weapons of mass destruction. There were nine battalions in all, up to five hundred men each, based in various regions and countries with orders to strike within those areas if war came to Iraq. Regardless of such a conflict actually on the horizon after the 9/11 attack on America, the crazy dictator was shipping the materials from Iraqi military stores into Syria and Lebanon and even Iran!

Saladin and his commanding officer had been called to one of Saddam's many palaces to report the status of the United States Battalion's mission to develop a virulent biochem nerve agent that could be deployed within the United States. The work had been going on since the 1980s, slowly and steadily, but with the many starts and stops of any major scientific research program. Much of the research had even been done within the United States itself, under the noses of the FBI and sometimes with the willing assistance of the CIA. In the years in which Iraq was fighting Iran, and Afghanistan was fighting the Soviets, the United States had been quite helpful.

They snapped to rigid attention before Saddam, who

was smoking a cigar as he stared at them. Flanking the
dictator were Uday and Qusay, his two murderous sons,
and at the end of the table was Ali Hassan al-Majid, the
man known as Chemical Ali. Those four had created
Unit 999 and kept its terrible objective as a secret among
themselves.

When Saddam quietly asked if the weapon was ready,
Saladin knew his life rode on the dictator's reaction to the
answer. Not quite, replied the commander of the United
States Battalion. Perhaps one more year of research and
development would be required. Maybe even two years.
Uday and Qusay exchanged glances and grinned. Saddam
tapped his cigar ash and nodded his head, as if in understanding of the difficulties involved.

A burly bodyguard stepped forward without a sound
and crushed a long iron bar onto the right shoulder of
Saladin's superior officer, who crumpled in agony when
the bone broke. Two more bodyguards joined in the pounding as Saladin struggled to remain at rigid attention while
his friend and colleague was beaten to death by his side.
He could still recall the crunching of the bones, the
spreading pool of blood, and the screams, with the uncaring eyes of Saddam Hussein watching him, not the man
being beaten to death. When it was done, Saddam leaned
forward and said, "You are now a full colonel and the new
commander of the United States Battalion of Unit 999. You
have three months to finish the work. You may go."

Saladin saluted, turned on his heel and marched out of
the palace, found a quiet place, and threw up.

Saddam Hussein was crazy, the plan was crazy, and if
he stayed in this job, he was crazy, too.

The new colonel was required to stay around Baghdad
for a while to help transfer much of the technology and
equipment comprising the Iraqi stock of weapons of mass
destruction onto railroad cars and refitted Boeing planes

to shift the components out of Iraq. He consigned some of it to go to America, through a front company in Jordan.

It had been at dinner in a quiet Baghdad café one night during that time that he was introduced to a unique young warrior called Juba, who, it was said, had been waging a one-man sniper campaign in Afghanistan and was a superb killer of infidels. The man was quiet, with a sense of spiritual loneliness, and Saladin, who was a scholar as well as a soldier, decided to exploit that missing piece. This could be his way out of the disaster that was surely coming toward Saddam Hussein's army.

At nights and in the mosques, he guided his new friend deeper into the Book, behind the words of the Koran and into the concepts of what it truly meant to be a Muslim. He steered the conversations easily toward the approaching war, and Juba agreed totally that Iraq would lose.

Since Juba was so bitter about his experiences in Afghanistan, it was not difficult to convince him that Muslims needed a goal higher than squandering their lives to achieve another round of fourteenth-century squalor.

"There will never be a rebirth of any united nation of Islam, unbound by colonialist borders and not ruled by worthless kings," he said. "But that does not mean the struggle should cease."

Juba snorted and sipped some tea. "We will lose. Iraq is doomed."

"What would you say, my friend, if I told you there is a better way that you and I can serve the Prophet?"

"I've heard that promise before, and it was worthless."

There were only the two of them in the room, studying the Koran. Saladin spread his fingers and laid his hand on the Book. "I tell you now, and take an oath on the Book, that we can carry on the battle no matter what happens to Saddam Hussein. I am building a weapon that will make the Crusaders weep for their children," Saladin said. "I need a strong man I can trust, you, to protect me while I finish the work."

"So we will not change the world?" the warrior asked.

"No. That is impossible," the scholar said. "While Saddam will be defeated, we will continue our work in secret. The project will belong to us then, and together we will unleash Allah's vengeance and fury upon the infidels' own homelands."

Then the Iraqi colonel inducted Juba into the secrets of Unit 999 and chose to assume a secret identity of his own, the name of the famous warrior-king of ancient times—Saladin.

10

After the debrief, Kyle Swanson dropped by the hospital to check on Double-Oh, who was still in surgery, then went over to the private quarters maintained for special operations, checked in, and took a shower. The television set in the small room was reporting on the London attack, and he punched up some pillows and lay back on the bunk to watch for a while, then catch some sleep. A pounding on the door ended the brief period of relaxation.

Captain Rick Newman and Sergeant Travis Hughes were there, still dressed in their cammies and covered with dirt from the mission. As they described the odd interrogation of Dalara Tabrizi, Kyle realized that by sharing her idea for another cross-border operation with the intelligence officers, she had unintentionally kicked down the first of a long row of dominoes.

The intel pukes would report up their chain of command, then planners would be brought in to examine the possibilities and would kick it to Washington for debate and approval, and then somebody would have to make a decision to send a U.S. patrol deep into Iran because some woman wanted to find her brother. Since the first raid had turned up so little in the way of hard evidence that a chemical device was being built, there would be great reluctance among the higher pay grades to sign off on a risky new mission on the word of a stranger. If any Americans were caught, the international repercussions would be severe. With every hour that passed, the attack in the UK was going to be viewed more as an investigative matter for police, and the military would be sidelined. Maybe a satellite could take pictures of the suspected site, or perhaps a spy plane could do some flyovers, but without having to put boots on the ground. Was it worth the risk?

"What's your opinion, Trav?" asked Kyle.

"She's telling the truth," he answered. "Every minute she was being questioned, she just kept getting stronger. Rawls is with her right now over at the mess hall, and she is cool and focused."

Swanson looked at Rick Newman. "I doubt if another mission will be authorized," the young captain said. "Too much potential fallout."

Kyle was already putting on his uniform, his mind whirring with possibilities while they watched the latest horrific televised report from London. "We have to do it, even if there is only an outside chance to get to the bottom of this whole thing. So I am thinking that my authorization for the original mission into Iran is still in force and we returned to Doha just to drop off our wounded man. We have to get out of here because this place is just too damned big and has too many competing interests."

Travis Hughes gnawed a fingernail. "The village she mentioned is in the west of Iran, about halfway up the border with Iraq and out where the agriculture gives way to the mountains. We could stage out of Camp Baharia, which is on about the same level in Iraq."

"Good," said Swanson. "Once we are among just Marines, things will get easier. Rick, you get us a plane to

take the team up to Fallujah and run the support side of
the show from Baharia. I'll get Captain Summers over
here, and we can slide it out of the military chain of command entirely and put it under Trident and General Middleton. By the time Sybelle lands, we want to have this thing
already moving. If we keep the momentum going, the
paper-shufflers will never catch up."

WASHINGTON, D.C.

Sybelle Summers arrived for work at six o'clock in the
morning. Like thousands of other commuters, she rode the
Washington Metro to the Pentagon station, patiently took
the long escalator ride up to the main entrance, and signed
in. As she walked the wide, polished hallway, the place
seemed like a giant tomb, and there was an overwhelming
feeling of barely restrained excitement as the men and
women of the United States military services were preparing to face what quite possibly was a new attack against the
homeland. She went directly to the Trident offices.

Major General Middleton and Lieutenant Commander
Freedman were watching television, with the general
switching from channel to channel as each network de-
voted its entire programming to the news from England.
No cheery and smiling wake-up morning show hosts today, just macabre news reports.

"How is Double-Oh?" she asked.

"The docs in Kuwait say that old warhorse is going to
live to fight another day," said Middleton and immediately changed the subject. "You up to date on this London
attack?"

"Yes, sir. Watched some at home and read the *Post* and
the *Times*." Sybelle dropped her purse on a desk. "How
do the news reports match up with our intel sources?"

"Got no fuckin' intel," snorted Middleton. "Once again,

billions of dollars thrown at them, few laws to confine them anymore, and the spooks still come up short. How come TV cameras can always be there when the intel professionals can't?"

General Middleton turned the sound down and made a quick telephone call to the Pentagon central command post that was monitoring the emergency in England. He asked for the casualty count, grunted, and hung up. "Less than a hundred and fifty dead so far, from the dirty bomb explosion to the stampede of people trying to get away, but a bunch of people are hurt. The royals were safely evacuated up to Balmoral Castle in Scotland. Lizard, show her what you're working on."

Freeman pulled a chair up to a small computer terminal and clicked some keys, and a chart replaced the news report on the television screen. He folded his arms and rocked back. An oval-shaped blob of red designated the most saturated area of the attack, then faded into bands of orange and yellow that followed the wind pattern. "The initial public panic kept things in gridlock for a while, and the authorities were prompt in swinging the emergency units into action. Traffic control, quarantines and showers, getting people into clean zones. Thanks to the warning from that fire chief, the first responders were in protective gear when they moved in, and they probably will have saved hundreds of lives when all is said and done."

"The Brits' 9/11," said Sybelle. "Worse than the World War II bombings."

Middleton was grim. "They picked on the wrong country. Not only are we their big brother and will kick the crap out of whoever did this, but the Brits are a tough bunch. They won't knuckle under. Ask Hitler."

The Lizard was out of his chair, moving nervously about the room as he spoke. "I did some statistical analysis to get a grip on what kind of biochem agent was used in the attack and found something I did not expect. Look." He pointed a finger at the scarlet oval of maximum devastation. "Look at the very defined edges of this red zone. The material is very concentrated here, as would be expected." Then he fanned his entire hand out over the other colors. "But the other bands of contamination are extremely narrow."

Sybelle caught it, for like all Force Recon Marines, she had been schooled in biological, chemical, and nuclear warfare. The weak point of any chem attack is atmospheric dispersion, for the moment the toxin goes into the air, it begins to dissipate and grows weaker until it is of no significance whatever. That is why prime targets for such attacks are normally underground or very confined areas, such as in subways, where the effects can be contained and multiplied. "The wind didn't carry it far!"

The Lizard stood and looked at her with a smile, a teacher gazing on a prize pupil. "Exactly." He slapped the top of the television set. "This looks like something new, a heavier-than-air gas that somehow morphs into a sticky liquid on contact with the air. The contamination readings at the center of the attack are still strong right now, many hours after the explosion. This stuff preserves its lethality even in open air."

"In other words, it stays at home and does what it's made to do."

Middleton nodded agreement. "Yep. And that is why we have to be worried. I think this attack was just a field trial. Imagine if huge containers of this stuff went off in the middle of a big city. The death toll could be enormous."

Sybelle went to a sideboard and poured a cup of coffee, then cocked her head toward Middleton. "Every intel service in the world has to be working on this, and the

Brits have to be going all out. Has anybody come up with anything?"

"Nobody has claimed credit yet. No demands have been made. All of the usual idiots are cheering, but none are raising their hands as being responsible because if they do, they get wiped out." Lieutenant Commander Freedman read some notes on his computer. "The explosion came from a truck in the press area, and the chemical canisters were attached to a second truck. The police identified both as belonging to a rental company out of Scotland called Edinburgh All-Media."

Middleton was bending a paper clip into different shapes, and it popped apart as he pulled on it. He tossed it aside. "Damned media again. That girl stuck a microphone in the fireman's mouth just as he realized what was really happening."

Sybelle wouldn't buy his anger. "Wasn't her fault, sir. The terrorists wanted this to be as public as possible, which is why they picked the press that was covering the wedding. It sent a warning straight into the living rooms of millions of viewers. Poor Kimberly Drake will always be the face of this disaster." She felt a shudder as she recalled the horrible death of the reporter on live TV.

The general stood and looked out the window. "Okay. You're right. I'm just trying to add it all up in my head. Get your stuff together, because we have to be at the White House in thirty minutes for a national security briefing on this attack and whether it may be related to what we are doing in Iran."

Sybelle asked, "And exactly what are we doing in Iran, sir?"

"You will find out soon enough. Swanson's taking another team in, and he wants you over there to ramrod the operation from Camp Baharia. The Lizard is setting up a flight, and you are out of here in a few hours."

"Aye, aye, sir," she replied, thinking: *Wake up in my apartment in Maryland this morning, go to work at the Pentagon in Virginia, visit the White House for a conference, do a drop-by at the CIA over in Langley for a final situation report, then out to Andrews Air Force Base and into the back seat of a screaming fast military fighter-bomber for a few hours, and sleep tonight in Iraq. Got to love this job.*

KINGDOM OF BRUNEI DARUSSALAM

Ambassador Richard Taffe was a professional diplomat who had been entrusted by the United States government with the crucial position of ambassador to one of the smallest, richest, and most strategic countries in the world. It was not a gift position awarded to some political party loyalist or to the friend of a friend of the president. Instead, whoever held the post had earned his spurs through years of experience in the diplomatic world. Taffe peeled off his sweaty orange shirt after a morning round at the Royal Brunei Golf and Country Club in Jerudong Park and concluded once again that the years spent in Nigeria and Bangladesh and Jordan had paid off handsomely for him. What was there to dislike about Brunei?

A Malay club boy in pressed black shorts and a white tunic buttoned at the collar brought him a stack of fresh towels. The ambassador wiped his face and chest, rolled the towel into a ball, and tossed it into a hamper ten feet away.

"He shoots! He scores!" called his playing partner for the day, Zul Jock Matali, a senior officer in the Ministry of Foreign Affairs and Trade. "Nothing but net." It had been a good day, and the ambassador had beaten Matali three-and-two in match play. Now they would shower and dress and have lunch in one of the club restaurants and talk about oil.

Brunei was attached by land to Malaysia but floated on a sea of proven oil reserves rated at about 1.35 billion barrels. The country shipped 206,000 barrels every day, and a great deal of it sailed across the Pacific Ocean to the United States. Taffe's primary job was to keep that black gold flowing.

Taffe took a sip of chilled water from a bottle that had almost magically appeared at his side. There was only one thing to really worry about in this little land where, true, nobody voted, but nobody paid taxes and the country had zero external debt. Oil money did that. The problem was not the human trafficking that masqueraded as migrant labor from other Asian countries, because who really gave a shit? Even human rights groups couldn't keep track of it. Just don't call attention to what was, in reality, a booming slave trade. Neither was there any problem with the mandatory death penalty for drug smugglers, which Taffe's people handled quietly when some stupid American kid got nailed trying to bring in dope in a backpack. There was no official arrest, so there was no trial or death sentence, and the tourist was just turned over to the U.S. Embassy, which sent him home on the next plane. At all costs, keep the black oil flowing.

The real diplomatic problem in Brunei was that the nation's religion was Muslim. The common law could be overruled in some cases by sharia law, and the sultan himself was the official defender of the faith. The same royal family had run the little country for six centuries, even after it was spun off as an independent nation by the British Empire. They displayed some enlightened leadership in spending great wads of cash on improvements and allowing at least the appearance of listening to the will of the population of 375,000 people, almost all of whom were literate. Things were politically quiet, and Ambassador Taffe wanted to keep it that way.

Still, there was discomfort about the overall anti-Muslim zeal that seemed to be sweeping through American politicians, whose words were studied by the Brunei policy makers. There was always the possibility, too, that al Qaeda would jump over from nearby Indonesia, make militant inroads here, and turn this fabulously rich nation into a powder keg of trouble. So far, nothing serious had happened. It was so quiet that a citizen of Brunei still did not even need a visa to fly to America.

After their showers, the two officials went upstairs to an elite restaurant and were escorted to a private table beside the huge windows, with a ring of empty tables around them. Matali was much more than just an official in the Ministry of Trade, for the graduate of Stanford University and the Kennedy School of Government at Harvard also held the rank of brigadier general in the Royal Brunei Land Forces. Part of his portfolio was counterterrorism.

They made small talk as the waiters hovered around to take their orders.

"Are you and Maggie going to the Japanese Embassy reception tonight?" asked Matali.

"Yeah, maybe we should sneak away to McDonald's and get some real food instead of sushi."

"I can't eat a Big Mac! It is unclean food."

"So put curry sauce on the chicken nuggets and french fries."

Jock Matali looked up as a waiter approached and handed him a large cream-colored envelope. "A gentleman at the front desk asked that you personally receive this, General."

He opened it. "Strange," he said and shook out a letter

and some photographs. The dark eyes became serious and scanned the restaurant, which was almost empty. No one was watching.

Taffe also peered around. "So, what's up?"

Matali lowered his voice. "It's a contact about London. Someone calling himself Saladin has claimed responsibility and is setting terms."

"Oh, no, not another Saladin. Let me guess," said Taffe. "This latest savior of the downtrodden Middle East wants direct discussions with the president of the United States. Same answer as always, Jock: We don't negotiate with terrorists."

Matali shook his head, reached over, and put a strong hand on Taffe's forearm. "No, my friend. That is not it at all. This is an invitation for the finance ministers of Muslim nations, terrorist organizations, and countries that oppose the United States to participate in an auction for the formula of the weapon used in England."

Taffe rocked back hard in his chair. Matali let him have the note while he looked through a set of photographs. As he read, Taffe's blood chilled.

The London attack was part of an experiment, the note said. A true demonstration of the weapon, which had been years in development, would be unleashed soon in a very public and well-known place, which was not identified.

Parties interested in bidding were to send a buy-in fee of ten million dollars to a Swiss bank account, all but one million of it refundable by the bank escrow officers if the potential bidder did not agree after the demonstration that the weapon was worthwhile. After all, for a measly million, they would be helping sponsor a huge attack against the infidels at no risk to themselves.

If they chose to bid, then the rest of the ten million dollars locked in as the final entry fee, and bids could be submitted. Details would be worked out with the winner to exchange the formula for the cash.

The United States and its major allies in Europe, Asia, and the Middle East would not be allowed to participate.

11

Juba caught a British Airways Boeing 727 out of Charles de Gaulle International Airport in Paris for the long jump to Tehran, more than 2,600 weary miles. He slept much of the way in the darkened first-class cabin, having learned as a soldier to grab sleep whenever it was available, but questions kept pestering him. The director of the site promised that the formula would finally be complete, but so many earlier pledges had been made, then something always went wrong and more tests, time, and money were needed. Unit 999 had labored for years in various places to piece together the extraordinarily lethal mix, something stable enough to transport to a target zone, then able to lock into the area and not blow away with the first puff of air. London had been good, but not quite good enough. Could this really be the time?

The BA plane landed at Mehrabad Airport, and Juba took a taxi to a four-star hotel. He could have pushed things and made the one-hour hop over to Sanandaj on the only Iran Aseman Airlines domestic flight of the day but chose not to. A long drive to the west of Sanandaj also was needed to reach the site and he would be exhausted by the time he arrived. Staying in Tehran also was much better than remaining among the Kurds over there any longer than he had to. They were a dangerous people and would be even more so when they found out what he had been cooking in their back yard.

The test was to be performed tomorrow afternoon. Tonight he would have dinner with three men who would make the trip with him. He would go to the site, watch it, make the decision, and get out, never to return.

THE WHITE HOUSE

Brunei was thirteen hours ahead of Washington, so it was late at night in Washington, D.C., as the president of the United States was climbing into bed in the White House. Every day was a long day in his job; he welcomed the down time, and his staff tried to protect it.

Secretary of State Kenneth Waring knew that, but after receiving the flash traffic from the ambassador in Brunei, he had no choice. Waring telephoned the president's chief of staff, Steve Hanson, and within twenty minutes, all three had gathered in the Oval Office for an emergency meeting.

The president slowly read the message. Smoothed the edges with his hands. Said nothing.

Steve Hanson had known the president for years, and part of his job was to be outspoken on any topic. The Boss wanted it that way. "Secretary Waring and I believe this to be authentic, Mr. President."

"A classic backchannel communication from Saladin, whoever he is," said Waring. "The police over in Brunei are questioning everyone who was in the hotel at the time, trying to find who delivered it. Nothing yet."

Chief of Staff Hanson moved to a different point.

"Why an auction? Why not keep this thing as his own little devastating secret, like the formula for Coca-Cola? Or sell a batch once in a while to al Qaeda and the other fanatics?"

The president crossed the spotless carpet, a giant depiction of the Great Seal of the United States, and leaned an elbow against the fireplace mantel. "Production, Steve. Think back to when we were earning an honest dollar out in the business world. We could have made some of our gadgets in the garage, but constructing them one at a time would never bring real success. We needed manufacturing plants, which is exactly what we eventually had."

Hanson agreed. "So this psychopath claims to have the magic formula for a super-deadly biochem weapon but can only churn it out in limited quantities. If he sells it to a nation, say, North Korea or Iran, then the state can produce any amount it wants to brew."

"Scary thought," said Secretary of State Waring. He closed his eyes and rubbed them. "What's next?"

Hanson had been thinking about that. "Standard policy would be to get the entire cabinet in for an emergency meeting and turn loose the military and CIA."

The president studied him. "You don't think that's the way to go? This is among the most important things we have ever handled."

The secretary of state said, arms crossed, "It will be impossible to keep it a secret for long if he is reaching out to bidders."

Hanson was excited. "It's already out there, Mr. Secretary, but we don't have to throw fuel onto the fire. The president can remain in the background for a while, and all press queries will be directed to you at the State Department. Your statement can be something along the lines that we have heard about some strange new terrorist demands but we have not been contacted directly. Although we take all terrorist threats seriously, we remain confident that our security forces are up to any new challenge, and we pledge again to do whatever is needed to protect this nation."

The president had been analyzing the information while the others talked, just as he had done when he ran one of the biggest electronic and computer companies in the world. Finally he said, "I think this Saladin fellow made a mistake. He gives no deadline for responses to the auction idea because he knew that any potential bidders will need time to get their acts together."

The secretary of state interrupted. "True. But what do we do with the extra time?"

"Find him. Kill him. Bury him." Steve Hanson pulled himself erect, all five foot six of him, and shoved his hands in his pockets.

"We don't assassinate heads of state," huffed Waring.

"He isn't a head of state, Ken!" Hanson said. "He's a fucking terrorist who has already attacked London and is now coming after us! Anyway, we won't be the only ones after him. Al Qaeda and other big players are going to try to take that formula for free. They don't want some bit actor like Saladin grabbing power away from them."

The president waved a hand. "Okay. Go easy, Steve. The secretary of state is correct: The United States does not assassinate people. You guys get things moving while I go upstairs and shave and put on fresh clothes. I want an NSC briefing in an hour." He shook hands with the secretary of state and thanked him for bringing the bad news.

Once Waring left the Oval Office, the president turned to his chief of staff. "Get General Middleton over here right away, Steve. I think we're going to need Kyle Swanson very soon."

CAMP BAHARIA
IRAQ

Swanson had to smile at the astonishment on the face of Delara Tabrizi when he walked into the special ops briefing room with Travis Hughes and Joe Tipp. They had collected new clothing on the way over and now, instead of American soldiers, they looked like Iranian farmers: baggy pants, long tunics, and wrapped head coverings. Each carried a heavy sheepskin coat. He went over to her. "Thank you for this new information, Miss Tabrizi. However, you really don't have to go in with us. In fact, it would be better if you stayed here."

Her gaze was steady. "No. I must go."

"We can find your brother, if he's there, and bring him out."

"You don't know that country," she said and walked over to a map hanging from the wall. She spread her hand over an area circled in red. "This is my home village of Kamveh, and I grew up roaming those mountains, tending our sheep and goats. I know the general location of this other horrible place where Iranian people are being tortured and murdered, and I know pathways that can get you there."

"It will be dangerous."

She shrugged her shoulders. "For us, every day we live is dangerous. I am going with you."

"Just try to keep up."

Delara Tabrizi bristled at the condescending tone.

She looked up at him with determination in her dark eyes, her face framed by wisps of black hair that escaped from the edges of the emerald green scarf covering her head. Kyle realized that she was beautiful. Less than thirty years old, she stood only about five-five and could not have weighed more than 115 pounds, but she carried a sense of self-assuredness that had been honed by being a woman with a will of her own living in a country run by men and religious police.

The previous year she had been ordered by police to attend classes on respecting the proper attire for Islamic women. Like many of her generation, she still bent the rules concerning the *shalwar kameez,* a boxy full-length coverall that fell from shoulder pads to ankles. Delara's coat was in a muted beige design, fell only to her knees, and was somewhat fitted, although it was still loose and had sleeves to her wrists. Instead of droopy pantaloons beneath it, she wore a pair of jeans and a rust-colored T-shirt.

"I just need a pair of good boots and I'm ready to go. Give me a pistol, something small like a Makarov, and you won't have to rescue me again," she said.

"We can do that," laughed Travis Hughes, enjoying the exchange of barbs between Shake and Delara. "You know how to shoot?"

"I grew up in the mountains. Everybody has to know how to shoot to protect our herds."

"Girl knows her guns. Cool," said Darren Rawls, stepping up beside Kyle. "Gunny, I want to go, too."

"You can't. You're black, remember? Ain't no brothers up in those mountains," said Joe Tipp.

"Shit," said Rawls.

"You and Rawls go by the armory and get us all weaponed up. In case we have to use them, we don't want to leave an American signature with the shell casing. I'll take an AK-47 and a Dragunov sniper rifle. Grab an RPK light machine gun and some RPGs. Get plenty of explosives, water, binos, and rations for three days. Travis, you outfit Miss Tabrizi with whatever she wants. I will make a final comm and logistics check with Captain Newman.

Rendezvous at the helo pad in thirty minutes. We are going to have to push it to get into position before daylight."

A few lights from Baghdad illuminated the bottom of the cloud cover far to the south as the Pave Low raced through the night, each mile seeming to Swanson to take forever. If they could not find a good position by the time the sun came up, they would just have to burrow in somewhere and wait all day long, and he believed that they could not afford the luxury of just staying put for twelve hours. The first site had been totally destroyed, and he wanted to see this second one before it suffered the same fate. He felt in his gut that the time was close. Whoever was running that operation was cleaning up loose ends, and somehow the entire thing was wrapped up with the attack in London. He fought the nervousness and settled into the racket of the Pave Low helicopter. He could not make this bird go any faster.

A crackle came on the radio in his ear. "Bounty Hunter, Bounty Hunter, this is Slider Base. Come in." Sybelle's voice!

"Slider Base, this is Bounty Hunter."

There was a comforting sense of crisp professionalism in her voice. "Confirming Trident on deck here. Mission is yours."

Excellent! The spur-of-the-moment special operation to return to Iran had clicked into place, with Rick Newman holding the fort until Sybelle Summers had arrived at Baharia to take over. Now Kyle could stop worrying that some colonel might find out about what he was up to and order a stop to it all or, worse, start meddling to change the mission. He now would report to Sybelle, who reported to Middleton, who reported to the president of the United States. That simplified things.

"Slider Base. Roger on Trident. Out."

He didn't need to go into any further explanation. Between Newman and Sybelle, all of the support elements would be in place, and whatever they did not have on hand, they could whistle up in a hurry. The best offense was still total secrecy, but it was nice to know that a pair of Marine Harrier jump jets might just happen to be flying near the border soon, along with a few Cobra gunships to protect the helicopter during extraction.

The Zagros mountain range in northwestern Iran was a natural geographical barrier that discouraged visits deep into its saddles and peaks. People only went into the stark and barren reaches if they had a purpose, and population centers were few. Adding to the isolation were roving patrols of the Iranian Revolutionary Guard, who were absolutely vicious in protecting an area that the government had designated to be off-limits because of its importance. Some people who wandered into the area were never seen again.

The mountains could be an advantage for interlopers, since it was impossible for the Iranian military to tightly control the entire rugged area. Roads petered out to paths, communications were difficult, and the villagers were sullen, even hostile, doing what they were told to do only under the threat of force. The mountains also were a resting place for small packs of bandits who enjoyed ambushing a patrol to ransack its supplies. As a result, the Iranian troops stuck close to their small bases during the night.

Because resupply was always a problem, the villagers of Kamveh paid scant attention to the brief clatter of a passing helicopter in the night. The low-flying craft were frequently in the area to transport goods to the soldiers, although the farmers still preferred their slower but more reliable pack mules. A mule did not need radar to get where it was going.

The Pave Low moved fast and close to the undulating terrain to reach its designated landing zone, the bald knob of a hilltop about three kilometers each way between the suspected biochemical site and the village of Kamveh. It flared to a halt and dropped down only long enough to let the three Marines and Delara Tabrizi jump out, two from each side, and then it spun out of the area and let the satellite mapping system carry it safely out of harm's way, dashing back across the border with Iraq, where a refueling plane was loitering to top it off for a slower trip back to Baharia. The special operations crew breathed easier.

Everybody on the ground hunched over and stayed put for a minute to assess whether any threats were in the immediate area, and then Travis Hughes led the way north, into the treeline. Kyle Swanson followed, followed by Delara, with Joe Tipp trailing. Once they were deep into the trees, they stopped to get their bearings, and Swanson opened a plastic-shielded map. He pulled a red-lens flashlight from his web gear, only to feel a light touch on his arm. "I remember this place," Delara said softly. "There is a shallow stream over to the left and a meadow to the right. We can stay hidden in the trees all the way around the field, but then there is a road to cross."

Too easy, Swanson thought, but he pointed for Hughes to check out the landmarks, and he was back in five minutes, moving unheard through the foliage. He nodded and took them to the edge of the calm and moonlit meadow. Judging by the height of the grass, it was a grazing area, and although all of the animals had been herded back to the village for the night, the smell of wet wool and sheep dung still permeated the air. Maybe this girl was the real deal with her directions.

Going downhill gave them a vantage point on what was below, and they came to the crest of the little road and paused again. Travis went one way and Tipp the other, slithering through a rocky ditch that ran alongside the dirt passageway. Again the two scouts with night vision goggles returned without seeing or hearing anything, and they all moved on. "We can follow the road for about half a kilometer north, then we have to cross it and continue down to the valley floor," said Delara. Her voice was excited, but quiet, as she guided them with certainty through the rugged area she had roamed as a girl. Passing decades did not bring much change to such places, and she was sure-footed and steady as she pointed them onward, recognizing ourcroppings of rock and sharp curves in a narrow path as familiar landmarks.

Kyle kept them all at a steady pace, not allowing Delara's unerring directions to hurry them into making a mistake. Security was as important as speed, but she had come up with a route that bypassed all activity except for the noise of an occasional night animal. They reached the valley floor without incident, caught their breath, drank some water, and started up the next mountain.

Going up was harder than coming down, but Travis Hughes set a brutal pace, aware that the darkness had changed with the passing of time. He looked behind him and saw that the others were thirty meters back, unable to keep up with his rate of climb because Delara was a civilian, a schoolteacher, not a trained warrior in peak physical condition. The other three could go only as fast as the slowest member. Hughes held up his right hand in a fist, and everyone stopped as he scrambled back to the group.

"What do you want me to do, Shake?" he asked.

"Get going, and be quick about it. Get up to the ridge-line and be able to give us cover if we need it, and look around for a hide."

Small and energetic, Hughes turned back and went into what would be considered an uphill sprint, his powerful legs pumping like pistons as he attacked the mountain, moving silently through the foliage.

Kyle, Delara, and Joe Tipp kept their distance, working through heavy underbrush beside a gulley, searching for firm footing with their boots and grabbing roots, pawing at rocks, and huffing for breath. Delara Tabrizi never asked for a rest, although her lungs were aching and her muscles burned with the strain. Once she stopped, and the big hand of Joe Tipp pushed hard on her behind as he whispered, "Go, dammit!" She went.

Ten minutes after Hughes had reached a position just below the summit, the three others crawled up beside him, gulping deep breaths. "This is the right place," he said and then pointed toward a group of boulders about fifty meters away that bumped out from the run of thick trees and undergrowth. They went toward it on their bellies, anxious to clear a place in which the four of them could hide during the coming daylight hours as the morning sun began turning the sky into a definite gray. Delara rolled onto her back, sucking in deep breaths, fighting exhaustion.

Swanson pulled out his binos and crawled to the crest, looked down, and said, "Oh, damn."

Below was the site, where frightened groups of people were being herded into small, barbed-wire cages.

Juba drove a Russian-made UAZ-469 jeep directly up to a military roadblock in a mountain pass, stopping slowly at a safe distance from the Rakhsh armored personnel carrier that blocked the road, with its 12.77 mm machine gun pointing toward the visitors. Another jeep halted right behind him, and all four of the men in the vehicles dismounted with their hands held high.

"We are expected," Juba told the young sergeant who approached, then handed over his identification papers. The soldier took the ID back to a guard shack and radioed the site, two miles away. When he received clearance, he ordered the big Rakhsh off the road and returned the papers to Juba with a crisp salute. The other guards snapped to attention, and the UAZ-469s were soon on their way.

"Are we going to have trouble with those boys on the way out?" asked the big man who was riding in the passenger seat beside Juba.

Juba laughed and shook his head. "No. The Iranians are in on it but have the erroneous idea that they control the situation. They have been excellent hosts and sponsors, but the time has come to say good-bye. We can fly out using a little helicopter that is kept at the site." The helicopter could not be used to bring them in because the jeeps were loaded with special equipment that might have been questioned by the crew or by people at the site.

All three of the men with Juba were mercenaries, tough guns from the old Soviet Union. Even so, this was dangerous. "The MOIS is going to be very upset if they are screwed," said the man. The Iranian Ministry of Intelligence and Security was so notorious and ruthless that its handpicked agents had to prove they could kill and torture before being admitted to the ranks. International boundaries meant nothing to the secret police, and the well-paid mercenaries understood that the MOIS would try to track them down.

"That already has been arranged. We bribed the minister." Juba saw the building when he came around a final curve. He drove past a series of tall cages, each holding a cluster of three people, men and women, with haunted looks on their faces. The small administration office structure was the only other thing aboveground, and a man in a white coat was walking out to meet the jeeps.

"Leave the weapons and the gear in the vehicles for the time being. I will tell you when." He got out and went to shake the hand of the site director.

12

Joe Tipp and Travis Hughes lay side by side, sketching the site below and building a range card. Tipp would focus an MLR-40 handheld laser rangefinder on a specific point and describe it, and Hughes would note the digital readout and write it onto their map. The rangefinder was a product of OIP Sensor Systems in Belgium and was used by military forces around the world. Swanson considered it to be a dinosaur in comparison to the rangefinding computer built into his favorite sniper rifle, but he had left Excalibur behind on this mission.

A line of small motion detectors, Sentinels out of a plant in China, had been arranged behind and to the sides of their hide site to prevent anyone from creeping up unnoticed. And a small box was rigged in a safe location nearby, with a small directional antenna pointed down at the site. It was a Swiss-made Grabber V401 listening device that would record up to twenty channels of voice and electronic data traffic. Anything that was said down below for the next fourteen hours would be on a tiny computer disk for later analysis.

Delara Tabrizi had the binos on the cages, shifting her

study from person to person, hoping to recognize her brother. So far, she had not recognized anyone.

Swanson was down behind the crest, his back against a tree and the map spread before him, talking by encrypted telephone with Sybelle Summers back at Camp Baharia. "The site is very active. Something is going to happen soon. A pair of Russky jeeps carrying four guys pulled in a few minutes ago, and a man in a white doctor's coat is leading them around."

"Can you get to the building?"

"No way. We're in a good hide about seven hundred meters away and uphill, but there is a big clearing around the site, the same kind of discoloration and dead foliage that we found at the first one. Too much ground to cover undetected in broad daylight, and we don't know how many people are in there. Some IRG are also in the area."

"How is your passenger?"

"Holding up good. We're all watching to be sure she doesn't get too weirded out and do anything stupid if she actually sees her brother down there."

"Okay. Call if you need me. Slider Base out."

As soon as he terminated the call, Travis Hughes was at his side. "We need you up there, Shake. The white coat dude is pointing at us."

"The wind normally comes from that wooded high ground to the north and pushes on down through the valley," explained Director Ali Kahzahee, sweeping his hand toward the range of foothills that led down to the plain on which the site was located. "Our weather forecast today is ideal, with some rain moving in this afternoon. You can already feel the breeze building up, and it will increase, coming from that way. Obviously, we have placed the experimental stations downwind."

Juba was not interested in a weather report. "Is this the final test?" He had left his men at the jeeps while the director gave him a tour.

"I believe so," replied Kahzahee, lifting his chin in the direction of the cages. "It worked perfectly in animal trials, and I have a high level of confidence that it will work down there today."

They strolled casually, discussing details, to the first cage, a six-by-six wire enclosure crowned by circles of concertina wire. Three men were inside, all emaciated and fearful of what the day would bring. Two had been arrested during crackdowns on government dissidents and the third was a common criminal, but it made no difference now. They knew they had left the category of human beings and were now just expendable laboratory rats, listening in horror to the explanation Director Kahzahee gave to Juba.

"At this station, there will be a one hundred percent fatality rate within five minutes. First will come an icy feeling as the liquid goes into their pores and attacks their pulmonary systems, which will make them strangle and suffocate. When they attempt to wipe it away from their skin, they spread it to uninfected areas. The effects are irreversible and very painful. Our autopsies have shown significant damage to the major organs as the oxygen supply is terminated."

Juba looked at the terrified dark eyes. They were scared, yes, but still there was a spark of defiance. Stubborn people, but it no longer mattered.

Another fifty meters and they came to the second cage, this time with a man, a teenaged boy, and a middle-aged woman with long gray hair as the experimental subjects. Juba had a faint recognition. She was a famous writer who had been heavily critical of the government. Once he placed her face, he ignored her. "This group will have the same reactions as the first. I anticipate complete success."

"They will all die within a few minutes?"

"Yes." The director made the same predictions at the next two cages, still spaced fifty meters apart, then they approached the next to the last enclosure, which was 250 meters from the first one. "This is where things change sharply. Even with the prevailing breeze today, all of the subjects in the final enclosure will survive for much longer and may recover entirely with proper medical help."

Juba liked what he had heard. "Well, Director Kahzahee, it sounds good. Let's get on with the test and see if you have earned your money."

They returned to the jeeps, where the rest of the scientists had gathered with their measuring equipment and a metal container the size of an oxygen tank. Everyone put on hazmat suits. They were upwind, but none wanted to take a chance with the deadly genie that was about to be set free.

"There he is! I see Mahmoud!" Delara Tabrizi grabbed Kyle Swanson's arm. "There in the second cage with the woman with gray hair. He's alive."

Swanson shifted his own binos over and saw the three people clustered together behind the wire. "It's impossible to get to them right now," he said. "We have to wait."

"I can go by myself. They will not suspect a woman, and then you can shoot them all from up here and call in airplanes." She started to stand, and Swanson pulled her down hard.

"Listen to me! I'm in charge here and you are a free rider. You don't do anything at all, *nothing*, unless I tell you to. You understand me? I thought that we made that perfectly clear before you even got on the helicopter." His eyes were fierce and the whispered command thunderous with his anger.

"I cannot just let them kill my brother!"

"You will not be allowed to compromise this mission, Miss Tabrizi," he warned. "Our job is to see what is in that building and what they are doing. We will save the boy if we can, but right now, we all stay put. Travis, sit on this woman if she tries to go anywhere."

Swanson turned back to the scene below. There was nothing they could do now but watch. When he saw the men below donning their biochem protective gear, he turned and softly said, "Everybody get the MOPP suits on. Right now."

All four of the watchers slid out of sight below the ridgeline and struggled into their protective gear, with Hughes helping Delara figure out the bulky outfit. Even the smallest size was too big for her and hung around her in folds.

Kyle ignored her. He needed a plan. Something.

Mahmoud Tabrizi knew he was going to die today. He had not really expected to live very long anyway after his awakening to the ideas passed along by some of his friends, subversive talk about establishing some other form of government in Tehran, a loosening of the police state tactics, and profound questions about the teachings of the mullahs. That was treason, and he knew it and didn't care, and he had become known in places where revolution was discussed. Three weeks short of his seventeenth birthday, as he sat on the dirt in a barbed wire cage, he believed that although his contribution had not been much, he had made a difference among the coming generation of students in Iran.

He thought about his sister, Delara, the only other surviving member of their family, and prayed that Allah would bestow many blessings upon her. Mahmoud never believed that religious nonsense that women were lesser than men, nor that he was going to live in some fairy-tale paradise once he died. What counted was what one did while one lived.

The teenager reached out and took the hand of the woman in the cage with him. She had made a difference in the struggle, and he felt honored that they would be together at the end. Although her clothes were now shabby and she was very weak, she had wielded the power of written words. Her poems and stories had bounded across international borders, and the government had been unable to stop them, so they arrested and tortured her. "Do not be afraid, Mother," Mahmoud said. "No matter what these dogs have done to you, or will do to us, you will always be one of our true warriors."

The woman looked at the boy with her watery eyes and tightened her grip on his hand. "Freedom, my young friend Mahmoud. Let us cry out for freedom, even with our final breaths."

A technician in a white hazmat suit drove a four-wheeled ATV to the first cage, pulling a cart with a pair of large containers strapped inside. He parked just beyond the reach of the prisoners and unhitched the trailing cart. He secured the canisters so they pointed in the correct direction, then adjusted a nozzle that would diffuse the gas inside when the valve was opened. When one was empty, the other would begin to unleash its deadly contents. The three men trapped inside the cage had lost their fear and were resigned to their fates and glared at the suited figure and cursed him.

The man had a radio headset inside the helmet and told Director Kahzahee that all was ready. The men at consoles inside the building gave other confirmations. A pause, then Kahzahee's steady voice ordered, "Begin the experiment."

An extremely loud signal horn groaned into a wailing

siren that blasted through the valley and over the hills, warning the Iranian soldiers to stay away from the area until the siren was heard a second time. At the roadblocks and on the patrols, soldiers looked nervously at each other and ran for shelter.

The technician twisted the knob atop the nozzle counterclockwise three full turns, jumped back onto the ATV, and raced away from the area. Over the barking whine of the little engine, he heard people yelling, calling out, and chanting.

The prisoners who were about to die in agony were standing at the wire, chanting at the top of their voices—FREEDOM!

The hissing gas moved unseen into the air, then spread as it was pushed by the flow of more compressed gas coming behind it. The slight breeze helped it stay airborne, spread apart, and rise higher for a while, but the heavy individual molecules began to chemically weld together and, yielding to gravity, slowly arced back toward earth as spots of liquid. The prisoners in the first cage felt cold droplets, as if a rain shower were passing. They covered their mouths and noses with the rags of their clothing and closed their eyes, but the droplets clung to their skin and coagulated into a sheen of clear gel that seeped into their pores. Two removed the cloths from their faces and tried to brush away the liquid on their skin, but it would not rub off, only spread out in a viscous covering over a wider surface area. The third man kept the rag over his face, watching as the others began to cough loudly; then he could take it no longer, feeling as if his skin were being penetrated by a million tiny drills of heat. He immediately had trouble breathing, as if he had swallowed a large piece of meat that was stuck in his throat.

The first scream was heartrending, but after that there

were just too many to tell one from another. All three men in the cage were flailing in torment, grabbing their throats and chests as the poison sped through their bloodstreams and into their hearts, lungs, and brains. Mucus membranes expanded and ruptured, and a clear liquid leaked from their mouths and noses. They were gasping for air, sucking loudly, but their lungs and air passages had filled to overflowing with the mucus discharge, and the fading hearts kept pumping the contaminated blood throughout their bodies. *No air. No air!* It was impossible to breathe.

The expanding bubble of gas moved on. By the time all three of the men in the first cage were thrashing on the ground, Mahmoud and the writer felt the first wet drops and their cries for freedom stopped. "Inhale it deeply, Mother! Gulp it all in and we can beat them by shortening the pain," he said, opening his mouth wide and turning his face upward. When the gel formed on his tongue, he lapped at the liquid eagerly, like a kitten at a bowl of milk, then toppled, coughing and gagging, but still holding the hand of the woman.

All three men in the first pen had ceased thrashing, and the bodies entered the final stages of destruction. The final conscious thought of each was sheer pain and the feeling that he had been eaten alive.

The gas moved on, the bubble expanding, and swept up the next three victims in the third cage and then the fourth. The people in the hazmat suits watched with clinical detachment as the ground in the pens was littered with moaning and thrashing human wreckage.

"Now this is where it gets interesting," said Director Kahzahee. As if it had hit a wall, the sticky gas stopped spreading after causing total destruction for two hundred meters. The three men in the final enclosure had stared at the certain death that had been marching steadily toward them and were wailing in anticipation of the grinding end awaiting them. Then minutes passed and nothing happened. They could still breathe. They were still alive.

"Wonderful," exclaimed Kahzahee. "Absolutely perfect. Total lethality in an exact space, with the contaminant lingering there in heavy doses. It could remain potent for up to twenty-four hours."

The director motioned to several of the workers in the hazmat suits, who moved forward and pulled one of the bodies from the fourth cage and hauled it to the final enclosure, which had not been infected. They dropped it inside, then used clubs to knock each of the final three prisoners to the ground and rub their hands and arms into the gel and mucus on the dead man.

"After an attack, the so-called first responders will show up, the police and medical people. With the poison being clear, there will be no pools of blood to warn them of danger, and they probably would not even be wearing gloves. Anyone without protective shielding who touches one of those people or that clothing will transfer the gel to themselves and can spread it to others. The entire zone becomes a death trap."

Juba was impressed. The weapon would not weaken quickly in a wind because it had been designed to create a specific cone of death and hold its position for a long period of time. He imagined driving a truck through a major American city, spewing the toxin into the air, and knowing that everybody for two hundred yards on each side of the street would be killed, all along his route. Or rigging a spray from a plane over a metropolitan area. The first responders entering the scene to help would be slain by the lingering, sticky gas, and they would spread it to the hospitals and emergency shelters. On the battlefield, the gas would be a targeted weapon with a specific kill zone that would devastate an enemy but not harm your own troops. Scientists and military tinkerers would dream up even more uses.

"That's it, then. Congratulations on your achievement," he told the director. "How will you clear it out down there?"

"We will just have to burn it all where it stands. It's the only way."

"Then let's go back into your office while your men take care of it. I need to report your success."

13

The four people in the snipers' hide had felt helpless and were horrified as they watched the experiment unfold, for there was nothing they could do to stop the murders of the innocents in the cages. Delara covered her ears and buried her face in the carpet of leaves beneath her when she saw her brother fall. Mahmoud was dying in great pain, and she was powerless to help.

Kyle Swanson's brain had kept churning, figuring out a plan. The mission had never been to rescue hostages but to get inside the building and its web of tunnels to document what was in there. When he saw how the experiment developed, he got the idea to turn the deadly weapon against its creators.

He gathered the others and explained what they were to do. Aggressive action was the best antidote for the useless feeling that had engulfed them all. Swanson, Tipp, and Hughes would execute a long-range ambush to kill as many of those cold-blooded bastards as possible and then steal their work.

There was no urgency at the site as the workers went about their jobs as if this were a normal day. Perhaps it was, for them. The man with the ATV, still in a white hazmat suit, zipped out to the first pen and turned off the valve to stop the escaping gas. Without looking at the bodies, he reattached the cart and brought the narrow tanks back to the site and returned them to a small fenced area near the building, the loading zone in which the canisters were filled. Another worker waited there with a water hose, buckets, and a scrubbing brush to wash down the driver, the ATV and cart, and the canisters.

The three Chechnyan mercenaries lounged around the jeeps, smoking cigarettes and watching, waiting for Juba to give the signal for them to grab their weapons and kill the scientists, their assistants, and then any leftover prisoners. After that, the boxes of explosives and incendiaries they had packed along would be placed at vital points and the structure would be destroyed. Juba had not yet given the signal. They waited, three hardcore fighters loyal only to the big paychecks, half already paid up front, half on completion. It was more than a fair deal as far as they were concerned. There were no threats among the busy men in the white coats, other than that extraordinary and lethal gas. The mercs were happy the wind was at their backs, blowing away the remains of the spray, and the sprinkle of rain had begun.

Director Ali Kahzahee was in his private office. He had spent many months coming in and out of the site and was glad to be leaving for the final time, the complicated work done. A number of laboratories scattered around the world had worked on various parts of the project, but it was Kahzahee and his team who had brought it all together and made it work.

His personal knowledge was invaluable, and Kahzahee knew that once the project was completed, his usefulness to the Iranian regime would be at an end. The soldiers who had been guarding the site would probably sweep up the entire team and demand the formula, particularly since Tehran thought they were part owners of the project. Juba and his guards would protect them on the swift journey into Europe, where Saladin had promised to help them all build new lives.

The director folded up his laptop computer, which contained his research, and stuffed it into a black briefcase along with his detailed notes. He then took a final turn around the office, checking every drawer and file cabinet. There were no mementos or reminders. A pile of discarded notes and reams of results was scattered in the middle of the floor, where it would be soaked with gasoline. Everything was to be burned.

The soldiers at the roadblocks might be curious about the smoke, but Kahzahee had not sounded the all-clear siren, and the military would not enter the area until they heard it. He picked up a pair of pliers from his desk and snipped the curling red, black, and green wires to the alarm. The all clear would not sound today.

There was no concern about the people he had killed in the experiment, just a sense of scientific satisfaction. The director grabbed his briefcase and headed for the door.

Juba was in the communications room, where he had placed a call to a number in Paris. Saladin had answered.

"It is ready," said Juba. "The test was impressive."

"Excellent. Do we have the material in hand?"

"The director gave me an envelope with a complete disk and matching set of printouts. I will bring them out."

"What about backup copies? Does Kahzahee have a set?"

"I would imagine so. The material is too valuable to entrust to anyone working for him."

Saladin paused. "Are you somewhere that you might be overheard?"

"Yes," said Juba.

"Very well. Make sure to destroy any backup material after you dispose of the staff."

Juba saw Director Kahzahee come into the communications area and smiled at him. "We will all be leaving soon," Juba said. "Yes, sir. I will tell him you said so." He terminated the conversation. "Saladin sends his personal congratulations, Director, and says there will be a bonus waiting for you in Paris."

There would be nothing sexy about the ambush, just total surprise by an unexpected enemy with overwhelming firepower shooting from a secure position on high ground only seven hundred meters away. "Kill everybody on site so we can get inside. You saw what they did to the prisoners," Swanson told the others, his voice low and determined. "They deserve to die. Take down all those fuckers." Then he laid out the targets and the firing sequence. "I'll take the bodyguards, and Tipp, rake the area for any targets you see. Hughes, you put some RPG rounds into the container storage area and we will see how they like a little of their own shit on them. Everyone engage on my first shot."

Kyle considered the Russian-made SVD Dragunov sniper rifle to be a serviceable weapon, but not in the same class as its American counterparts, and certainly far behind his personal Excalibur. The synthetic buttstock fit comfortably against his shoulder, and his right hand eased around the pistol grip. The canvas sling seemed archaic, but the magazine could hold ten rounds of SVD 7.62×54 mm ammunition. It was semiautomatic, not a bolt action, and was almost fifty inches in length, upgraded to a POSP 8×42 sniping scope that worked well in harsh environments. It was an old hog, dating back to before the Vietnam era, but it would do what needed to be done on this day in Iran. He slowly pushed the barrel through the foliage and scanned for his first target.

He chose one of the bodyguards who had come in this morning and was now sitting on the hood of a jeep, facing away from Kyle. He looked like he was trained as a fighter and therefore presented a primary threat. For a sniper, a back shot is a golden opportunity, since it gives the target no chance to notice that he is taking his last breaths. Kyle had already checked the range card and had done the other calculations in his head for windage and the bullet drop going downhill. He put the reticle just below the man's neck, exhaled, let his heartbeat slow, and squeezed the trigger straight back until the Dragunov barked and the bullet hurtled toward the unsuspecting man at 2,700 feet per second.

The Chechnyan fighter jerked forward as if he had been slugged in the back by a big hammer, his eyes opening wide with surprise as he fell facedown in the dirt. The bullet severed his spine and exploded within him, tearing his organs to pieces before pushing a mass of tissue and blood out through a big exit wound in his chest.

Kyle shifted his aim to another Chechnyan who was spinning around at the familiar sound of a shot being fired. Swanson was cold and smooth, not hurrying. This guy was just reacting, he wasn't going anywhere. Kyle aimed for center mass, and the Dragunov spat out another powerful bullet, which took the second man in the chest. The victim remained still for a moment, then slumped to his knees, grabbing at the fatal wound as blood poured between his fingers. He fell over dead.

Off to Kyle's right, Joe Tipp opened up with his RPK light machine gun, with the long barrel braced on its fold-

ing bipod, slapping out three-round bursts throughout
the general area . . . *Clack-clack-clack* . . . *Clack-clack-
clack*. Several men were sent sprawling. Tipp had two
spare big banana clips for the gun nearby so he could reload quickly. He was not going for any random fire to keep
their heads down. As a trained sniper, Joe Tipp was taking
enough time to aim and kill people. The gunpowder smell
of burned cordite rose in the hide.

To Kyle's left, Travis Hughes came into a kneeling
position with an RPG-7 launcher on his shoulder and fired
a grenade that burst from the tube with a loud *whoosh!*
Four sharp fins popped out to stabilize the flight, and ten
meters away, the grenade armed itself. Sizzling at the tip
of a hot red exhaust tail, the high-explosive round zoomed
into the storage area and exploded hard when it hit metal,
setting loose a spray of the poison gas.

The crashing symphony of the ambush was fully under
way, and none of the people at the site had yet fired a
shot in return. In fact, none had yet even reached a weapon.

Watching through binoculars from beside Kyle, Delara
Tabrizi viewed the destruction with a burning fury on
her face. "Kill them," she said through gritted teeth. "Kill
them all!"

Inside the building, Juba heard the shots, and three seconds later the RPG explosion shook the concrete structure, blowing around a layer of dirt and debris. An attack
was the last thing he had expected, and he instantly recognized that his situation had totally changed.

"What's happening?" Director Kahzahee, who had been
heading for the door, stopped in midstride and turned back.

Juba stepped closer, looking through the door and then
glancing out a side window. Men were running around trying to find shelter, and smoke was spreading along the

ground while a misty haze rose into the air. "Either the Iranians are coming to take over this place, or some dissident bandits are making a raid. Either way, it is not good for us."

"The fools are shooting at the container loading area! Some of those canisters are still filled with the gas!" The director dropped his briefcase and grabbed for a fresh biohazard suit hanging on a wall hook as another RPG grenade whumped into the containers and rattled the building.

Gas! Juba was beginning to feel a pull of panic and forced himself to slow down enough to think and act. There was no time to go through the complicated procedure of getting a full biosuit back on, and to just stand where he was would be a death sentence. He had to get out!

In one motion, he pulled a Heckler & Koch 9 mm pistol from his belt holster and fired two bullets into the skull of Director Kahzahee, picked up the fallen briefcase, and dove through the side window in the wall across the room from the exploding storage area.

He tucked his head and shoulders and hit the ground with a roll, in a shower of splinters and glass that sliced at him. *This wasn't the Iranian government,* he thought. *It was dissidents who were determined to capture the site and expose its secrets to the world, making the government in Tehran be viewed around the world as monsters.*

Juba rose, bent at the waist, and ran toward a little gulley in order to put terrain between himself and the shooters while hoping he was moving faster than the spreading and invisible cloud of gas. The wind was on his right cheek, not directly behind him, so that improved his chances of escaping. Wet droplets splashed on his arms and face.

The sustained chatter of an AK-47 being fired on full automatic broke the rhythm of the incoming rounds. One of his Chechnyans was returning fire, taking the attention

of the attackers and buying Juba a few more steps. The
hired gunman was covering the escape in an effort to
protect his own paycheck and called out, "Juba! Start the
helicopter!"

Juba was standing completely up now, panting and
sprinting hard toward the field where an old UH-1 Huey
helicopter was stationed, his heels pounding hard. The
droplets continued to splash on him. The chopper's rotors
were sluggishly beginning to turn, and the engine was
coughing. Almost out of breath, he reached the bird and
jumped into the cargo area, rolling flat on his back, his fist
tight around the briefcase handle. "Go!" he yelled. "The
gas is escaping."

The Americans had sold a lot of aging Hueys to the old
shah before he was deposed, and the helicopters were a
common sight around Iran. The pilot had been running
his checklist even before the shooting started. He wasn't
worried about some stray bullets, because the Hueys had
proven in Vietnam that they could soak up gunfire and
keep flying. Bullets were not the threat, but there might
be a veil of deadly gas outside his cockpit.

Juba slammed the big side doors shut, found a dry
towel, and wiped his face and arms and hands hard, staring straight ahead at the big drops hitting the broad front
windows, some of them coalescing into pools. *Rain or
gas?* He didn't know.

The pilot made an emergency takeoff, kicking the
helicopter to full throttle to let the powerful downdraft of
the overhead blades dissipate any gathering fumes. They
had to get out of the zone. The tail of the Huey rose sharply
up and the heavy nose was almost pointed at the ground;
then the lift began as the skids came off the ground. The
bird, slowly at first and then more rapidly, sailed along
the meadow and then made a sudden jump into the sky,
climbing high and fast away from the burning site. No

one else had made it out to the field, and the pilot didn't really care.

Kyle saw the third bodyguard hiding behind a Jeep and spraying wildly with an AK-47. The man did not know what he was shooting at and was just throwing out a hail of bullets in hopes of making the attackers duck, or at least pause. Above the racket, Swanson had clearly heard the man shout the name of Juba, but he could not take time to analyze who he was calling to. Swanson pinned the scope on him and saw something happening to his target that made him pause before squeezing the trigger.

The Chechnyan not only stopped firing but dropped his weapon and slapped at his skin. His face was twisted in surprise and then in pain. The bubble of poison gas released by the attack had crawled over the bodyguard, and he was trying to rub it away. Then he began to breathe it, and he stood and ran, as if there were some shelter, grabbing at his throat as if strangling. Kyle understood that the man was trying to reach the water hose and maybe scrub away the lethal drops that were congealing into a gel on his body.

Not going to happen, Skippy. Swanson adjusted the scope, following the movement, and fired. The bullet dropped the bodyguard in his tracks, hitting low on the back, just below the kidneys, and the man crashed and bounced on the dirt. Kyle had not wanted to make a kill shot, just to bring him down. In the view of the sniper, the bastard was not a candidate for an easy death. The man tried to crawl but gave up and rolled on the ground as the gas went into his lungs. He lay there with his chest heaving, turning purple in the face as he choked to death on his own fluids.

"Cease fire. Cease fire," Swanson called to Tipp and

Hughes. "The gas has them now. Let their little miracle finish them off."

"Shoot them!" demanded Delara.

"No need," Kyle replied. "What those men did to your brother is now happening to them. I will kill any who might survive."

"One got away on the helicopter," noted Joe Tipp. "I tried to nail him, but he was low and moving fast."

"Yeah. I took a shot at the Huey, but it was too far away for the Dragunov." *Juba? Now that would be an interesting twist to things.* Kyle stood up. Fire raged in the container area but was not spreading to the building. A dozen bodies lay on the ground, three still twitching in the embrace of the poison in their bodies. "Anyway, the site is open. We'll wait for a little while to let that shit burn off or blow away before going in."

A slow thirty minutes passed and an uneasy stillness came to the area, as if nature were eager to take back the dead zone. Things someday would grow here again. No curious soldiers came looking for the source of the shooting and explosions because the all-clear siren had never sounded.

The light rain began falling heavier, which would help dampen the traces of the gas.

"I want to bury my brother," said Delara.

Kyle was eating an MRE ration. "I don't think we can do that. The body is contaminated now, and we don't know what the stuff is. In fact, you probably should not even look at it, and you definitely cannot touch him."

She was also standing. "I don't care. He was my brother. I cannot just leave him out there."

"As much as I hate it, we have to leave them all out there. We are taking a huge risk just going into the building for a few minutes." He stuffed the half-eaten ration back into his pack. "Look, Miss Tabrizi. Whatever was being concocted down there obviously is one of the greatest weapons-grade poison gases ever created. A real terrorists' cocktail, and we don't know its properties—sarin, ricin, anthrax, whatever. We have seen how it kills without conscience, and the bad guys have it, which means thousands of people are now in jeopardy. Your brother gave his life fighting these maniacs, so don't you think he would want you to do everything you can to bring them down?"

She was near him. Delara knew what he said was true, but . . . "He is my brother," she whispered softly.

She looked so small, and there were tears in her eyes. Kyle stepped close and wrapped his arms around her. "I know. I am so very sorry."

"Our chopper will be here in ten minutes, Shake. Let's do it." Travis Hughes had his MOPP suit on.

"Right. Tipp, you cover us from up here with the RPK, then take Miss Tabrizi over to the field where that other helo was. Make that the designated landing zone."

"I want to go with you!" Delara's response was immediate.

"No. You really don't," Kyle answered, but with a gentle tone instead of that of a combat commander. "You will want to remember your brother as who he was. You don't want your last memory of him to be a close view of what they did. Please, Delara, I'm asking that you stay here with Joe. Travis and I are doing a quick search and then we're out of there. Speed is necessary, and you would slow us down . . . maybe put us all in danger."

He and Hughes were already moving, leaving no time for discussion. Delara watched them go and turned to Joe Tipp, who was scanning the area with his binos. "He's right. Let's finish this and get out of here," said Tipp. "Kyle is good at this stuff. Trust him."

"Kyle? That is his name?"

"Oh, shit," Tipp said. "Forget I said that."

Swanson and Hughes moved as cautiously as if skating on frozen glass, determined to touch nothing unless absolutely necessary. They ignored the bodies and the exterior destruction and, wading through a thin film of lingering smoke, moved into the building. The mist was gone, but rain was coming down harder.

The body of the man they recognized as the leader of the scientists was on the floor, killed not by the gas but by two bullets to the back of the head at close range. Hughes had his camera running and took pictures as Kyle probed deeper into the office area, his weapon at the ready. A pile of papers had been thrown onto the floor. File drawers hung open. Desks were empty.

The door at the far end of the room stood open, and the two Marines started downstairs. The lights were still on, and they entered a spacious area of several rooms crammed with laboratory equipment and electronics gear. Every computer had been destroyed, the screens smashed and the hard drives removed and crushed. Shelves were lined with covered containers, and at one end was a sterile room that could be entered only through an airlock. It was empty except for more counters and scientific gear.

The place seemed to Kyle to mirror the one they had been in earlier in southern Iran, only this one was still intact. He shuddered to think of the experiments that went on in this place. Through another door and down more stairs. A storehouse of material, and smaller areas that indicated mess and health care facilities. The place was like an underground pyramid, with plenty of space at the bottom and narrowing to that single administrative area on the top. Down low was where the really dirty work was done, and Kyle, followed by Travis, went carefully to the bottom floor and finally into the individual spokes and tunnels. He breathed easier when they found that the dungeon cages were empty. All of the prisoners had been taken out and executed this morning. On the side of one of the cells, they found someone had used a rock to scratch numbers into the concrete wall—999. Hughes took pictures.

"Nothing more down here, Trav. Let's go back up and gather those papers, then get out of here." Kyle led the way back into sunlight, almost feeling the dark shadows pulling at him from down below, trying to take him into a cell and lock the door. He shook it off.

Travis stepped to the front door and waved up to Joe Tipp. It was time to get moving. "All clear," Tipp acknowledged on the radio. "Bird inbound."

Kyle took down a pair of white biohazard suits hanging on the wall and tossed one to Travis, and they both stuffed the papers on the floor into the garments. Scientific records, notebooks, computer disks and office documents, letters and notes, but they did not know if it was treasure or trash. Finally, Kyle searched the body of the director and found a cell phone and a wallet. He threw both into the makeshift sack. "Let's go," he said.

They trotted through the rain, letting the water wash off anything that might have clung to their suits. Joe Tipp was in the open, guiding the helicopter down, while Delara Tabrizi stood to the side.

Kyle and Travis stopped just outside the radius of the powerful rotor blast and peeled out of their biosuits, leaving them on the ground before they climbed into the Pave Low.

"What did you find?" Tipp asked, pointing to the two bulging white biosuits on the floor. The sleeves and arms were folded tight, but loose papers stuck from the neck openings.

"Don't know. I'm not a scientist," said Travis, "but whatever it is, I think the intel pukes will be having wet dreams for the next month or so."

14

PARIS

Juba had never been so scared. Not in his entire life. In the first twenty-four hours after escaping from the contaminated biochemical weapons site, he took five showers and still was almost mad with worry that he would never be truly cleansed.

His helicopter had landed at a small airport, where he showered and found fresh clothes, then abandoned the aircraft. The helicopter pilot was killed and the body hidden in the equipment shed; then Juba hired a small plane and flew back to Tehran. He was out of Iran on the first available international flight.

Only when he checked into the Four Seasons Hotel in Qatar did he begin to breathe easier, and immediately after being shown into the suite, he got into a shower with water as hot as he could stand, imagining that some of the deadly gel particles were sticking to him even then, burrowing beneath his skin, reaching for his guts and his brain.

He repeatedly coated himself with soap and shampoo, working the suds hard beneath the downpour of scalding water until his skin was red and raw. He turned his face into the falling stream and felt it cook. He vigorously scrubbed between his toes, the bottoms of his feet, deeply into his ears, beneath his crotch, fingernails, nostrils, everywhere. Shampoo the eyebrows and under the armpits, and even the pubic hair and the crevice of his butt.

Steam rose from his body when he turned off the water and stepped from the stall onto the cool tiles and wrapped himself in thick white towels. Wait—what if he had swallowed some of it? He brushed his teeth until the gums bled and gargled with antiseptic mouthwash. He studied the blood on the toothbrush and threw it away.

Moving into the bedroom, he noticed the full-length mirror. He dropped the towels and stood before it for a long time, examining his entire body, turning slowly, looking for rashes and lesions. Then he climbed beneath the covers, only to be seized again by unreasoning panic and break into a sweat. He rushed to the bathroom for another shower, his thoughts anchored on the memory reef of the prisoners dying, trapped in the small cages as the gas ate at them. Every itch he felt was magnified a thousand times, the lingering fear intensified by the knowledge that he had helped make the monster that was trying to devour him. Juba was new to fear, for he had never been frightened by any enemy. This invisible slayer was different, hungry and uncaring about who was right or who was wrong, nor obedient to its creator.

After a few hours and another shower, he calmed enough to have the concierge send someone to purchase new clothes from the nearby mall, and later had a nice dinner at a table overlooking the expanse of the Arabian Gulf. When he returned to his room, he called for a massage, then lay still in bed between clean sheets while the masseur pounded the twisted muscles, loosening the knots with pressure and pain. Afterward, Juba turned out the light, and to avoid thinking about the invisible gas and the wet drops that brought certain death, he concentrated on the long and tangled journey that had brought him to this place on this day.

As a boy, back when he was Jeremy Mark Osmand, he was teased at school in England for having a foreign father and for being a Muslim, although that stopped as he grew taller and stronger and fought anyone who belittled his family. Despite his superior abilities in rugby and soccer, he still heard the ridicule that swam just below the surface of many of his classmates' polite geniality.

In the summer of 1988, his parents took him to Peshawar, in the North-West Frontier Province of Pakistan, where his father joined the surgical staff at a Red Crescent hospital while his mother helped at the refugee center. They lived in a house among the eucalyptus trees of University Town, and from there, Jeremy set out each day to explore the boomtown spawned by the Russian invasion of neighboring Afghanistan. Spies and journalists, Russian planes overhead, distant explosions, the hubbub of the Smugglers' Market and a crush of people, animals, and vehicles of all sorts and every color. Weapons and ammunition were strapped to the backs of trains of mules headed for the border.

The war was an awakening of an Islamic spirit within the boy, and in mosques and youth meetings, Jeremy discovered that London was not the center of the universe after all!

He learned much more about the Prophet and the holy places and was astonished to discover that the mighty Ottoman Empire was not an ancient myth. Although it had begun back in 1300, it lasted until 1924. Its creation was led by the venerable Osman I! His family's original last name was the same as that great caliph, and Jeremy questioned his father's decision to bastardize and anglicize it. "Come with me to the hospital today and I will give you the answer," his father said one morning as they sipped strong black coffee. "One of my fellow physicians wants to meet you."

Within the hour, Jeremy was at a small table in the rear of a coffee house near the hospital, deep in conversation, in English, with Dr. Ayman al-Zawahiri, the Muslim firebrand who had been jailed and tortured following the assassination of Egyptian president Anwar Sadat. He had come to Peshawar to help the mujahideen freedom fighters, and Jeremy was spellbound by the intense man with the large eyeglasses, who made sense with his stern and unforgiving religious and political views.

Then someone else joined their group, a tall and slender man who wore common robes although he possessed great wealth. Osama bin Laden was from Saudi Arabia and was famed for lectures that painted a dark vision of Islam and reasoned that it was not only permissible to kill infidels: Under the Koran, it was a Muslim duty. Bin Laden extended a hand and uttered a soft greeting, then encouraged the boy to speak, and Jeremy's new dreams of revenge and hatred spilled forth. Jeremy promised that he was a true Muslim and ready to die, today if necessary, for Islam.

The tall Saudi touched the boy's forearm. "No, not today. Not for a long time." He glanced at Dr. Osmand. "Were you aware that your father has long been one of us?"

Jeremy blinked as his father bowed at the compliment. "It was at our request that he has endured such shame among the infidels, and the Prophet will reward him."

"Father? I don't understand. What is he talking about?"

"Our name, Jeremy," the father replied. "You believe I changed our name for mere advancement in English society. That is not what happened."

Al-Zawahiri interrupted. "Many years ago, I formed

the Muslim Brotherhood in Egypt and brought it forward into the Islamic Jihad, and now into al Qaeda. Part of our early work was to create what intelligence services call 'moles' who would infiltrate foreign countries and be ready to strike when needed. Your father volunteered to help in this cause and was asked to eradicate the automatic Muslim link of his name so that you, Jeremy Osmand, would have a true British name, speak like a native of England, and act British. Your father has been a loyal soldier." The dark eyes burned into Jeremy. "Now it is your turn."

"So, young man, you will not become a martyr today," added Osama bin Laden. "Praise be unto Allah, we have plenty of recruits ready to do that vital work. Yours is a special task that will require years to accomplish."

Jeremy stared at the two leaders of the most violent sector of militant Islam. They wanted him!

Al-Zawahiri's tone changed. No more polite chitchat or explanations, just a stream of orders. Jeremy was to become as English as he could be, join the British Army and become skilled in its ways, let the army give him as much specialized training as possible.

Osama bin Laden said, "You must shed any trace of Islam. Your present knowledge of the Koran must sustain you, for you must not read it again for many years, nor even have a copy. You will eat the flesh of the filthy animal, drink alcohol, walk without a beard, be profane, and fornicate with their women. At times, you may even have to fight against Muslims, and you will do so with your utmost ability, for there must be no question as to your loyalty. When the time is right, we will call you."

"Turn away from Islam? I don't know if I can do that, sir."

"That is the answer we expected from you, Jeremy. To satisfy that disturbing thought, a council of holy men has granted a special absolution to excuse the many sins you must commit in the future." Bin Laden leaned close. "Follow us, young man. We have heavy hearts in requiring someone to abandon the Prophet here on earth in order to sit with him in paradise. Sadly, you will pretend— and live—as if we are your enemies. The forces of the Prophet are already defeating the atheist Russians in Afghanistan, but we must plan ahead. Great wars will come against the Jews and Crusaders before our final victory. Will you help us protect Islam?"

"Yes. Of course I will," Jeremy replied, and his father squeezed the shoulder of his sixteen-year-old son.

"Then we will give you a new name. To everyone else, you will continue to be Jeremy. But when we summon you, you will become Juba, named for a village created by fierce warriors many years ago along the White Nile in Africa. You will be our own fierce warrior."

Jeremy graduated from school the very next year and joined the British Royal Marines. When the shooting instructors saw his skill with a rifle, he was sent to sniper school and then moved to advanced training for special operations, including workouts and instruction at the U.S. Marines Scout Sniper School at Camp Pendleton over in America. Every fitness report glowed with praise, and senior sergeants said they had never worked with anyone so dedicated. He rose in rank to color sergeant ahead of his peers and earned the badge of a master sniper, along with other gongs and citations.

Just a natural, said the other bootnecks. Best stalker and shooter in the game, and in a firefight, I want to see the green lid and Lovats of Color Osmand from 42 Commando at my side.

Early in the spring of 2001, Dr. al-Zawahiri sent the message: It was time for Juba. He resigned from the Royal

Marines, dropped out of sight, and was in Peshawar on the first day of September.

It was there that he watched the attacks on the World Trade Center and the Pentagon, which were shown continuously on television. Thousands of Muslims took to the streets in mad celebration. *Enjoy it while you can,* Juba thought. The Taliban was only a mob of thugs, not a real army, and had never even been able to defeat the ragtag Northern Alliance. He knew the oncoming international force of professionals would have no trouble rolling over them. *You're going to take it right up the bum, mates, and there's really not a damned thing you can do about it.*

He was standing ready, finely tuned and bred for battle, but he was dispatched instead to set up training camps in Afghanistan and Pakistan. Volunteers were pouring in to fight the expected invasion, but there was going to be no time to train them. Anyway, they did not want to be trained: They just wanted to blow themselves up in the faces of their enemy and become martyrs. Juba tried to convince them they probably would never even get close enough to an American soldier to do that. No discipline, organization, tactics, or marksmanship, just the wild firing of bullets. He even killed several of the fools as punishment, but even that made no impression on the others. When he asked for new assignments elsewhere, he was ordered to do the job assigned to him.

The air campaign smashed in like a thunderstorm and slashed the Taliban with everything from superb man-hunting Apache helicopters to F/A-18 Hornet fighter-bombers to Daisy Cutter bombs that weighed seven and one-half tons to AC-130 gunships that spewed bullets in incredible swaths. Not a single plane was lost, but the Taliban front line peeled open like a tin can.

Incredibly, in the face of the disaster, a Taliban leader patiently explained to Juba that things were really going well. The strategy was just to draw in the American army and bleed it slowly over the years, not defeat it. Eventually, Washington would give up, just as they did in Vietnam and the Russians had done in Afghanistan.

Juba argued that it might not happen that way and pleaded to be allowed to create a special strike unit that could exploit the Americans' vulnerabilities. He knew this enemy! He was ignored.

The Afghan capital of Kabul fell only two months after the 9/11 attacks, and the developing ground campaign then destroyed Taliban units all through the country, until they found safe refuge in the defensive positions of Tora Bora and the White Mountains along the Pakistan border.

Juba at last was allowed to form a guerrilla group to attack supply lines and targets of opportunity, but his small team was soon swept back into the overall force, and Juba found himself in charge of troops who had no stomach for real warfare and retreated under the slightest pressure. There were many caves in which they could hide.

In frustration, Juba cursed the day he had met Osama bin Laden and Dr. al-Zawahiri. Their whole grand plan was a bust. He believed there should have been an entire series of attacks and responses ready to follow up on September 11, while the United States was almost totally unprotected, unsure, and reeling. Why weren't bombs going off in cities across America and around the world to keep the enemy off balance? Attack! They should never have allowed the U.S. military to catch its breath. Lies. Al Qaeda had fed him lies. He believed in continuing violence to accomplish military goals, while bin Laden and al-Zawahiri believed in . . . what?

He had no desire to spend a bitter Afghan winter holed up in some freezing Tora Bora cave, waiting for a cruise missile to fall on his head. The war had evolved into a gigantic game of hide-and-shoot, and that was something that ex–Color Sergeant Jeremy Osmand, a master sniper of the Royal Marines, could do better by himself. He did not want, nor need, to be around this mob. He decided to carve a personal, ruthless, and bloody path into the heart of the enemy.

After the disaster at the biochem site in Iran, Juba spent two days luxuriating at the Four Seasons in Qatar, pampering himself and letting the fear of the deadly gel recede from the forefront of his consciousness. To his surprise, he did not die.

He booked a Lufthansa flight to Paris, with a brief layover in Frankfurt, Germany, and took a cab straight to the house in the Nineteenth Arrondissement.

Saladin was concerned the moment he laid eyes on Juba. He looked like a man who was crawling out of a pit of despair. "Talk to me, my son," he said. "What has happened?"

Juba handed over the briefcase. "The experiment was successful, and I confess it was difficult to watch. Afterward, we were attacked and the canisters of the gas exploded. I barely made it out alive."

"Who did this?"

"I don't know. Maybe some politicals trying to free some of the test subjects." He rubbed his palms over his eyes. "No one survived except me and the helicopter pilot. It was too dangerous to allow him to live."

Saladin walked to the windows and looked out. It was a bright and pleasant day. "Can you continue?"

"Of course," Juba said. "I was just shaken by the thought that the gas had gotten to me. I am ready."

Saladin opened the briefcase. "This is everything about the formula?"

Juba nodded. "Yes. The site was almost empty, and the rest of the computers and paperwork were destroyed during the attack. We should go ahead and transmit this data to the facility in Mexico. Prepare enough of the gas for the demonstration."

"And you are certain that you will be able to continue on schedule?"

"Without a doubt," Juba replied. "I can be in the United States by the end of the week."

That brought a smile to Saladin. His man was still strong. Anyone can stumble at some time. "There is no urgency about that, so I would like for you to stay here for a while. We will study and talk and let you prepare for the mission ahead. I will send the formula today, but our lab in Mexico will still need some time to produce the gas and transport it."

"Thank you, Father."

"And you look as if you could use some good news, my son, so let me give you some: We already have six entries for the auction. That's sixty million dollars before the real bidding even begins, and I expect more."

"They will all come after us."

"They can try." Saladin laughed. "They can certainly try, but with you running our security, they will certainly fail. We will leave this house together and return to America in a few days, so if our enemies want us, they will have to first enter the U.S., which will be on very high alert. Then, after we collect the money, you and I shall just disappear."

15

On arrival back at the Marine base outside of Fallujah, Swanson turned over the captured material to an intelligence officer who had been awaiting the helicopter. Sybelle Summers was also at the pad, wearing a dark green sweater and black jeans, a small pistol tucked into a black leather waist holster. She looked over the Marines as they hopped from the bird. They seemed okay. Her first look at Delara Tabrizi made her smile, for the small woman seemed like a child among the heavily armed special ops team, but her walk was steady and confident. For a woman who had been a civilian schoolteacher only a few hours ago, and had since endured two major raids and seen her friend and her brother slain, she had done okay, Sybelle decided. A sister.

Swanson, Tipp, and Hughes brought Delara over, and Sybelle led them to a small office she had used in supporting the mission. "Not that I care, but the brass is raising hell about this unauthorized job," she said, plopping into the chair behind the desk and putting her boots on the top. "We didn't get enough papers stamped and authorized and all that bullshit."

Kyle dropped his gear on the floor. "Doesn't matter.

What we found and brought back will more than shut up the critics. Loads of recordings of voices, papers and records, some computer disks, pictures. And eyewitness accounts of how this new poison gas works."

"Can Tipp and Travis do the debrief by themselves?"

"Sure. They saw everything I did, and Trav took the pictures."

"Good," said Sybelle, "because you and I are out of here."

Kyle agreed. He needed to keep his cover intact, and that would be hard on a base filled with Marines. "Then I want to take Miss Tabrizi along with us. I don't want her falling into the system. Once she is debriefed, the intel pukes will hand her to the political types, and God only knows where she will end up. She helped us a lot. We owe her."

Delara was seated, watching the exchange. The woman was obviously an important person and spoke to the Marine like an equal, but they were talking about her fate. "I cannot return to Iran!" she said. "I want to kill these people who made this poison!"

Sybelle laughed quietly and looked over at Kyle. "So let's take her out to the boat with us and let Jeff figure it out. He has a ton of diplomatic contacts and is good at that sort of thing."

"Who is this Jeff?" Delara asked. "What are you going to do with me?"

Kyle touched her shoulder, and she immediately relaxed. "Jeff is a good friend, and by the time he finishes working his magic, you will pretty much have anything you want. A new country and a new future. A new you."

Sybelle was on her feet. "Joe and Travis, we'll leave you here. Good job, guys. Thanks for the help."

"Sure, Captain," said Tipp. "Anytime."

"Y'all take good care of our girl Delara," called Travis Hughes. "I already taught her how to say Semper Fi!"

A Humvee was parked outside, and the three of them got into it, with Sybelle at the wheel. "I didn't want to mention it in there, but there's another reason we have to get back on board the *Vagabond*." She glanced back at Delara, whose eyes were already closed.

"The Lizard has flown out from Washington to meet us there. You have a Green Light package."

"I would like to get some sleep first."

"And I would like to be thinner," Sybelle said. "Neither is likely."

The Lizard had everything ready when Swanson, Sybelle, and Delara flew out to the *Vagabond*. Delara was turned over to Lady Pat for the time being, while Sybelle and Kyle met in Sir Jeff's private office with Lieutenant Commander Freedman. A big pile of documents was at the Lizard's side, and his computer was already running on secure circuits.

"This is the voice of Ahmad Hikmat Aseer, a known al Qaeda operative, in conversation with another al Qaeda leader. The NSA Big Ears picked it up. The caller is so furious that he ignored normal security precautions and made contact from his home telephone." The Lizard tapped his keyboard and turned up the volume. A torrent of French sprang from the speakers in an angry and threatening tone, so fast that Kyle could not follow the words. It sounded like the guy was spitting on himself in his rage.

The Lizard handed transcripts to Sybelle and Kyle. "It seems that Ahmad had a brother named Youcef, who happened to be the head of al Qaeda operations in France. Youcef's body was found floating in a Paris canal several days ago. That's when Ahmad made this call."

Kyle read carefully. Ahmad said that his brother was last seen alive before an important meeting at his home in Paris with the outcasts Saladin and his bodyguard Juba.

"They killed him and his own guards in his own house!" Ahmad Hikmat Aseer sputtered. "Not only that, the arrogant pigs have confiscated the house as their own!"

He demanded revenge, insisting that al Qaeda send in an execution team, and that was when the other man realized the danger of the call and challenged Ahmad about making it. He hung up.

"By then it was too late; the Big Ears had it. NSA gave it to the CIA, and they turned up an address in Paris for the deceased Youcef Aseer."

"So why give us a Green Light? Let the CIA handle it." Sybelle skimmed the transcript again.

"I don't know that. Too far above my pay grade. I could guess that if the CIA mucks up the arrest of Saladin, there would be an embarrassing trail back to Washington. Anyway, General Middleton gave me the assignment to brief you and get you on your way. I have a military jet standing by on shore. You're going to Paris."

"What about me?" asked Sybelle.

"We go, but to a support point in a separate location. Kyle comes back there when he finishes."

"When do we leave?"

"Now," the Lizard said.

PARIS

The Lizard had reserved him a businessman's suite at a nondescript and out-of-the-way hotel that catered to executives of companies that did not allow lavish expense accounts. Paris on the cheap. Kyle checked in without any problem. He called down to room service for a steak and salad and a bottle of water. The sun would be setting soon and he could move. Then he stripped down and got under a shower, alternating hot and cold water.

He let it cascade over him for five minutes. Drying off

afterward, Swanson stared into the brightly lit bathroom mirror and did not particularly like the man he saw looking back. Bleary-eyed, tired, the mouth a grim line, and blue-gray eyes as hard as stones. The tanned body was nicked with scars and the puckered skin of healed bullet holes. His hair had returned to its normal shade of brown from streaky surfer blond. He splashed more water on his face and went back to bed, with the Glock 17 pistol handy on the night table. *Are the weapons still just tools, an extension of me, or have I become an extension of them and what the fuck kind of question is that, anyway?* He laced his fingers behind his head on the fluffy pillow. A psychiatrist would have said he was undergoing severe depression. Swanson believed this was deeper than any shrink's diagnosis. *I think I am about one step away from going nuts. One small step for man, one giant leap for me.*

There was a knock on the door, and he put on a robe, picked up his Glock, and answered. A waiter pushed in the food cart. Kyle unwrapped his hand from around the Glock in the pocket of the robe and signed the check with a generous tip. He pushed the plastic DO NOT DISTURB card into the exterior electronic key slot and closed the door.

He surfed the television channels while he ate the steak, watching British newscasters, CNN and Fox, and American sitcoms translated into French. Nothing. Kyle pushed away the food cart, washed his hands again, and then smoothed a white towel over the tufted bedspread. He spread out his personal weapons, which he had been able to keep in his possession because they had come in on a military flight and did not have to go through customs.

Glock, Ruger, Gerber. Marine armorers had given both pistols Limited Technical and Procedural Firing Inspections before he had left for the Middle East, but they needed a good cleaning after the raids into Iran. He opened a small gun-cleaning kit and arranged the toothbrush, the bore brush, cotton swabs, the vial of oil, and a soft rag.

The push of a lever in front of the trigger took off the slide of the Glock, leaving the pistol in two pieces, the barrel assembly and the butt. With the slide out, he removed the spring and began a careful examination to see that nothing was frayed or chipped. A look down the barrel confirmed it was neither dented nor warped. He only wiped down the butt section, because doing a proper job on an intricate trigger assembly was the task of a gunsmith. Swanson spent five minutes cleaning it, then reassembled the Glock and did an ops check to make sure it worked. He pointed it at the mirror on the back of the door. The trigger clicked on empty.

He had four magazines with fifteen rounds in each clip, and Kyle thumbed out the bullets one by one to personally examine them for any defect. The shiny brass cartridges were laid out side by side on the white towel, gleaming in the overhead light, each a marvelous little piece of engineering built precisely by Beretta to fit the barrel of the 9 mm pistol. They were all soft-tipped rounds designed to avoid a ricochet indoors. The bullet would create an entry wound as small as a dime, but once it slammed into bone, the soft nose would splinter with the impact of a small grenade and shred everything around it. It was not supposed to exit the body. Swanson always enjoyed watching movies in which shooters used their knives to carve an *X* on the tip of a bullet to make it open up. Fantasy. The rounds were already designed to do that. Start screwing around with your rounds and you will screw up the barrel and the accuracy of the weapon; then you are the one who is screwed. He reloaded the magazines.

The little Ruger five-shot revolver was even easier, but the maintenance was performed with the same amount of care. Open the cylinder, visually inspect it, clean it, load it, and bingo, it was ready. The Gerber knife was easier still. Just wipe down the blade, which gleamed along the cutting edge that had been honed in the armorer's shop. Field strip and op check on all weapons. Good to go.

Comfortable with his personal arsenal, he slipped into his night outfit: black jeans, black sneakers and socks, long-sleeved black turtleneck T-shirt, and black windbreaker. A woolen balaclava mask was rolled up into a watch cap and adjusted for a firm fit and so his eyes could see out of the openings. The Gerber went into one pocket; the Ruger was on his ankle and the Glock snug in the shoulder rig. He turned out the lights and lay on the bed to let his eyes adjust to the gathering darkness.

Swanson closed his eyes and lay there for thirty minutes, breathing slowly, trying not to fall asleep because he had work to do tonight. Thoughts of Shari Towne flitted at the edge of his consciousness. As a lieutenant commander in the Navy, she had been given a hero's funeral at Arlington, her coffin rolled to the gravesite on a horse-drawn carriage. The box was virtually empty because she had been riddled by gunfire and blown apart by two satchels of explosives. There was no family present at the funeral. Shari's father had died years before, and her beautiful mother died in the same attack that stole Shari's life. Shari was the end of the family line.

Kyle wasn't there for the ceremony because he had been stashed in a secret medical clinic abroad recovering from bullet wounds of his own. He now considered it ironic that he and Shari were both officially buried at Arlington, yet neither was really in that hallowed dirt. He felt that they were still together, and she occasionally visited him in dreams that were so vivid he could describe exactly what she was wearing. They could not speak to each other, they could not touch, but they could be together for an almost tangible moment, no more than a heartbeat, and she always had that glorious smile. Now another face was also showing up, unbidden, in his thoughts, that of Delara Tabrizi.

Stop it, he commanded himself. *This is getting me nowhere. Keep on the mission, and the other stuff will sort itself out. God, I need some rest.*

Green Light. That order came straight from the top. Finding out so unexpectedly where the man known as Saladin was provided a very narrow window of opportunity. This was the person responsible for the poison gas attack on London, and he was now blackmailing the world. The decision was made to take him off the board while there was a chance and to seize the formula and plans for the weapon. The president was absolutely right that the United States did not assassinate people. But the dead man who used to be Kyle Swanson did.

Darkness had fallen, and it was raining when he opened the window, a nice French rain that alternated between a fine mist and a wet mop in the face. Anyone watching would avoid looking upward, and amateurs would seek shelter. Since he had turned off the lights, the assumption would be that he was sleeping. Three floors below, an alley stretched along the back of the hotel. Empty. No darker shadows huddled within the other shadows.

Kyle stuffed a hotel towel into his jacket, stepped through the window onto a ledge, faced the wall, and closed the window behind him.

The Lizard had provided maps and layouts from satellite imagery and building blueprints, and the room had been chosen because of its proximity to steel latticework erected for some outside renovation. The Lizard had measured it to be exactly eleven feet from the window. Kyle scooted carefully along the wet ledge, grabbed the scaffolding, and was down in the alley in seconds. He went into the shadows of a garbage bin, dried off with the towel, and tossed it.

Turning his back to the street and cupping his hand to shield the light, he pushed a button and the dial of his watch illuminated with a soft blue glow. It was almost 2200 on the dot, two hours before midnight, and Paris was open for business.

Swanson used a combination of taxis and the subway system, frequently doubling back and walking through stores to check for followers, and only when he was convinced that he was alone did he edge to the northeast and into the Nineteenth Arrondissement.

The first time past the house, he had a cab drive aimlessly around for ten minutes, and they passed the small compound without slowing. He got out of the taxi four blocks away at a small restaurant, where he went in, ordered a glass of red wine, and made a cell phone call.

Sybelle arrived within twenty minutes, dry and playing the part of a girlfriend. "Hi," she said and touched his hand. She sat down at his table and also ordered a glass of wine, and Kyle explained what they needed to do. Urban warfare is a sniper's specialty because all windows and buildings and fences offer places to set up a hide. He had no intention of allowing the coming fight to be fair, and he and Sybelle could check out the place as a couple on the street without arousing suspicion. They would look for ways to tilt the playing field in Kyle's favor.

Swanson put some money on the table, and the two of them left, squeezing beneath Sybelle's small black umbrella. They approached the house from the north, walking slowly along the old sidewalk, with Kyle's arm around her waist. She snuggled closer and giggled, working on the cover as both of them swept the area with their eyes and ears.

Saladin had strong security. Two sentries stood in the courtyard, and newly mounted cameras were at all corners to watch the surrounding streets and the interior grounds. Guard on the roof. A street person stumbled past them, drinking from a bottle. External surveillance. Plus whoever was inside. Probably an alarm system. Not just good security, Kyle thought, but too much. Like they were expecting someone. *Me?*

Sybelle and Kyle walked back to the restaurant, and she pulled a pair of night vision goggles and small binoculars from her purse and handed them to Swanson. He would go back out onto the rain-slick streets now for a deeper recon from the shadows. "I'll have some coffee so I can be close by if you need backup," she said.

"I assume you saw everything that I did," Kyle said. He had a puzzled look. "But did you feel that something seemed out of place back there?"

She crossed her arms. "That flicker of light at the window of the corner building. Somebody else is watching that place."

"Yeah," said Kyle. "We're not the only game in town."

16

Kyle Swanson did not try to intellectualize the assassination. He had been ordered to do the job and given free rein to carry it out. Besides, he believed that the bastard had earned this as the price for organizing the London attack on a crowd of innocent people and for slaughtering prisoners in awful experiments. The only question that Swanson had was how soon he could pull the trigger, then go into the madman's lair and get the data on the poison gas. It had eluded him in Iran, and he did not want to miss again.

The morning after his scouting mission, he had decided on a plan of attack and needed some things. After a quiet breakfast of coffee, a warm croissant, and fresh fruit, he went downtown to find a good sporting goods store that specialized in alpine equipment. Explaining that he was heading off to do some climbing, Swanson bought a mountaineering axe, some good gloves, a pocket set of Zeiss binoculars, a puffy down jacket, and a black hard hat with a battery lamp attached.

He returned to the area near Saladin's house and scouted for a small quiet street, finding just what he needed only three blocks away. Two warehouses backed against each other, and their windowless rear walls were separated by a shade-filled alley. Using the sharp, curved end of the new mountain axe, he quickly pulled up a sewer lid, climbed down and slid the lid back into position, and put on the hard hat with the bright lamp. With the beam of light boring a hole in the darkness, Swanson began to walk.

Paris had 1,400 miles of sewers, and compared to some places he had hidden during his military career, they were almost comfortable. The sewers were usually as wide as the streets above them, and a channel of water carried the waste down the middle. The walls and ceilings held an orderly array of cables and pipes for electrical circuits and drinking water. Street signs in the caverns were the same as the street signs above.

He easily found his way through the tunnels for a few blocks and stopped at the grate on the curb directly across from the courtyard of Saladin's place. He stepped up on a ledge and brought the Zeiss binos to his eyes, settling in to watch the place and build a range card.

Promptly at 11:30 A.M., two burly guards entered the courtyard, looked around, and unlocked the parked sedan only after searching beneath it for explosives by using a mirror on a pole. One got into the driver's seat, and the second returned to the house and returned beside a slim, well-dressed, dark-skinned man. *Saladin?* The man was heading for lunch. Kyle watched throughout the day and about midafternoon chowed on a baguette with some cheese and an apple. Only when night fell did he return to the hotel and wash off the stink. He needed some help for the next step and went over to meet Sybelle and the Lizard. They had to work fast.

Lieutenant Commander Freedman stretched in his chair before the all-seeing eye of his laptop computer. "Interpol came up with the sketch of the guy they believe is Saladin, based on several sources, including the two al Qaeda operatives who were on the telephone. They were arrested yesterday."

Kyle only had to look at it for a moment. "That's the guy I saw in the courtyard," he confirmed. "The thin face and well-trimmed beard are pretty unique. That's him."

"Are the French cops going to hit the place?"

"Not yet," said the Lizard. "Everybody is still standing around creating elaborate plans. Being the French, I don't think they really want to make the arrest. They just want him to leave because he is a political embarrassment."

"Yeah." Time was ticking faster if others were getting ready to move. He had to be done before the authorities were in place to figure out what happened. Swanson finished a sketch of his plan, using maps that the Lizard had printed out, and gave them their assignments. "We're doing them a favor. When Saladin sticks his head out for lunch tomorrow, they won't have to worry about him anymore. Lizard, you find us a little SUV?"

"Waiting downstairs in the lot. A gray Peugeot 4007."

"Okay. Sybelle, give me a ride back to my hotel, then you do your thing and come back here. I should see you both tomorrow about noon at the front of the Air Museum, and we're gone."

Kyle returned to his room, showered, and took some time to clean the Dragunov sniper rifle he had brought along from Iraq. As soon as he had heard it was a Green Light mission, he had wanted a disposable and untraceable weapon. Then he lay down to sleep, telling his mind to awaken him two hours later, before dawn came.

Sybelle Summers telephoned an all-night mechanic and spoke in angry French. A neighbor had parked his blue BMW Mini in her assigned space again, after many requests not to do so, and she wanted to teach him a lesson by having the car towed and dumped in a vacant lot somewhere.

The mechanic said he was not interested and mentioned that it also was illegal. He was not a car thief, he said. She offered a hundred euros with no paper transaction that might lead back to him, and he wavered. At two hundred euros, he changed his mind. Business was slow this late at night.

Soon the tow truck arrived at the intersection the woman had designated, and she waved him down. Still angry, the driver thought, taking the money and watching as she pointed out the little car that was causing her troubles. Neighbors, he shrugged. He went to work, and within a few minutes, the tow truck vanished down the street with the little Mini hanging from its big hook. Sybelle slipped the rented Peugeot SUV into the spot, got out, locked the door, and walked away. The SUV was parked with its rear wheels just beyond the sewer grate and the high rear end shielding the opening from view, directly across from the gate to the courtyard of Saladin's house. A long, dark ribbon was tied to the rear bumper and moved in rhythm with the passing breeze.

Just before the sun came up, Kyle had disappeared again beneath another sewer lid, clicked on the light of his hard hat, and found his way back to the proper grate, this time with the Dragunov across his back. He snapped off the light before looking out of the grate, keeping the darkness as a guard against being spotted. He was satisfied with the protected and clear view of the courtyard.

The problem was going to be with the timing, for the target would be exposed for only a few seconds, while walking from the house to the automobile. Based on what he observed the previous day, there would be some warning when the bodyguards came into the courtyard first to be sure the area was clear. At that point, Kyle could bring up the rifle, but not before then. Sticking the barrel of a sniper rifle out of the opening of a hide was done only in movies, for it was almost as good as waving a flag. It would be seen, even as well concealed as he was.

The range could hardly be better, close enough to do the job even over the iron sights of an ordinary rifle. The target would appear huge and close in the Dragunov scope. He rolled up the big jacket he had bought and placed it along the ledge just inside the grate opening to provide a more stable shooting platform. He could keep an eye on the windage by watching the ribbon fluttering from the bumper of the Peugeot.

Swanson did not really want to think about how the task would change if Saladin did not go out for lunch today. Then he would have to use the rifle to pick off any outside guards and fight his way into the house, which was as strong as a fort. Too much noise, effort, and danger. But who could resist a nice lunch at a Paris café on a beautiful day such as this?

He drank some fruit juice, picked up his binos, and stood back in the shadows. He glassed the courtyard with intense concentration, for he knew the moment he let fatigue or boredom pull away his attention, the target would appear and then vanish before he could act. Cars and trucks rolled by, the wheels blowing trails of dirt and rocks behind them. The occasional pedestrian hurried along the sidewalk, and the cameras on the corner posts followed. Swanson stood motionless back in the darkness of the wide sewer, his center perfect over slightly spread legs, a position he could hold for incredible lengths of time. He emptied his mind as the minutes went by. For two hours, he remained immobile, except for an occasional stretching of his muscles. Then he changed position, moving closer to the narrow rectangular opening, leaning on the little shelf of molded concrete with his elbows, and continued to watch.

The first guard came out at 11:28 A.M., a muscular young man in pressed jeans, a white shirt, and an open sport coat. He walked out to the street, looked around, and searched the car. Unlocked it and got inside. Turned on the ignition.

Kyle put down the binos and raised the Dragunov, putting the end of the barrel onto the soft, rolled jacket at the inner edge of the sewer grate, with the Peugeot 4007 overhead hiding the opening. The ribbon moved only sluggishly, telling him the wind was not enough to change the scope. He let his breathing slow, and his heart rate, feeling the strap of the rifle dig into his left arm.

The second guard appeared, a large man in a cheap suit, also with no tie. His hand was at his back, beneath his jacket, probably grasping a pistol. This one stepped out of the courtyard and checked the street both ways. He went back to the front door and said something Kyle could not hear.

Saladin stepped into the open for the short walk to the automobile, no more than ten steps. The bodyguard moving ahead of him opened the door. Only forty meters separated Kyle from Saladin, who was talking on a cell phone as he walked, and the shot, when Swanson took it, was simple. Five steps, six steps, squeeze the trigger, and Saladin never made the seventh step. He was hurled upward by the force of the rising bullet and was tossed backward like a puppet whose strings had been cut, dead before he hit the ground. The bodyguard stared in surprise long enough for Kyle to shift the scope onto him and make a head shot.

The driver threw open his door and rolled out, with his

pistol drawn, but unable to see a target. Everything beyond the gate looked normal, and the tendency was to look up to find a sniper on a rooftop or in a high window. Kyle had him centered in the scope as the man searched for somebody to shoot at, and Swanson once again smoothly pulled the trigger. Since they were almost on the same level, the flat trajectory sent the bullet ripping into the guard's shoulder, then down through the chest and rib cage before exiting at the hip. He bucked under the impact, and the round wrecked his heart and lungs.

There was no time to waste now, and Kyle pulled the Dragunov back inside and dropped it into the deep sewage channel flowing behind him. A manhole cover was just above him, and he pushed it aside, grabbed the edges, and hoisted himself up and out, staying low behind the Peugeot. He pulled the silenced Glock from his waist and ran across the street, through the gates, and into the sun-dappled courtyard. Three shots, one into the head of each of his targets, and he was on his way inside.

"You see that? Who the hell is that?" asked a big man with binoculars pressed hard against his eyes. "He just shot our suspect!" Special Agent David Hunt of the Federal Bureau of Investigation was rocked back by the surprise attack and turned in disbelief to Carolyn Walker, an agent with the Department of Homeland Security. She had been seated, watching a small television set that was linked to the adjustable telescopic lens of a camera that had been recording all movements in the courtyard for the past two days. They, along with the CIA, were part of a joint task force assigned to watch the man believed to be Saladin, the person responsible for the London nerve gas assault. When word came from Washington, they would arrest him. The JTF room was on the fourth floor of an apartment building on a corner overlooking Saladin's house, which they believed gave them a total view of the entire area.

But the assassin had come out of nowhere, unseen and with no warning. Nevertheless, Walker now had him on the camera and was recording. She adjusted the focus on Kyle's face, and a USB connection fed the images onto a computer hard drive.

"I got him," she said. "What the hell is he up to? Let's go pick him up."

Dave Hunt threw down his powerful binoculars. A total stranger had barged into their operation and it had all gone to shit, right in the heart of France. "Can't do that, Carolyn. The French cops are going to be all over this place in ten minutes, and all hell will break loose if they find us up here."

He stuffed their equipment into large zippered bags, and Walker radioed the joint task force office within the U.S. Embassy to warn them what was happening. As Hunt and Walker ran down the back stairs and got into their dark SUV, more telephone calls were made and agents swung into action, happy to have something to do rather than sit around the office.

Juba was up and moving at the first loud *craaack!* of the Dragunov sniper rifle, knowing exactly what it was. Pistol in hand, he backed against the front wall and peered around the edge of the window, looking down into the courtyard. Saladin was down flat on the stones, in a spreading puddle of dark blood. As Juba watched, there was a second shot and one of the methodical, experienced, and handpicked bodyguards was blasted in the head, the bullet plowing all the way through the skull in a spray of blood and brain matter. Juba looked but could not see the sniper.

There was no time! It might be anybody, even the French,

and the house might now be assaulted by counterterrorism agents. It did not matter how they got this address or the name of Saladin. They just had it, and now Juba had to save himself. He stuck his pistol into his waistband and moved across the Persian carpet to the living room table.

He jerked the printer and power cables from the laptop and folded the computer into its black carrying case. All of the information about the deadly weapon was in that little case, and it had to be removed from harm's way. Outside, there was a third *craaack!* and Juba did not have to look to know that the other bodyguard was now dead, too. Neither of the guards had gotten off a shot at the sniper, which meant they never saw him.

The burgundy leather briefcase was beside the table, and he pulled it up and opened it, dumping out the contents except for travel documents and some passports bundled with a rubber band, along with a stack of American hundred-dollar bills that was in one corner. He put the small computer inside and closed the case.

The room was littered with documents and other computer gear that needed to be destroyed, but there was no time to individually shred or burn the items. The entire house would have to go. Juba had spent quite a bit of time planning for just such an emergency, and blocks of explosives were planted at key support points throughout the structure and wired to a detonator connected to a wall switch. He slapped the switch closed without hesitation, which gave him five minutes to leave the house before it blew up.

The noise of three soft, coughing shots came from the courtyard. Juba took the briefcase in his left hand and carried the pistol in his right. He went out, paused at the top of the landing, and snapped off some quick shots downstairs to discourage the intruder.

Juba spun around and headed down the back stairs,

putting solid walls between himself and whoever was at the front of the house. In thirty more seconds, he would be clear of the area and in his car, which was parked around the corner. With luck, he could make the 5:55 P.M. British Airways flight to Dulles International in Washington. He looked back over his shoulder, up the stairwell.

Kyle Swanson pushed his pistol around the corner of the front staircase and fired blindly, twice, then charged up the stairs as he heard the pounding of running feet, retreating in another direction. He took the stairs two at a time, his weapon in front of him, searching for a target.

A door slammed in back and he went that way, noticing the pile of papers in the living room, wondering if the magic formula was among them. Saladin was dead, and that formula was the remaining part of the mission, but he first had to be certain there was no other threat. Whoever was on the run had not continued the suppressing fire, but the footsteps were growing faint. Kyle kicked open the rear door and dove onto the landing of the staircase so the fleeing man below would not have a clear view. He was on his back and then rolled onto his belly with his Glock grasped in both hands as he looked over the top step. The wrought-iron supports for a long railing hindered his view.

Their eyes locked for an instant, and Juba and Shake recognized each other.

"You!" screamed Juba, who was already disappearing around the outer door. He put his back against the concrete wall, reached around and emptied his clip at Kyle.

"Goddamn!" shouted Swanson, off balance and ignoring the bullets as he also started to shoot, although the angles were wrong and his target was out of view.

Bullets whanged against marble and stone, and chips of rock ricocheted in the tight confines of the rear stairwell.

Each man knew his opponent's capabilities, so there would be no more headlong charges, for any rash move would be suicide.

Juba dashed through a small gate and disappeared around a corner.

Swanson heard him leaving but edged down the stairs, wary of deception and places that danger might be hiding. He had to suppress his reflex to go after Juba and bring him down. The mission was still unaccomplished. Those papers on the main floor had to be examined, and he had to be gone himself before the cops came. He holstered his weapon with a curse: a golden opportunity missed.

Kyle hurried back into the main room, where papers were strewn wildly across the furniture, the sign of someone who had left in a hurry. They were bound to contain the secrets, and Kyle was about to call for Sybelle and Freedman to come around with the SUV when his peripheral vision caught the blinking of a tiny red light on the wall. He stopped.

The detonator had only two minutes left and was steadily counting down. Any attempt to disarm it would take longer than that, and Kyle knew that Juba had probably rigged it to a booby-trap alternate igniter to protect the explosive sequence.

He ran. The door at the bottom of the stairs seemed a mile away as he rushed toward it, counting seconds as he went. Minute-thirty. In the distance, he heard the dipping whine of sirens that meant the French cops were coming. He jumped over the body of Saladin, went out of the gate, crossed the street, and crawled back into the manhole. A minute. The stinking sewer system was his friend now, for the blast could not reach him belowground, and it would be a while before the police discovered the open manhole cover. Every step he took got him farther from the blast zone. Forty. Thirty.

At fifteen seconds, he found a small side room where workmen could store their tools and used his Glock to shoot the lock. The door wobbled, and he hauled on the heavy wooden panel with all of his strength, pulling it open far enough so he could burrow inside and kneel, opening his mouth so the blast would not rupture his ears. He hoped the cops had not arrived.

It went off with an earthshaking roar in a repeated series of explosions as Juba's booby traps blew up in deadly sequence, one after another, and the big house crumbled and shattered. The blast wave knocked down the old walls of the courtyard, clawed at the nearby brick buildings, and ruptured the neat lines of parked vehicles. The shock wave came pounding down the sewer openings and raced along the main trunk line, tearing down everything in its path, pushing aside debris, causing a small tsunami in the sewer water itself, and slamming the door to the room in which Kyle was crouched. He was knocked to his side and bounced hard against some large equipment.

When it was done, he lay there for a minute, dazed and catching his breath in the darkness. Then he struggled to his feet and opened the door to see a thick cloud of dirt and dust hanging in the tunnel like a curtain. Slapping his handkerchief to his mouth, Kyle was about to leave the little room when he noticed the object he had been thrown against was really the steel rungs of a ladder built into the side of the concrete, leading upward. He climbed and found another door, an entrance to the service tunnel. *Why didn't I find this before?* He moved into the sunshine and looked back over his shoulder at the huge, rising ball of flame and smoke behind him.

Then he walked away, and each stride convinced him that he was uninjured. By the time Swanson arrived at the Fort d'Aubervilliers station, he was walking normally. He would catch the Line 7 train for the five-minute trip north to the next stop at La Courneuve/8 Mai 1945. Nearby, Sybelle and the Lizard would be cruising in a car out in front of the sprawling and popular Air Museum tourist attraction.

They took him at the station when the train rushed up to the platform in a howl of screeching brakes, pushing a blast of air ahead of it. The crowd moved almost as one toward the doors, jostling for position while trying to avoid being touched.

Two needles of a Taser X26 penetrated Swanson's jacket and shirt from the rear, and multiple pulses of electricity totaling thousands of volts hit him with volcanic pain and rendered his motor systems useless. Kyle toppled toward the dirty station floor, aware of a man kneeling beside him, on the left, calling out in English, "Hey, this guy's had a heart attack!"

As the subway doors closed and the train moved out, two ambulance attendants trotted down the stairs. Kyle was placed on their rolling stretcher, where he was again hit with the Taser to keep him immobile while one of the attendants jammed a needle in his arm.

Commuters parted to let the stretcher bearers exit, carrying some man lashed to the gurney to the ambulance waiting up on the street.

17

Juba was certain that no one was following him because the explosion would have turned all eyes toward the disaster. He hoped Kyle Swanson was buried in that smoking debris. Swanson was supposed to be dead, but there had been no mistaking that angular face that had absolutely no fear on it when they were trading shots in the stairwell. Maybe Shake really was dead now, a thought that made Juba smile. *The only man who ever really beat me.*

Juba used his time well before the flight to America. An executive hotel near the airport rented rooms by the hour for businessmen in transit, and Juba used a Dutch passport to get a room and clean up. Downstairs, he got a close shave, then had a stylist trim his hair to a neatness that would be welcome in a company boardroom. He had her put in a little lighter color, joking that he wanted to look younger because of the competition for a new vice presidential opening at his finance firm. A clothing store furnished new slacks, shirts, underwear, socks, and a blue sport coat with gold buttons. What he did not wear fit snugly into his large briefcase. Unfortunately, he would not be able to take his weapon, but there were plenty of guns waiting on the other end of the flight. As a final move, he bought a disposable cell phone with plenty of prepaid minutes.

Carrying only the briefcase and the computer bag, he passed through security without a problem and took his seat in the first-class compartment of the British Airways flight to Washington. A hostess brought a glass of chilled water for him while the rest of the plane loaded, and once the plane was moving, gathering speed, and lifting as the wheels left the tarmac, Juba let himself relax. There was no danger now, so he stretched his seat back and ordered himself to catch some sleep. The quiet, steady hum of the engines helped him relax. He dreamed of Scotland.

A special ops team of American Marines had been pitted in a war exercise against a similar team of Royal Marines, and Color Sergeant Osmand was in his element. He had racked up a couple of mock "kills" and then decided to take the game to a higher level.

For a full day he and a spotter tracked the American Blue Team, then slithered through their sentries and lookouts and set up an invisible hide on a low ridge that overlooked the enemy headquarters and a road the Americans would have to use the following morning. He hoped a general would turn up in his sights. The two of them spent several hours erasing all traces of their passage and improving their hide, then shared a tin of cold meat and drank some water as the night closed around them like a starlit glove.

It was raining, but that meant nothing on a mission in Scotland, where it was always either raining or about to rain. Juba was on watch during the early morning hours while his spotter caught a nap, and it was not only wet but cold, too, and absolutely silent. A fire to warm his hands, of course, was out of the question.

Instead, he remained still, the thistles and weeds sprouting from the slits of his ghillie suit turning him into just another bush on the rugged Scottish landscape. Dawn would come in two hours, and the American Marines would begin moving around. Color Sergeant Osmand intended to slaughter as many as he could and possibly even capture their headquarters, which would give him bragging rights forever over the vaunted United States Marine Corps.

Something even colder than the night, the barrel of a pistol, touched his neck just below his ear, and a quiet voice whispered, "Bang, asshole. You're dead. So is your partner there, Sleeping Beauty."

Osmand spun around to see the grinning, blackened face of the sniper they called Shake, Gunnery Sergeant Kyle Swanson. "I thought you two were never going to get settled. Sounded like a couple of elephants stomping around. You almost stepped on me when you came up," the American said, casually putting the weapon away. "Come on. Let's go down there, get warm, and have something to eat."

On the British Airways plane flying across the Atlantic, a hostess noticed the first-class passenger twitching in his sleep. A dream. She lightly spread a blanket over him.

The dream shifted to what had just happened a few hours before in Paris, when again Swanson had gotten the better of him, ambushing and killing Saladin right under Juba's nose. He vividly recalled hearing the shots and seeing the body of his spiritual father sprawled on the courtyard stones, and that brought sadness and a flare of anger. *What now?* When his mind started tugging at that question, he woke up.

Right now, Juba could disappear. Eight bidders were seeking the formula, at ten million dollars each, nonrefundable. All of that money had already been rerouted to other banks, hidden beneath folds of false accounts in smaller accounts, and he had those account numbers and access codes. His own personal investments were worth about five million dollars and there was still about another ten million in the reserve and operations accounts that Saladin had organized. That meant that Juba could put his hands on almost a hundred million dollars, a life-changing amount.

With so much money, there was no need to continue as a professional killer or as a bringer of death to masses of people. He could go anywhere in the world and buy anything he wanted. With Saladin dead, the entire scheme was compromised and carried much greater risk. The bidders would still want the formula, but now they would be more willing to use guns rather than their checkbooks to get it. They also would want their deposits back.

It would be best to take the money and leave now. The Middle East was afire with Islamic fanatics to carry on the fight against the Crusaders. There was no real reason for him to try to run a one-man reign of terror.

In the end, he decided there were three reasons to continue. The first was that Juba still had the gas, the formula, and several factories in which it could be manufactured. It was he who handpicked the undercover operators to support the attacks, personally distributed the weapons, and communicated with the terrorist cells. Few of the others had ever heard of Saladin before the London attack and the auction. They answered to Juba and would still obey his orders. Second, he did not really believe Kyle Swanson had died in the explosion, which meant the two of them were on an eventual collision course. If Swanson was after him, the man would never give up the chase. The American was an insufferable pest. Third, Juba knew he would get bored sitting around doing nothing.

Why not use it? The attack on the United States would be spectacular and bloody, and he would expand it for years to come with strikes all over the world. Carrying out the demonstration that had been announced by Saladin would cause the bidders to fall back in line.

That left Swanson, and Juba realized just how badly he wanted to kill the sniper. The threat of the man would always be present, like an unwelcome shadow. No matter where Juba went, he could never relax as long as Swanson was alive. On top of that, the Marine had murdered the one person who really understood Juba, and the death of Saladin could not go unavenged. Kyle Swanson had to die.

He adjusted his seat and brought the laptop from beneath his feet, placing it on the adjacent aisle seat. The first-class cabin was only half full, and the hostess came to ask if he wanted a meal. He ordered vegetarian, put on a headset, and found some classical music, which helped his thoughts roam free. He had an attack to plan. Preparation of the weapon was already under way in Mexico, and he would call later today to make certain the work would continue. All he needed was a target, and he needed to decide quickly.

Las Vegas was a good possibility, a city of sin that tainted the society of the entire world, beckoning to him like the painted harlot she was. Numerous Muslim men had been corrupted by that impure city and its gambling and whores. Juba considered Las Vegas loathsome and cheap, glowing like a carnival in the desert night, and destroying it would have been a personal pleasure. Satisfying but not very effective, for he believed that not many people would truly care. With its flashy girls, card players, and high-rolling rubes, its destruction would not gather much sympathy after the first week of headlines. Hotel entrepreneurs would just bury the dead, then build new casinos right outside the contaminated radiation zone, close enough to let tourists view the destroyed city through powerful telescopes, for a small price.

He would not waste the weapon by killing the wrong people. After all, he remembered, look at New Orleans. A major city was destroyed by a hurricane, and the United States government wrote it off after only a few months. New Orleans was populated by poor residents who did not have political power, so Americans just continued going to the malls and movies as if nothing had happened. The city was still rebuilding.

He finished the meal, placed his computer on the little table, and scrolled through the news sites. Not much yet about Paris, but London was still going on. Kill the right people! He checked the international news, where the lead story was a typhoon pulverizing Bangladesh, and then went to the sports results, for he was still a soccer addict.

Juba read with interest about how violence had broken out at a stadium in Germany during a match, and the idea came to him as the camera panned around to show the thick crowds of fans surging onto the field or fleeing for the exits or just standing around watching. Thousands of people. Thousands of targets.

A sports arena would be an ideal place for the gas attack, for it would bring confusion, destruction, mayhem, and televised horror. It was baseball season in the United States, and he could turn a big game into a nightmare. The Internet let him study the details of every major league baseball stadium in the States and look at the upcoming schedules. Although he did not follow the sport, there were several obvious possibilities. Still using the Internet, he made a flight reservation.

When he arrived in America, Juba lingered at the U.S. Customs portals until he found a place in a line just ahead of a Turk with dark skin and a beard who was wearing a suit with a shirt buttoned at the neck and no tie. The eyes of the authorities were focused on that man, a ceramics trader out of Istanbul, and not the European businessman in front of him. The Turk looked like a possible terrorist. Juba showed a well-used passport, was cordial to the customs officer, and passed through with astonishing ease. A camera recorded his arrival.

Clear of the final barrier, he strolled out into the waiting area, which was crowded with families and friends and business associates welcoming the flood of people who were arriving from abroad. Rental limousine drivers waved hand-printed signs that bore various last names, but he ignored them and made his way all the way to the curb to catch a cab.

He had the cab drop him at a Metro station and used the subway to get out to Reagan National, where he used an American Express card in one of the lobby computers to obtain his e-ticket for a domestic Delta Airlines flight from Washington to Florida. Juba had never seen a major league baseball game and was looking forward to the experience.

OVER THE ATLANTIC OCEAN

Kyle Swanson returned to consciousness slowly as the drugs ran their course. He had no idea how much time had passed, and his last memory was getting ready to ride the subway and then . . . sudden pain, people yelling, followed by an empty nothingness. No dreams. He remained still, eyes closed until his mind cleared enough to suppress the automatic fear of the unknown.

It was not completely dark when he cracked his eyes just a bit. Some light penetrated the area to give shape to objects, but he remained essentially blind, so he allowed his other senses to sort out whatever available information he could gather. He had a slight headache, a hangover from the sleeping drug, but felt no wounds.

The first thing to make itself clear was the steady whining of jet engines and a slight shaking that told him he was in an airplane. He could almost smell the nearby bulkheads, and there was a chill on his skin that matched the hum of air-conditioning. Not a prison cell but a controlled environment. Whoever had him was taking him somewhere in a small, modern jet.

Using his body, he tried to explore further but quickly concluded he was lashed to a small bed. His fingertips told him that he was naked but covered with a blanket. Abnormal. Not the treatment usually given a prisoner in foreign lands. A condom-like device pinched on his penis, a motorman's friend that would let him urinate into a tube. Some thin wires touched his skin. Electrodes for heart and pulse monitors.

For a few moments on first awakening, he had thought terrorists might have snatched him, which would have meant some pretty uncomfortable times ahead. As he lay there on the soft mattress without moving, he could hear muffled voices from a nearby compartment: English. Kyle concluded that he was a prisoner of the United States government. They weren't going to kill him, so there was nothing else he could do at present. There was an almost inaudible click, and another dose of the drug flowed through the IV and into his veins. He controlled his breathing and let it tug him back to sleep.

"This guy is a damned ghost," said FBI Special Agent David Hunt, the man who had watched Swanson through his binoculars back in Paris. He removed his glasses and rubbed his eyes. DHS Agent Carolyn Walker was seated across from him in the Gulfstream, studying some papers on the table between them. More than four hours had passed since they had grabbed the assassin, and there was still nothing in the way of a solid identification.

The man who was drugged and strapped down in the rear cabin had carried no credit cards in his old black wallet, just some five hundred dollars in cash and an Arizona driver's license that was a phony. There was no Social Security number. Empty pockets. They had photographed the face, full on and both profiles, digitally enhanced it, and transmitted it to Washington along with the fingerprints to be run through the government's entire computer base. So far, the computers were throwing up blanks. Nothing.

Walker spread out the digital photographs that had been taken of the suspect while he slept. "His body gives us the only real information we have. No tattoos or other identifying marks, but those scars are from bullet holes, knife wounds, and medical operations. Battle wounds."

"Which means military." Hunt started pacing. "Okay. Active or ex? A merc? Damn, Carolyn, we don't even know if he's American."

She chewed a fingernail. "My gut feeling is that he's one of ours, because nobody has the ability to scrub an identity from U.S. databases so thoroughly without help from the inside, and that presents the real problem. We have pictures of him shooting Saladin in the head with a pistol, which indicates he also was the one who fired the kill shot with the rifle. He assassinated the man, and that is not sanctioned by our country. That's why we are hauling his ass back home. That's where the answer is."

"Doesn't make sense," Hunt said. "Even if he was on the inside, we should have known about him snooping around in Paris. He is as sterile as they come. That's no accident."

* * *

Another government Gulfstream was also streaking back to Washington that evening, and its only passengers were Captain Sybelle Summers and Lieutenant Commander Benton Freedman. Both were worried. Swanson had not turned up at the designated rally point, and according to protocol, they abandoned the plan after waiting fifteen minutes.

They saw the smoke plume and drove toward it, viewing the destruction of the house with a fear that Kyle might have been buried inside. The debris was mostly confined inside the grounds, as the building had been brought straight down, one floor pancaking upon another, but damage was visible on surrounding buildings, too. Windows were shattered, and bricks littered the sidewalks.

Sybelle had hopped out of the car and moved to the Peugeot, then dropped into the open manhole. No one in the gathering crowd had paid her any attention because the main attraction was across the street. She walked a hundred meters in each direction down the tunnel. No Kyle.

Their orders were to bail out if the mission was compromised, rather than risk getting caught on foreign soil, which would only make things worse. They hated to obey, but they had no idea where Swanson was or what had happened to him.

The Lizard took them to a military airport, where their Gulfstream was being readied. Once they had taken off, he filed a brief report in code to General Middleton in Washington. There was an acknowledgment that the message had been received, but there was no other reply.

All they could do now was get back home as fast as possible.

18

MARYLAND

An ambulance was waiting at Andrews Air Force Base when the FBI Gulfstream landed and taxied over to a distant hangar. The unconscious patient was transferred to the vehicle, and it drove away at a normal speed, inconspicuous in the morning traffic around Washington. Special Agents Hunt and Walker followed in a black SUV.

The ambulance stayed on the Beltway, then broke away onto less busy highways and finally onto the streets of a town and an even narrower road that led to a Coast Guard station on a rocky promontory that jutted out into the Atlantic Ocean. A storm front was moving in, and rain drummed heavily on the roof of the SUV. Dave Hunt had the wipers on high but still had to lean forward as he drove slowly along a narrow road that was bordered by a mosaic of waist-high walls of rocks.

Both vehicles pulled into the parking area of a weathered old building that was two stories tall, its bare concrete walls dingy from the gravel, grit, and saltwater that had scoured it for half a century. The masts and aerials mounted on the roof were pegged tight on the surrounding rock but strained against the tension of the support wires as the wind whistled around the big masts. The building had been abandoned by the Coast Guard in the 1960s for improved quarters nearby and was now a safe house shared by several government agencies.

Hunt and Walker parked and hurried through the rain into the house, where a team of CIA agents was taking charge of the sleeping man delivered by the medics.

"What do you think, Carolyn? Should we go wake him up and have a talk?"

Agent Walker shook her head. "Not yet. We're exhausted and need some rest. Let him be for now so he can wake up in there and wonder what has happened to his little life." She gave instructions to one of the other agents. "Turn off the air-conditioning and switch on the heater. Have the urine analyzed. In three hours, hit him with the lights and the a/c again, only put it two degrees lower. Alternate that about every hour, and then start the noise about two o'clock, off and on. Give him water only during a dark phase. We want him disoriented, hungry, and thirsty." She stretched. "He can sit there and stew while we get some sleep upstairs and come back in, fresh as daisies, and hammer him. By then, the identification will probably have popped out of the computers, and that will make our job a lot easier."

ST. PETERSBURG, FLORIDA

That afternoon, Juba attended a baseball game between the Tampa Bay Rays and the Toronto Blue Jays at Tropicana Field in St. Petersburg, Florida. The weather was hot, but a breeze from the Gulf of Mexico kept it from being scorching and it was easy to understand why retirees flocked to the place after spending their lives in cold climates. It never snowed in St. Pete, and the locals called the city "God's waiting room."

Despite the kind weather, the stadium was an old domed

arena that was home to a poor team, and the relatively few fans attending that day's game were mostly older men and women. Most of the seats were empty. Thinking tactically, Juba decided this was not the kind of crowd, nor a suitable place, that would gain the attention he wanted with the attack. In fact, Tropicana would be a waste of time and energy. Don't kill the wrong people.

That evening, he flew out of Florida, and as he crossed the Great Plains Juba's thoughts again turned to Swanson, who was supposed to be dead and buried at Arlington. Juba had been in the military long enough to realize that the entire burial, posthumous Medal of Honor and all, could have been just a charade, a staged black operation event. So, Swanson was actually alive and totally undercover. Was there a possibility that Juba might find a bonus in this situation by having another chance to prove who was superior? After all, Swanson had tarnished the reputation of Color Sergeant Osmand, back in the day. Juba would like to serve a dish of cold revenge to the man. Why not add a one-on-one showdown with Swanson to the agenda, even if it meant leaving a trail of breadcrumbs to help his enemy along? It would be interesting.

His mind was made up by the time his plane began to be buffeted around the sky by the turbulence of the Rocky Mountain air prior to landing at Denver International Airport.

Sybelle Summers and the Lizard arrived at the Pentagon only to find that General Middleton was out at Quantico for an emergency conference of Marine leaders. The president had increased the national alert status to orange.

Freedman went to his desk and logged on to his mainframe computer while Summers put on a pot of coffee and checked the unopened mail. They would have a concise report for Middleton by the time he returned.

"Here's some good news," called Freedman. "The medical status of Double-Oh has been upgraded to 'Good,' and he'll be flown back here in a few days." He went back to the screen. "And here's an e-mail from Sir Geoffrey saying that Delara Tibrizi is doing okay but is wondering about Kyle."

"So are we," Sybelle said and went to her own desk and flipped through copies of the *New York Times* and the *Washington Post*.

"Whoa! Sybelle, would you please come over here?" A pulsing chime was repeating from Freedman's computer, and a small red rectangle flashed in the upper right-hand corner. Something had pinged the automatic warning system he had designed to track any queries about members of Trident.

He clicked some keys and the NCIC/Interpol symbol appeared, along with the expanded data. "Somebody is checking Kyle's fingerprints in the FBI's National Crime Information Center system! The request lists him as a John Doe and an 'unknown suspect.'"

"Unknown suspect? That would indicate he's alive and being held prisoner. Does it say who has him, or where?"

The Lizard was frantically scrolling through data, calling up new screens of information. "No. It doesn't even carry a high priority. Bingo. Look at this link to some photos that are being run through the government's face recognition software. Kyle, for sure."

"I'm calling Middleton," Sybelle said, reaching for the encrypted telephone. He was in a car being driven back to the Pentagon and answered on the first ring. "Gunny Swanson is alive, sir, and someone is checking his fingerprints."

Middleton paused before answering. "That fucking

Swanson. Where is he and who is checking up on him?"
The general could hear the Lizard clack the keyboard,
and Sybelle switched them all onto a conference call.

"It looks like the original ping came from the FBI but
has since branched out to cover databases around the
world, under the flag of the Department of Homeland
Security. The ping registered about noon, so we are several hours behind on this." Freedman tapped a pencil on
his desk.

"Stay on it, Liz," said Middleton. "Get into the system
and sidetrack whatever you can. Do what you can to slow
them down. I will be in the office as soon as I pay a visit
to the Hoover Building and talk to the Feebs."

"Yes, sir. Got it."

Middleton replaced the car's secure telephone in its
cradle and stared at the surrounding traffic. Rush hour
never ended around Washington, and thousands of cars
and trucks were creeping along bumper to bumper. "Sar'nt
Johnson!" he barked at his driver.

"Sir!"

"Turn on your fancy spinning lights and that siren and
get us out of this mess and over to the FBI place pronto."
The general buckled his seat belt and was thrown back
against his seat as Johnson launched the big sedan across
a thick band of traffic and into the lane especially reserved for emergency vehicles. He roared around the cars
ahead, tapping bumpers when necessary. Middleton held
on, hoped for a safe landing, and repeated to himself,
"That fucking Swanson."

Carolyn Walker checked the big wall clock in the office
that was adjacent to the interrogation room: 5:10 P.M. The
clock was a discount store special, and a federal agent
precisely adjusted it twice a day to the correct atomic
time. Why not just buy a better clock? She blinked and

turned her attention back to the man strapped into the chair on the other side of the one-way mirror. "We've got bupkis. Nada. Diddly-squat. Three damned hours and he hasn't said a word."

"That's not exactly true, Carolyn. He has told us to go fuck ourselves at least a dozen times, in several different languages," corrected Dave Hunt.

"He doesn't look like someone who was scared out of his wits after hours alone in that room, buck naked and motionless."

As if he knew they were watching, Kyle Swanson yawned. Since his head was also strapped to the chair, it was mostly just opening his mouth and flexing his jaw muscles.

"We've got to report in soon. I can't believe that we've caught an assassin red-handed and he's mocking us."

The urgency they felt to identify him was not shared by everyone in law enforcement, for they were being very cautious about making a splash until they could do so without infuriating the international community. The French had not even known they were in the country when they made the arrest on a public street. Now safely back home, they had run into a stone wall. Since the national alert level had been raised, traffic had picked up on the computers, and they felt their efforts were falling on deaf ears. They had made a routine blood draw from the suspect to furnish DNA samples but were curtly informed that the backlog was so great that their samples might not get tested for a week. Other requests were being similarly delayed, and their entire system was slowing down, the memory being packed with reams of useless data.

Walker pushed rimless glasses up on her head and fluffed her brown hair in frustration. In her early forties, she was a thorough intelligence professional who had come over to the DHS from the CIA in the big reorganization after 9/11. With a doctorate in psychology and years of interrogation practice, she believed she could get to any suspect. She sighed. "We still don't even know his name."

"Nope. Still Mr. X."

"We have to do more, Dave. If we can't scare him with words, then we must employ some physical stress. I recommend that we use Level Two techniques."

"I agree. Should we file it up the chain of command?"

"Not yet. Not yet. I can order a Level Two decision on my own authority. Let's crack this guy."

"Dangerous game, Carolyn," Hunt warned. "I can almost hear a special blue-ribbon commission questioning us now. At least let's file a short summary saying our John Doe may be on the terrorist watch list, just to get a time stamp on it and protect our asses."

"Life was easier when we didn't have so much power," she said, recalling the time when the agency did not worry about such particulars. "Okay. They get a synopsis, but I'll keep the particulars vague to buy us more time."

Agents Evan Brown and Kealoha Kepo'o were large men who had been specially trained in advanced interrogation techniques, ways to intimidate people and make someone hurt like hell without leaving a bruise. Both had played football in college, Brown at Florida State and Kepo'o for Hawaii, and their imposing size was part of the drill, for when they sauntered into an interrogation room, they carried a sense of menace. The subject immediately knew that polite questioning was over.

Everything was choreographed. They were federal agents, not thugs, and their job was to persuade the prisoner to answer questions. Walker and Dave Hunt had briefed them well and let them read the transcript of what had been asked so far. They studied the man through the mirror and decided their next move.

The unidentified subject finally seemed disoriented by the cold, heat, sleep deprivation, bright lights, and hours of questioning. Mixed music, yelling-loud rap lyrics followed by classical melodies so soft that they could barely be heard, had also taken a toll. Walker now shifted the music to a soothing concerto for flute and violin, let the room go dark, and set the temperature just a shade above normal. Comfort. Within five minutes, the man's head sagged to his chest. At that moment, she switched off the cameras and the music and turned on the bright lights, and the two big agents stepped into the interrogation area.

Kyle Swanson had been running through a series of isometric exercises to keep blood flowing to his extremities, muscles, and brain, straining so hard that he had broken into a light sweat.

He had recognized the chair as soon as he had awakened and gotten his bearings, for he had strapped a couple of guys into one just like it in other places, in other times. Stamped into the base of the round metal frame would be a stamp that read PROPERTY OF THE UNITED STATES GOVERNMENT. Kyle had remained still, knowing he was probably being monitored with an infrared camera, and had given the man and woman who questioned him nothing to work with. They weren't going to kill him, so all he had to do was hang on until the cavalry arrived.

He also had been expecting this new tactic, because he was being so uncooperative, and centered his mind on how to deal with it. There would be physical pain, and standard practice was to get the subject out of the chair for a Level Two so the apes could toss him around.

Agent Kepo'o threw a five-gallon bucket filled with cold water onto him, and Kyle did not tense up. He was relaxed and fully alert. Waiting for an opportunity.

Brown stood beside him, hands on hips, and Kyle

glanced at the diver's watch on the agent's left wrist. The hands were almost at six o'clock, but a small dial indicated the military time. Almost 1800, which would make it six in the afternoon. Free information. *Thanks, big guy.*

"We are required to ask you one last time to cooperate with the special agents who have been questioning you," said Brown. "So I just did that, you little shit." He slapped Kyle hard with his open palm, and Swanson's head snapped around.

Kepo'o hit him with a return volley, using a fist that seemed the size of a volleyball. The first punch had split Kyle's lip, and blood oozed from it. He shrugged off the pain.

"Now we are going to drag you up out of the chair and kick your skinny ass around this room until you decide to cooperate." Brown roughly undid the strap around Kyle's right arm and leg while the giant Hawaiian unbuckled the left side. Then Brown released the chest restraint and unsnapped the Velcro head band.

Before the agent could lean back, Kyle grabbed the man's neck in a tie-clinch and jumped up in one fluid move. Brown was instantly off balance, and Swanson pulled down hard on the head while smashing his knee upward. The agent fell, grabbing his shattered nose and fractured eye socket.

Swanson was now able to face Kepo'o, who had recovered from the momentary surprise and moved forward, just close enough for Kyle to lean back and telegraph that a kick was coming. The 275-pound Polynesian saw the slight position change and put his arms down to protect his stomach and groin. Instead, Kyle snapped into a complete fast spin and landed a roundhouse kick that sailed over the lowered arms and slammed against the man's temple so hard that it knocked Kealoha Kepo'o unconscious on the spot and dropped him sprawling to the floor.

Swanson stepped forward and kicked the fallen man hard in the unguarded balls. "That's for the punch," he said.

Then Swanson grimly faced the mirror and sat back down as Walker, Dave Hunt, and two other agents burst into the room with their guns drawn. Kyle allowed himself to be strapped back into the chair without a struggle.

"Okay, so you're a tough guy. Are you willing to talk to us now?" asked Carolyn Walker.

Kyle stared back. "No. Fuck all of you. It's almost six o'clock. Can I have some dinner?"

"You're a real bastard, you know that?" Dave Hunt snarled as he turned on his heel and walked out, passing an EMT team coming in to tend the agents. The suspect had taken down Evan Brown and Kealoha Kepo'o as easily as swatting a couple of flies. Hunt said, "We go to Level Four, Carolyn."

"No Level Three?"

"It would be idiotic to unstrap him again to make him kneel on a broomstick or hold his arms out with weights attached. We can't take the chance, so we waterboard him instead. Then probably the battery and electrodes, too. Hell, I may even take a baseball bat and a meat cleaver to the son of a bitch! How did he know what time it was?"

"Cool down, Dave. What about getting permission?"

Hunt sighed. This thing was escalating, popping up out of the ordinary run of business and therefore likely to get noticed. The bosses would want to know how two agents had been injured and what was going on, but somebody in Washington would have to sign off on the waterboarding, and few would want their names on such an authorization.

Walker was also disgusted. "It may take a few hours, but it will be worth the wait. No way should you and I take the fall for this all by ourselves." She spent some time drafting the request message in careful, legal language, then signed it.

19

General Bradley Middleton was in the spacious office of the director of the Federal Bureau of Investigation. Dark furniture. Framed handshake pictures on the wall. FBI symbols everywhere. It bespoke power, as did the quiet and competent man across the desk from him, who never took off his dark suit coat, even while he was sitting.

"What do you mean, Mr. Director? You've lost one of my people and can't tell me where he is or even if you have him? How does that work?" Middleton cocked an eyebrow.

Director Samuel Banks spread his arms wide, palms up. "I can only repeat what I just told you, General. As of now, I have no report whatsoever of any unidentified suspects being picked up yesterday."

"Our alert came straight from your FBI computer system, Mr. Director. Your machine talked to my machine and said one of our hot sets of prints was being examined. The link activates only for that specific reason."

The director nodded in affirmation. "And our system shows that indeed a query was made, and that we replied that there were no such prints on record in the NCIC. But our people were not the ones who initiated the inquiry!

Anyway, you are military. How can your people not have fingerprints on file?"

"Sorry, Mr. Director. Need-to-know basis on that one."

"I'm the director of the FBI!"

"I apologize and suggest you take up any questions you have about this with the White House. I do not have authorization to discuss it. Back to business. If the FBI system was pinged last night, where else could it have come from? Can just any hacker or country cop do it? Or could the NSA or a foreign government run something without a trace?"

"No, of course not. There are high-level security protocols and firewalls and passwords that I can't discuss with you. Need-to-know." The eternal Washington game. My dick is as long as yours.

Middleton smiled, and the director grinned back. "Mr. Director, I don't care about the inner workings of your computer and databases as long as we continue to have authorized access. I just want my operator back."

"I understand that, General. Here's my suggestion. I will put a tag on the query. If anything pops up, I will personally give you a call." He scribbled on the back of a business card and handed it to Middleton. "Here's my private number in case you need to contact me directly." The general looked at it. There was no telephone number, just *DHS??*

Middleton put the card in his jacket pocket and rose, shook hands and left, wondering why Banks had chosen such an odd method of communication. Was he concerned that the office of the director of the FBI might be bugged? No, it was simpler than that. Banks *knew* the conversation was recorded, because he was the one recording it. Just in case questions were asked later. *Weird world we live in*, Middleton thought, getting into his waiting car.

"Sar'nt Johnson!"

"Yes, sir!"

"Do you know where to find the Department of Homeland Security offices in this hick town?"

"Yes, sir! The Department of Homeland Security. Uh, down at the far end of the Mall in that really tall, skinny building with the pointy top?"

"That is the Washington Monument, Sergeant, and I have no time for your smart-ass comments this evening." Middleton noted that it was past six o'clock. He had just wasted hours working his way through the FBI chain of command in order to reach the director for their brief, private conference. He didn't want to repeat that process over at the DHS, starting with some flunky at the front door who would explain that everyone had already gone home for the day. "Let's just go back across the river to the Pentagon. If I'm going to be sneaky, I want a whole bunch of Marines around. You do know where the Pentagon is, don't you, Sar'nt Johnson?"

"Aye, aye, sir."

MARYLAND

They had turned the thermostat down again to be sure that Swanson, in the interrogation chair, was thoroughly chilled before beginning the water procedure. They were not about to unstrap him again, because bad things had happened the last time they tried that.

As far as Special Agent Carolyn Walker was concerned, the bastard could lie there and freeze to death. She gave a look of disgust through the one-way glass and swiveled her chair around to face Dave Hunt.

"Okay, I'm not waiting any longer. We can't dodge our responsibilities while the bureaucrats argue about conducting a Level Four interrogation on American soil with someone who we think may be an American citizen. An assassin working for a terrorist organization is the most likely scenario."

"Still a dangerous precedent, Carolyn."

Walker's eyes were sharp and her mouth a thin line. "No more waiting, Dave. We can't afford *not* to do this. We have to find out how he is involved. Anyway, screw my goddam career. I want to know what that bastard knows! We will proceed with the first phase while we wait for authorization. I will take full responsibility."

"I never said I didn't want to do this, Carolyn," Hunt said quietly, trying to keep her calm. "I concur, as long as it remains a limited and supervised situation. He has brought it on himself by refusing to talk and putting a couple of our people in the emergency room."

The room was cold. Both Walker and Hunt wore dark blue windbreakers as they watched other agents set up the procedure. The suspect, shivering from the icy air-conditioning, had been blindfolded; his chair was laid back and a large galvanized tub clattered into place beneath his head. This was just the first phase and would be done with no talking, no questions.

A thick towel was draped across the face. Walker pulled out her stopwatch, nodded to an agent standing beside the chair, and started the timer as he tipped over the first bucket.

Kyle was already shivering, and with his eyes covered, he depended on his other senses to keep track of what was happening. The metallic noise of the tub on the tile floor told him it was probably time for some water, and he sucked in deep, regular breaths. Instead of fighting back when the towel was laid over his nose and mouth, which would have expended both energy and air, he hauled in even deeper breaths. He heard someone pick up one of the heavy buckets, and shoes beside the chair squeaked on the tiles as the agent shifted for better balance. Water sloshed as the bucket came up. Kyle got a final deep breath and heard the click of a stopwatch, and five gallons of water was sloshed onto the towel in a single rushing torrent. He remained perfectly still and let his brain be a clock. At fifteen seconds, he intentionally squirmed, but there was little real discomfort.

Carolyn Walker detested doing what she was doing. Only fifteen seconds had passed and the suspect was already wiggling, showing signs of oxygen deprivation. She pushed her personal reaction aside and pressed on with the procedure, signaling the waiting agent to pour a second bucket over the drenched towel.

Kyle lurched against the straps when the cascade of water washed over him. The towel was thoroughly drenched, and no air would come through, even when the waterfall passed. When his count reached thirty-five seconds, he struggled again, harder, pushing against the straps.

He's drowning under there. Carolyn held up a finger. Still another bucket was dumped on Swanson, and he struggled while the straps dug into his arms and ankles. When her stopwatch hit one minute, Walker held up her fist. Stop. The agent yanked away the towel, and Carolyn looked down at the suspect, who was coughing and sputtering, gasping for air. A full minute underwater. Let him know what was in store if he refused to cooperate. Now give him some time alone to think about it. The chair was elevated to the sitting position to help him catch his breath, and everyone left the room, leaving the suspect alone to fear what might happen next.

Kyle was wet and shivering. He opened his eyes and blinked and allowed his breathing to return to a regular rhythm. Only a minute under the towel? Piece of cake. Any surfer would think so. Cold and wet? He thought about his big surfboard and the frigid waters at the Wedge in Newport Beach, where he usually had to wear a wet suit and booties even on a warm day.

Wet? This was nothing compared to being scrubbed along the sandpaper bottom of the California shoreline after being blown out by a big wave. It could take a minute or so just to get back to the surface. Or being sealed in a fifty-five-gallon drum half-filled with water and rolled down a hillside during a training exercise. Cold? Try trekking over an ice-sheeted mountain during a blizzard with people trying to kill you. In this room, he knew that the water torture was only a mind game to force his cooperation by making him think he was drowning. He would play it out and let them believe they were getting to him. He was, however, cold and hungry, and time was being wasted. *Where's my damned cavalry?*

THE PENTAGON

The Lizard, well aware of how the computer age could be made to work against itself, had been jamming useless data down the information superhighway to the unknown computer where the requests about Kyle Swanson were originating. For the past two hours, he had been reprogramming, cutting down that computer's ability to reach out to others without first going through him.

With the help of a friend at the National Security Agency, he eventually narrowed it all down to a half-dozen lines of communication, all of it encrypted on the sender's end but popping back into readable English on his screen.

Sniffing around the U.S. Department of Homeland Security violated a dozen or so laws, but General Middleton had been very clear with his order: "Find Shake."

The message for Level Four permission came up. Unidentified terrorist suspect related to Saladin inquiries is in custody at location Delta Two One Sigma. No identification, not even fingerprints. DNA tests were incomplete. Probably ex-military. Subject may have information re poison gas attack. Extremely uncooperative, two DHS agents injured and hospitalized. Urgent request for authorization to conduct a Level Four interrogation. Signed by Special Agent Carolyn Walker of the Department of Homeland Security, with her identification code.

The Lizard didn't know what a Level Four was, but it sounded rather dire. He went to the general's office and knocked on the door. "I've located Gunny Swanson, sir. He is being held by the Department of Homeland Security at a safe house over on the Maryland coast, used to be a Coast Guard station."

Middleton was on his feet, walking across his office, and called out, "Captain Summers!"

Sybelle came in. "Sir."

"Round up some Marines and go get our boy," he said. "The Lizard will fill you in and arrange a helicopter from here to there." Middleton was at his private safe, spinning a dial. He opened the door and found an envelope containing a special letter. "You know our charter, and this is your authorization. Show it to the person in charge, but nobody stands in your way, got it? Bring him home."

At the safe house, Hunt and Walker let an hour pass, waiting for permission that never came, before they went in to question Swanson again.

"You can end this right now. Just talk to us," said Special Agent Dave Hunt. "What's your name?"

Swanson remained silent. He was cold, but he would be warm again, someday. This was only temporary. No matter what they did, it was only temporary. He said nothing.

"Damn you," Hunt muttered. "We need answers—now! Do you understand? It is no small matter, and you're not in that chair because of back taxes or some fucking parking ticket. Our national security is at risk."

Carolyn Walker stepped before him and held up the photograph of a man. "This is Saladin. You killed him in Paris. Even if you were not the sniper who first brought him down, we have you on video putting a bullet in his head at point-blank range. We were right across the street at the time, and Saladin was under close surveillance."

She shuffled that picture to the bottom of a small stack and held up another head-and-shoulders photograph. "Here's your second victim, a bodyguard." Then she showed him still another. "Your third was the driver. You massacred three men and then ran inside that house, and that was followed by gunshots and the big explosion."

She held up a final photograph. "This was the only other person inside, another bodyguard, and I assume you killed him, too, because you came out and he didn't." Carolyn Walker stopped talking and stared at Kyle. He had blinked when shown the final photograph. "What is it? You recognize this man?"

Kyle said nothing. *Oh, yeah. I know him all right.* He had been using the entire time since the last procedure to pump in deep breaths to store up oxygen, because he knew more water was on the way. As a sniper, he had been trained to slow down his life in critical moments, to breathe regularly under stress, and, most of all, to never panic. The picture had thrown off his rhythmic breathing pattern.

"You'll talk," Walker said. "Sooner or later, everyone talks." At her signal, the wet towel was thrown back over his face.

He heard water slosh as a bucket was hoisted and he gobbled air, ordering himself to relax rather than fight it this time. *Temporary. Temporary.* His brain ticked off the seconds as the buckets emptied, pouring over him and into the big tub below. The soaked towel was to simulate the feeling of being smothered but actually helped keep the water moving instead of flooding into his nostrils and lungs. He could hear and sense everything but after the first minute decided to turn off the sound for a while and just lived in his head.

The gnarly pipeline wipeout in Hawaii was one favorite memory. One moment, standing in control on the board with the bright sun overhead and the big wave roaring its protest at being ridden, then the curl catching and dumping him. Down he went into the swirling, powerful wash, and a strong underwater current pushed him beneath a rock. Thought he would never be able to climb out of that hole where the green water was trying to kill him. Two minutes. Chest getting tight, and he let some of the old air bubble in his lungs escape to ease the pressure. Two and a half.

When the towel was removed, he switched on his own lights again. Nothing had changed except his freedom to breathe. Kyle looked up at the agents and brayed a loud and challenging laugh as streams of water streamed down his face. One of his defense mechanisms when he was in a tight spot was to turn it into a game, something that was not so serious. "Come on, you pussies! Can't you do better than that? Feeling sorry for the prisoner? Damned amateurs."

Hunt and Walker stormed from the room. "Did you notice that he didn't even move this time? That first session, he shook like a leaf." Hunt said.

Walker peeled off her windbreaker and hung it over the back of her chair. "He was playing with us," she said. "I'm bringing the doctor and the crash cart down here to stand by for resuscitation. This time, I'll drown the son of a bitch, if I have to."

"I just had a thought, Carolyn. We've had him for almost a full day and he has not once asked for a lawyer.

Any normal American would be screaming for an attorney by now."

"Any normal person would have broken by now. He is too well trained to resist pressure and pain. I'm worried that he would rather die than talk."

"So I will take away that option. If the water fails this time, we resuscitate, then use chemicals to knock him out and push through those defenses."

"Might be fatal."

"Might be."

"Wish that authorization would come through."

Thirty more minutes passed before they went back into the room, this time with some white coats tagging along with them.

Medical staff, Kyle realized. He no longer gave any pretense of being subtle and started to loudly huff and puff to fill his lungs. One medic filled a syringe with propofol, a white liquid that would erase the last few minutes of Kyle's memory. As soon as he blacked out, the "milk of amnesia" would be administered, and he would not be able to recall what had happened to him during the drowning moments.

A dry and thinner towel was spread over his face this time. He closed his eyes and relaxed as the water began to pour, this time an almost unbroken stream, bucket after bucket. He raged silently in his mind: *Bring it, you shitbirds! Bring it on!*

A minute. Two minutes. Three. He was paddling off the Baja coast near kilo marker 57, going out several miles and just lingering in the hot sunshine. He was diving without scuba gear along the Australian watery wonderland of the Great Barrier Reef. He was in full rig, practicing planting explosives on the hull of a ship at night. He needed air now, just as he had needed air then. *Running low on fuel here, gang.* Bubbles. Gagging building in his throat. Water winning, seeping into his lungs. Four minutes. *Hold on*. Then an acceptance of death as the body's defenses caved in, the physical machine demanding air. *Temporary*. Five minutes and counting. Nothing left. He gasped and opened his mouth to suck in oxygen and the water poured in. He was drowning.

As he began to black out, he heard sounds, shouting in the room, and the towel was jerked away. *Air!* The chair popped to an upright position, and one of the white coats was there to help him regurgitate the water he had swallowed. His senses returned, blinking on one at a time like a series of switches, as he shivered violently against the straps, vomited water, and sucked in life-giving oxygen.

More people were in the room, heavy boots, yelling, moving like shadows. His eyes focused on a slim figure, a woman with short hair, dressed in black jeans and a black sweater: Sybelle!

She had an envelope in one hand, a pistol in the other, and a wicked gleam in her eyes. The questioners, along with the two agents that he assumed had been the bucket brigade and one of the white coats, were lined up along the far wall with their hands up, covered by four Marines in full combat gear. Sybelle had brought along overwhelming power for backup.

"Hey there, Dead Guy," she said. "I have your Get Out of Jail Free card here, and I'm supposed to give it to some chick named Carolyn Walker. What say we just pop these motherfuckers, get you dressed, and go find her?"

"I'm Agent Walker," Carolyn said, raising her voice to try to regain control. "What's going on? Military troops cannot be used in America."

Sybelle sailed the envelope toward her and told her to pick it up but stay by the wall. She kept her pistol trained on them. "You medics unbuckle this man and get him warm, right now. Blankets, towels, your own fucking clothes, whatever. Move!" Her voice was steely with anger, and the menace was not lost on the medical team.

Walker's look of surprise was total. "Dave, it's a direct order from the president and countersigned by the attorney general to give her the full and unconditional interagency support of the U.S. government."

"Jesus," said Hunt, reading the letter. He handed it back to Walker. "Okay, so you are some kind of undercover agent. We still should have been told you were coming onto our turf. And if you have this kind of pull, why didn't you just say so?"

Kyle had a jacket over his naked lap, and a medic was vigorously massaging his shoulders with a towel to get blood circulating again. As his voice returned, he issued orders. "Give us all documentation—written, video, and audio—of your surveillance operation in Paris and my interrogation. You keep nothing, no copies or backups." He nodded toward Sybelle. "We're special forces operators, so I still can't give you my name or reveal any details. It would be best for everyone if you just go back to your other business and pretend you never saw me."

Sybelle holstered her pistol and had the Marines stand down and leave. The agents relaxed, but when Dave Hunt started to talk, she snapped, "No questions. Just gather up that material so we can all get out of here."

Kyle stood unsteadily as Walker and Hunt left the room. He whispered to Sybelle, "I know who Juba is."

DENVER

The taxi spun along mile after mile on the long route between Denver International Airport and the city. The afternoon was clear, and the range of jagged and purple

Rocky Mountains, some still topped with snow, commanded his attention. They could be a problem.

After checking into a hotel, he strolled into Lower Downtown, LoDo, which had been a run-down part of the city until the Colorado Rockies were given a major league franchise. Coors Field was dark tonight because the Rockies were playing out of town, but Juba studied how the big stadium had been built right in the heart of the area, near Mile High Stadium, the home of the Denver Broncos football team, and the Elitch Gardens amusement park. Redevelopment flooded in and gentrified the entire former warehouse district. Nightlife now throbbed in fashionable LoDo.

Juba slept late and about noon showed up at Coors Field and joined a group of tourists being given an escorted visit through the ballpark by a charming young woman in a cowgirl hat who was a fountain of information. He watched the flags beyond the outfield, which were stuttering in the steady wind from the mountains, gusts that his sniper's eye judged to be about thirty miles per hour. The guide said high winds were not unusual around the city.

He considered the situation. Looked west beyond left field to the ridges of mountains. That kind of wind would blow the bubble of poison gas . . . where? Kansas? New Mexico? Empty states. It wouldn't work. He had misjudged this one, too.

Denver was the metropolitan area, but the real population of Colorado lived far out in the suburbs, and commuters thronged the big highways after work, driving seventy-five miles an hour to reach their homes many miles away in bedroom communities.

The West was too spread out for his purpose, big enough to swallow some small nations whole. He could cause severe damage, but even the new and stable gas

would dissipate too quickly on those mountain winds.
Coors Field was not the answer.

He was looking for more than just a baseball stadium—
something that was more of a net, a trap, somewhere with
no way out. He checked out of his hotel and headed back
to DIA and bought a ticket to California.

20

THE WHITE HOUSE

The president of the United States looked over the top of his rimless reading glasses as his chief of staff, Steve Hanson, came into the Oval Office through the door on the left, which led into the staff offices area. Almost at the same moment, the door on the right opened and Secretary of State Kenneth Waring came through the visitors' entrance. The president tossed his glasses onto the big desk. "Whatever it is, tell me outside."

The three moved out the double French doors to the right of the president's desk, across the narrow covered stone walkway, and into the Rose Garden. Secret Service guards shifted their stations accordingly along the columns of the walkway to the living quarters as the president moved down the few steps and onto the perfect rectangle of grass, raising his face to catch some of the bright sun after being indoors all morning. As he stretched his big arms over his head, then bent from side to side, he could see other black-clad agents on the roof of the White House. Sniper teams. Troubled times. "What's up? Ken, you start."

Secretary of State Waring's eyes gave away his excitement. His manner remained formal, but his foot was poking at some grass. "Mr. President, we have good news."

"Well?"

Waring spoke. "It looks like the whole Saladin thing has been resolved. Fizzled." He snapped his fingers like a stage magician. "Poof and gone."

"What the hell are you talking about?"

"There was a shooting in Paris a few days ago, and some gang lord took a bullet or two in the head. So did a couple of his bodyguards. Police ran his prints and identified him as an Algerian Muslim leader, a rich guy with a lot of terrorist contacts."

"Why is that important?"

"It took some time to make the real identification. The dead gangster was Saladin himself!"

The president pumped his fist like Tiger Woods sinking a twenty-foot put for an eagle. "Awwright!" *Swanson was successful.*

"And the best part is that we didn't have anything to do with it," Steve Hanson said. "The French are laying the shooting on al Qaeda. Cops found a sniper's lair in a sewer right across the street, beneath an abandoned car that was rented with a phony credit card and driver's license."

The secretary of state said, "The enemy of my enemy is my friend . . . but who really was our enemy on this one?"

"All of them were, and remain, our enemies. We remain at war with terror as a whole, not with a specific name or group." The president headed back to the Oval Office, taking big, confident strides, and plopped onto a sofa.

The secretary of state took a wingback chair, crossed his legs, and straightened a perfect crease in his trousers. "This started with an extremely deadly device in the hands of a crazed fanatic," he said. "Now the fanatic himself is dead."

"But where is the poison gas? Has it fallen into the hands of someone or some group we know nothing about?"

The president was somber, leaning forward with his elbows on his knees. *Did Swanson find the papers? Why haven't we heard from him?* "Guys, we have to make sure that monstrous thing does not reach America. If we have won some political leverage in this mess with Mr. Saladin, we need to cash it in now."

"So go on television with an address to the nation." Steve Hanson was already arranging the details in his mind. "No politics at all, no swipes at our critics, just a direct appeal to all Americans to pitch in and help. Better than that, make it a worldwide appeal, because the other nations also remain at risk until that poison threat is nullified." The secretary of state nodded agreement.

"Pulpit time," said the president. "We need to warn the people without unduly alarming them."

"Yes, sir," replied Steve Hanson.

"Ken," he asked, "what's the international community doing? Anything?"

"They are all keeping their cool right now, Mr. President. The strike in London sobered them all, and none of them want to be on the wrong side of this issue. Until that weapon is located, nobody wants to create problems. They may need the help of their neighbors in a big way if they are picked as the next target."

"Anything new on the Saladin auction?"

"Apparently that is at a standstill. Any nation or group that entered the bidding is keeping its actions very private, but who would be around to orchestrate that show now? With Saladin dead, the auction may be dead, too."

"Hopeful speculation," said the president. "There is always a number two man who becomes the number one man. If he has the plans, he can just step in and run the show. How do you rate the chances that somebody else is going to get hit?"

"Honestly, Mr. President, my gut tells me that it is going to happen."

The president nodded and went back to his desk and sat down. "Yeah. We'll keep up the pressure. I don't like having the United States of America in the crosshairs."

"We are doing everything we can, sir. We will lay out all the details at the National Security Council briefing. The news of Saladin's death will be leaking out of France by then. Pressroom will be in an uproar."

The president put his glasses back on and picked up a pen. As always, paperwork awaited. "Thanks for coming by, Ken. See you downstairs in a little while." When the door closed, the president touched the intercom and told his secretary not to let anyone in for the next fifteen minutes and to pass the word along to the Secret Service guards on all the doors.

Hanson stood before the big desk. "I just finished the debrief with General Middleton. Kyle Swanson got in and did the job, but the house blew up before he could grab any papers. Then he was snatched by our joint task force, brought back here, and worked over a bit, even waterboarded. He kept his mouth shut until Trident got him out. He's okay, and the operation is safe."

"We tortured our own guy?"

"Swanson is fine. Kyle had a brief firefight with some other guy at the house. He recognized him, but with a bomb ticking down inside the house, Swanson did not have time to pursue. Later, when he was being questioned, he was shown some photos and was able to confirm the identification. Apparently it was Saladin's right-hand man, a British-trained sniper who goes by the name of Juba. Kind of a legend in the dirty warfare trade."

"He may have the weapon, then?"

"Yes, sir. Or at least control of it." Hanson paused.

"We're going to have everybody working to find him, so should I keep Trident rolling?"

"Absolutely. And tell them I said they did well in France."

When the president was alone in the Oval Office, he looked at the paintings on the light vanilla walls: confident Franklin Roosevelt, somber Abraham Lincoln, elegant George Washington. Each had led the nation through times of crisis and into a brighter future. *I'd sure like to talk to those guys,* he thought. *Too bad this job didn't come with a training manual.*

His shoulders slumped; he pushed the papers aside, took off his glasses again and buried his face in his hands. He rubbed his eyes hard.

That weapon of vile poison was coming this way. He could almost feel it vibrating or doing whatever the hell those things did. America was a big place, a gloriously spread-out country with more freedom for individuals to roam than any other nation in the world and a security net that had gaping holes. He thought about how previous administrations had not even been able to stop millions upon millions of poor laborers from sneaking undetected across the southern border, and he understood that the northern border with Canada, although perceived as safer, was much longer and just as unprotected. The coasts and ports were funnels for dangerous men and cargo. So what chance did he really have against a skillful and determined team of terrorists? The tragedy of 9/11 had only proven the seriousness of the problem. The president sat there with the lives of 304 million men, women, and children weighing upon him and knew that he could not guard them all.

America could never be totally protected from those who wished to do her harm. To think she could be was an impossible dream.

SAN FRANCISCO

Juba was enjoying himself in the grandstand at AT&T
Park, eating salty peanuts and drinking cold beer as a cool
and steady breeze sailed up the bay and spilled over China
Basin Park. Canoes and kayaks floated in McCovey Cove
to await the splash of home run balls. The San Francisco
Giants were playing baseball against the team from Arizona, but that was not the point. He was there to recon a
potential target zone.

Almost as soon as he entered the arena and walked past
the monstrous, skeletal Coca-Cola bottle tilted at a twenty-
five-degree angle next to a huge four-fingered old-style
baseball glove, he knew he had found just the place. From
the mezzanine level, Juba could see downtown San Francisco and the long bridge across San Francisco Bay. Oak-
land was only ten miles away. There was a medium crowd
that evening, about twenty-five thousand fans, but the New
York Yankees were arriving in two days and all of the
stadium's 41,503 seats would be filled. The decision made,
he used his cell phone to call a number in Nogales, Mexico, and gave the man who answered a brief message.

After the game, Juba wandered down to Chinatown for
a hot and spicy meal of garlic chicken before returning to
his hotel and tuning in the world news on the thirty-two-
inch LCD high-definition television set in his room. The
news readers were still carrying on about London and the
death of Saladin in Paris. Soon they would have a fresher
subject. A better kill zone was being staked out at AT&T
Park.

Then he turned to his laptop and transferred a retainer
fee to the account of a private detective in Connecticut
who was hired occasionally for discreet jobs and background checks. The detective believed the client was a
major computer company that required the utmost confi-

dentiality. When the money transfer was confirmed, Juba sent the detective an e-mail telling him to find former U.S. Marine Kyle Swanson.

That night, Xavier Sandoval was in the confessional of a little church in the hills outside of Nogales, Mexico. The religious quandary was nothing new to him, a mysterious puzzle that had haunted him for the past three years. He was not a Muslim, and in fact didn't believe in any organized religion, but the ancient pull of the Roman Catholic Church still tugged at him. It was difficult to give up the teachings of a lifetime.

As a younger man, he had made his way to the United States to find work, only to end up in a bar fight in Texas and be arrested, deported back to Mexico, and slammed into a cell with other failed immigrants. It was shortly after the 9/11 attacks on the United States, and the government in Mexico City was eager to show common cause. Many of the prisoners, including Xavier Sandoval, were declared to be suspected terrorists, and vigorous interrogations followed in locations that were beyond prayer. By the time he was released, he really was a terrorist. He again crossed the border and this time made his way to Michigan, settling into a Muslim area with friends of friends he had known in prison. They were bound by an intractable hatred of the United States.

One day an Englishman appeared and plucked him from the crowd, and Xavier Sandoval went to work for the man everyone respectfully called Juba. He was kind and generous and quite talented at killing.

Still, there was a bit of conscience left inside Xavier, enough so that on the evening of the telephone call from Juba in San Francisco, he bathed, combed his hair, put on his best dark suit with a matching somber tie over a blue oxford-cloth shirt, and went to mass. The deep feelings of the liturgy and tradition and guilt seeped into him and drew him to the next level, staying after the service to give his confession. The priest was puzzled at the vague admissions of carnal and other little sins because it was obvious that the parishioner was greatly troubled, but Xavier knew when to stop talking. He did not expect absolution for his crimes; he had just wanted to hear the calm voice of a priest one last time. Then he walked calmly out into the warmth of the late summer night.

The next morning, he said a final prayer and asked God, if he was really up there, to grant him courage and forgiveness. It was a lot to ask, since he was about to murder several thousand people. The small man put on khaki pants and a yellow shirt and headed off to his job as a truck driver for the Diablo Gourmet Seasoning Company.

Diablo Gourmet was a *maquiladora* success story, owned by Americans and operated by Mexicans. Suppliers all over South and Central America cleaned and processed their spices and seasonings and sent them to Nogales, where the company blended and packaged the finished products and sped them on to some of the best restaurants across the American Southwest.

The Diablo operation had been established more than twenty years ago as a false front, a vital part of Saddam Hussein's Unit 999 operations in North America. The only traces of ownership were a lawyer's name and the post office box of a shell corporation in the Cayman Islands. Years of legitimate operations had made the familiar blocky buildings of Diablo Gourmet a welcome money generator in the Nogales area and allowed Unit 999 to smuggle almost anything it wanted to across the border.

About noon, every day of the week, three yellow trucks left the loading docks carrying fresh loads of Mexican spices and herbs. The guards at the international frontier could smell them coming, for the vented cargo holds exuded the powerful odors of sweet cinnamon and ancho chile pods, pungent epazote, overpowering vanilla, chile negro, and the citrusy blast of habaneros, considered the hottest chiles in the world. All were encased in plastic bags, glass bottles, or metal containers and shipped in cardboard boxes, but it was impossible to capture all of the smells. The arrival of the spice trucks reminded the inspectors and guards it was time for lunch, and the veteran drivers regularly left samples for the guards. Everyone loved good Mexican food, and the signature company logo of a little red devil prancing on a background of yellow was synonymous with quality, hot, authentic spices from south of the border.

Three yellow trucks at noon, day after day, year after year.

The trucks were familiar, the drivers known to the inspectors, and the company owned by Americans, so there were never serious delays when the vehicles came to the border, which had every conceivable security device. Big fences, new television cameras, dozens of computers, sniffer dogs, and experienced inspectors worked both sides of the line. The dogs, however, were useless when the small convoy of yellow trucks arrived, because their sensitive noses would twist in agony if they inhaled the scents of peppers and raw chiles. They whimpered, their eyes watered as if they were weeping, and they batted their paws against their muzzles, sneezing. As a courtesy, the lead driver would use his cell phone when the trucks were about a half mile from the border so the handlers could take the dogs for a nice walk away and protect them from the intolerable aromas. Day after day.

Today, one of the vehicles, number 14, had been especially engineered to contain several ranks of high-pressure storage cylinders that stood against the cab wall in the cargo area behind the boxes and containers of spices. Some of the tanks were plugged into small pipes that fed up to and out of the roof of the truck, and at the turn of a dashboard switch by the driver, the contents would flow out of two exhaust fans. Others were sealed for later use. All were filled with the toxic gas that had been perfected in the Iranian lab. From Paris, Juba had transmitted the final formula to a laboratory attached to the Diablo Gourmet factory, and a small production run was assembled.

At noon, all three yellow panel trucks with the dancing devil logos rolled through the checkpoint unmolested. Number 14 was the last truck in the line and was driven by Xavier Sandoval. Three miles from the border, when he passed the Mariposa exit on I-19, Sandoval placed a call to San Francisco and confirmed that he was on his way.

21

BALTIMORE

Sybelle Summers called General Middleton on a secure phone from the safe house and did a quick report to assure him the situation was under control and they would both be back at work tomorrow. Kyle needed rest tonight. Middleton accused him of just being lazy but authorized them to take the rest of the day off. It was already dark outside when one of the government types took them back to civilization, into the swarming normality of Baltimore and the comfort of a large hotel on the waterfront.

After taking showers, they met in the bar. A storm had moved in from the east, and a steady rain whipped by the wind provided entertainment beyond the big window, where pedestrians and traffic did erratic battle at intersections and, beyond that, small boats rode the incoming swells.

"What next?" Sybelle asked, tasting a tame scotch and water.

"Try to find Juba again," Kyle responded. He had already drained a cold pale ale microbrew and was on his second. The water treatment had left him dehydrated.

"That's not what I meant." She looked hard into his eyes. "This whole thing has gotten its teeth into me, Kyle.

Action, worry, violent ups and downs, and not knowing whether any of us will be alive tomorrow."

"We'll be alive. At least for tomorrow. Can't guarantee after that."

"How do you know?"

"If Juba had wanted to set off a demonstration gas attack in Paris, he would have done so by now. Why wait? He's hauling it somewhere else. Probably coming this way."

"See, that's just what I mean. Tomorrow is going to be just as bad as today until we stop this bastard. Thousands of people are at risk of dying, and you and I are racing to put ourselves right in the middle of the next ground zero in order to stop him." She reached across the table and grabbed both of his hands in hers. "Right now I need to stop being a Force Recon Marine and just be a woman for a couple of hours. I want a man's arms around me and some sweet nothings whispered in my ear."

"I see your point, Sybelle, but I ain't that guy."

"Oh, I know that. I outrank you anyway, and sleeping with you would almost be like incest. But I don't want you to be concerned if I'm gone for the next few hours. I am going to hit a club or two and look at the lights and dance and have a couple of drinks. Then some smooth-talking and beautiful man is going to pick me up and take me back to his apartment. I suggest you do the same."

"Pick up some dude?"

"Don't be weird. Call Rent-a-Blonde, or maybe buy a drink for that little brunette at the bar. Just don't be alone tonight." She squeezed his arm tightly, rose from the booth, and walked out, toward the music that she hoped was waiting for her somewhere uptown. She stood in the doorway to struggle into a raincoat and belt it tight. Kyle wondered what the pickup guy was going to think about the ankle holster and the Gerber knife.

The brunette watched Sybelle leave, then looked over at him. She wore a silk blouse with a subtle Chinese print and a matching brown skirt and shoes, with gold accessories. The triangular face was Midwest pretty, and her hair was shoulder length and layered. The brown eyes were questioning.

He ordered another beer and settled back, letting his mind roam. *We know who Juba is now, so the problem becomes finding him. What is he looking for? How can we put a net over him so I can kill him?* He closed his eyes and ran the mental loop again, everything he could recall about Juba and the earlier Trident discussions about how to nail the enemy sniper back when he was just the scourge of Iraq.

"Do you mind if I join you?" The soft question made him open his eyes.

"Sure. No. I mean not at all," said Kyle, snapping awake. "Please. Sit down. Nobody should be alone on a night like this."

Sybelle dropped her wet coat, slid in beside him, and ordered a drink.

GUILFORD, CONNECTICUT

Christopher Lowry firmly believed that he could find anybody; it was impossible for any American to completely disappear. When the ten-thousand-dollar retainer came in with the request for a location trace, the private detective poured another cup of coffee, put aside the *Courier,* and got to work. He and his wife, their five children, and two dogs lived in an old house on one of the many crooked, twisting roads around Sachem Head Harbor, and he always had bills to pay.

United States Marine Gunnery Sergeant Kyle Swanson. Trying the obvious first, he typed the name into several search engines, looked over the mass of hits, and decided that couldn't be right. He refined the search and got the same result. Then he switched to a restricted military database and again received the same information, along with a personnel jacket that ended with the man's burial at Arlington National Cemetery. The archives of several major newspapers, including the *Post* and the *Times,* contained stories covering the event and awarding the Marine the Medal of Honor. A friend in the state police entered the name into the NCIC database.

This Swanson guy was dead and planted. Lowry drank some more coffee and took the dogs for a walk. They tore around through the thick trees chasing squirrels and went splashing into the shallow water where fields of cattails grew tall, and Lowry let his thoughts go free as he limped along behind them. He had been on the New York Police Department for fifteen years and carried the shield of a detective before a bullet from a crack addict took away much of his left knee and forced him into retirement. Chris Lowry doubted if his client was going to be satisfied with a newspaper report that the man they were thinking about hiring had been dead for some time, buried in Arlington.

Okay, he thought, *so we start at the beginning.* The stories said the man was from South Boston. By noon, he was easing his blue Toyota sedan onto the Connecticut Turnpike, heading for Southie.

BALTIMORE

"Swanson! Where is that asshole and his poison gas?" The voice on the telephone brimmed with authority. Kyle blinked himself awake, shook Sybelle's bare shoulder, and silently mouthed the word "Middleton." She threw the bedcovers aside and sprinted, naked, to the open door between their rooms, as if the general could see between Washington and New York. She took nothing for granted, particularly where the Lizard might be involved. He had eyes and ears everywhere.

"General? Jesus, sir, what time is it?"

"Almost 0600. Gimme something that Wolf Blitzer doesn't already know."

"Can't do it, sir. I've been asleep. Just spent a day getting tortured, you know?"

"Bullshit. You went through stuff worse than that in boot camp. We've got a session at 0900 with the alphabet agencies, and it would take too long for you to drive, so the Lizard has laid on a helicopter to bring you and Summers back here. Where is she, anyway? Tried her room and no answer."

Kyle took time to yawn and sound sleepy. "I don't know, General. Probably out for a run. I'm not her keeper."

"Excellent. I ran three miles before breakfast myself and have been at my desk since five. Go get her and get on that bird."

"Three miles before breakfast. You are one hell of a Marine, sir," Kyle said.

"Hoo-ah," said the general and hung up.

Sybelle leaned against the adjoining door, a white towel around her and her beeper in her hand. "I have a message to call him."

"Forget it." He was leaning on his elbows, looking at her. "He has a helicopter coming in to fetch us back to the Pentagon."

"Damn, Kyle. This is what I meant last night when I told you the stress was getting to me. It never ends. Last night was great, but both of us know there is no future for any relationship. There is only room for work, and I almost feel like a traitor for having sex with you."

"Yeah. It would only complicate things." It was the first time he had had a serious sexual interlude since the death of Shari Towne. "But thanks for rescuing me yesterday, in more ways than one."

She let the towel fall and dropped the beeper on top of it. "Hoo-ah."

Precisely at 0845, a shining black government SUV was waiting at the Pentagon and all four members of Task Force Trident climbed aboard. "Sar'nt Johnson! Take us to the Old Exec and go in through the gate. It's next to the White House. You know where that is, I assume."

"Excuse the general's abrupt manner, Sergeant," said Kyle. "He ran three miles before breakfast and then drank too much coffee."

The driver managed a smile. They were already out of the parking lot and into traffic. "Fast or medium fast, sir?"

"Fast," replied the general, and the sergeant clicked on the siren and lights and swerved into a hole between two yellow cabs, setting off a round of horn honking.

In the rear, the Lizard looked at Sybelle with a strange smirk.

"What?" she said. *The little fucker knows!*

"Oh, nothing. Just thinking." He blushed and looked away.

A private and secure conference room had been set aside for them on the second floor of the Old Executive Office Building, and it was empty when Middleton led his team down the checkerboard-tile hallway to an office that was guarded by a uniformed member of the U.S. Secret Service. From the outside, the location seemed no different than any other in the busy office building, but the old wooden door opened into an airlock, and just inside, a step put a visitor above a false floor and into a slightly smaller room that also had a false ceiling and soundproof glass. Sound was imprisoned within the room.

"Send them in, please," said General Middleton as they entered, and the Trident group went ahead and took chairs around a table. The Secret Service agent opened the door again, and two more people entered.

Agent Carolyn Walker looked refreshed, in a starched white blouse with a crisp collar and tailored gray pinstriped trousers. The night at home had helped her. Dave Hunt of the FBI still appeared disgruntled but was in a different suit. Their eyes took in the four people waiting for them, and puzzlement was written on their faces because they had put one of them through the wringer the previous day and another one had threatened to kill both of them.

"Please, have a seat," said Middleton, sweeping his hand toward vacant chairs. He smiled. "Thank you both for coming over on such short notice."

"General, what is this about?" asked Walker. The urgent summons to attend this meeting had left her in a foul mood. The Old Exec was neutral ground, neither Pentagon military nor government granite. It guaranteed no home field advantage for bickering agencies.

"Simply put, you two are back in the game." Middleton leveled his gaze at them but did not raise his voice.

"And what game is that, exactly?" asked Hunt.

"Probably the biggest of your careers." The general opened his file and slid out the picture of Juba. "You took this in Paris, right? The subject's code name is Juba, and he is a motivated and extremely skillful terrorist operative. We believe he is about to hit the United States with a poison gas weapon much larger than the one that went off in London. We have to stop him."

Walker nodded but put the picture aside. "We want to

help, believe me, but I don't take orders from you, General."

"Me either," said Hunt, his voice not much more than a growl. "I'm FBI, and she is Department of Homeland Security. We have our own chain of command. I know the letter that woman waved at us yesterday outranked us for the time being, but that was then. Big difference."

Middleton was unperturbed. "Earlier this morning, the directors of both of your agencies signed authorizations of temporary duty assignments for you. Now you're mine." He slid a document to each of them to verify his statement. "You are veteran and experienced agents, cleared for Top Secret material and beyond, so here it is. Everything I am going to tell you is above top secret."

"Way above," agreed the Lizard, pointing a finger toward the ceiling. He had opened his laptop. "Big way."

The general glanced over. "That is Lieutenant Commander Benton Freedman, our do-it-all electronics and communications officer. Next to him is Marine Captain Sybelle Summers, whom you met yesterday. And finally, the man you captured, Gunnery Sergeant Kyle Swanson, also USMC. The four of us make up Task Force Trident, and that is what you are now attached to."

"So it's a military black op outfit?"

"Is Swanson an assassin? We saw him shoot Saladin."

"Let's just say he is a specialist," Middleton replied smoothly. "And, no, we are not really a military unit at all. We just carry the baggage for Swanson. Now, the reason you could not identify him yesterday is that he is officially dead, with a headstone at Arlington to prove it. Every record was scrubbed clean a couple of years ago. Swanson was the best scout-sniper in the Marine Corps and specialized in black ops. His death was staged to create a unique place in which he could still operate under the deepest of covers. He simply ceased to exist. The Invisible Man."

"Excuse me, General," said the Lizard in a quiet voice.

Middleton ignored him, concentrating on the sales pitch. "Trident was set up to support Swanson. We work for him, because he needs specialized backup, and putting him under the Department of Agriculture didn't seem appropriate. Don't worry, this is totally legitimate, just way off the books."

Walker rubbed her eyes. "This is confusing. Why do you want us involved when you have all of the Pentagon resources under your thumb?"

Kyle finally spoke. "Because you both impressed me. You not only snatched me off the street in France and got away with it, but you also were willing to bend the rules to get the answers you needed. I want that kind of help for this job."

"General Middleton." The Lizard again tried and was ignored.

Kyle continued, "You continue to run your normal operations and use every trick in your books, but cut us in on everything and help push things along with any special needs we might have. Nobody knows about Trident, but everyone jumps when the FBI or DHS shows up on their doorstep. You two bring a lot to the table for this job."

"You're going to kill this guy? We can't go along with another assassination. That Saladin hit was obviously illegal, but it was done on foreign soil."

"Of course." Middleton smiled again. "If a congressman ever asks, we want to arrest Juba, same as you. I'll back you all the way."

Dave Hunt grunted. "I can live with that, but let's look at this from the other side of the line. Even Swanson here admits that we are pretty good at what we do. So why do we need Trident?"

Kyle placed both hands on the wooden tabletop. "All

due respect, Agent Hunt, but you guys are never going to catch Juba if he doesn't want to be caught. He is a master at this sort of thing, and I think he has slipped over a psychotic edge to a point where he doesn't really care who he kills. I want to find him and get his attention enough so that I'll be at the top of his list. The two of us have a bit of a history, so it will be more than a matter of professional pride for him. It's personal. He will want a clean hit and the satisfaction of seeing me fall."

Walker looked at Swanson. "You want to set up a duel with this guy? You can make someone that mad?"

Sybelle and Middleton nodded in the affirmative. "Recall how angry he made you yesterday?" Sybelle said. "Pissing people off is perhaps what he does best."

"General!" Freedman interrupted again, his voice urgent, and he would not be refused a third time.

"What is it?" Middleton snapped.

A red warning light was flashing in the corner of Freedman's computer. "The Connecticut State Police just pinged the NCIC for any and all available information about Swanson."

BOSTON

Private investigator Chris Lowry spent all afternoon gathering the remarkable life of Kyle Swanson: birth records, family genealogy, education, mentions in wills, Social Security number, job history, a couple of scrapes with the police, driver's license, and then into the Marines. All of it was down in black and white, even with pictures of the young man in the yearbooks of South Boston High. The military file from the Marines was precise, and all of the dates matched. It was odd that the service had been so willing to help when usually there are iron rules against giving a service jacket to a non-family-member. He had listed it all on a yellow legal pad, and everything locked together like a neat puzzle. That was what bothered him. Life was never this neat. Clerks screwed up. Papers were misfiled. Memory played tricks. Information did not always match. This was too clean, as if it had been made that way on purpose. Sanitized.

With the data logged into his laptop, he started hitting the sidewalks, looking for those whose names had been linked along the line with Swanson back in the day. The good thing about a place like South Boston was that many family members stayed in place for generations, and it was easy to track them down. His cover story was that he was a magazine reporter putting together a piece on this true American hero and he needed personal anecdotes. Most were happy to share their memories, and steered him to Kyle's schoolhood chum Michael McLaughlin.

McLaughlin, a short and scrappy man, had been Swanson's best friend in high school and his baseball teammate. Kyle and Michael had been friends for years, and Swanson always felt better when he was pitching to know that McLaughlin was roaming behind him at shortstop. Those nervous, fast feet and incredible reflexes helped Mike make double plays out of hard-hit balls that taller players could not have even reached. Michael also had a remarkable combative streak that went far beyond mere competition. In a day when schools were moving to rubber cleats, Michael stayed with the metal ones, persuading the coaches that they improved his footing. Kyle would often see Michael sitting close to his locker, hands inside and out of sight, sharpening his spikes. Kyle Swanson had always made a point of hitting an opposing batter early in the game, just to set the tone for the day. That tactic would put a runner on first base, who would try to retaliate by taking out the shortstop on the next ground ball, and Michael would grind the runner up like hamburger. Swanson kept score of the players spiked by Mike.

They stayed in touch after high school, when Kyle went into the Marines and Michael tried the minor leagues for a few years before returning home to South Boston. Then Kyle slowly withdrew from the Southie crowd, because when he came back he could not tell them where he had been or what he had been up to. Still, Swanson stayed in distant touch by sending postcards from far-off lands and then birthday and Christmas gifts for his godchild, Mike's daughter, Mary Elizabeth. The nine-year-old girl thought the world of her uncle Kyle and missed him terribly, Mike explained.

The detective thanked McLaughlin for the interview and left. Not much to report after a full day of investigating, using both high-tech and low-tech methods. He found a wi-fi zone at an Internet café and wrote his report, attaching copies of documents and logs of the names, phone numbers, and addresses of the people he talked to and a synopsis of each conversation. He included his own opinion that it seemed someone had made sure that everything pointed to the conclusion that the Marine had been fatally wounded in Syria and buried in Arlington. No further action was possible, the detective wrote, short of going out there and digging up the grave. He sent the e-mail and drove back to Guilford. Traffic was a bear heading out of Boston during rush hour.

A team of FBI agents was waiting in the driveway when he got home.

"I knew this was too easy," Lowry said to himself as he got out of his car and approached them, holding his hands out from his sides in plain view.

22

A command center had been established in the Hoover Building, and agents from various national security agencies were working computers and telephones. Printers and faxes churned through reams of paper. Wiring curled around the floor to power the armada of electronics. Maps were pinned on cork boards along one wall, and white greaseboards marched side-by-side down another wall. There was clatter enough to make everyone look busy. All looking for Juba.

Kyle was in an adjacent room with the Trident team, away from the main force of civilians but watching the operation on several television sets. The Lizard complained that the equipment that was being used was practically antique, but Kyle had been impressed by how Dave Hunt and Carolyn Walker had pitched in and mobilized their massive resources so quickly. Things were moving fast now that they were all on the same page and knew who they were looking for.

With Kyle's identification of the man who got away in Paris, British police swooped in and arrested Dr. Allen Osmand and his wife, Martha Goodling Osmand, at their home. A montage of photographs was built of their son,

Jeremy, from his sports days at school through the time in the Royal Marines to the fuzzy picture from the house in Paris. A computer smoothed out the details, made comparisons with key points, and created an accurate and up-to-date image.

That was fed into a database of facial recognition software that examined the image against the airport photographs of everyone who had entered the United States in the past few days. The computer did its work at blazing speed, but it still took time to check the digitized photos of tens of thousands of newcomers.

Meanwhile, a nationwide alert was issued for Jeremy Osmand, a known terrorist who was to be considered armed and dangerous. The Department of Homeland Security photograph was given to all of the television networks.

"We've got a hit," said Agent David Hunt as he entered the Trident enclave and closed the door behind him. "He came in at Dulles three days ago as a businessman on a Dutch passport. The customs officer and the airplane's crew will be interviewed, but it is doubtful that they will remember him unless he did something to attract attention, which is unlikely."

The Lizard pulled up the security camera picture of Juba passing through the gate. "Looks ordinary," he said.

"That's the point," said Kyle. "He disappeared into the background. Nobody would have noticed him."

"Now we're switching the computer to scan domestic flights to see where he's gone."

"Good luck with that," said Kyle.

Hunt took offense. "We caught you, didn't we?"

"But you got the wrong guy."

Dave Hunt left the room, muttering beneath his breath.

General Middleton shook his head. "Play nice, Gunny. What are you thinking?"

Swanson walked around the table and looked out of the only window to the street, where civilians were going about their daily routines in the heart of Washington. Behind him, the image of Juba was still on the three television screens. "This is all out of some James Bond movie. Those people out there have all the toys, but they still don't know who they are really dealing with. Juba is a damned good sniper. He is not running away to avoid prosecution, he is moving with great speed and deliberation toward a specific objective."

"He's stalking a target," Sybelle added.

"And he knows I am coming after him, which is why he had that investigator in Connecticut checking me out." Kyle picked up the transcript of the exhaustive FBI interview with private detective Chris Lowry, who had been totally cooperative. Discretion was one thing in keeping a client's confidentiality, but a federal subpoena was much different. He gave them everything he had.

"Look down where Lowry reported back to his 'client,' who has to be Juba using another false front. He listed everyone he spoke with during the day and a brief outline of the conversations. When he was talking with my old high school buddy Mikey McLaughlin, the detective also mentioned that I was godfather to his nine-year-old daughter, Mary Elizabeth. Juba sent an e-mail right back to thank him and added that he would talk with Michael and the girl, Mary Elizabeth, personally." Kyle dropped the transcript. "Now why would he do that?"

Carolyn Walker from the DHS had been following the conversation without adding anything, but now she spoke up. "He did not have to respond at all, and in fact, he did terminate that entire e-mail link after sending that message. The conclusion is that he intends to attack that little girl in order to draw you into the open."

"And how have you responded to that threat?" Swanson asked.

"Boston is being flooded with extra agents to help secure the area, and some HRT countersniper teams are standing by. He won't get near her." Walker looked steadily across the table. The routine was in place, concentrating overwhelming manpower on a trouble spot, building a protective web around the target.

"It is a waste of time, money, and resources, Agent Walker," said Kyle. "Juba has no plans to go after my goddaughter and couldn't reach her even if he did. What you people aren't mentioning is that you have a file a foot thick on Mikey. His uncle Tim runs some of the healthier criminal enterprises in Boston, everything from gambling and girls to dope and supplying money for what's left of the Irish Republican Army. Mikey is Tim's chief enforcer. No, Mary Elizabeth is quite safe."

"So why did he send the message, if that is indeed what happened?"

"A diversion. It is a sniper's habit to make pursuers chase their tails instead of him. He took an action with minor risk that caused you people to have a major reaction."

Dave Hunt came back into the room. "We now have him in the domestic air system, flying from Washington to Tampa."

SAN FRANCISCO

Juba's warning antenna was quivering. He had rented a spacious, fully equipped automotive garage in a small industrial park on the outskirts of San Francisco, and while he was working, he kept an eye on a small black-and-white television set perched on a workbench. His picture was on part of the screen, and he walked over, wiping his hands on a greasy rag, to turn up the volume. A colorful SPECIAL ALERT logo was imprinted below the woman news reader giving the report. National security authorities had issued a request for all citizens to watch for this man, Jeremy Osmand, a known terrorist believed to be somewhere in the United States at the moment. Do not approach him by yourself, she said. Call the police.

Juba had purchased a 2004 Ford Excursion, the biggest sport utility vehicle ever produced in the United States, for a 20 percent cash down payment and his signature on a lot of legal papers. It shone dull silver beneath the overhead lights of the garage, where he had been clearing out everything behind the front seats to create a long, flat deck. Now he got in, rolled up the big front door, and drove to his motel, a nice mid-priced facility. He parked two blocks away and walked down a narrow alley, with a dirty 49ers cap tilted low on his face. At the corner, he went into a health food store, bought a cup of vanilla chai, and sipped it as he scanned the area.

He had been there for two nights but had only been seen by the night clerk. Had the young man already recognized the picture on the screen and called the authorities? It did not seem that way, because there were no unmarked police cars in the neighborhood, no vans with tinted windows, and no strong young men pretending to do work. No cops, but they would find this place sooner or later. He had to take the chance.

The pistol was snug in the waistband of his jeans, beneath the floppy T-shirt, but he needed the contents of a plastic bag that he had left in the bathroom and the big gun that was hidden in the air-conditioning vent of his room.

It was difficult to buy a good weapon in the People's Republic of San Francisco, but back in the late 1980s, American law enforcement had turned a blind eye toward al Qaeda representatives who had made many open purchases at gun shows around the country. Those guns were believed to be for export to Afghanistan and the war against the Soviets, but a number of them went into secret caches such as the one that had been stored in northern California. He had picked up an Armalite civilian knockoff of the famous .50 caliber Barrett, which had been purchased from a gun show in Sacramento. There was a little .22 Bushmaster, too, but Juba wanted the big kick.

He dumped his drink and circled the block to approach the motel from a direction that could not be seen by the front desk, sauntered up the single flight of stairs, and was quickly into the corner room. The maid had already been by to clean up and prepare the bed, and the room had fresh towels and the smell of pine aerosol. He stole the towels and pushed them into the plastic bag with the box of Clairol Nice 'n Easy hair coloring, then unscrewed the wall vent with a tiny screwdriver on his army knife and pulled out the Armalite in its carrying case. Four minutes after entering the room, he was out. Time mattered now, and he still had chores to do.

A hospital located twenty miles from the baseball stadium was commonly known as "the Saints." It had been founded by Mormons as a business and charitable venture; the Latter-day Saints sold it to the Catholic Church in 1993, and it was renamed St. Mary's Hospital. Sick people did not care which saints were in charge as long as the doctors and nurses took care of them. The Saints encompassed four floors of a modern building and had earned a reputation as a top-rated trauma center.

The previous day, Juba had picked out an apartment about two hundred yards away from the Saints, and now he drove there and parked in an empty space behind the low building. He went up the inside stairwell and needed only thirty seconds to pick the lock. It was the middle of a sunny afternoon, and the dead bolt had not been engaged by the young mother watching television. She only had time to turn in surprise when she heard the door open; Juba shot her before she could scream. He carefully went through the apartment and found a little boy playing in a bedroom. The kid looked up just before the trigger was pulled. Juba pulled the dead woman into the light blue bathroom that smelled like daisies and dumped her in the white bathtub. Her four-year-old son was placed atop her body. The gunman dipped a washcloth in the boy's blood and wrote his name on the tile: *JUBA*.

In the refrigerator, there was some leftover chicken in a covered bowl, which he heated in the microwave and brought into the living room with a dish of cold potato salad. As he ate lunch, he studied the unobstructed view from the window: a large white sign with EMERGENCY ROOM printed in large blue letters and a concrete ramp that jutted into the driveway to allow ambulance drivers to back right up to it and wheel their gurneys smoothly from the vehicle and straight into the trauma unit.

Then it was back to the garage.

WASHINGTON, D.C.

"About seven hundred and fifty million passengers flew on some eleven million flights from U.S. airports last year," said Lieutenant Commander Freedman, surging around the Internet. "That's a lot of faces for the computer to look at, and they won't find anything if he rented a car and drove somewhere."

"Damn, Liz. Don't even think like that," said Sybelle Summers. The Trident group was bored. They liked answers crisp and quick. The coffee was stale and so was the air.

"We have people on it down in Florida," said Carolyn Walker. "If he's there, we'll find him."

"That means Juba has split our resources yet again," Kyle said. "First Boston and now Tampa–St. Pete."

"Not much down there," said Walker.

General Middleton looked up from working the *New York Times* crossword puzzle. "Right. Nothing at all. Just sunshine and MacDill Air Force Base and the headquarters of the U.S. Central Command, which runs the wars in Iraq and Afghanistan. We've jacked security to the max around them."

The doorknob turned and Special Agent David Hunt came in. "He is still on the move. Flew from Tampa to Denver."

Middleton swept the newspaper from the table and stood up. "Oh, fuck," he growled. "That's Cheyenne Mountain. Lizard, get me a secure voice link to the Joint Chiefs at the Pentagon so they can lock 'em down."

Walker knew the incredible importance of the system that was the electronic heart of the nation's defenses. "That facility is buried two thousand feet underground. It's heavily guarded and can be completely sealed off. Those people are totally safe from any gas attack."

Kyle Swanson grimaced. "Their families aren't. Even so, I can't see that as the attack point. Not a big enough crowd, and the security level is always high throughout that area."

"Then where is he going to hit?" asked Walker. "What is drawing him to these places?"

"Think about targets," Kyle answered. "Juba wants a huge splash, something bigger than London. We don't see it yet, but he does. He is not moving at random."

SAN FRANCISCO

Xavier Sandoval found the garage address without difficulty, stopped the yellow Diablo Gourmet truck, and honked his horn. Juba pushed a button inside and the main garage door rolled back. Sandoval steered the truck inside and parked beside a huge SUV.

"Welcome, brother," said Juba, embracing the man as a friend. "How do you feel after such a long drive?"

"Tired, but not too bad. I have grown to hate talk radio." Sandoval laughed. He drank from a cold bottle of water offered by Juba. "You are aware of the police bulletins that are out with your name and description?"

Juba pointed to the little television set. "I have been watching most of the day. My parents have been arrested, but the Crusaders still have not figured out what is going to happen. We remain in control, but we must hurry. I hope you have a few more hours of work left in you."

"That is why I am here, brother."

They put on coveralls and stacked four fifty-pound sacks of ammonium nitrate fertilizer across the width of the SUV cargo compartment, which could handle up to a ton of payload. A small fork lift was used to hoist a single, heavy fifty-five-gallon drum of liquid nitromethane and carefully nudge it forward against the barrier of bags; then they packed four more sacks of fertilizer along the near side of the drum. Their work was fast and silent, and they moved with determination, climbing inside the Excursion to secure the deadly pyramid of explosive components with strong fabric straps. A blue and white striped awning, common at tailgate parties, was arranged over the stack and anchored by several plastic picnic coolers, lawn chairs, and a folding table. The forty-four-gallon gasoline tanks were topped off with a series of five-gallon cans.

Then both took quick showers and washed off the stink and any residue from the dangerous mixture.

Once Juba and Sandoval were clean and dressed in fresh clothing, they pulled a rug from the little office area and spread it out, knelt down facing toward the east, and offered prayers to Allah. Two hours until game time.

Juba tested the circuit of a digital detonator, set it for four hours, and plugged it into four bricks of C-4 explosive that were tied together.

"Let's go to the ballpark," he said. The big door rolled up, and Juba drove away in the Excursion, followed by the Diablo Gourmet truck. The smells inside the SUV were overpowering and forced him to crank up the air conditioner all the way. He sprayed a couple of cans of air freshener back over his shoulder. Even that wasn't enough, and he reluctantly opened the front windows for circulation, but not the blackened rear portals.

At the stadium, he joined one of the lines entering the parking lot, and the nineteen-year-old cash collector twitched her nose at the odor coming from the big SUV. "Gosh, mister, that's some kinda smell!"

"Uh-huh. I run a lawn service," said Juba. "Ordinarily I would have cleaned it, but I wanted to get here early to set up the tailgate. Me and my buddies got seats right by the Yankee dugout." He smiled at her. "Hey, you looking for another job? Pay you good wages to muck out this truck every day."

She took the money and gave him a ticket to put on his dashboard. "No way. Not with, like, that smell. You ain't got that much money. Enjoy the game."

He followed the striped lines until he found a parking spot near the edge of AT&T Park, where he got out and closed and locked the door. The truck had an American flag decal on a heavily tinted window, and a green bumper sticker proudly announced: MY DAUGHTER IS AN HONOR STUDENT AT TURNER MIDDLE SCHOOL. Juba considered those signs to be urban camouflage. The Excursion weighed seven thousand pounds, was almost nineteen feet long, and stood six and one-half feet tall but would not draw a second glance in any parking lot.

Still an hour before the first pitch. Beautiful evening. Sellout crowd.

Instead of entering the stadium, Juba walked across the parking lot and found a taxi heading out after dropping off a passenger. He gave directions to go to the apartment building across from the Saints. When he was in position, he called Xavier Sandoval, who was parked about a mile from the ballpark. The game was about to begin.

"Another match! He's hopscotching all over the place," said Dave Hunt. "He went out of Denver on a flight to San Francisco. Anything of great military value out there, General?"

"No, not anymore."

"We are scrambling the West Coast people to check the hotels and motels, and the cops are getting a readout that he might be in their area. Maybe he's just passing through there, too."

"Could he be going after some other government installation, say, a courthouse, like in Oklahoma City?" Sybelle didn't believe it but was just throwing out ideas.

"Every city has government buildings. He would not have to keep moving around so much to attack one."

"Maybe a big mall? A theme park."

"Anywhere in the U.S.A., but none that are unusual or noteworthy in those three cities."

Kyle Swanson was barely listening. There was nothing he could do but wait and try to think like a sniper stalking a target. He picked up the sports section of the *Times*. The newspaper was great at covering the rest of the world but totally hometown oriented when it came to sports. The lead story was the pitching rivalry for today's game between the Yankees and . . . *Tampa–St. Pete. Denver. San Francisco.* The cities tumbled around in his brain like dice in a cup, and when spilled onto a table, dice always form a pattern.

Stalk the target. Forget a hit on any military installation because the word was out and the guards were alert. *Tampa–St. Pete. Denver. San Francisco.* What do they have in common? No huge conventions going on. No presidential visit. Vacation time in the summer and people in a laid-back mode. Old people in Florida, modern cowtown in Denver, political antiwar nutcakes in San Francisco. Nothing remotely connecting them there. Denver Broncos, San Francisco 49ers, and Tampa Bay Bucs in pro football, but in separate conferences because they were spread across the country. The Devil Rays, the Rockies, and the Giants in major league baseball. Big stadiums. Can't-miss targets. *Yes. That's what I would do.*

Swanson poked his finger onto the newspaper story. "The game. I'll bet that he's going after the baseball game between the Yankees and the Giants. More than forty thousand people will be there, sitting around peacefully in neat rows, waiting to be killed, with hardly any security to protect them."

The room went silent for a few heartbeats as they stared at each other. Then Carolyn Walker and David Hunt crashed out of the door and started yelling orders to their people.

The bomb in the Excursion exploded during the third inning, raking the parking lot and shattering the broad edge of the urban ballpark, collapsing part of the wall into a pile of bricks. The first thought for San Francisco residents was that it was an earthquake, a feeling that lasted only a moment, until some people recognized the explosion and started yelling, "Terrorists!" Ballplayers ran from the field, and fans stormed the exits, leaping over seats, pushing up and down the stairs, and trampling the slow, the infirm, and the small. The stampede steered away from the destroyed side of the stadium, and there was no thought by those in the outfield bleachers of waiting for a slow ferryboat to take them back across the bay. Run! They poured across the green field and out through the concrete tunnels looking for a way out, fighting for a place in the mob to reach a front exit, and adding to the panic.

Police warnings were ignored. Arguments flared, fists and elbows were thrown, and several shots rang out and people fell, ignored by those who were still running. Safety was at the end of the tunnels. Just get out of the stadium and everything would be okay. Screams howled behind them, rising from the stands.

Two minutes after the big car bomb explosion, Xavier Sandoval drove his yellow truck away from the vendors' loading docks at the stadium and stalled it in the path of the fleeing crowd. He ripped out the ignition wires and activated the roof vents and fans, jumped from the cab, and ran for the street. With a hissing sound that could not be heard above the noise, the aerosol spray rose from the poison canisters in the truck bed and spewed into the air, riding the slight breeze into a slow, lazy arc as it settled onto the frightened men, women, and children who were running right into the misty veil that was softly falling across the kill zone.

23

Xavier Sandoval was a nervous man by the time he arrived at the apartment complex. He had run as fast as he could for several blocks, ignoring the chaos creeping behind him, until his breath and limbs began to falter. Traffic had slowed, then stopped as drivers gaped in astonishment at the smoke roiling from the ballpark explosion. He punched one, threw the man out of the way, and jumped behind the steering wheel, hijacking the car. A sharp turn down an alley and Sandoval accelerated from the danger zone, his shirt soaked in sweat.

He parked in the apartment lot and sat still, breathing deeply and trying to convince himself that he had escaped the poison gas. Leaving the keys in the ignition as instructed, he staggered up the concrete stairs and found the door that Juba had designated. When it opened, he almost did not recognize the man.

Juba had showered and changed the color of his hair to midnight black. The hair itself had grown ragged around the edges since he had left Iran, and he had not shaved since entering the United States and had several days' growth of beard, giving him the distinctive look of a foreigner. He wore owlish glasses with round gold frames. If police were profiling suspects to identify suspicious Middle Eastern males, Juba would have fit the image.

Sadoval came inside and locked the door, then sat on a chair and looked up. "The package was delivered. I will never forget this day."

"You did a perfect job," Juba told him with a pat on the shoulder. *The man's courage is slipping.* "Almost finished now."

A television set was on in the corner, showing wide shots of the carnage from a helicopter while reporters who were safe within their studios broadcast the warnings for everyone to avoid the area of the ballpark. It was a poison gas attack, and authorities were saying the material was still in the air. Police had established barricades and were evacuating people as fast as possible. The high camera showed the flashing lights of ambulances, police cars, and fire trucks popping bright colors across a multitude of bodies. Among those fallen at odd angles were the uniformed figures of first responders who had tried to help and transferred the poisonous gel to their own skins. The entire rescue effort had slowed to a crawl until the emergency personnel were ordered into their hazmat suits.

In the apartment, Juba heard sirens wailing, coming to the Saints. "Are you ready?"

Sandoval gulped. "Yes."

"I have set up this position carefully for you. The rifle is loaded and ready, and you have a clear line of sight. When the ambulances arrive, open fire on the hospital personnel, the patients, the police, bystanders . . . anyone. We want to create pandemonium in a place that everyone perceives as safe. Keep firing until the clip is empty, then reload and use the second clip, and then the third. Take your time, because no one is going to be coming over here in the face of such hostile action. Then drop the rifle, take the car, and leave."

"And you, my brother? I do not know about being a sniper, but you do."

"I'm going to another position higher up and wait until after you shoot. Let them get back to work, thinking the danger is over. That is when I strike. It will be devastating." He moved to the door as the sirens came closer. "I will be in contact soon. Good hunting, brother. You have done well."

Sandoval watched a police car roll up, lights flashing, with a bright green fire truck on its bumper, their sirens gliding to a finishing growl. He was hidden in the shadow of the room. The scene was frightening, as everyone was wearing the bulky hazmat suits, some of different colors but moving like awkward ghosts with no faces, helping injured people they had ferried over from the disaster site. Workers in similar protective gear rushed out of the trauma center, facing the problem of working on horribly injured patients without touching them.

Two ambulances came shrieking in, only to find their way to the ER door narrowed by the emergency vehicles. Everything came to a halt for a moment, and Sandoval had his rifle resting on pillows stacked on a small ledge that separated the kitchen and the living area. His eye was at the scope.

Three nurses, an orderly, and a doctor, all in suits, gathered behind an ambulance, and an attendant swung out to open the rear door. A stretcher was pulled free, the wheels popped down, and the doctor leaned over to make a triage decision on a patient who had been lacerated by the car bomb and was bathed in blood. Another patient was taken out of the back of the vehicle, and a second team moved in on him. Sandoval heard more distant sirens.

He pulled the trigger. The first bullet took a nurse in the back and drilled downward from her shoulder, tearing through her heart on the way out the other side. She bounced against the stretcher and slid to the ground. The second bullet slammed into the temple of the doctor and splattered brain matter and more blood onto the wounded patient.

He stopped for a moment. This was easy. Juba had set it up so that he could hardly miss! He ranged over the stunned first responders and shot a firefighter in the throat and another nurse in the stomach.

Then Juba was beside him, pointing a pistol at his head. Xavier Sandoval never heard the explosion of the gunshot that took his life.

Juba left the rifle where it lay, removed Sandoval's wallet and identification, and walked out the door. The investigating police would find the body, eventually identify it through fingerprints or dental records, and then expend valuable time chasing a false trail toward Mexico.

Juba made his way down to the stolen car. In moments, he was out of the lot, driving north toward Canada.

WASHINGTON, D.C.

The command center was in crisis mode, as if it had personally suffered a body blow even though the attack was on the other side of the nation. The United States had finally been attacked again by terrorists, with horrendous results, and everyone in the big room knew that it had happened on their watch! They would be held responsible! They shuffled around or just stood by their desks with their eyes glued to the television screens. All were trained law enforcement personnel, and their sense was to automatically get to San Francisco, get on the ground, and help the victims and find the bad guy. They were stunned and demoralized, and failure clung to them like sweat.

"I can't believe we let it happen," said DHS Agent Carolyn Walker, slumped in a chair in the Trident office.

Kyle was at the end of the long table, running his hands back across his head above the ears, frustrated. He could not believe how the civilian professionals were freaking out at the very moment they needed to be at the top of their game. "We didn't let anything happen, and you cannot undo what has already happened," he said.

"If we had only moved faster," Walker said.

"Bullshit," responded Kyle, growing angry. "Yes, it is a horrible tragedy, and yes, a lot of people are dying, but there is not a goddamn thing you can do about it but stay focused. Our job is to stop it from happening again by getting Juba. That goal has not changed."

Dave Hunt looked across at him, his hound dog face containing even more lines than usual. "And I suppose you have a plan?"

"No, of course I don't. All I can try to do is to think like Juba, put myself in his shoes."

Sybelle got into the conversation to prevent it from getting personal and accusatory. "We are looking at this attack from a combat point of view, Agent Hunt. The enemy sniper, for that is what Juba is at heart, stalked his target, picked it out, carefully planned his attack, and then struck fast and hard. That is standard sniper doctrine."

"So what the hell does he do next, this supersniper that nobody can find?"

"He's going to get the hell out of Dodge," said General Middleton. "We should consider San Francisco only to be the place that he *used* to be. He is going to exfiltrate that area, and he knows that if he stays in U.S. territory, sooner or later he is going to get caught. Hell, your people were closing in fast, and you know what he looks like."

Another agent knocked and entered the room, handing a message slip to Carolyn Walker as Dave Hunt asked, "Then where would you go?"

Kyle had his hands on his hips, looking thoughtful. "I'd go international again. Run with the purpose of finding a place where I can defend myself."

Walker passed the message across to General Middleton and told the rest, "Maybe not. We just got word of a sniper attack on a hospital where patients were being taken. Several more people are dead, but cops found the hiding place and IDed the shooter."

"This says they got him," the general announced. "Juba's dead."

VANCOUVER, B.C.
CANADA

Juba sat in the international departure terminal at the Vancouver International Airport, trying not to look at his wristwatch, nor the clocks on the wall, nor the digital time reminders above the gates. This was the most dangerous part of the trip, a calculated risk that had to be taken. He would be fine in another twenty-four hours, but until then, the most hunted man in the world was open and defenseless.

There had been no problem getting through the security procedures leading to the departure lounge on level three of the airport because the description being circulated among police and customs officials concerning Juba was of a Briton who had entered the United States as a Dutch businessman. A white man.

He had not shaved since arriving in the United States, had changed his hair color, wore gold-rimmed spectacles, had visited a tanning salon to darken his skin even more, and had put a rubber lift in one shoe to make him walk with a marked limp, which drew attention to his feet instead of his face. No one paid much attention to him in his new identity as a mild, polite college professor from the faculty of agriculture at a university in Damascus. The passport was in order, as were the university identification card and supporting documents such as a lengthy study of Canadian wheat production methods. It had been in place for more than a year, waiting for the time he might need it. The paper about wheat-growing was important to the disguise because it carried the official seal of the Canadian government on the cover, a tacit acknowledgment that he was a trusted academic and accepted by the government in Ottawa about something, even as minor as making bread. That would register on security agents.

Plus, the "terrorist syndrome" had automatically kicked into the consciousness of many people in the airport, albeit subconsciously for a number of them, and they cast suspicious glances at all of the dark-skinned passengers gathering to fly to Damascus, a planeload of Middle Eastern people. *Just get them out of here as fast as possible!* None of the passengers looked even remotely like a Dutchman.

So Juba sat quietly, on his own, reading a news magazine, waiting for the morning flight to Damascus.

Complementing the disguise was his recognition that the expected security crackdown had yet to materialize. It would come, but he had learned as a sniper how to bank time by leaving destruction and distraction in his wake, and time was what he needed most.

The Austrian Airlines flight was called, and Juba boarded when the courtesy announcement was made to allow first-class passengers to get on first. He pulled out the news magazine and put his nose back into it, keeping his peripheral vision busy for possible threats. The herd in coach boarded noisily; then the doors closed and the plane began to move. Ten minutes later, they were airborne.

He was safe for the next twenty hours on the one-way flight. Would the enemy figure out his ruse and escape route before then, and if so, would the Syrians be agreeable to the anticipated demand to seize him at the airport? Escape and evasion is a step-by-step process that could not be planned too far in advance. Syria was the next step, and he would concentrate on that when he got there.

He ordered an orange juice from the hostess, and it was presented chilled, with moisture still on the glass. Draining it in sips, he then asked for a bottle of water. He had to hydrate. In all, Juba was satisfied with the way the mission had turned out, but that part was now history. The San Francisco attack should not only mollify the bidders for the poison gas who might be restless over the death of Saladin, but they would be eager enough again when his next communication was transmitted to resume the actual auction of the formula. Of course, they would not get it, but they did not know that.

It was time for him to turn to the money option while things were falling apart, put the money in safe and accessible places and then vanish. He had years of learning how to become invisible, and this time it would be easy because he had millions of dollars available for the job.

The only real loose end was Kyle Swanson. Shake would never give up, and Juba could not rest comfortably until he killed the Marine. That was the only true option, because no matter what the other authorities might do, say, or decide, Swanson would never let up.

WASHINGTON, D.C.

"I don't fuckin' believe it," Kyle exclaimed. "How do they know he's dead?"

"Says here that he wrote his name in blood on the wall of an apartment he turned into a sniper's hide," replied Middleton, passing the note around. "Killed a mother and her little boy."

"Too easy. Another diversion," Sybelle said as she read it. She handed it to Shake and told Walker, "No identification on the body itself. We need a picture of the corpse to compare with what we have on Juba."

Swanson grunted a laugh. "So somebody, they don't know who, snuck up behind one of the best snipers in the world and put a bullet in his head with a pistol? No way. Run the guy's prints. This stiff ain't our boy."

Walker rapped her knuckles on the table, a nervous, repeated gesture. "Yes. I agree. It does seem too convenient. The problem is that with the stadium attack, law enforcement out there is stretched to the limit and snarled beyond belief."

The Lizard joined in. "Not only that, the entire comm system is becoming jammed. The time stamps indicate that it had been taking about three minutes for a message to get through. Now it's more, and the delays are climbing fast as people fight for the available cyberspace. Several relay stations are probably going to shut down soon from traffic overload. Even the military channels and backup routes are busy. The governor has called out the National Guard, and the president has declared a state of national emergency. I haven't seen it this jammed up since 9/11."

Walker said, "So communications are slow, and everyone with a badge or a crime kit is busy around the stadium. At least two thousand people have been pronounced dead already, and the figure is climbing fast. I will detail a special team to get a firm identification on this body and take over that crime scene and send us a picture, but it's still going to take time."

"How much time?" asked Middleton.

"Dunno, General. We'll move as fast as possible. Realistically, under the deteriorating conditions out there, it will be a while."

Swanson ripped a page off of the yellow legal pad before him, balled it up, and flipped it across to a trash can in the corner. It hit the rim and bounced onto the floor. He studied it with resignation and said, "He's gone."

24

WASHINGTON, D.C.

General Middleton, Captain Summers, Lieutenant Commander Freedman, and Kyle Swanson took a final look at the command center, which was slowly coming back to life. "We're done here," said the general.

"Okay," replied Carolyn Walker. "Thanks for your cooperation." Her tone was neither warm nor cold, but she was glad to get rid of the secret military unit. Now things could get back to normal and law enforcement could do its job without second-guessing by people who were not trained as investigators.

"Anytime. Just keep us in the loop if you catch a break and when you identify the corpse they think is Juba." Handshakes all around, and the Trident team left by a side door. "Come on. I'll buy us all a big breakfast. There's a good pancake house over in Alexandria."

They were all tired and frustrated, lost in their own thoughts as they drove over the bridge and into the red-brick section of Old Town, then on west to where the neighborhoods were not as ritzy and there were fewer antique stores, and then to an area that was rather seedy. The sun was bright, and the day was warming as they got out of the car. The restaurant parking lot was half full, mainly pickup trucks among two big rigs, because the eatery was popular among the over-the-road gang. A long wooden trestle table, worn smooth by generations of elbows of hungry working men, was empty in a rear corner by the kitchen, and the Tridents slid onto the benches. Napkins and silverware and a rack of syrup were already on the table. Coffee appeared as if by magic from a passing waitress, followed soon by platters of pancakes, sausage and bacon, warm biscuits, and scrambled eggs, served family style. Everybody ate the same limited, delicious menu here.

"So, none of us believes that Juba is dead, right?" The general stated. "We unanimous on that?"

Everyone agreed.

"Pass the blueberry syrup, please," said the Lizard. "The communications net is absolutely overloaded, there is probably not an investigator to spare in San Francisco, and the disaster is going to be sucking up all of the resources. If the DHS agents don't get to it in a hurry, the other officers won't get around to doing our corpse anytime soon. Juba always seems a couple of steps ahead."

Kyle refilled his coffee cup. "He is no longer in the U.S. I'm confident of that. The air system was not shut down, and the West Coast airports dump dozens of international flights into Asia every hour. More to Europe. He needed a disguise and new papers, and he had to move quickly, but I would bet he made one of those planes."

"Mexico? South America?" asked Middleton.

"He doesn't specialize down there. Maybe he has connections, probably does, but right now he is looking for a comfort zone. As a sniper, he is extracting after completion of his mission. South America would be alien to him." Sybelle ate a mouthful of eggs while she thought, then continued. "Same thing with most of Asia, from Japan to New Zealand. The only Muslim safe zones would be in the Philippines or Indonesia, and they would not risk the wrath of the United States by knowingly giving him shelter and protection. Maybe North Korea or Iran might shelter him, but he's a pretty hot potato right now, and they could make points with Washington by turning him in."

Middleton said, "Know what? I think the final destination for this crazy, murderous shitheel is Iraq. That's the only place where he can disappear."

"That's my bet, too, boss. He is going to hide in the war. And that's where I am going to find him."

"Okay. So go get him. Sybelle will go along to keep everything under the Trident umbrella, and the Lizard will do his keyboard magic from our office here. Take whoever or whatever you need, but remember that there are no orders for anything, there is no paper trail, nobody ever heard nothin' about nothin'. Then be clear on this, Dead Guy: I want Juba's fucking scalp."

"Aye, aye, sir," said Kyle Swanson, already feeling the rush. Sniper against sniper. Me and Juba. *Bad shit comin'*.

AUSTRIAN AIRLINES
FLIGHT 512

Ten hours. Halfway. Juba was feeling talons of claustrophobia seizing his flesh, as if the airplane were shrinking in on him. The spacious first-class seat had narrowed and the bulkheads seemed closer, but he had work to do, so he popped open his briefcase and removed the laptop computer and a single condom in its sealed plastic container.

The diagrams, the formula, and the instructions for assembling the weapon were spread over several files, and he had spent some time in Paris putting it all together for future use. It was in several folders, to meet different contingencies. From the briefcase he removed a tiny memory stick, attached it to a USB port, and downloaded the final file, which included the updated material from the Iranian laboratory, the final step in the process. The folder containing the date for the poison weapon used in London was in a file by itself, called File 999, and contained no indication that it was incomplete. The product would kill, but not do what was done in San Francisco. When the ultimate formula file was downloaded, he sighed with resignation and erased it from the hard drive.

Then he spent time transferring the various bank accounts and codes to the tiny memory stick and erased most of them, too. He pulled the memory stick free and he pocketed it, then stashed the computer.

When he got up to go to the bathroom, his head whacked the overhead storage bin. In the narrow bathroom thirty thousand feet in the sky, Juba washed his face and hands and under his arms and stared into the mirror: The disguise was still good.

Stop this nonsense! He stared hard at the reflection, an edge of his mouth slewing downward, angry with himself. He was a professional, and this was all part of the plan. It had been expected, just as a sniper has to remain immobile and idle for hours at a time in a hole. *Sweat it out. Losing personal control is not going to get this big damned airplane to Damascus one second earlier. Turn the glass over and instead of being only ten hours away from North America, you're halfway to freedom!*

Remember that you are no mild little college professor. You are still a sniper, a killer of men. You are still Juba. You can do this. You will do this.

He took a deep breath, allowed his bodily rhythms to settle, and then unbuckled his belt and dropped his trousers. Moving swiftly, he tore open the condom packet and removed the lubricated rubber contraception device and slid the computer memory chip in as far as it would go, folded the condom over, and tied the end. Another deep breath and he bent over the sink, spread his legs, and pushed the condom deep into his anus. Uncomfortable, but not impossible. Drug mules did it all the time, so he could do it, too.

He readjusted his clothing, washed his hands and face again, opened the door, and returned to his seat. A movie was playing on a little screen that he could tilt, so he put on the earphones and tuned it in. A tray of food was presented. Lunch. When the movie was over, he pushed up the covering of the window and watched the blue sky that stretched out forever, but he refused to look at his watch.

Halfway. More than halfway there.

WASHINGTON, D.C.

"Middleton is going to be up to his eyebrows in bitching generals. We can't run this mission as a usual black op because we are going onto other units' battle space and crossing boundary lines. They don't know who we are; they could open fire on us." Sybelle was at her desk in the Pentagon, and Kyle was across from her.

Operating beyond the shadow of secrecy presented problems, but Swanson figured it was worth the exposure because they were going to need the entire might of the U.S. military establishment to make this work. Iraq was a huge country, and they needed to shrink the number of places where Juba could feel secure, which meant using intelligence assets from satellites to local informants. First chase him across continents, and then across nations, then into a city or town or village, onto a certain street, into a specific house. Make the rabbit run for his burrow.

"We'll work around it. No big deal. How big a package should we field?"

"Do we want mobility or firepower or both?"

Kyle thought about that. "Mostly mobility. A small team can move faster, and we will have support troops all over the country we can call on. Even get air support in a tight spot. But we will be moving in the cracks, chasing one man, and I just need to get close enough to get a shot."

"So we have enough to cover your ass and call for help if and when we need it? Ride in on tanks?"

"Use the whole available force, Sybelle. You run the show from a mission command post in real time."

"Bullshit. I'm going in with you."

"Bullshit right back at you. You're a damned good operative, you don't have to prove that to anybody, but your real value is in coordinating the show."

She stared at him, hard. "I'm no little damsel in distress, Kyle."

"That's not the point. Juba is dangerous and he can bite. If I have to call for help, I want you on the other end of the horn, not someone without the warrior smarts who might not deliver when the shit hits the fan. Shooters I can get elsewhere."

She pushed her legal pad aside. "Getting in some field work is important for me now, Kyle, because I don't want to be tied to a desk for the rest of my career. I've been selected for major . . ."

Kyle interrupted. "Selected below the zone? That's great, Sybelle. Proves my point. Even the Pentagon thinks you're something special."

"General Middleton recommends that my next step be a tour as a White House military aide." Sybelle Summers was clearly displeased that she was obviously being groomed for higher rank, moving up ahead of her peers. "Very nice, but it's not what I signed up for, or why I went to the Naval Academy, and certainly not why I put up with Force Recon training. When I try to look over the horizon, all I see is desks, desks, and more desks! The men get field commands and I get another glass ceiling."

Swanson grinned at her. "Golly. That's really awful. I'm very sorry that your career track is pointing you toward being a general someday. That is not today's problem, however. We are trying to catch this mass-murdering terrorist son of a bitch Juba, remember?"

That made her laugh. She could only talk about that sort of stuff with Kyle. "Right on, Gunny. I think we should do this with some of the same MARSOC guys that we used in Iran, since they are pretty much up to speed on it. Captain Newman to be the ground commander again."

"Yeah. Rick is good people. I'd like Travis Hughes along as my spotter, then Darren Rawls and Joe Tipp as shooters. Five of us should be plenty to move fast or hold tight while you bring in backup and blow the hell out of whoever is bothering us."

"I can do that," she said with a nod. "But I'd rather be a shooter."

"We all got problems."

DAMASCUS, SYRIA

Juba was buckled in his seat and eagerly looking out of the window of the passenger jet as if he were a first-time flier. After the announcements were made for landing, the plane descended with a professional smoothness; the wheels came down with a hum and locked in place. The wheels kissed the tarmac and the nose came down and the engines roared and the brakes took hold. Normal, normal, normal. His senses were alive, and the bulge in his anal tract seemed enormous. This was the last point of danger, but he was back on friendly turf. Or, if not friendly, at least not unfriendly.

As was his habit, he unbuckled as soon as the plane

came to a halt so he could have freedom of movement, although there was really nowhere to go on the big Boeing. It coasted toward the terminal without delay, meeting the printed arrival time. Juba knew the Damascus airport was a hard place for passengers lining up for departure, but the arrivals seldom had much difficulty, and part of what the purchase price of the first-class ticket bought was being allowed to get off of the plane first and gain an advantage in the customs area. Once he cleared customs, he finally would be able to breathe easier.

The crew unlocked and opened the doors, and the covered exit ramp oozed out from the side of the terminal like some great worm. "Please remain seated until the doors are clear and secure," came the overhead announcement in three languages. "Passengers in the first-class cabin will be able to depart and . . ."

Juba never heard the rest of the announcement. Three large men in civilian suits with pistols drawn and two uniformed soldiers with submachine guns came running aboard and into the first-class section as the crew stood aside. They surrounded him. "You will come with us," said the leader, with a tone of outright menace. *Mukhabarat*, Juba thought. Secret police.

They placed him in the middle of the guards and picked up four more security operatives on the way out of the airport and into the waiting convoy of husky Land Rovers. Motorcycle police rolled out on their bikes with sirens wailing to lead the way over the eighteen miles into the city, and Juba heard the distant *wocka-wocka* of a helicopter overhead. They were taking no chances.

He settled back in the seat, a guard on each side, and considered the situation. Were they keeping him from escaping, or preventing the Americans or other covert operators from snatching him? The arrest had been abrupt and disappointing but not rough. Damascus International Airport was a known entry point for young men sent from other countries to be martyrs in Iraq, to strap explosives around their bodies or drive car bombs into targets. The arrival of another terrorist would not cause much concern there. But, Juba reminded himself, he was no longer just a terrorist but the most wanted man in the world. Nothing was certain.

The Land Rovers swooped into the city, and he began to pick up familiar landmarks and got his bearings, for he had been to Damascus many times in transit to other places. The convoy pulled to a stop at an ugly gray office building across from an open area with a few palm trees, a tall monument, and a small domed mosque, the Sahat al-Marje, Martyr's Square. Uniformed guards popped the doors and fanned out in a protective cordon while the three civilian agents hustled him inside the Ministry of the Interior, took him up two flights of stairs, and placed him in a nondescript office with orders to sit down and wait. He asked for some water and was ignored.

For almost thirty minutes, he sat still in the chair before a desk, gazing out the window and meditating to keep his heart and pulse under control. If they were going to kill him, they would have done it by now. This being Syria, they still might do so. Wait and see.

Behind him, the door finally opened, and a cheery voice called out, "Jeremy! It has been a long time since we have talked!"

A man who stood no taller than five foot five came in, white teeth gleaming in a smile beneath a thick mustache but with nothing showing in the dark, intelligent eyes. General Yousif al-Shoum, head of operations for the Syrian Military Security Directorate, came forward and tossed a blue-covered folder onto the desk, then took a seat. A young man in a white tunic followed, carrying a tray of cold drinks and hot tea. He placed it on the table and left.

"Please, have a drink. You must be thirsty after such a long flight." The English was flawless, thanks to al-Shoum's tours of duty as a diplomat and spy in London and New York.

Juba unsnapped the white cap on a bottle of water and drank. "General al-Shoum. I did not expect to be seeing you today."

The small man laughed. "You were coming to Damascus but would not pay me a courtesy visit? I am shocked." He flipped open the folder and removed a copy of a message from Interpol. "The facial recognition program got you boarding in Vancouver, despite the disguise. You almost made it, but close doesn't count."

"What happens now?"

"Did you notice on the drive in that you passed the Tomb of Saladin? The real Saladin, not your former partner. I really do not want to also have a Tomb of Juba here."

Juba did not squirm although he knew that al-Shoum would carry out the threat without batting an eye. He was being told to deal or die. "I had few choices. My plan is to go back into Iraq and kill Americans."

"Now you see, Juba, that, unfortunately, is not my plan at all." Al-Shoum backed against the desk and leaned there with his arms crossed. "Every country in the world will soon know that you have landed in Damascus, dragging along the stink of what you did in San Francisco. The death toll there, by the way, is now at four thousand five hundred people. Amazing. The Americans want you back badly."

"So you can make points with Washington by giving me

up?" Juba cocked an eyebrow. Al-Shoum was a complex man, adept at playing several games at once.

"That is one option."

"General, let's get on with this. What is your preferred option?"

"You are in such a hurry, Jeremy. Well, first of all, we want our ten million dollars back."

"Done," said Juba. "Plus another million for you personally, because of the inconvenience I have caused."

"I don't know. There is already immense pressure."

"Two million, then. Bank account of your choice." Bribery, *baksheesh*, was the most stable currency in the Middle East.

Al-Shoum went around the desk and took a chair, looking even smaller until he tucked a pillow beneath him. "Can you do that from here?"

"If your people will bring in my laptop, sure."

"Then there is another point, the matter of the auction itself. I have decided that we won the bidding, so you turn over the formula to me. That is indeed a mighty weapon that was deployed in California. I want it."

"Wait a moment, General. I give you all of your money back, plus two million more, and the formula for free?"

"That sums it up very well, Jeremy. Either that or you will be killed trying to escape . . . after we force the information out of you." The dark eyes were stones now. "We will get that formula. Voluntarily, chemicals, or skinning knives, it is of no matter to me. The best choice is to remain friendly so you can leave this building alive."

Juba looked down at his hands for a moment, quiet in his soul, even while negotiating for his life. The secret hidden in his body seemed to be pulsing signals to him. "I don't have any choice, do I?"

"No, not really." The little general smiled.

Juba feigned reluctance. "I hope that your government will use the information to strike the infidels?"

"What we do is not your concern, my friend."

"But I get to keep the other money that was put up for the auction?"

"And your life, Jeremy. I think that's fair," said al-Shoum. "Turn it over and you leave this meeting rich and healthy."

"I still don't like it."

"I don't care. Give it up. Now."

Juba stared at the general and let his shoulders slump. "You win, General. I think it may be best anyway because the project has become too unworkable for one man. You will see what I mean."

"How will you get it to us?"

"Right here, right now. It's all encrypted on my laptop. I will transfer the money and download the formula so your chemists can check it out."

Now it was al-Shoum's turn to think hard. This was too simple. Juba was willing to give back the ten million, hand over the formula, and transfer a sizable sum into the general's personal account. It was not in the man's character to give up anything without a fight.

"You have something else, don't you, my friend? Something that prevents me from taking all of the things you offer and then still hanging you from a meat hook in Martyr's Square? What is it?"

Juba showed a hint of a smile, almost flashing fangs with the anger boiling within him. "Back before the war started in Iraq, Saddam moved many of his special weapons and special ammunition into your country under the supervision of Unit 999. The Americans never found those records, but I know where they are, General al-Shoum, because my boss, the man known as Saladin, helped move them and had me hide the records somewhere in Tikrit—

Saddam's home territory. Even if you tortured me to get the information, you still could not retrieve them because of built-in safeguards. That is my insurance policy. Should I not return safely, those documents will automatically find their way to the Americans. Imagine how happy Washington would be to finally know exactly what happened to those WMDs. You let me leave Syria alive and I will destroy them and send you proof."

Al-Shoum laughed aloud and slapped the desk. "Excellent! I knew you would not disappoint me. So we have an agreement. The only condition is that you remain here in Damascus as my guest at the Four Seasons Hotel until our chemical experts examine the formula. One day. Then we will help you get back to Iraq to eliminate that WMD data."

"And kill more Americans."

"Yes. That, too."

The computer was brought in for Juba, and he shifted the funds, put the bank material onto a disk, and downloaded File 999, the London poison gas recipe. He slid the computer over to al-Shoum, and the deal was done.

25

General al-Shoum kept his end of his bargain with Juba, which might or might not be important in the future. As soon as the government's science experts concluded that the formula provided by the bloodthirsty maniac was as deadly as advertised, the task switched to spiriting the killer out of Syria. Two Land Rovers from the Ministry of the Interior picked Juba up at the hotel the following afternoon and headed out on the long drive from Damascus to the border town of Abu Kamal on the Euphrates River. There were many places along the route where Juba could have been killed and buried, but al-Shoum wanted those WMD papers, although he had doubts as to their existence. He did not bother to say good-bye.

At the border, Juba was given one of the Land Rovers and drove off on his own into the bleak country. Once word was received that he was gone, the shrewd little general triggered the next part of his plan. He had kept his word to Juba, but now he had more to do.

The diplomat was waiting, scarecrow-thin Foreign Minister Rustom Talas, when he entered the conference room. The intelligence chief did not begin with formalities.

Al-Shoum put Juba's laptop computer onto the slick,

polished table and shoved it toward the foreign minister. "Here it is. Everything about how to make that devil bomb."

Talas asked, "And the money?"

"The wire transfer has already been made. All ten million is back in the treasury."

"Your decision on this, General al-Shoum, is most unusual, and I say that with all respect. As a diplomat, I always look for leverage in political negotiations. This information about the weapon could help me pry substantial favors from the United States."

Al-Shoum switched to English. "Mr. Foreign Minister, you are a fucking moron! If they find out that we have this formula, the United States of America will come after it. They have lost almost five thousand American lives because of this and want to hold somebody responsible. They would not bargain, they would demand, and we could be the next country invaded! Is that what you want?"

"No, of course not." The foreign minister coughed. "I was speaking in the broadest terms."

"Just listen, you old fool, and stick to the story. We pulled Juba off the plane as soon it arrived, but he killed two security guards and got away. Are you with me so far?"

Minister Talas was almost grinding his teeth over being spoken to like a schoolboy. "Yes."

"Then we launched our own search, and a security camera outside the airport showed him getting into a waiting vehicle, a Land Rover. We issued a nationwide alert and discovered that he has crossed the border into Iraq. We deeply regret that this mass murderer slipped through our security net, but he is indeed a formidable opponent, as the Americans know."

"So what do I tell Washington about the weapon?"

Talas said. "That information is worth its weight in diplomatic gold if we hand it over."

"Tell them nothing! We don't know about any formula, because Juba got away from us! Understand that? Instead, deal them this information: Our informants tell us that Juba may be headed toward the city of Tikrit in Iraq." Al-Shoum scribbled a note and handed it to Talas. "This is the license number of the Land Rover he was driving."

"Why Tikrit?"

"You don't need to know that, Foreign Minister Talas. Just tell Washington that we hope they find him soon and make him pay the ultimate price for his monstrous deeds." He leaned forward menacingly. "And you tell no one, not a soul, about our having the formula. If I hear a whisper that you have revealed this information, you and your family will die."

Al-Shoum was through with diplomats. They bored him. He turned on his heel and walked from the room, back to his office, humming a little tune, two million dollars richer and in sole possession of one of the most powerful chemical-biological agents ever devised. He would hold on to all of it for a while. Saladin had a good idea about the auction, but he had made it too public, and the time was no longer ripe for such a play. Who knew what deals were to be made in future years?

COMBAT OPERATING BASE SPEICHER
IRAQ

The Army briefing officer with the scraped-clean scalp wore spotless and creased camouflage BDUs and had a 9 mm pistol strapped into a leather shoulder holster. Kyle Swanson wondered why everybody wanted to look like a warrior, even the ones whose jobs kept them safely inside the wire at all times. The man flashed aerial photographs on the white wall. "We have ascertained a suggested target that fulfills the requested parameters to facilitate your mission," the officer said. Swanson groaned but paid attention rather than interrupt the intel puke. The other members of the Trident team were having the same dual reactions.

"Somewhere along the way, the hajjis came into possession of an M120 heavy mortar. Normally this 120 mm weapon is carried on an M1100 trailer attached to a Humvee, or by truck or tracked vehicle, but the insurgents have developed a suitable alternative method of transport."

Darren Rawls spoke up, in his Mississippi drawl. "You mean the ragheads stuff it in the trunk of a car."

The officer cleared his throat. "Yes. Anyway, once it is mobile, the mortar can be moved into position to provide high-angle organic indirect fire support across a wide area with high-explosive, illumination, or smoke rounds. It requires a crew of four men."

Swanson knew the M120 weapon well and respected its ability to lay down good fire support. It was not only able to be put into a car but also could be broken down and man-humped by the four guys on the crew. One would carry the tube, another the base plate, the third took the bipod, and the fourth would have the lightweight sight and the ammo. Even assembled, the thing only weighed a little over three hundred pounds. Once in place, it could fire up to four rounds a minute, then be torn down and moved to a new location before counterbattery fire could find them.

From Swanson's viewpoint on this job, it would be almost ideal because that four-man crew would train and fight together, which meant they would be together during the down time, too. He wanted them all. It was important that he have more than one target in order to get the message to Juba.

Middleton and the Trident team had guessed right that Juba had fled to Iraq; then the net was narrowed even tighter, to the Tikrit area, through a diplomatic communication from Syria. Somebody in Damascus had dropped a dime on Juba, and now Kyle had to draw him out.

"And you have this one located? A solid ID?"

The briefer was back on stride. "We have a high confidence in the location." He clicked on a narrow laser pointer and a red dot ran across the photo on the wall. "There's the car, and there's the house that the crew is in. Humint confirms the photo reconnaissance."

"Humint" was military-speak for human intelligence, which meant somebody actually saw it. The best kind of intelligence there is. He looked over at Sybelle, who glanced his way and nodded.

"How fresh is this?" she asked the briefer.

"The photograph was taken this morning," he said. "We consider it to be actionable intelligence."

Sure you do, Kyle thought. *You aren't the one that has to get out there and kill them.* "I'm go with it, then," he said. "We need to move fast."

The area was the hotbed of Iraqi opposition during the opening battles of the war and the violent aftermath, and enemy eyes were still always watching what was happening in and around Combat Operating Base Speicher, only three kilometers outside of Tikrit. Swanson felt that he was always being watched from the other side of the wire, although Task Force Hammer of the U.S. 1st Armored Division kept security tight.

Swanson knew that security and secrecy were two different things, and loyalty to Saddam Hussein ran deep in the dictator's hometown on the Tigris River. Saddam built his biggest presidential palace there, drew the members of his inner circle from his home tribe, and was now buried near there. Tikrit, a hundred miles northwest of Baghdad, was an anchor point of the hostile Sunni Triangle.

Even at one o'clock in the morning, as Swanson led the Trident assault team aboard the helicopter, he felt as if some Iraqi diehard were counting noses and radioing an alert. They all wore loose local clothing and face paint. As a precaution, the helicopter took off in a direction ninety degrees different from the true target area. It would circle back to the attack path only when it was well clear of the base.

They were dropped in an empty area four kilometers from the town that contained the suspect house and automobile, and Travis Hughes took point as they trotted forward in silence. No talking, no metal jangling, no hard breathing, just a half-dozen shadows moving steadily in the dark of a moonless night. A steady wind helped mask their approach, keeping their scent away from the animals.

Few lights flickered in the windows during this dead time of night, and the group steered clear of them, carefully threading through the outlying streets and clinging to the shelter of walls and alleyways. They seldom paused and entered the tangled neighborhood where the suspects were without detection. Joe Tipp snaked forward on his belly, elbows, and knees to scout the house. No one was on guard, and the old white Ford sedan with a rusting roof sat just where it had been shown in the intel photo, right outside the gate of a small wall around the house.

Hughes fell in beside Kyle to be his spotter, and the two of them scurried away to set up a stable firing position while Captain Rick Newman fanned out the others in a protective arc and messaged Sybelle that they were in place.

"You sure you want to do it this way, Shake?" asked

Hughes. "I don't like being so exposed." They were in prone position in the middle of a street.

"We want to be seen, Travis. This time, I want people to know that a sniper was at work here."

"Still. Just saying."

"I know. Come on. Let's build the range card."

At four o'clock, Kyle clicked his microphone twice, and Newman and Rawls set off at a lope around the front of the house. Swanson nestled his cheek into the custom-made stock of his personal sniper rifle, the Excalibur, and brought the scope to rest on the engine of the car. His world began to slow down as the moment of action neared.

Rawls started kicking at the front door, hard and noisily, and Newman smashed his rifle into the glass of a window, shattering it. Voices were heard yelling inside. Newman popped in a red smoke grenade. Neither man had said a word while causing the occupants of the house to head for the back door.

Out they came, some of them coughing and wiping at their eyes as the trails of red smoke followed them. Hughes had his binos on them. "One, two, another, four. That's all of them. Nobody else coming out." The mortar crew made straight for the car, and Swanson waited until they were all inside and the doors were slamming. "Fire. Fire. Fire."

He let his finger pull back slowly on the trigger and Excalibur roared, snapping a .50 caliber round down the street. It burrowed into the engine block, and the car shook with the impact. Now it was a matter of reloading and shooting fast, but accurately, at men trapped in a ruined car only a hundred meters straight ahead of him. He took out the driver first, before the man released the steering wheel.

"Target down," reported Hughes. The man seated

behind the driver jumped out and filled the sight. Kyle shot him in the chest. "Target down!"

Swanson shifted to the other side of the vehicle and nailed the man scrambling from the passenger seat. He was part of his rifle, the world a black-and-white place of mechanical action and reaction, and he felt the new bullet reloading as the old brass ejected out. "Target down."

There was one more, and he ran. Excalibur roared again and the bullet tore out the Iraqi fighter's heart as the forward momentum propelled him into the courtyard. "Target down," Hughes said. "Let's get out of here, Kyle."

"Follow the plan, Travis. Stay with the plan." Swanson watched the Marines form up near him, in the shadows, and Hughes joined them. Rawls and Newman were back.

"Helo inbound," said Newman.

Kyle Swanson stood up in the street, holding the ominously long Excalibur at his side with his left hand, and moved without hesitation toward the car. Lights were coming on, but no one was yet on the street. Fear and confusion were making them pause. He paced deliberately forward until he was standing beside the body of the man who had been behind the driver.

Swanson propped Excalibur against the car and used his knife to cut off part of the dead man's shirt, which he twisted into a knot. Squatting beside the car, he dipped the shirt in his victim's blood and slowly wrote a single word on the driver's door: *JUBA*. Wherever he found Juba, the secrets to the poison gas would be nearby. The terrorist would never let that information be far from his side, and it was more dangerous than he was. A matched set, and Kyle had to get them both this time.

He picked up his rifle and strode away, a perfect target but also a fearsome figure in the darkness. The neighbors had heard some noise, but no talking, then a volley of five steady shots from a high-velocity rifle. That meant "sniper," and while no one wanted to stick a head out the door, they did watch from the windows.

When he reached the Marines in the shadows, Darren Rawls grabbed him by the shirt and pushed him forward, making him run, and Kyle's senses rolled back into normal time. "You a crazy mutha, you know that?" called Rawls into his ear, running right beside him. "Now haul your ass!"

26

The city of Tikrit is hemmed in tightly by a dirty necklace of small towns and villages, and in one of them, a tangled little place called Hargatt, a tense meeting was under way. Light razored sharply through the window of a bullet-pocked two-story building, illuminating a husky, bearded man who sat in a worn green chair in the main downstairs room. Guards were at every window and on the roof, and one stood directly behind him. The area commander of the Iraqi insurgency asked, "Why did you do this thing, Juba?"

"I told you. I did not do it. What reason would I have to kill four of your men, who are helping to protect me?" Juba had been staying at the man's spacious and comfortable home since arriving in Tikrit. He had already secured a new laptop computer and filled it with the data from the disk that al-Shoum had provided in Syria, plus the vital material from the memory stick that he had carried for three days in his rectum. Juba was back in business.

"The townspeople have described in detail that a man wearing our style of garments and carrying a long rifle had the courage to walk down the middle of the street after the murders. He wrote your name in blood—*Why?*— and then walked away again. *Walked,* as if he owned the town! No Shiite dog would take that chance, and certainly no American."

"One would. His name is Kyle Swanson, he is a Marine sniper, and he wants to personally kill me."

The commander took a few breaths before speaking again. "You did noble things in London and the state of California, Juba, and for that, I have granted you sanctuary. But death follows you like a plague."

Juba motioned toward the guards and the windows. "How long has this war been going on? You and the people of Tikrit are no strangers to death. I didn't bring it. It was already here."

"Why would this Swanson Marine do this thing last night? It was foolhardy. He would be aware of what we do to captured snipers, but his audacity stunned and delayed the fighters who might otherwise have swarmed outside and taken him. That was why many of them thought it was you out there."

"Swanson was, ah, communicating with me. Telling me he was around here and looking."

Finally a glimmer came into the man's eyes. "So he will be back?"

"Yes. No doubt."

"Are you afraid?"

Juba softly laughed. "No. Of course not. I want him to find me, because I am going to kill him."

The commander's mind was suddenly busy with ideas. "Then we shall lure him in close and hope that he brings many friends. You kill him, we kill them."

"I like that," said Juba. "Just be sure to leave him for me." Once he cleared away the Swanson obstacle, he would find a safe haven and resume the auction process. General al-Shoum would not be pleased to learn that he had been swindled, but Juba planned to be a long way from Syria by then. Tahiti and Fiji both sounded good.

"First, let us show the Swanson Marine that what he did will not be tolerated." The commander smiled. "Go and communicate with him."

COB SPEICHER

Kyle Swanson was in a bunk, fast asleep after the night's work. The rest of the Trident strike team was doing the same thing, while beyond their separate building, U.S. Army troops were going about their daily routines.

An armored patrol rumbled out through the front gate of the combat base, large warfighting machines clanking in the lead and helicopters zipping ahead to look for threats along the wide road. A short time later, several smaller patrols went out, spreading to different directions and different roads. Iraqi civilians were also on the move, wary when approaching American roadblocks. Unemployed young men and kids congregated on some corners in the towns as American troops moved through on foot. Shops were open. Business as usual.

Swanson snored peacefully. He had made his move, and now, while sleeping without dreams, he was still at work, a sniper lying in wait for his target. Army psychological operations teams were in high gear all around Tikrit, handing out paper flyers with Juba's photograph and broadcasting over the radio and loudspeakers mounted on vehicles, promising a five-million-dollar reward to whoever turned him in.

Kyle had nothing to kill but time. It was Juba's move.

HARGATT

The insurgent commander and Juba stood on the flat roof of the tallest building in town while guards listened for marauding American helicopters that might see them.

The advantage of height increased the distance they could see, and they had a good view of the spot where a road crested a small ridge and then came down into a little valley and a bridge under which a canal flowed to the Tigris.

"The Americans always vary their routes of approach, but there are only so many routes they can take. Repetition is inevitable." The commander pointed toward the ridgeline. "Before they approach our area, they usually stop at the top of that high ground, as you see, and take time to study what is going on before moving forward."

Through his binoculars, Juba studied the site. A pair of gigantic M1A2 Abrams tanks were on each side of the road, with their 120mm cannons and array of machine guns having total command of the area. Other armored vehicles, both tracked and wheeled, rolled arrogantly down the main road, occasionally stopping to let a patrol dismount.

The commander had it all figured out. "See? When they stop, you can shoot them."

"All right," said Juba, shifting his binoculars around the zone. "See that farmhouse about halfway down the slope? I want your people to clear it out tonight so I can use it tomorrow morning."

"Of course," said the commander. "We all look forward to seeing a display of your skill against the Crusaders."

Juba gave a slight bow of appreciation but said nothing as they went back downstairs and into another building for some lunch. If he took a shot from that farmhouse, those big Abramses would be on him in a heartbeat with a hurricane of plunging fire, then the Humvees, armored personnel carriers, and troops would run over him, unless they decided to let an Apache helicopter gunship take care of the job. He had no intention of telling anyone, including the commander, where he would set up. Not with that five-million-dollar reward on his head.

During the afternoon, he borrowed a car and went out alone. As the commander said, there were only so many roads that the Americans could take into the area. Out of the bleak terrain and houses, an opportunity rose like a mirage at a little crossroads, and Juba stopped the vehicle beneath a few tall palm trees, got out, and walked around. His eyes studied the isolated area and the single Iraqi government traffic policeman on duty. The deep ruts made by the passing of numerous tracked vehicles spiderwebbed the crossing. The Americans came this way often.

Then he restarted the car and drove some more to find the second site he wanted. This was payback for Swanson's daring raid, and the method in which the challenge would be answered had to be special. The scorecard would be kept in human lives not their own.

Back at the safe house before nightfall, he studied a map, ate only a bite of food, and went shopping for the few supplies he needed for the coming hours. He retired to his room about eight o'clock and spent a long time cleaning the weapon he had chosen from the insurgents' stockpile, a beautiful HS .50 Steyr Mannlicher long-range, single-shot, bolt-action, precision-fire sniper rifle that could punch right through the body armor worn by the Americans.

A few hours after midnight, he left the house. He had a small backpack that contained some rations and his compact computer.

COB SPREICHER

"He's out there tonight. I can feel it," Kyle Swanson told Sybelle Summers as they sat atop a sandbagged bunker and watched a pair of bright flares drift down on small parachutes to the west. A moment later came the chatter of an automatic weapon and the loud booms of a big gun. "He will hit back soon."

"I don't know, Kyle. Task Force Hammer has things pretty well buttoned up. Patrols were rolling in and out of the gate all day, and the surrounding bases report nothing unusual."

Swanson pulled his knees to his chest and wrapped his arms around them, rocking back and forth, feeling the muscles stretch. "Would all that stop you, if you were him?"

She picked at a rip in one of the bags, and the sand beneath was hard. Been there a long time. "No. Just slow down and take my time. Pick my spot."

"Umm. That's what he's doing, too."

A shadow appeared beside them and Travis Hughes flopped down. "Hey."

"Hey," said Sybelle.

"Let me pick your brains here," said Swanson. "Juba is pissed off and wants to get even, right? But what is going to be his target, and can we stop him?"

"Hell, Shake, we can't stop the bastard until we know where he is. As for the target, my bet would be that he is going to want to match your number of kills, if not surpass it." Hughes spit over the side of the bunker.

"Classless jarhead," said Sybelle, disgusted. "Travis is right. He's going to want a nice body count, so he will be looking for somewhere that American troops are bunched together."

Travis laughed quietly. "Hell, maybe he's going to come in here. Lots of people gathered at the Subway. They're even giving Latin dance lessons over at the Morale Building. Hell of a war."

"No. He might be able to get inside the wire, but it's too dangerous. The man is not stupid."

Darren Rawls crawled up and joined them. "Just visited a friend for a couple of beers," he reported. "Man, the buzz is all about what you did last night. That is interesting, because nobody on our team would say anything, which means informants are spreading the word about the badass snipers in town."

"We wanted the word to spread," Sybelle commented. "Part of the game. What we don't want is for the whole of Task Force Hammer to go charging out, trying to track Juba down, because he will take off and we will have to find him all over again."

"They won't," said Kyle. "Remember, Sybelle, that you and I specifically let Colonel Withrow know during our introductory briefing that Juba and the poison gas formula was our assignment."

"So where the hell is he, Shake?" Hughes asked.

Kyle laid back on the bunker and stared up at the stars. "I don't know. He's out there somewhere. I can feel it."

HARGATT

Juba had no way to really know if an American patrol would come through that crossroads seven hundred yards away from his hide today, but all those track trails and torn berms and crushed vegetation indicated that it was frequently used. Just like animals create paths through a thick jungle by padding along the same route, the steel animals of the American tanks and other vehicles were following a familiar pattern, apparently thinking the lone Iraqi cop directing traffic there was adequate security. After all, it was just a way station; the fighting forces were just passing through.

He had a position in the rubble of a destroyed shop that had collapsed upon itself in a jumble of timbers and stones. Many of the cement blocks were painted white on two sides, the outside and inside walls before it all came crashing down. During his scouting, he had found a narrow entrance that dropped into the shop's storage basement, and by moving aside a few big rocks, he had opened a good view down to the crossroads. He had put the rocks back in place when he left, returning with his gear a few hours ago.

Working in the narrow beam of a flashlight, Juba built a sturdy hide that provided maximum protection on top and to all sides. Stacking stones and wood, he created a firm platform on which to rest the Steyr Mannlicher. The tip of the muzzle would be four feet back in the room. Turning off the light, he practiced his escape route several times, returned, and walked around the devastated shop to re-arrange more debris. A dirty piece of blue and white canvas that had once been an awning was spread across the rear opening and anchored in place with loose rocks.

Dawn was coming, and, with luck, so were the Americans. After planning and prayers, luck helped. At first light, Juba slowly removed the loose stones that would create a ragged window facing the crossroads, one by one, inch by inch, until the hole was about two feet wide and two feet high, just behind some scraggly underbrush outside. When a sniper fires, it is an automatic response for the people in his target zone to look up in order to sweep the rooftops, where the attacker may have the height advantage. Juba had chosen a place with a two-story building nearby. That was where he expected them to concentrate during the critical moments that he was firing three shots, no more, following standard doctrine that shooting more than three times from the same place allowed the enemy to pinpoint your position. And kill you. Three and out.

The previous day, during his scouting ride, he had noticed that the children in the neighborhood were eating candy from America, scribbling in notebooks with ball-point pens, and playing with silly plastic toys. Gifts from U.S. soldiers. A relationship was being built. Good.

There was a distant grinding rumble, and as he expected, his juvenile early warning system began to shriek as a dozen kids took off running toward the intersection. A pair of bulky M2 Bradley Infantry Fighting Vehicles surged down the road, raising big roostertails of dust behind them, where three up-armored Humvees trailed. Juba made a mental note that the 25 mm Bushmaster chain guns on the Bradleys were his biggest threat. *Don't give them a chance to engage.*

The kids were running alongside the vehicles, dodging the tracks and the wheels with ease and calling up to the soldiers in broken English. Sure enough, little packages of gaily wrapped candy showered down on them. The convoy pulled into the crossroads and into a line along one axis. The policeman steered traffic around them. Everyone was relaxed, and Juba focused his rifle on the second Bradley, which had a number of aerials sticking up from it, clearly the command track. The turrets were open, but the gunners were at ease, bantering with the kids. Then the soldiers got out, their rifles hanging loosely, some squatting down to the children's level. They came here often to rendezvous with other convoys before heading out on individual missions. Only two troopers took sentry positions, one at each end of the convoy. Iraqi adults stayed away, clustering in doorways or just going about their business.

Luck. Juba let his mind wash itself clean of outside noise. The command track was a tempting and militarily significant target, the place where the officers lurked. Kill the officers, tilt the battlefield. No. That was not what he wanted today. Just take the easy ones and go before they knew what hit them. Give them something to remember, to enrage them, to drive them crazy with rage. He brought the Steyr rifle to him like a lover and remembered his schoolboy Shakespeare, a line from *Julius Caesar,* "This foul deed shall smell above the earth."

The scope was on a small boy, about seven years old,

with dark hair and a smiling face, all white teeth and dirt, who stood beside a kneeling American soldier, talking to him. The rifle stilled its movement. The boy turned enough for a back shot, and Juba pressed the trigger with four pounds of pressure. The snap of the gunshot was loud inside the hide but was barely heard on the outside, and the big bullet smashed hard into the child, knocking him in a bloody heap onto the American soldier, who grabbed the boy and fell atop him to shield him from further harm. He was already dead. *One!*

The moment of frozen realization that danger was upon them occurred when Juba squeezed the trigger the second time and brought down an American who had been smoking a cigarette, the bullet ramming through his armored vest and into his vital organs. The man staggered, a look of disbelief on his face, and fell. *Two!*

Now came the chaos of children screaming, soldiers yelling and getting their weapons up, and the ugly Bushmaster cannon looking for somebody to shoot. *Sniper! Where?*

Now he wanted a good shot, a difficult shot, to put his seal on this attack, and he found it with the soldier who had made the mistake of grabbing a telephone handset from a radioman. The officer, calling in for help with this ambush. He was on his belly beside one of the Bradleys, peering out around the track, searching for the threat, just enough for Juba to see his eyes beneath his helmet. Easy, smooth trigger squeeze and the Steyr snapped again. *Three!*

The firing began in his general direction, but there was no target. The bullets were just chewing dirt and rearranging rocks. The soldiers and the Bradleys would be on the move in seconds. Juba wrapped his rifle beneath his loose robe, tore away the old awning, and walked into the morning sun, down the alley and around the corner. No one was on the streets because of the sudden eruption of gunfire. He got into his car and drove away.

Fifteen minutes later, he was snuggled beneath some bushes that lined the top of a hard mud fence some four feet high at the edge of an irrigation ditch. He peered over the berm and saw the crossroads, which had become a bee-hive of activity as the Americans swept into the neighbor-hood he had just left. It was hard for them to keep their professionalism, for the murder of a child does something to the American psyche. Snipers have to know about emo-tions. They were after the shooter who killed the kid, and he was somewhere in that neighborhood. Even their new defense perimeter was oriented toward the original hide, the place of the perceived threat, and not toward his new location behind them.

He had a plain view of the medical personnel working frantically with the three victims, who were laid side by side, trying somehow to keep them alive long enough to get them back to the aid station at COB Baharia. Juba was not depending on luck now but on expected responses. Sup-press the threat and evac the wounded. The troops were in the village, and no more shots had been fired, so a medevac chopper was coming in.

He heard it before he saw it. Then the helicopter zoomed in low toward the battle site, flared to a stop in the air, and settled to the ground, the rotor wash throwing up a blizzard of dirt. Red crosses were painted in large white squares on the green chopper. Mercy flight. Juba aimed.

Two soldiers picked up a stretcher that carried one of his earlier victims. A medic leaped from the helicopter to give them a hand, and Juba shot him in the stomach to tear out the liver and a kidney. *One!*

The Bushmaster gunner atop one of the Bradleys was facing toward the village, exposing his back. Juba put the scope on him and fired a bullet that hit center mass. The soldier threw his hands up on impact and fell straight down into the vehicle. *Two!*

The medevac pilot had realized they were under attack and started winding up his bird for an emergency takeoff, but Juba had a clear view through the side window. Tight head shot. The pilot turned his head, and Juba, using the dark sunglasses as his aiming point, once again gently squeezed the trigger. The bullet crashed through the pilot's helmet and destroyed his head. Immediately, the helicopter began to power down while the stunned copilot took command. *Three!*

Juba ducked away behind the wall, carried his rifle back to the car, and quickly vanished into the streets again. *I am here, Shake. Come and get me!*

27

Captain Newman had the Trident team in a tight security perimeter while Kyle Swanson and Sybelle Summers probed through the sniper hide behind the mud wall like crime scene specialists on a TV show. As soon as the attack was reported to the base, orders rocketed back to hold in place, and an uneasy silence engulfed everything up to a mile away on every side. Extra troops were dispatched to bolster the available firepower, and the Trident team hustled in aboard a helicopter.

The mud-wall sniper's hide was the closest to the landing zone, so they went there first. A trooper had marked the spot with a yellow cloth tied to a stick, and the slash of bright color was stark against the bland brown surroundings. Kyle went in from one side, Sybelle from the other end, looking for booby traps, but they found nothing. Some bushes had been crushed where the sniper had lain on them, and there was a crease in the wall on which he had braced the weapon. Three hefty .50 caliber brass cartridges were scattered off to the right of the position, flipped out by the weapon during the reloads.

"Excellent field of fire," Sybelle said, looking over the wall to the bloody crossroads, still the center of activity.

"Particularly if you have the enemy looking the other way," said Kyle, kneeling in the dirt to study the placement of the attacker's body. He would have had a solid base and fired with an economy of movement. Swanson reached out and touched a dirty piece of cloth that was still in front of where the rifle muzzle had been. Wet, spread there to tamp down the dust, which otherwise would have been thrown up when the weapon fired and given away the position. A thorough pro, taking care of the little things. Boot prints led away from the wall, toes deeper than heels, indicating he was moving fast but not running. Those prints vanished at the small road almost hidden by the wall. A vehicle was waiting for him.

They all walked as a group across the action zone to a destroyed building that had been marked by another yellow flag, and Kyle and Sybelle again went into the sniper's hide. The canvas curtain had been torn down, and three more .50 caliber brass cartridges blinked in the light. Sybelle turned them over in her fingers.

"Same as the others," she said. "One punched clean through the armored vest. My guess is it's an M8 armor-piercing incendiary. He was going for a big wallop."

Swanson agreed. A velocity of 3,050 feet per second and a range of 6,470 yards. It was overkill to use such a weapon from only seven hundred meters. Was the shooter trying to prove a point? There was a makeshift rest for a rifle in the middle of the room, well back from the opening in the far wall. He went closer to the odd window and looked at the sparse vegetation that had been broken and singed by the muzzle blast.

Rick Newman came into the basement hide. "What do you think, Shake? Was it Juba?"

"No doubt," Kyle replied. "He left his shell casings behind, which he does as sort of a signature. Then, this double ambush was the work of a single professional, because not even two average shooters would be able to pull it off with perfect coordination. Three shots maximum, then move, that's standard doctrine."

Kyle crouched behind the table and aimed along the viewing line that the sniper had. He could almost reach out and touch the men at the crossroads. "Finally, he waited to attack the first responders who came in to help. He did the same thing in San Francisco because it's such an immense shock to everyone else. For a while, every soldier who comes around here is going to be thinking about snipers, and that will inhibit their freedom of movement."

"Well, we gotta go. I just had a call from Colonel Withrow. He wants to meet us back at the base pronto," said Newman.

The three of them walked out into the light, and the entire team went back across the field to a waiting helicopter. "What are you going to tell the colonel?" asked Sybelle. "He's not going to like sitting around and having this kind of attack on his men without fighting back."

"But that's exactly what we have to get him to do, Sybelle. Withrow is no fool, and he realizes that catching this terrorist is the most important mission on his list right now. This mess today was bad, bad shit, but it proves that Juba is right here in this area and is not hiding somewhere in the urban maze. We are getting closer, and the funnel is narrowing. First we tracked him across the United States to Canada, then to Syria and then into Tikrit, which meant we did not have to search the rest of Iraq. Now he is here, for sure. The bottom line is that it is still a fight between the two of us: I called, and he has answered. Now we just have to make a date."

Army Colonel Neil Withrow, commander of Task Force Hammer, was standing with his executive officer before a large plastic-covered grid map of the town of Hargatt. Black and red marking pens had slashed and stabbed to mark positions and events. "Two days ago, this area was quiet. Real progress had been made both politically and militarily." He turned to face Kyle and the flinty blue eyes bore into the sniper. "Now it looks like World War III outside my front gate again."

The XO pointed to marks on the maps. "Here's the ambush site this morning. Since then, we've had two IEDs take out vehicles, with one man KIA, four wounded. An ambush by a militia organization we thought had been tamed left another two of our troopers wounded. Sectarian violence has flared in one part of the town, and a suicide bomber hit a market street. Two mortar rounds came into the camp but caused no damage. All this in broad daylight. It's getting hot."

The colonel ran a hand flat across his crew-cut hair, then crossed his arms. "We're going to have to go in there and settle things down, sooner rather than later, if we want to keep a lid on. How much longer do you people think you will need?"

Kyle saw the dilemma facing the colonel. The job of catching Juba was undoing a lot of good work. "Sir, I have to ask you to hold back for two more days."

Withrow groaned aloud. "Look, Mr. Swanson, I have followed the orders in your letter of special authorization and provided your team with maximum cooperation here. Unfortunately, you have ignited a powder keg." He pointed toward the window of his office. "My soldiers died out there today, and morale is sinking because we have all of this power at our fingertips but are not responding. Your mission is hampering my ability to protect my force."

"Yes, sir. I understand that completely and feel just as strongly as you about the loss of life, and that the best defense is a good offense. Unfortunately, our job still remains more important right now. The key to how he pulled off the San Francisco attack is with him, and if you throw a bunch of Abrams tanks and Bradleys into the game, Juba could just fade back into Tikrit or possibly return to Baghdad and we will lose him. I'm sorry, sir, but we need that material, and the only way we get it is to get him. We need two more days before you turn loose Task Force Hammer."

Withrow looked back at the map. "This one asshole killed six people out there today in a matter of minutes, but he killed thousands more innocent Americans before he even got here. The most dangerous terrorist in the world is in my sandbox. Do me a big favor when you find him, Mr. Swanson: Don't arrest him."

"Oh, hell no, sir. I'm going to blow his fucking head off."

The colonel exchanged glances with his XO. "Very well. We will keep the troops on a short leash for another two days. Meanwhile, what can we do to help?"

Kyle moved to the map, picked up the red marker, and drew a great circle around Hargatt. "Close it all off. Roadblocks on all major highways, secondary roads, and cowpaths, and put roving patrols in the open fields. Nobody in or out for the next day, no passes honored for any reason. Iraqi police and troops will work only within the task force perimeter. Juba is somewhere in that circle, and I want to keep him there."

Withrow said, "You got it . . . for forty-eight hours, and then we have to reevaluate the battlefield. But our hand may be forced if the violence continues to increase. We may have to start kicking in doors."

"Yes, sir. Agreed. We will keep each other informed."

Sybelle and Rick Newman flanked Swanson as they left the headquarters building and walked down the neatly kept road. "Can we do this in only another two days?" Rick asked.

Kyle Swanson looked up at the sky and adjusted his cap against the hot afternoon sun. "I don't know. I had to tell him something to give him some hope, and he is right that his task force cannot sit on the sideline forever. We can try. See what happens."

HARGATT

The commander of the insurgents smelled opportunity. A few minor attacks during the day had drawn some American blood, but they had not responded in force as usual. The presence of Juba made a difference.

Juba, however, just wanted to kill the Swanson Marine, while the commander had a much wider agenda. The big force stationed at the camp three kilometers southeast of Tikrit had enforced the uneasy peace, allowing the time and space needed for the political process to move forward. The residents of the villages and towns in the entire area were feeling safe beneath the umbrella of tanks and helicopters and soldiers. They were imagining what peace might be like, and for the commander, that was the most dangerous thing of all.

"Are those houses ready?" he asked the man in charge of helping plan attacks.

"Almost. The people have been removed, and we have begun the storage."

"How long?"

"Transporting and placing the gasoline, the explosive plastics, the propane tanks, and artillery shells require caution and skill. We should be finished in a few hours," said the aide.

"Let me know as soon as you are done. We don't have much time." This would be a fine operation and should not interfere at all with Juba's own personal vendetta. The commander had a war to fight, and he would ask a favor of Juba tonight.

It was a fine day outside, the temperature holding around one hundred degrees, but dropping as evening approached. He wondered where Juba was.

Juba had carefully cleaned the Styer Mannlicher rifle during the long afternoon hours, caught a power nap during the hottest part of the day, and then went back on the prowl. It was cooling off, and he was ready to work again, far across town from where he had been that morning.

Hargatt was not a large city, but big enough to draw in potential customers from the surrounding area, and many of the buildings remained in surprisingly good condition. He drove down the broad main avenue, an unremarkable presence in the late afternoon crowd of pedestrians, cars, and trucks. There was a tension in the air, and people in the shops were talking about the growing violence. There was some confidence, too, that the Americans and the police would bring things back under control.

The symbol of that confidence stood at the end of the wide boulevard, the blocky new police station that had been built with a $3.4 million grant from the United States government. The location obviously had been chosen carefully to show that the Iraqi police force had come of age as a trained unit and was present, ready to help. It was a point of pride for the emerging new government, and Juba considered it a worthy target. He could crush that rising spirit of safety.

A three-story building was on a corner about a thousand meters away, a place of shops and small offices. He parked around back and jogged up the steps and into the building. The doors were unlocked because the merchants were begging for work and did not want locks to keep customers out.

The door to the sewing shop on the top floor was not only unlocked but slightly open, too, to create a cross-draft through the stuffy rooms. A middle-aged woman with a wrinkled face was at a sewing machine, a round cushion full of needles and pins pushed high on her arm. Juba smiled in greeting, closed the door, turned, and shot her twice in the head with a silenced pistol. He spun the CLOSED sign around, locked the door, dumped the body out of sight, and arranged multicolored bolts of cloth into a crude rifle rest away from the open window. He retrieved the Steyr from his car, settled into the back of the room, and checked the scope; a clear view of the police station. Several American Humvees were parked out front, indicating that there were some discussions going on, probably about him.

He studied the building at the end of the street and sketched a range card while he waited. After an hour, he drank some water, then returned his eye to the scope, watching people go in and out of the ornate main entrance of the station. Some American soldiers, probably the drivers, were talking with some Iraqi policemen. Laughing. Cordial. Friends.

A stir rustled the small crowd. The soldiers shook hands with the cops and climbed behind the steering wheels of the Humvees. Two men were at the door, then at the top of the steps. Juba focused on the Iraqi officer dressed in dark blue trousers and a light blue shirt with rank epaulets on his shoulders. He was squaring away a blue beret on his head. A final check of the range card, eye back to the scope, a squeeze of the trigger, and the explosion of the shot filled the small room as the big gun kicked back against his shoulder.

Without waiting to see the fate of the policeman, Juba worked the bolt smoothly to rack in a second round and shifted his aim to the U.S. Army officer. He was wearing a vest, but that would not matter, and Juba brought the scope to center mass and fired. Two targets down.

The third round was fed into the chamber, and he looked for one more victim. The bodyguard with the sunglasses? The young sentry in the guard post? One of the Americans rushing out of the building with their weapons ready, searching for the sniper? He paused a few seconds to let the scene develop, like the image on a photograph in a darkroom. One American was pulling the fallen officer back inside, his weapon dangling uselessly as he hauled with a hand on each of the man's wrists. A medic? Juba shot him in the heart.

This time, he left the rifle in the room as he walked away. The military and the police would be looking for anyone carrying anything suspicious, and Juba had access to other rifles to use in the future. He disappeared into the crowd that was running away, scurrying for their homes.

28

The Army soldiers were starting to mutter beneath their breaths in the chow lines and in the barracks, feeling that they were losing control of the area. It was no longer a secret that the dangerous terrorist and sniper Juba, once an evil legend down in Baghdad, was out there roaming their turf with a big motherfucking rifle. The fact that everyone now knew his name and background did not detract from the reputation but made it even more ominous. The guy was no raghead shooter popping off rounds from a rooftop but a former master sniper and color sergeant in the British Royal Marines, one of *us,* a real professional, not one of *them.* Could shoot the hairs off a gnat's nuts. He had done Baghdad, he had done London, he had done San Francisco, and now he was doing Task Force Hammer and every soldier venturing beyond the wire felt a target on his back. Count the bodies, button up tight, do your job, and keep an eye peeled for the nearest armor in case Juba comes to play.

Albeit, the Army could not do its mission that way. It had to have men in the gun turrets when they went out because you could not sail blindly into dangerous territory. Then the soldiers eventually would have to dismount and go on foot patrol, out in harm's way with a pucker factor of ten. Snipers cause problems even when they are not around.

In his office at the sprawling camp, Colonel Neil Withrow was in a tense and private meeting with his XO and his top intelligence officer. The blinds were twisted to let in light but keep out the heat, and an air conditioner churned hard to keep the air clean and the temperature in the eighties, which was twenty degrees or more lower than outside. The machine was overmatched.

A new map of Hargatt was spread on the colonel's desk, and the intelligence officer, a major, used a big magnifying glass on a sliding mount to make the images jump out. "We've been looking for these places a long time, and finally it has all come together," said the major.

Two square dwellings were colored in bright red, about a half mile apart on the scaled map. "Each one is a safe house where the new foreign fighters and al Qaeda types are gathered before being sent down into Baghdad. The fighters are usually the young suicide bomber fanatics. Al Qaeda sends in better-trained men to help coordinate and run the show down there."

The XO, a lieutenant colonel, added, "Your sources say that both houses are full right now?"

"Sources, as in plural, and not just some joker off the street with a grudge against his neighbor and looking for a quick cash payout?" The colonel stared at the map, his mind running through the options.

"A good source that we have used before, and a separate backup. Both are locals." The intel officer had vetted the information carefully before presenting it. The last thing he needed was some turncoat informant giving false information at this point. The backup source not only confirmed the information but added a sense of urgency. It was authentic, and the aerial recon photos showed men moving in and out of the houses.

"Colonel, we estimate maybe twenty-five fighters are in each house. They filter them out a few at a time as more come in. As we have suspected, Hargatt is a major stop on the insurgents' underground railroad to get fresh fighters and arms into Baghdad."

Withrow remained cautious. The Juba mission was still paramount, but this was a golden opportunity. His overall mission would continue long after the Juba situation was gone, and bringing down these two houses and bagging fifty bad guys would chop a major insurgent resupply line. Still, it might compromise the other thing.

"Okay." He made a decision. "Now that we have the informants' material, I want some American eyes on it for confirmation. Send two scout-sniper teams out to recon on both target buildings and report back."

"Why not use those special ops types who are after Juba? They look pretty competent."

"This doesn't have anything to do with Juba. If he happens to be in one of those houses, then we take him, too. Task Force Trident doesn't need to know everything we do."

"Yes, sir."

The colonel ordered, "Get your planners busy. The sniper teams go in as soon as it's dark enough. They are not to engage, just scout out the houses and report back. If the targets are valid, then we roll out and hit both places at 0500."

The XO was in total agreement. He, too, was tired of getting punched around without striking back. "What kind of force, sir?"

"A full package on each house. Abrams on the corners, Bradleys bring in the infantry, with Apache choppers overhead. Way up overhead, I want a couple of flyboys with smart bombs targeted to those places in case things go to shit."

"What about the Tridents? We told Swanson they would be kept in the loop."

"And they will. They will be notified if and when we are ready to roll. Right now, we are just trying to gather actionable intelligence on some insurgent strongholds. Get to it."

HARGATT

An M40A1 rifle, the exquisite weapon of U.S. Marine snipers, lay on an unzipped gun bag on a table in the commander's kitchen. Juba picked it up gently and made sure the safety on the right side of the receiver was fully to the rear before handling it further. Satisfied, he observed that a lightweight oil covered the surfaces instead of normal lubricating grease and Break-Free, which tended to hold grit in desert climates. Then he disassembled it on a clean cloth.

He depressed the bolt stop in front of the trigger and pulled the bolt straight back to remove it and check the inner surfaces. Clean as a whistle.

"We took it from a Marine sniper who died in a roadside ambush, and we have not disturbed it," said the commander. "A gift for you."

At first glance, it seemed the weapon had been well cared for and protected. That meant it had been cleaned with a .30 cal bore brush from the receiver end, not the muzzle end. No pits in the muzzle or dents or bulges in the twenty-four-inch stainless steel barrel. The chamber, the entire bolt assembly, the receiver, the Winchester modified Model 70 floor plate, the sling swivels, the magazine follower, and the spring, trigger, and trigger guard had been tenderly handled with soft patches and brushes and cotton swabs. The springs were taut, the stock was free of cracks, the bottom of the barrel had been shoe-shined with a cloth, and the Pachmayr recoil pad was new. The bolt slid freely when he put it all back together. He put the safety off and pulled the trigger to check the hammer fall. No trigger creep.

It was almost as if a Marine armorer had handed him the 7.62 mm rifle. Fresh ammunition was plentiful, with each round to be loaded individually. The rifle could hold up to five bullets, but in action, the sniper would put one in the chamber, leave three in the magazine, and then, after three shots, stop and reload. Never let it run dry. A ten-power Unertl scope crowned the package, and its lens was still pristine although it had been kept in the bag.

The weapon seemed to be asking to be set free of the confining gun case and allowed to kill. It had to have put five rounds within a three-inch shot group at a distance of three hundred yards just to get out of the armorer's shed. Up to a thousand yards, the M40A1 was considered by many to be the best sniper rifle in the world, and this one was aching to do its job of killing people. Juba approved.

"Now I have a task for you and this beautiful new rifle," said the commander. "We are finishing a massive trap for the Americans, two entire houses that are filled with explosives that will be triggered by remote control. Earlier, we led a couple of men whom we know to be informants for the Crusaders to believe that the houses are secret rest stops and rendezvous points for jihadist fighters headed toward Baghdad. Those dogs went running to their masters with the news."

Juba looked puzzled. "You want me to kill a couple of informants? You can do that with your own men. I do not want to risk exposure for such minor targets."

The commander chuckled. "Oh, no. No, indeed, my

friend. If the Americans operate with their usual thoroughness, they will want to confirm what was said on their own before committing to an attack. We have watched this before. Air reconnaissance will not work, so they most likely will send in scouts to validate the information. These men are invisible and move like ghosts."

"Scout-sniper teams," said Juba. "A spotter and a shooter working together, probably one team for each suspect house, probably tonight."

"Yes. I want you to find them all. Kill them all. Use this weapon." The commander put his hand on the M40A1 and gave it a friendly pat.

Juba winced. *Shit, now I have to clean it again.* "May I suggest an alternative, Commander? It is an old custom in your part of the world to leave one victim alive to carry tales of horror back to his army. Suppose I kill just three, and then you have women desecrate the bodies with long knives. We make the fourth man watch and then throw him out on the road so he can be found by the Americans. They will be absolutely enraged. If your goal is to lure them in to attack those houses, you can bet they will be coming hard. But I will not take part in that fight."

The commander looked hard at Juba. Brilliant and bloody-minded, extremely proficient and totally mad. He clapped his hands with enthusiasm. "Yes. We will do it. Darkness will be on us soon."

COB SPEICHER

Colonel Withrow was waiting four hours later when a Humvee ambulance with the big red crosses painted on the sides rolled up to the hospital. Doctors and nurses were ready to work, but when they loaded the young soldier onto the wheeled gurney to get him into the operating theater, Withrow put out his hand. "Stop," he commanded in a soft voice.

The soldier was the spotter for one of the scout-sniper teams sent into the town, the only survivor, and although he was covered in purple and yellow bruises, he had lived through the experience. A lump the size of an orange surrounded his closed right eye from where he had been clobbered. The problems were not physical but mental, and he was in shock. Tears carved paths in the greasepaint on his face. He looked up with his one good eye and recognized Withrow.

"Sir, they butchered them. We never got near that house. The bastards *butchered* them, sir!"

A patrol on the outskirts of Hargatt had found him wandering on the road, beaten and dazed, wearing only his pants and boots. The colonel saw the circle welts of cigarette burns on his chest. Rope burns around the biceps and wrists. Trigger finger broken.

"Try to tell me what happened, son."

"It's that fucking Juba, sir. We never saw him coming. He's crazy good."

"Easy. Details, please." The colonel looked at a doctor standing there with a syringe of painkiller and shook his head. Not yet. This was too important, and the boy wanted to talk.

The soldier also shook his head at the doctor. He had to report. Had to. "Jenkins and I were doing our thing, Colonel, and everything went fine from the drop-off from the tank until we were about thirty minutes into the village. We found a drainage ditch and were crawling up the block, with no lights on anywhere. Really, really dark. Then Jenk ducked under a little bridge, had to hold his breath in that crappy water, and when he popped up the other side, there was a single shot and Jenk took it in the head. I managed to snake down under the bridge to pull the body back, but somebody came up and coldcocked me. Knocked me out cold."

The colonel closed his eyes and patted the scout on the shoulder. Fucking Juba. "Then what?"

"I came to in the street, aw, Jesus, sir, it was awful."

"Come on. I need to know."

"Three bodies were piled up, and somebody flashed a light so I could identify the faces. Jenk, Tony White, and Ian Grable, and they all were obviously dead. I saw a lot of shadows milling around them, as if waiting for something. That's when I actually saw Juba! He told me in British English that everyone had been waiting for me to wake up. They had shoved a gag in my mouth so I couldn't scream, and Juba went behind me and held my head so that I had to watch what happened next. You know that scream that Muslim tribal women do, that quick *la-la-la-la* tongue clicking? Well, that started up and got loud, like it was some kind of celebration, and then a few more lights were turned on."

The words were pouring out, as if the soldier believed that by telling the story he might force it from his mind. The colonel knew, though, that there was a good chance the boy would see the same scene every night for the rest of his life. Still, despite the horror, his training had kicked in, and he was giving a good, solid report before accepting medical treatment.

"Old women, sir, and young girls and mothers. Just women. They fell on those bodies like a pack of wolves, stripped them naked, and then went to work with big sharp knives, cutting and cutting . . ." The tears started again. "They cut off Jenk's head and threw it at me. They flayed chunks of skin and meat from all of them and hacked off arms and feet. Men were laughing and encouraging the women. Then somebody hit me hard on the head again and I was zonked, thank God. Next thing I know, I was being helped toward the sound of a Bradley that was idling behind a patrol. The ragheads shoved me into the street and left. Sir, I'm sorry. I fucked up and got them all killed."

The colonel motioned to the doctor, and the needle punched into the soldier's arm. As the sedative took hold and the eyelids fluttered, Withrow took the boy's hand. "Bullshit, trooper. None of this was your fault."

The patient was rolled away, and Withrow stepped back and stood silently for a moment before turning around. The XO was there, as were Kyle Swanson and Sybelle Summers. "We're going to go get those bodies," said the colonel. "Bastards wanted my attention, and now they have it. Nobody does this to my people."

Swanson had listened to the young soldier talk. He also had reached his limit.

29

The colonel had made his decision and was not going to change it. The escalating violence in Hargatt had nullified the forty-eight-hour deal he had made with Kyle Swanson. Withrow had to plug this bleeding sore before Hargatt, and perhaps Tikrit, fell back into their old, bad ways and the locals lost confidence that the Americans would respond. Another Fallujah was looming out there.

"We can't wait any longer, people," he told the small group in his office. "There is no time for collecting and analyzing information. We are going to hit those houses hard with a full company package on each one: tanks, Bradleys, and Apaches. If that fucking sniper opens up, we will send the Abrams tanks after him and crush the son of a bitch into the rubble. Apache gunships will hose down the escape routes."

"There will be substantial collateral damage, sir," reminded the XO.

Colonel Withrow's face was an angry shade of red, remembering what the women had done in cutting up the snipers. "Right now, I don't give a shit. As far as I am concerned, anyone still in the area will be considered to be enemy combatants. Those suspect houses are seeping hatred like spreading cancers and *I ... WANT ... THEM ... DEAD!!*"

Kyle Swanson stared at the latest map pinned to the wall of the office and let his thoughts jump ahead to the action planned around the two houses that were circled in red. Four massive M1A2 Abrams tanks would lead the charge through the streets just before dawn and advance to within a hundred yards of each corner of a house, blasting away with their 120 mm smoothbore cannons. A dozen Bradley Fighting Vehicles with Bushmaster chain guns buzzing would then swarm forward and disgorge three platoons of infantrymen, or "dismounts" in cavalry talk. Support vehicles would zoom into the area on the ground while the Apaches roamed overhead. Brute force.

"Mr. Swanson? You disagree?" The colonel was almost daring Kyle to challenge him.

"No, sir. It's your show. If you get him, we will go in afterward and try to find his information. He doesn't have to be alive for that." Kyle disagreed a lot, but there was no use butting heads on this one. The sniper deaths and torture had set off a firestorm of reaction. It could not wait any longer.

"Very well. You and your people can go along with us in a support capacity." Withrow turned to his XO and intelligence staff and planners. "We launch at 0500 hours. Remember, no man left."

As Kyle and Sybelle walked back to the special ops area, he looked up at the crescent moon, then at his wristwatch. It was thirty minutes past one in the morning. Not much time. "You're coming with me," he said. It wasn't a question.

"Yeah," she answered. "Of course."

Sybelle and Kyle spoke with the rest of the team while saddling up to go into Hargatt and finish the recon job and see what else they might turn up. The rest of the team would cover for their absence in case the Army started asking questions. Then Captain Rick Newman would join one of the strike packages for the predawn raid, and Travis Hughes would ride along with the second one.

A blacked-out Humvee driven by Newman pulled up to the camp's front gate fifteen minutes later, with Hughes in the shotgun seat with the radios. Crouched unseen in the back were Kyle and Sybelle, dressed in local clothing, and Rawls and Tipp, whose faces were covered with grease-paint and who wore black combat clothing beneath their web gear.

"It's dangerous out there in the dark, Captain," warned the corporal who checked them through the gate. "You guys be careful."

"Thanks, Corporal. We are just going to do a quick recon of the main road up to the intersection. See what we can see. Be back in about fifteen minutes."

From the depths of the sprawling camp behind them, everyone could hear the rumble of the big tracked vehicles moving about and getting arranged for the morning's attack. Fuel and ammo were loading.

Newman kept a steady speed up to the intersection, where he made a three-point turn and drove right back the way he had come down the road, at the same speed. During the turn, the four people in the rear tumbled out of the doors and lay still. Joe Tipp and Darren Rawls belly-crawled up to the mud wall that had shielded Juba the previous day and swung into an observation position, ready to go in and support Swanson and Summers if necessary.

Kyle and Sybelle went into the jagged window of Juba's first hide and waited to see if anyone had reacted to the passing of the Humvee. There was no clatter of running men, no shooting, no bright lights, but the air was thick with tension and there was a steady undercurrent of quiet noise. As their senses adjusted to the night, they could make out the sounds of people moving and some low talking. They flipped down the night vision goggles and slid out the front entrance and into the shadows at the edge of the town. Suddenly, it seemed as if some giant had kicked over an anthill and streams of green ants were moving everywhere. Both recognized the familiar pre-battle scene. Everyone in the area knew the Americans would be coming in with deadly force soon, and refugees were getting out of the way. Men, women, and children were shuffling along, carrying a few belongings, looking to get into the perceived safety of Tikrit before the American tsunami arrived.

It made the job of Kyle and Sybelle a bit easier, for with so much movement, no one would notice just a little bit more. Things were being kicked, and people were bumping into objects and each other, talking in low tones, but never stopping in their flight. Making a little noise was not a problem for the two snipers, and they removed the goggles, tucked their weapons and gear beneath their flowing clothing, and stepped into the tail end of the sporadic march, allowing the surge of frightened refugees to carry them straight into the middle of town. Sybelle wore a scarf over her head.

Rounding a corner in the thickest part of the village, the line of refugees bent to the right as it approached a couple of armed guards standing in the street and waving the villagers to the side. Kyle and Sybelle did not break stride or look at the men, but when they were about twenty yards beyond the guards, they swerved into a tight alley and pulled out silenced pistols. They had reached the first suspect house and anticipated that it would be bulging with insurgents, but it wasn't. Sticking with the shadows, they split up and circled the structure and still saw only the two guards out front.

Sybelle pointed to her eyes and then the building. *Look inside.*

Swanson went off in a low trot to the rear wall, and she covered him. He crouched and put his night goggles back on and let his eyes adjust to the strange glow before standing up, pressing his back against the wall, and slowly peering around the edge of the open window. He inhaled deeply, then waved to Sybelle, who ran to join him.

"The place is empty, but you get that smell?" he whispered.

She took a breath. "Gasoline fumes. Chemicals."

Kyle levered himself into the window and balanced on the sill but did not drop inside. There was a nightmare collection of explosives stacked around the walls, ready to blow. Cans of gasoline, boxes of ammunition and grenades, bricks of C-4, and a collection of artillery shells were all ready to obey the spark that would explode it all. Looking at the door, he could see no thin wires stretched taut, awaiting the boot of an American soldier coming in. No wires around the windowsill. The bodies of the three Americans were stacked in the middle of the ground floor.

He dropped back outside. "No insurgent troops in there, but a hell of a lot of explosives, and it doesn't seem to be booby-trapped," he told Sybelle. "Looks like they want to get a bunch of Americans in the middle of the place before setting it off. Let's go check the other one."

This time it took about a half hour to make their way to the target building because the line of refugees was thinning out and it was dangerous to continue to use the streets. The best way to go house-to-house was out one window and into the window of the home next door. With the buildings standing empty, progress was clumsy and tiring but uneventful, and they got there unseen by any rooftop observers.

Two guards were at the front of the second house, too, and another circled the building at random. Swanson and Summers squeezed into a shadowed alcove, and when the sentry disappeared around the corner, Kyle ran to the building and looked inside. He did not expect to find anyone looking back, and he was back with her in fifteen seconds. "Same thing," he said. "Damn big bomb. Let's back off and call it in."

They were both sweating by the time they found a safe zone about halfway between the two houses. It was four o'clock when Sybelle got on the Trident secure radio link back to the observation post, where Joe Tipp relayed the message back to Camp Speicher.

Captain Newman was standing beside a Bradley, drinking lukewarm coffee, when his earpiece buzzed. He listened intently, dumped the coffee, and jogged up to the command track, throwing a quick salute to Colonel Withrow.

"Colonel, Captain Summers and Swanson just reported in, sir. They are inside Hargatt and report that both of the suspect buildings are stacked to the rafters with explosives. It's a trap, sir, to draw us in and blow up the buildings right in our faces. The bodies of the three snipers are in the first house, probably booby-trapped."

"Your people are in the town?" The colonel looked at Newman in surprise. "You let them go in without telling me first?"

"We had a tip about Juba, sir. They just decided to finish the recon on the houses along the way when they saw an opportunity. Lots of refugees are moving out and covered their approach." Newman and Withrow both knew that was a lie, but it was a discreet way out of the problem.

"Swanson recommends strongly that you hold off on

entering the town for a little while longer but make a big feint at first light, growling about on the outskirts to draw the attention of any fighters who are still there. That will help him and Summers continue snooping."

The colonel looked at his XO and a smile creased his leathery face. "Well, I'll be damned. Okay, we'll do it."

A soft dawn spread over the quiet town. The streets were empty, the shops closed; the last of the refugees had padded away. The insurgent commander and Juba stood atop the distant rooftop of the commander's home, watching the storm build.

"Here they come!" said the commander. "They are so predictable."

The ground vibrated as the mighty armored armada waddled down the roads approaching the village, throwing up clouds of sand in its wake. The monstrous Abrams tanks fanned out from single file into one long row and took their time parking wheel to wheel, and the Bradley Fighting Vehicles maneuvered behind them in V-formations. Overhead, Apache gunships swung around to the west of town, darting close, then withdrawing to a safer and higher distance. Behind the armor came marching columns of infantrymen who wheeled about and spread out, almost in parade formation. A task force was on the move.

"Is this what you wanted?" Juba asked. "You think you can stop all that?"

"I do not intend to stop it, my friend. Let them come in. I want them to try to retrieve those bodies. We have a few fighters planted around to deliver just enough fire to channel the Americans toward the two houses. When their soldiers fight their way inside, the houses detonate on them. It shall be a great victory, praise Allah."

Juba's more practiced military eyes saw what the commander did not. All of that armor out there snarling at the gates was not actually doing anything but making a lot of noise. The Abramses normally operated in violent but precise choreography, and their crews were extraordinarily well trained with the machines. Now they were having difficulty *parking* the damned things? Not bloody likely. And all that marching, like some old army forming up in a straight line for an attack? The hair on his neck prickled, as if touched by a cold hand. This was, somehow, Swanson at work.

"Bingo," said Kyle. "I got the spotter. On the roof of that building five doors down on the diagonal street to our left."

Sybelle checked the rooftop through the scope on her rifle and caught the sunlight flickering off the lenses of a set of binos. "Uh-hunh. He's got a good view of both places from there and is safe, back out of the attack zone. Has to be the triggerman."

"Yeah. Let's go get him."

They squirmed out of their hide in the back of an abandoned house, checked the outside, and went into a cautious lope alongside the walls. The place had the look of a movie set, lots of empty buildings but no activity. Still, they took their time and proceeded with great caution: stop, observe, assess, move.

The building was a three-story affair of concrete blocks, with the third story added much later to the original structure. It leaned slightly to the right, and mortar had oozed out between the bricks before drying. A shop was on the first floor, and residences probably were above it. They stopped for almost ten minutes and waited in silence, watching for movement inside.

"There has to be a guard in there," whispered Kyle. "Just can't see him."

Sybelle handed him her rifle and got her local clothes

back in order with the scarf over her hair and a veil pulled across the lower part of her face. "I got it." She stood and walked along the side of the building, stepping boldly through the front door.

The guard was seated in a straight chair, leaning against the wall of the shop with his AK-47 balanced on his lap. He looked up at her silhouette in the doorway and barked, "Woman, what are you . . ."

Sybelle whipped the pistol up from her side and shot him twice in the face, and Kyle came ducking inside at the soft coughs of the silencer. They rotated through the cluttered store, finding no one else, and Swanson pointed to the stairs. Sybelle took a moment to step out of the cumbersome gown and scarf and followed Kyle up.

A closed door was at the head of the short staircase, and Swanson eased it open. He went to the right and Sybelle went left. Nothing. There was only one other room. With Sybelle covering, Kyle pushed hard through the closed door, and it flew open but did not bounce off the wall. He immediately double-tapped two rounds through it, and the guard hiding behind the door gave a little cry of pain and surprise and toppled to the floor, where Kyle shot him in the head.

They moved on. The third floor was empty, and when they crawled up to the roof, they saw the triggerman standing nine feet away, exposed in the morning sunshine, binoculars to his eyes, watching the sideshow being put on by the rumbling beasts of Task Force Steel. Kyle Swanson kicked him behind the knees and jerked back on his head at the same time, forcing a fall. As soon as the surprised man was on the deck and out of sight from the street, Kyle shot him in the eye and dragged the dead man inside. Sybelle jumped over the corpse, swept up two cell phones that lay side by side on the top of the wall, and also hurried back through the door.

Inside, she examined them as gently as if they were diamonds. Normally, a cell phone used as a trigger would be pre-dialed to a number and the operator only had to press the SEND button to complete the circuit. "Whoa, girl," she said to herself. "Easy does it."

"Look at this, Kyle," she said, pointing to the ١ and ٢ marks scrawled in black greasepaint on the faces of the phones. "The Arabic symbols for 'one' and 'two.' Got to be the houses."

"Good to go," Swanson said. "I checked this guy out and he's nobody. Probably a midlevel type who could be trusted with just enough responsibility to carry out this job, but I doubt if he had anything to do with the planning."

"So how do we get higher up the food chain?" she asked.

Kyle grinned. "Let's blow some shit up and see who comes calling."

"Oo-rah," said Sybelle, picking up the number two phone. She pushed down on the SEND button.

The entire town seemed to jump on its foundations as a bright and blinding flash of light ignited like the wink of a miniature sun and was followed by a deafening, crashing roar. The three outside guards were swallowed in a hell of fireballs that cometed into the sky and rolled out into the street while debris scythed through the air, chopping at everything in its path. Then came the rolling concussion, giant fists slamming across the landscape and splintering windows.

Swanson and Summers were burrowed in the corner against the interior wall when the concussion rolled through with freight-train power. Rafters sagged and plaster cracked. Toys and dishes and furniture tumbled around, and they breathed through open mouths to equalize the pressure pounding at their ears. A flying lamp cracked Sybelle on the head hard enough to make her see stars, and Kyle was punched in the gut by a table leg.

When the initial explosion was done, a secondary series of smaller detonations began cooking off with loud booms, and when Kyle and Sybelle finally crawled outside on the roof, they saw that the target building was utterly gone, leaving behind a blackened hole in the ground from which smoke rose in filthy columns. Destruction ringed it. Dozens of U.S. troops might have been killed in a raid on the place.

Three blocks away, the commander of the insurgents was knocked flat by the explosion and jumped back to his feet with a shout of exasperation and fury. "He set it off too early! That stupid, ignorant son of a whore! The Americans are not even in the streets yet and now they have been warned! I am going over there and kill him myself!"

Juba laughed. "You're a fool. If you go out there, the only one who will die is you. Your crude ambush attempt is over."

The commander spun around in anger. "Don't call me a fool! You cannot accept the hospitality of my home and then dare to insult me! Do not forget that it is you, Juba, who is under my protection, not the other way around." The bearded man vaulted down the stairs, grabbed an AK-47, and sprinted toward the triggerman's building, trailed by a bodyguard.

Juba raised his eyes and looked beyond the edge of the village at the armored vehicles bumping about over a couple of miles of ground. Nothing but a feint. *Shake,* he thought. *Getting closer.*

30

"Couple of guys running this way, and they don't look too happy," said Sybelle, peering around the edge of the door.

"Right." Swanson dug a finger into each phone and levered out the batteries and then smashed the instruments with hard stomps of his boots. "Let them come in and we grab them."

The insurgent commander was the first through the door, and he was allowed to rush into the center of the room, but when the bodyguard crossed the threshold, Sybelle clocked him hard in the mouth with the butt of her M-4. His head snapped back, his feet flew out from beneath him, and he collapsed. At the same time, Swanson launched onto the commander's back and rode him to the floor, rolled him over, and popped him hard on an ear to daze him. By the time the man collected his senses, a strip of duct tape was across his mouth, plastic flexicuffs ensnared his wrists behind his back, and more duct tape had been wound around his ankles. Between the colors and shapes dancing in his eyes, he saw that the bodyguard was sprawled unconscious, also being wrapped like a mummy in black duct tape.

"You speak English?" Kyle asked, peeling back the tape across the mouth just enough to let the man speak.

"Who are you?" The words came out in a garble, as if he were talking around a cigar.

Kyle slapped him hard. "I ask the questions."

The commander shook his head. He understood the seriousness of the situation. His attempt to trap the Americans had failed, the town had been penetrated, the remaining explosives would be neutralized, and he had been captured. The plan to bleed the Americans badly and write the name of this village in the annals of resistance had failed. Without his leadership, his fighters would fade to other locations and the village would return to peace.

"I will tell you nothing," the commander grumbled. "Nothing."

"Then you are of no value to me." Kyle stood, took out his pistol, and fired a shot that ripped away part of the man's ear. The commander jerked at the pain and the impact. "Last chance," Swanson said.

Sybelle spoke. "Kyle. Hold on. No use wasting more time on him. He may have some intel, but the interrogators will wring it out of him. Let's just leave them tied up here while we go find Juba."

The commander looked strangely at them and shook his head vigorously, grunting for attention. Kyle lifted the tape again.

"Now you suddenly got something to tell me?"

The man bounced his head in understanding. "The woman just called you by the name of Kyle. Are you the Swanson Marine?"

"Maybe." Kyle ripped the gag all the way off with a swift pull that yanked out patches of beard.

"If you are, then I can tell you exactly the location of your enemy, my friend Juba. He wants you to find him, Swanson Marine," said the commander, a slit of a smile on his bloody face. Here was a chance to repay Juba for calling him a fool. Maybe both of them would die. "He is waiting just down that street."

Juba was in a mouse hole. Over the past few days, he had used some of the idle hours in the commander's home to create a unique sniper's hide, oriented along the most likely line of approach, and now he crawled into a prone position and made himself comfortable.

The moment was finally approaching, and without realizing it, he had started losing perspective. He was so intent on killing Kyle Swanson that his thoughts rejected anything but that one goal. The smart play was to leave now and fight somewhere else, some other day, but he wanted to finish it here. Never would he have a better opportunity. Swanson had to come up that single road and straight into the crosshairs.

Each decision he made now contained a trade-off, because a defender cannot defend against everything. The situation he had created was imperfect, for a mouse hole opening was so narrow that the shooter could not remain too far back in the darkness. The muzzle of Juba's rifle was no more than a foot behind the opening.

Nevertheless, arranging a battlefield of his choice had been important, for Swanson would have to be the one risking exposure. The biggest advantage was Juba's intimate knowledge of his enemy, the operational concepts of a sniper and the combat habits. He could get inside of Swanson's head and think along with his adversary.

Juba had opened all the windows in the three-story house and pulled the curtains almost closed so they would flap in the air. He chipped out several cinder blocks up high as decoy hides and stacked another dummy emplacement on the roof behind a barricade of loose wood. A sheltered animal pen stood to one side of the house. Swanson would have to be wary of all of them and might make a mistake while doing the recon. Snipers always scan a target house from top to bottom, and the higher the defender's position, the more it stands out and the more likely it is to draw attention. The mouse hole was only on the fourth row of cinder blocks up from the foundation of the house, below eye level. Juba would be watching for a slight movement of a rifle and a scope as Swanson ranged over the possible hides higher in the building, an advantage of a few microseconds.

An added bonus was the spider hole. Almost every house in Iraq had a small pit in which a family could seek shelter if and when bullets started flying outside. Juba's position was right beside the hole that had been constructed below the commander's home, which normally was kept covered by a small door and a rug. Once in the pit, there was a narrow tunnel some twenty feet long that led away to a dry well next door as an emergency escape route.

Juba had rolled away the rug and removed the wooden hatch to leave the hole uncovered. He placed the computer in the backpack and laid it on the far side of the hole. Once again, he had downloaded the important information on the memory stick as a backup, and the small device was in his breast pocket.

It was going to be a one-shot battle, and whoever fired first probably would win—but that shot had to score. Otherwise the advantage, however miniscule, switched to the other sniper. Juba would be patient, take the critical shot, and then grab the backpack, roll into the spider hole, and leave. Shoot and scoot, the Americans snipers called it.

He racked a round into the chamber of the M40A1 and settled behind his scope to wait.

They wrapped both of the captured men tightly in rings of duct tape. A hand-drawn map of the area had been pulled from the commander's pocket, and Sybelle and Kyle spread it on the floor, compared it with their own maps, and worked out the grid coordinates of the house where Juba was said to wait.

"I don't like this *High Noon*, mano-a-mano bullshit," Sybelle said. "The guy is too good."

"Hey, I never said that I want a quick-draw contest. He's the one fixated on taking my scalp to show he's the baddest sniper around. That ego is forcing him to stay put instead of hauling ass." Kyle sat on the floor, with his legs crossed and his M40A1 resting in the crook of his right arm. "I just want to kill the bastard any way we can."

Sybelle, down on one knee, brushed some hair back from her eyes. She was sweating, and it was still morning. "You're not going to play fair?"

"Nope. Never happen. As much as I definitely want to personally blow him away, we have a lot of other gadgets in our toolbox."

When he explained his plan, Sybelle relayed the orders back to the task force.

The big armored force that had been moving awkwardly suddenly fell into exact positions and nosed casually into the village streets, heading in to secure the area, disarm the remaining house lined with explosives, and retrieve the bodies of its dead soldiers. Sporadic small arms fire whanged off the thick armor plate and was answered with booming cannons and machine guns.

Fifty thousand feet overhead, a strange-looking toothpick of an aircraft received new commands from its controller on the ground at Balad Air Base and tipped over to descend to a lower altitude. The MQ-9 Reaper hunter-killer unmanned aerial vehicle had been on station for nine hours and had plenty of fuel left. It wore a pair of GBU-12 Paveway II laser-guided six-hundred-pound smart bombs beneath its wings.

* * *

"Let's do it," Kyle said. "You go high and paint the building, and I stay down on the dirt to draw his attention."

Sybelle gave him a long look. "Take it easy out there, pardner. And remember we have exactly fifteen minutes, not a second more. Do *not* go in that building." Then she rolled through a side window and was gone.

Kyle gave her a minute's head start and then went out the back door, hooked a left, and ran across the road and into a doorway. The rumble of the approaching tanks and Bradleys shook the stones on the surrounding streets, and Kyle used that to mask the noise of breaking windows and jumping to the adjoining house. Juba's hideout was no more than a thousand yards away, an easy shot for either of them.

As planned, a Bradley Fighting Vehicle suddenly came around a corner on the far side of the building, scraped alongside it in passing, and then screamed down the street at high speed, crunching over an automobile parked in its way. Kyle ran to another building on the right-hand side of the street and dove through the door. Good diversion. Juba had to feel the hard whack of the armored vehicle against the side of his house. *Surprise the enemy. Force him to conform to your plan.*

As soon as the Bradley passed, Sybelle lobbed a smoke grenade down from the roof of a nearby building, and it bounced once in the street before igniting. Kyle let the gray blossom smolder and spread, then sprinted back across and climbed a low wall. He was about eight hundred yards away now. Close enough. He went inside the building and spent time clearing both floors and checking his watch. He had less than ten minutes left.

He pushed an eating table close to the rear wall opposite the window facing up the street and began stacking up a pile of pillows, then fronting it with overturned furniture to break up any regular lines. The sun was on the back side of the building, at an angle that did neither sniper any good, other than keeping them obscured in darkness.

Kyle pulled up a solid wood chair behind the table, sat down, and found a comfortable and firm rest for his sniper rifle, with the muzzle poking through the latticework of debris. He pulled the weapon back, checked the load, and pushed it forward again. His eye went to the scope.

Sybelle's progress had been easier. After throwing the smoke grenade, she took a roundabout route over rooftops and through houses, then angled back to the target zone. An Apache gunship hovered a few blocks away, securing her flanks and back. No one shot at her.

She went prone when she reached a rooftop on the left side of Juba's location, cleared it for safety, and clicked her radio as the helicopter swung into a new protective position.

"Good to go," she said. A double click meant that Kyle had heard her message and was also in position.

Putting her rifle to her left side and laying her pistol within easy reach on the right, Sybelle removed a small monocular from a rubberized carrying case. Since she had been working as Kyle's spotter, she had packed along the laser rangefinder, which now had another use.

She edged her eyes above the top of the small revetment running along the edge of the roof and had a clear view of the cream-colored target house. Bringing up the monocular, she focused and pushed the switch to activate an invisible laser beam, which bounced off the sturdy target house and came back to the electronics packet with an exact reading. She secured it into a firm position. "Target is painted," she reported, and at Balat Air Base, the controller linked the information to the circling Reaper UAV, which then descended another ten thousand feet. From that point on, Sybelle's laser was married to the Reaper's guidance system. Where the point of the laser rested, the bombs would hit.

"Confirming that target is lit and weapon is armed," came the voice from Balat. "Three minutes."

Juba let his breathing slow and felt his heart beating normally in his chest, not thumping with excitement. This was his house. This was his safe zone. And he was Juba! He was the Sword of the Prophet, and he intended to become an even sharper sword by brewing the terrible poison gas! He let the scope run down the street to where the American troops and vehicles surrounded the other house of explosives. They had gone in and nothing had happened, so the trap had not been sprung. Both the triggerman and the commander were probably dead by now, but that was beside the point.

Kyle Swanson might be somewhere in that milling crowd of American soldiers, and while Juba could have shot several of them with ease, the only person he wanted in his crosshairs was his old nemesis, Shake. Since Swanson always liked to be in on the action, maybe he was down there checking out the strange bomb.

Juba's trigger finger tightened momentarily when a figure in black walked across the scope, but it wasn't Swanson. He eased off and kept searching, facing the target zone, in his hide, waiting like a patient spider.

No, Swanson would not be down there. He was stalking, coming closer. The unexpected, noisy passing of the Bradley and then the smoke grenade was enough confirmation. Up in one of those many windows facing him on a street filled with buildings and homes? Low on the ground beneath a bunch of junk? A doorway? A shadow? He moved the scope slowly across the most likely danger zones.

* * *

Swanson studied the various openings in the Juba building. The shitbird knew his business and could be in any one of those places except on the roof, where the helicopter would have taken him out. Slow and steady scan, top to bottom, left to right. He couldn't fire without a target because the first shot would give away his position and draw a return bullet in instant retaliation.

The radio spoke to him again. "One minute." Out of time. He could put down the rifle and let the bomb take care of it, but hell, he *did* have some pride invested in this hunt to the death. He cursed himself for even thinking about something that ridiculous. Who is the better sniper? Horseshit. Nobody cares. Whoever walks away is better. Keep the scope moving. Nothing. Nothing.

Juba thought about saying a prayer. No. Stay focused. The butt stock of the rifle was cool against his right cheek. Plenty of time to pray later. *Where would I be hiding if I was Shake?* That window looked a bit curious. The others had ordinary lines in the rooms behind them. The shadows in this one seemed jagged and jumbled, as if a storm had passed through. A hide?

The impersonal voice in Kyle's headset said, "Weapon free. Weapon released." The big GBU-12 fell away, and the Reaper jumped higher at the sudden subtraction of weight and then curled back onto its course. There was no pilot getting tired, and the controllers at the base would simply swap off to a fresh shift as soon as this job was done and the UAV would perform some other job, somewhere else.

The bomb was in free fall, with big fins on the rear providing lift and the four smaller fins on the front allowing the guidance unit to steer it. The internal guidance system locked on to the laser beam that Sybelle had affixed to the side of the house and transitioned the control services from simple ballistics into a precise line-of-sight flight path. The bomb twisted into a smooth spiral motion, gaining speed as it plummeted nose down toward the target.

Kyle took up the slack on the trigger and held it so as not to require that extra fraction of a second if he found the target. Then he saw dark against darker in the small hole left by a missing cinder block almost at ground level. *There! A movement!* A rifle muzzle was on him!

Their rifles fired at almost the same moment, but Kyle had been a hair faster.

His 7.62 mm bullet went through the mouse hole opening and struck Juba in the left cheek just as the terrorist pulled the trigger of his own weapon. Kyle's round bored in straight along the jawline, taking out a line of teeth and a chunk of the left side of Juba's face before shattering the jawbone and exiting.

The return shot had been deflected at the moment of firing, and Juba's bullet crashed into the wall just above Kyle's head.

In the mouse hole, Juba rolled away from the jarring pain, feeling as if his head had been torn off. *Kill shot,* he thought. He toppled into the spider hole, fighting to remain conscious to pull the wooden door into position. When it fell into place, he lay back with his hands holding his destroyed face and agony racking his body as blood rushed through his open wound. He could see the light of the tunnel beckoning, and began to crawl.

The heavy, speeding bomb smashed through the roof and penetrated the ceilings before the warhead detonated in the kitchen. Everything in the immediate vicinity was vaporized in a gigantic explosion, and the concussion blew the walls apart. Support beams and interior walls were torn to pieces, and the house collapsed into rubble, with thick layers of wood and dirt and junk piling up over the spider hole, sealing it shut and totally obscuring it from view. At the bottom lay a shredded computer.

Juba, bleeding heavily, was thrown against the walls of the narrow tunnel like a doll by the explosion. His head, already savaged, now felt like it was being kicked from his body, and his eardrums ruptured and began to bleed. His mouth and eyes filled with dirt, and when he cleared his vision, he saw that the frail walls of the tunnel were giving way and the light was disappearing. He put a hand to his breast and felt the slight bump of the memory stick secure in the pocket as the world collapsed about him.

Down the street, Kyle had been rocked from his chair by the explosion but quickly got up and went to the window. Fire had broken out in the wreckage of the house, and flames licked out of the mouse hole as a curtain of smoke climbed out of the rubble. He was satisfied. If he had not killed Juba, then the bomb had obliterated him. And with Juba gone, so was the formula and the overwhelming threat of the poison gas. Probably. He had to believe that.

Kyle put down his rifle and took a deep breath, staring at the scene of destruction. "Burn in hell, motherfucker," he said.

EPILOGUE

The white yacht was alone on this deep swath of the Atlantic Ocean, churning a lazy wake in the late afternoon. Kyle rested his elbows on the rail and watched with awe as a huge whale broke the surface of the sea, launched a third of its black bulk into the open air, and fell back with an immense force that threw curtains of water high into the air. Then it was gone, burrowing into the depths of the ocean, and the disturbed water on top settled back into a normal rhythm. An instant of action followed by a disappearance. *My kind of whale,* he thought and raised his beer in salute to the beast. A two-week holiday was just starting, and he felt good.

"What are you doing?" Delara Tabrizi joined him at the rail, and the sea breeze stirred her dark hair. The multilingual schoolteacher from Khorramshahr, Iran, was now the beautiful personal secretary of Lady Patricia Cornwell, well on her way to becoming a British citizen. The government was appreciative and discreet about her help on tracking the device that had struck London.

"Did you see that whale leap up a second ago?"

"Yes. We see them frequently out here, far from the

shipping lanes." Her voice was quiet, her British accent thicker. "Amazing creatures. How can anyone put something like that into a tourist attraction?"

Kyle looked over at her. The brown eyes were devoid of worry, the lines of stress from the mission and her brushes with death were gone, and she wore slacks and a casual white blouse, with minimal makeup. She didn't need makeup, he decided. "So you're okay?"

"I am fine," she replied, and her voice was firm with decision. "I think about my family, my former students, and my country. It's like that part of me is dead, and a new Delara is being created."

Swanson laughed. "I know the feeling."

Delara blushed and also laughed, a hand shading her brown eyes. "Oh! I forgot that Kyle Swanson is dead, too. You *do* know the feeling."

"Yeah. Welcome to the club."

"Lady Pat and Sir Jeff told me the story, Kyle. They swore me to secrecy, but since you are such a frequent visitor, and such an important part of their own lives, they felt that I should know your background. I am very sorry about Shari Towne. She sounds like a wonderful woman."

"That she was. That she was." *Such a long time ago,* he thought to himself. *Long time.*

One deck above them, Pat and Jeff were watching, drinks in hand. "Couple of strong kids, healing," Jeff said.

"Sir Geoffrey Cornwell, you are a blind old bat," his wife said. She put a hand on his shoulder and leaned against him. "Even you should be able to see the sparks flying between those two."

"What? Patricia, they're not even standing very close together. Just having a friendly conversation."

She smiled. "Of course, dear. Right as always."

BALI, INDONESIA

The dreams were a vivid new form of existence, sustained by strong opiates and undulating waves of soothing incense. Shiva, the destroyer, pursued, his four arms and the third eye and the hair of snakes. Then Shiva would dissolve into the golden-feathered Garuda with the bulging eyes and hooked beak, bringing some calm of the all-knowing Vishnu. A flash of pain, then more and stronger opiates and more horrible dreams. The pattern went on for a very long time as the mystery patient bordered on constant hallucination. The doctors at the special clinic wondered how he was still alive, shrugged, and went about their work.

Then one day, the weeks of massive facial and dental reconstruction were finally over, and the patient, his left eye blinded forever, was allowed to awaken. Only a week later, he was out of bed, walking the clean wooden floors of the clinic, helped by nurses, as bright sunlight played through long, slatted windows. Physical therapists guided the recovery, but the patient seemed to suck up pain and constantly pushed the boundaries of exhaustion, several times passing out from doing too much. Within a month he was walking on the nearby beach, alone, hobbling because of the broken leg, but determined to stride out strongly, and day by day, he got stronger. At night, he fell asleep to the noisy mumbles and chirps of jungle creatures and insects. He fed a curious gecko wall lizard, and it became his friend.

After a few months, he was moved from the clinic to a villa that overlooked a plain of rice paddies and forests that stepped down to the sea, and the medical specialists came to visit. Servants tended him and were amazed at his regimen of sit-ups, push-ups, crunches, running, martial arts exercises, and practice with knives and guns. He ate a perfect diet.

Two men who were not doctors came to the villa one day, wearing thin and decorated short-sleeved shirts over dark trousers. They did not remark on the partial paralysis around the mouth and jaw, or on the latticework of facial scars, or on the black patch over the left eye. "We have a job," one said.

"Excellent," said Juba, who was tired of paradise. "I'm ready."

Read on for an excerpt from

CLEAN KILL
A SNIPER NOVEL

by Gunnery Sgt. Jack Coughlin, USMC (RET.)
with Donald A. Davis

Coming soon in hardcover from St. Martin's Press

1

PAKISTAN

For only a moment, less time than needed to take a breath, Gunnery Sergeant Kyle Swanson lifted his eyes from the dark path uncoiling before him and looked above the surrounding snow-covered peaks. A crescent moon rode in the cold night sky, with a shadowed edge so clean that the Marine sniper could make out the pimpled edges of individual craters with his naked eye. An early astronaut once described the lunar emptiness as magnificent desolation, and Swanson thought the same description was a good fit for the sheer and ragged mountains of western Pakistan. Up, down, or sideways, no matter where you looked, there was nothing in these badlands but more nothing. His eyes went back to the narrow trail, and he used his left hand to brush the stone face of the mountain, feeling for outcroppings of rock or tufts of weeds that could provide handholds, while he kept his boots at least six inches from the edge of the trace. Beyond that was only a sheer drop of perhaps a thousand feet into a black chasm.

"I vote that next time, we just dump a bunch of cruise missiles on this place," said Staff Sergeant Joe Tipp, who was climbing right behind him. "My legs are on fire. Cupla cruise missiles would have saved us from humping these damned mountains."

The six Marines from Task Force Trident had been on the move for three consecutive nights, following a surly Afghan guide along impossible trails, up into the high elevations where the air was thin, then down into boulder-studded valleys, then up again. Before the dawns, they would take hide spots, set a guard rotation and fall asleep exhausted, with every muscle sore and their weapons at hand. The only way through the Spin Ghars was to put one boot in front of another.

"A cruise missile wouldn't deliver the proper message, Joe. We don't want to just whip their asses; they have to know they've been beaten. This has to be up close and personal," Swanson said over his shoulder as he forced his protesting legs to make one more step, then another. Two short grenade launchers rode atop his heavy pack, while an AK-47 submachine gun was hooked on the chest harness, and encased in a special bag over his shoulder was a Russian-made SV-98 sniper rifle. Balancing the seventy-pound load was as important as the footwork.

"You really get off on sending this kind of message, don't you?"

Swanson snorted. "Bet your ass. Now shut up and climb."

This was their fourth black raid on hidden training camps across the border in the past three months. The official version of the mission stated that it was just a snoop-and-poop job by scouts from the U.S. Marine Special Operations Command, MARSOC, and the men would stay clearly inside of Afghanistan and under no circumstances venture into Pakistan. American and other NATO troops made such sweeps every day, probing for the elusive Taliban and al Qaeda terrorists.

They had ridden out from a forward operating base in three closed Humvees, gone through a couple of small villages of mud huts so they would be seen by curious eyes and been reported up the terrorist grapevine as heading north. Once in the wilderness, darkness fell and things changed. The Humvees turned east at a dim intersection known as the Camel Crossroads and drove without lights for an hour over a rotten road, following deep ruts up the incline toward the mountain passes. They stopped. Eight Marines and the guide dismounted, and the vehicles returned to the crossroads and continued north to another forward operating base, again intentionally attracting the notice of enemy spies who concluded it was a routine resupply run, not worth worrying about.

By the end of the first night, the commandos were deep in the mountains, at an isolated and abandoned observation position that overlooked some of the most forbidding terrain on the planet. They rested all day, and things changed again that night. Two Marines were left behind to set up a communications station that would transmit periodic false mission reports back to headquarters. The rest stepped out, wearing old clothes purchased in Afghan bazaars, carrying a variety of weapons that were not made in America and without any identification. Then they fell off the map.

Soon, not even the radio team knew where they were. No colored pins on maps at any base showed their position or their target. No unmanned Predators circled overhead for surveillance, and if things went bad, no fighter-bombers would be zooming in for air support and there would be no rescue helicopter. There was absolutely no indication that any Americans were in the Paki backyard, which meant there could be no leaks to the various tribal warlords of questionable loyalties.

Kyle climbed on, in the company of fighting men that he knew and trusted, all of them fully aware that there would be no after-action reports, no medals for bravery, no mentions in the media, no memoirs later in life when they were all grandfathers and retired. Whatever happened out here, stayed here.

The only unknown was the Afghan guide, who was only about as trustworthy as any of the locals. He had worked for the Agency for five years and was given a plastic-wrapped brick of $100 bills in payment to take them into the forbidden zone. He would not be a problem. Either he did as he was told or he would be killed and left in the mountains. Such was Kyle Swanson's unforgiving world.

Climbing the rugged terrain with him now were five experienced commandos, none below the rank of sergeant or with less than seven years in the Corps. Joe Tipp was right behind him, occasionally bitching about life in general. Next was Staff Sergeant Darren Rawls, a tall African-American who was a natural athlete and hardly felt the muscle pains shared by the others on the mountain. Captain Rick Newman was in the middle of the line, technically in command of the operation but with the primary task of doing officer stuff, like talking to other officers when required, so Swanson could do his job. The fifth was red-haired Staff Sergeant Travis Stone, a grinning little killer rat. Trailing and covering the rear was the wiry and always-silent Sergeant Eliot Brenner.

Just before the mission's fourth daybreak, as the serpentine trail descended toward a broad plateau, the guide suddenly stopped, then scurried back to Swanson. The patrol froze, instantly alert as the possibility of action replaced the drudge of climbing.

"What is it?" Kyle asked.

The Afghan pointed toward a long and rocky ridge and said in fractured English, "Al Qaeda, mister. Taliban. Just there."

Swanson shed his pack and crawled forward on elbows and knees to a cluster of big rocks that allowed him to peer downward without exposing his head on the horizon. At the foot of the steep mountainside was a valley floor about five miles distant, where a crude camp of tents and small structures had been built.

Captain Newman crawled up and flopped beside Kyle and scanned the valley with his binos. "Bingo. We're here."

"Yep," Swanson confirmed. "Let's get settled."

The Tridents spread out and found individual hides for the day, caught some sleep and spent their waking hours counting enemy noses and charting range cards to the various huts and landmarks. They did not speak, just watched the base camp in which the terrorists believed they were invulnerable. The six silent men were deep in the forbidding mountains, where their enemy had been protected by a truce between the local warlords and the Pakistani army, left alone for so long they felt free do as they wished.

In the late afternoon, three civilians were brought out from one of the huts, their hands tied and their eyes covered with black strips of cloth, stumbling as guards shoved them forward. A fighter who looked like a member of the training cadre called out to the terrorist trainees and pulled a knife from his belt. Obviously giving a demonstration, he crouched at the knees and thrust quickly forward and back with the blade to show what he wanted done. A dozen of his eager students formed a circle and one of the prisoners was pushed into the middle.

The instructor then shouted out the names of individuals, and the summoned trainee would step into the circle and repeat the lunge attack, but making sure to only slice lightly into the terrified prisoner. The man had to live long enough for everyone to get a turn. When the first trainee finished, then another name was called, then the next, and the crying prisoner's garments turned crimson with blood until he finally collapsed. After a final bit of instruction from the senior fighter, one of his younger acolytes bent down and cut the victim's throat.

Another circle was formed with other trainees, and the ones who had already finished the knife exercise became spectators, cheering and catcalling to the others while the second bound civilian was slashed. The exercise ended when the third prisoner had been slain. The instructor gathered his men for a verbal review of their work, then dismissed them. The three bodies were hauled away for burial.

Swanson swallowed his rage. Emotion could not be allowed to enter his thoughts, and the slaughter of those three prisoners made him focus even more. Still, he waited, chewing nuts and dates, and thinking until, finally, the sky darkened. Almost time.

The moon had reached the crescent shape three nights ago and now shone like a sign to mark the start of the ninth month of the Muslim lunar calendar, the holy month of Ramadan. Thirty days of fasting. In the valley, the forty terrorists and their half-dozen instructors settled down to break their day-long fast and enjoy the first food, water and sweet chai they had been allowed to consume since before dawn. Their voices swam up the mountainside, the giddiness of a small celebration. Afterward, they would offer the last of the five daily prayers, the Isha.

Swanson drank some water, wiped his hands and passed the word to prepare to move out. He called for the guide and when he approached, Kyle kicked the man's legs from beneath him and dropped him to the ground.

Joe Tipp was there to wrap duct tape around the ankles and put plastic flex ties on the wrists. Another strip of tape went over the mouth.

"You have done well so far to get us here, my friend, and we do this not to harm you but just to insure your silence," Kyle told the guide. "We cannot afford to trust you. Stay still and quiet and you will be fine. I promise that we will pick you up on our way out. Attempt to warn those bastards down there and you will wish you were dead long before you actually are."

The guide stared into the set of the gray-green eyes and the cold face and nodded. He understood.

The six Trident Marines picked their way downhill, carefully planting their boots to prevent stumbling or sliding on rocks. There was no hurry. It was dark and the terrorists in the camp were still milling around, finishing their food and drink.

This was exactly when Kyle had wanted to strike. He felt no alarm at all about violating any sacred religious rites, because the men in that camp were killers, through and through. This had nothing to do with religion, and everything to do with tactical advantage, for Swanson considered the fasting and prayer times of his enemy to present extraordinary opportunities, small openings during which their guard was down, their alertness dim, and they were extremely vulnerable. He knew those terrorists would do the same to him if given the chance, and believed that it was savages just like them who had flown passenger jets filled with innocent Americans into office towers.

Beneath a broad thumb of boulders about five hundred meters from the camp, the Tridents stopped so Kyle and Captain Newman could study the area one last time. Things remained normal and security was loose.

"One close sentry straight ahead and another on that ridge about five hundred yards away," said Newman.

Swanson broke out his sniper rifle and peered through the PKS-07 seven-power scope to satisfy himself that the moon was providing enough light for him to see clearly. He whispered to Newman, "Take out the close sentry and I'll drop the other one at the same time. Joe Tipp, you spot for me."

Newman passed the word to Darren Rawls, who slithered off into the darkness, his long arms and legs propelling him forward at an astonishing pace and in total silence, with only his strong fingers and toes of his boots touching the ground.

The sentry lazily walked his position, his senses dulled by the cool night temperature and the big meal of lamb and rice he had just devoured. A dot of flame flashed from a match as he lit an opium-laced cigarette until golden ashes glowed at the tip. The fasting period also meant no smoking during the day, so he hungrily inhaled, held it in his lungs and stared up at the moon as the drug's pleasantness spread through his body.

In an instant, a shadow rose behind him, a big hand cupped over his mouth and yanked the head back, and then the heavy blade of a sharp Ka-Bar, an old-school combat knife, ripped through the exposed neck, sliced the jugular vein and dug for the brain. Darren Rawls eased the man to the rocky ground and knelt on him as he bled out. He clicked his radio transmitter once, breaking squelch to confirm his task was done.

Joe Tipp and Kyle Swanson had calculated the distance, elevation, and windage numbers for their target. Upon hearing the click in their earpieces, Tipp whispered, "Fire." Swanson applied a smooth four pounds of pressure to the trigger and the SV-98 coughed once, the flash suppressor eating up the sound of the gunshot. An instant later, a 7.52 mm bullet slapped into the broad back of the distant guard and tore out his heart and chest, dropping him without a sound.

Swanson put the sniper rifle aside and turned to Newman. "You find their commo shed?"

"Um. Yeah. It's that center building, looks like the overall headquarters. They really grouped all of those tents and buildings close together. Hooray for sloppy work."

"Shit, why not? They aren't worried about any air strikes on sovereign Pakistani soil, and the Paks sure as hell aren't coming after them. We're here to show they aren't safe, no matter where they sleep."

Tipp unstrapped a rocket propelled grenade launcher. "I still think cruise missiles would be a good idea."

"Let's go." Swanson growled and led the way down the trail, unlimbering one of his own RPG-7s. The old weapons were notoriously inaccurate and had a short range, but had been modified and updated, and in the hands of trained commandos firing down slope, they were effective and deadly. With both sentries out of the way, the group closed on the camp until they were less than a football field away, then at Kyle's signal, moved into a line, side-by-side, about ten yards apart.

They were in position within seconds, invisible in the darkness against the mountain backdrop, all with RPGs ready to fire. The terrorists were grouped together outside in the open area of the camp, kneeling in five lines on their prayer rugs and facing Mecca.

Swanson took a final range measurement, just a flicker of an invisible radar beam and spoke into the small microphone on his headset. "Set your detonators at one hundred meters. On my count of three, send the first volley into the crowd and then hit your assigned buildings with the second shot, again on my count. We want both salvos to arrive as a package. After that, we move into the camp and fire at will. There will be no survivors."

Captain Newman had assigned each commando a specific segment of the crowd of worshippers, so as to maximize the damage rather than having all of the rockets bursting in one place. The terrorists were no longer men, as far as any of the Marines were concerned: Just targets. Kyle aimed at the center of the cluster, and counted it off, "Three . . . Two . . . One!"

The six RPGs spoke with a loud, rippling bark and the rockets leaped from their shoulder-mounted tubes, whining instantly toward the gathered men below. The few who looked up saw six rocket trails etching smoke in the night sky and then the missiles exploded in a hellish roar. The odd-numbered rockets carried high-explosive warheads that ripped through unprotected skin and internal organs, while the even-numbered ones were thermobarics, which erupted just above the crowd to spew a fine mist of underoxidized fuel that detonated in air bursts which sucked the air out of lungs and created massive fireballs that consumed bodies.

As the explosions ricocheted up the mountains, the Tridents were already firing the second rounds, ripping the other RPGs at the few buildings and blowing the fragile structures apart. Flames from the fuel-air explosions swept around corners and into doorways and windows and potential hiding places, vacuuming life out of every human it touched.

Kyle was moving before the roar ceased and relentlessly led the other Tridents in a mad scramble toward the shattered campsite. He estimated about 90 percent of the fifty-two-man terrorist force was already dead, and was glad that no return fire was coming back toward the Marines.

"Split up!" he hollered when they reached the perimeter. The team divided into two-man units and worked rapidly through the burning ruins, firing three-round bursts at anyone who looked as if he may have somehow survived the initial attacks. There weren't many, and even the wounded drew the momentary but deadly attention of the raiders. It was not work for the weak of heart, but mercy had no place in the mountains of Pakistan on a night like this.

At the far edge of the camp, Kyle yelled, "Back!" They all turned and worked their way through the charnel houses to their starting point. Fewer shots were needed this time.

The fire was chewing everything in the camp and an ammunition dump erupted like a small volcano, but the surrounding high mountains shielded the fire and detonations from the outside world. The Tridents pulled out after leaving behind a few booby traps in case of pursuit.

They climbed the trail, picked up the guide and disappeared like ghosts back into the unfathomable reaches of the rugged border.